CONNECTICUT BRIDES

THREE-IN-ONE COLLECTION

PAMELA GRIFFIN

BARBOUR
PUBLISHING

In Search of a Memory © 2009 by Pamela Griffin
In Search of a Dream © 2010 by Pamela Griffin
In Search of Serenity © 2010 by Pamela Griffin

ISBN 978-1-61626-456-7

All scripture quotations are taken from the King James Version of the Bible.

This book is a work of fiction. Names, characters, places, and incidents are either products of the author's imagination or used fictitiously. Any similarity to actual people, organizations, and/or events is purely coincidental.

Cover Design: Kirk DouPonce, DogEared Design

Published by Barbour Publishing, Inc., P.O. Box 719, Uhrichsville, Ohio 44683, www.barbourbooks.com

Our mission is to publish and distribute inspirational products offering exceptional value and biblical encouragement to the masses.

 Member of the
Evangelical Christian
Publishers Association

Printed in the United States of America.

Dear Readers,

Forgiveness. Renewal. Devotion.

All of these actions are important in the Christian walk, but they are sometimes difficult to live. In these last three stories of another generation of the Lyonses, the Thomases, and the Fontaines (the final chapter of their lives will appear in *'Til We Meet Again*, *In the Secret Place*, and *New York Brides*), not only are such mandates difficult to manage, but they have become impossible to give. However, several traits bind many of these conflicted souls in their quests for a better future: a strong loyalty to family, lasting friendships, and the hope for abiding love.

It is my prayer as you read these tales of "impossible" romances that you are touched in your own lives, that desired reunions beyond all hope come to pass, and that God once more proves He is the Master of time. He knows every heart, and all things work together for good for those who love and serve Him.

God bless you always,
Pamela Griffin

IN SEARCH OF A MEMORY

Dedication

To all those searching who have lost something special and to all those wishing to find a better way and the truth, this is for you. Many thanks to my critique partners, Theo, Therese, and my mother. Without you guys, I would be lost. And to my Lord and Savior, Jesus Christ, who found this lost lamb and brought her home, to Him I owe everything.

Chapter 1

Lanville, New York, 1935

A ngel Mornay couldn't pinpoint why she felt uneasy, but every nerve inside screamed out a warning to keep away from this man. He was definitely not the typical sort to appear at their door.

The tall, dark stranger in the black suit continued to stare, ignoring her two cousins. "I'm pleased I could be of some assistance." He tipped his felt fedora. "Ladies." At once he moved away, his fluid stride a strange mix of confidence and caution.

She remained just inside the entrance of her aunt's New England home and watched the departing visitor close the gate to the short picket fence that enclosed their cottage. "That certainly was. . .peculiar," she whispered, unable to voice a more suitable word to describe the unexpected encounter. Never had she known anyone who could make her feel in the span of seconds as if she were both floating above the earth and falling into its depths, an experience most unnerving.

Regardless of his apparent consideration, his furtive manner disturbed her. Charming. Yes, he was that. Attractive. Quietly compelling. But she couldn't fathom how or why his mysterious dark eyes—strangely familiar eyes—had seemed to reach into her soul. That is, if she had anything left of a soul, still tattered and bruised after her most recent quarrel with her aunt, regarding what Aunt Genevieve considered yet another of Angel's faults. She was just glad the dark stranger had gone. He seemed. . .dangerous. That was the word she sought. This day had been difficult enough without adding to its troubles.

Angel firmly closed the door on the stranger and on her thoughts.

"You didn't have to be such a flirt," her cousin Faye reproved bitterly. "I saw how you all but pushed yourself in front of him. Just like you did with Charles."

At the ridiculous accusation, Angel turned to gape at Faye then directed her disbelieving stare toward the foot of the staircase where her other cousin, Rosemary, stood. And glared.

"I answered the door as I always do. With courtesy. The same courtesy

I would give to any visitor, whether it's the postman or a member from the women's society or. . .or our most recent guest, who was kind enough to return your parcel."

She wondered why her cousins never extended the same courtesies or acted maturely, for that matter. Though she was younger than Faye by two years, and Rosemary by three, when the stranger rang the bell, returning the package Faye had accidentally dropped on the sidewalk on their way home, Faye acted with all the composure of a silly goose. She had rushed to stand beside Angel and asked the young man a number of meddlesome questions, making Angel wonder if Faye's lost package had been the accident she claimed or a ploy to gain his attention. Rosemary behaved no better, insinuating herself into every sentence when Angel stopped to take a breath in giving the man his requested directions.

In reply to Faye's question about the reason for his visit to their small town, he distantly admitted he came to see a friend. Before Faye could query further, he tipped his hat, expressed relief that he noticed her drop the package, and left. Faye's behavior had been ridiculously childish. She was acting childishly now, and Angel was in no mood to argue about the afternoon's occurrences.

She headed for the stairs.

Rosemary blocked her way.

"You think you're so high and mighty, and the fellas all flock to our door to see you just because some say you're a doll. But that's not enough, is it? You want all the men to notice you. Men like my Charles."

Angel sighed, weary of explaining herself. "I wasn't flirting with Charles at the druggist's, and I certainly wasn't flirting with that stranger. I asked Charles how his mother was since her fall on the ice last winter, and with the man who was just here—well, you heard. He wanted directions to Mayfair Lane, so I gave them to him."

"You did more than that," Faye interrupted. "You smiled at him!"

"I beg your pardon? Since when is smiling considered a crime? I was being polite."

Angel didn't add that the stranger had gotten a more-than-adequate view of Faye's teeth from the many smiles she had directed his way. Such a reminder was petty; besides, it didn't matter what she might say. She had learned long ago that what her cousins considered acceptable for them they regarded as taboo for Angel, no doubt aided by their mother's strong opinions. "For the last time, I have no intention of trying to interest Charles. He isn't my type." Though she wasn't exactly sure what sort of man was.

"Why?" Rosemary's face colored a shade of persimmon as she switched tactics and went to his defense. "You think you're too good for him, is that it? Ha! A lot you know. You're no better than Charles or me or Faye—or anyone in New York for that matter." A cruel smirk lifted her painted red mouth, making her seem like an evil clown. "In fact, you're worse."

"I haven't the time or the desire to continue this conversation." Angel graciously didn't mention that Charles had shown no interest in Rosemary to cause her to become so possessive of him.

She tried to push past, but Rosemary mirrored her action, again blocking her.

"You're such a stickler for the truth? Well, maybe it's high time you had a taste of it, instead of making trouble for others."

Angel sighed. "This is really about what happened the other night, isn't it? I had no idea when your mother came home early and asked where you were that you would be about to cut your hair and she would catch you. You can hardly blame me for what happened."

Her aunt detested the fashionable short bobs for her daughters and had an iron will that Angel's cousins preferred not to cross. Aunt Genevieve didn't care what Angel did. Nor did she bat an eyelash in disapproval when, in an act of self-defiance two years before, Angel cut her easily tangled, waist-length curls into a short, crimped style that stars like Myrna Loy had made popular. Aunt Genevieve even smiled when she noticed the uneven ends of Angel's pathetic attempt.

Rosemary narrowed her eyes. "This is about so much more than Mother taking away my privileges. It has to do with your past. The past you know nothing about."

"Rosemary, don't." Faye's initial malice shifted to abrupt anxiety, as often was the case when she was instantly sorry for her rash words and behavior. "Mama wouldn't like it."

"Mama's not here now, is she? And I think it's time Miss High-and-Mighty was put in her place. What I have to say is the truth. And that's something of which our dear, darling Angel is a strong advocate." She turned cold eyes on Angel. "Isn't that right, Cousin? It's the truth or nothing with you." Her tone gave the pretense of sweetness, while underneath lay something ugly.

"I prefer the truth to a lie." Angel swallowed over the lump of worry clotting her throat. Something odd was going on—her cousins fighting a battle of wills over a hidden disclosure Angel wasn't sure she wanted to hear. "There are also times when it's better to say nothing at all."

"Really?" Rosemary sneered. "Well, too bad for you this isn't one of them. You could have done the same—chosen not to say a word—but you didn't. Now I won't get to dance with Charles at Sharon's party because I won't be able to go!"

Faye stepped forward. "Maybe you should calm down before you say more, Rosemary. You're not thinking clearly."

"On the contrary, I'm thinking very clearly, Faye. I only wish to give our dear, blue-eyed Angel all she deserves and desires—the absolute truth. She's almost eighteen and has a right to know just what a grand lie her life has been."

Disgusted with Rosemary and more than a little nervous about her revelation, Angel turned away. Rosemary grabbed her arm in a grip that made Angel wince. "Oh no, *Cousin dear*. Don't go just yet." Her words came deceitfully sweet. "Wouldn't you like to know the truth of who you are? Of who your mother was—or rather, who she is? Of the freak she turned out to be?"

Faye gasped. "Rosemary, don't!"

"You're lying, as usual." Angel worked to keep her face bland and her voice emotionless, not wanting either of her cousins to see how Rosemary's words tore into her orphaned heart. "My mother is dead. She died when I was three."

"Died? Oh no. Our mother lied to you, Angel. Your mother didn't die, as Mother led you to believe. She gave you to our mother, that much is true. Because she didn't want you. And do you know why?"

Her voice rose in pitch as she stepped closer, her hate-filled eyes burning into Angel's wary ones. Faye grabbed her sister's arm.

"Rosemary, stop it!"

Rosemary shook off her sister's hold, her attention never wavering from Angel.

"She didn't want you with her because she's a sideshow freak in a traveling carnival. You've heard of the bearded lady, haven't you? Well, if I were you, I'd check the mirror daily, because it might be hereditary. Your mother has a beard thicker than Dr. Meeker's. I know; I've seen pictures. She's nothing but a freak, and she's still very much alive. She sent a letter to Mother two years ago."

"I—I don't believe you." Angel felt her world begin to tilt and grabbed the banister in a white-knuckled grip. Rosemary noticed and bared her teeth in another cruel smile.

"It's true. I saw the letter. Uncle Bruce kept clippings of his years at the carnival. Mother keeps his albums in her room. He worked there as a strong man. He married your mother, likely because he pitied the creature since no other sane man would go near her—she was half a man after all, a *bearded* lady, and who knows what your true father was. Likely some other monstrous freak. You're no relation to our uncle, no relation to anyone in our family—and you know what that means, don't you?"

"Rosemary, that's enough!" Faye's warning shriek hurt Angel's ears. Worry glinted in Faye's eyes as she pulled on her sister's arm with both hands. Rosemary ignored Faye, struggling to remain in place.

"You're nothing but a nameless foundling! Without a true father. With a freak of a mother who never wanted you. You're an illegitimate piece of garbage. A nobody. Hardly normal. And would you like to know the truth of how you came into being?"

Faye jerked Rosemary hard enough to pull her away from Angel and slapped her. Rosemary rubbed her reddened cheek and looked with shock at her sister.

"You know what Mama said would happen if we told. You've said too much already."

Feeling like a witness to a slowly evolving nightmare, Angel watched the usually cowed Faye stand up to her sister. Rosemary sneered at her. "We're not children anymore. It's time someone set the record straight. Mother should have told her ages ago."

Angel felt as if she'd been sucked into a void; she could scarcely think. Could barely believe what Rosemary said was true. Faye's uncharacteristic behavior seemed to make it all the more horribly real and not some hurtful prank for which Rosemary was known.

"Come upstairs," Rosemary invited with another hateful smirk. "The albums don't lie."

Dread made Angel hold back.

"What?" Rosemary taunted. "Afraid to see the truth with your own eyes? You can spout it about everyone else, but when it's turned around on you, you run away like a coward!"

Angel clamped her lips and straightened her spine, refusing to sink to the stairs in tearful self-pity, as Rosemary no doubt wished. It had been years since she'd shed a tear. She had learned at a young age that crying never helped and often made things worse.

"Very well," she agreed. "Lead the way."

Faye eyed Angel with unease while Rosemary regarded her in triumph.

Determined not to bolt, Angel directed her attention to the stairs, trying to ignore her cousins, who might not be cousins at all; they certainly had never treated her as family, though Faye at least seemed to have a conscience. Angel felt surprised her legs could move—they'd begun to tremble so—but she led the sisters to their mother's bedroom. Momentary unease made her hang back on the threshold while they brushed past.

As a child, she'd been forbidden to enter her aunt's personal domain, and not since Rosemary's malicious trick in childhood to lure Angel there and lock her inside to get her in trouble had she ever attempted it. But the sight of the worn leather album her cousin pulled from beneath the bed captured her curiosity. . .and released a wave of foreboding.

Against her better judgment, she moved closer.

Rosemary opened the album's wide pages. A letter fell to the floor. Angel caught the town's name—Coventry—before Faye snatched it up and held it to her breast, as if the envelope contained secret government documents. In the album, newspaper clippings had been pasted on the heavy black pages, along with old photographs.

Rosemary thrust the book under Angel's nose, her index finger pointing to a photograph. "There she is—your mother, Lila! Look and see if you don't believe me. And the brat Uncle Bruce is holding must be you."

With her heart pounding madly, Angel eyed the images, worn and faded from the years. The candid shot showed a group of carnival performers clustered near an erected tent; few acknowledged the camera. The little girl in the bald, heavyset strongman's arms was one of three people posing. Her eyes and smile sparkled as she tilted her head and modeled for whoever held the camera. Surely that couldn't be her! The dark-haired child with the long, tight ringlets seemed much too lighthearted and happy to be Angel.

Stunned, she tore her gaze from the ebullient child and stared at the solemn, dark-haired woman standing at the man's elbow. Young and slender, she wore a veil, Arabian style, hooked across her nose and extending over the lower part of her face. Huge dark eyes, shaped like Angel's, were the only feature clearly seen.

"What is the meaning of this?"

At their mother's forbidding words, Faye scrambled off the bed. Rosemary dropped the book. Numb from so many revelations in so short a time, Angel didn't jump in guilty shock like the others, didn't do anything but blink and stare.

A scowl darkened Aunt Genevieve's features. Her gaze dropped to the open album on the floor. Immediately her snapping dark eyes lifted and ensnared Angel's.

"M—mother," Rosemary gasped, "we didn't expect you back so soon."

"The meeting ended early." Her eyes glittered. "Girls, go to your room. I'll deal with you later."

Angel snapped out of her trance and moved after them, also hoping for escape.

"Angelica, you will remain. I must speak with you."

With a heart that furiously pounded and sank deeper each moment that passed, Angel stood, rooted, and awaited her fate.

✍

Five long hours later, when all was dark and the occupants of the house lay sleeping, Angel tiptoed downstairs, clutching a train case and one bigger satchel—all she could carry with all she owned in the world. In the larger case rested her uncle's album, which her aunt practically shoved at her when Angel quietly asked if she might look at it. She felt no remorse in taking the album, one of three, since it contained only clippings of her mother and husband and their life at the carnival. As much as she hated Angel's mother,

Aunt Genevieve would have no wish to keep the memento and likely had forgotten she owned it.

All that Rosemary said was true; Aunt Genevieve verified it in cutting, concise words. Equally distressing, her aunt informed Angel that she owed it to her to marry the man of her choosing, and her aunt's choice made Angel shiver with revulsion: Benjamin Crane, one of the meanest, oldest, and richest misers in all of Lanville, who'd often leered at Angel. According to her aunt, Angel, being nameless, would never make a better match or find another man who'd want her, and Angel should consider it an honor to be presented with such an "auspicious opportunity." Auspicious for her aunt, maybe, but not for Angel. Her aunt went on to say that the Depression had hit all of them hard, but she'd provided for Angel, who should consider herself fortunate not to have been kicked out on the street to fend for herself.

Except for her companionship with the friendly cook, Nettie, Angel almost wished her aunt had kicked her out. She certainly wouldn't marry Mr. Crane, old enough to be her grandfather, and felt a bit like Cinderella escaping her evil stepmother and wicked stepsisters. But no glass slippers existed for her, no magical ball to attend, and certainly no prince. Only the distant memory of a forgotten mother urged her down the silent road, along with the faintest recollection of her sweet scent and the gentle wisps of a song, perhaps an old lullaby, crooned in a voice that soothed Angel. The fleeting memory visited her both awake and asleep, and Angel reasoned any woman with such a voice couldn't be the vindictive monster her aunt described.

She wasn't sure how she felt to have a mother people thought of as a traveling carnival oddity, but above all else, she wished to find her. Even the ambiguity of her quest was preferable to the certainty of her future if she stayed in Lanville. Perhaps she might learn what it felt like to be happy like the little girl in the picture.

Her emotions dictated every action; reason had long fled. She refused to think beyond the flicker of hope that her mother might want to know her, that somehow her absence had all been a dreadful mistake.

The streets remained eerily quiet; not even a dog barked. Angel kept close to the elm trees, should the need to duck behind one for cover present itself. The neighbors thought highly of her aunt, who involved herself in charitable endeavors, and would no doubt report Angel's whereabouts should they peek through their curtains and see her skulking in the night with her luggage.

The windows of the houses remained dark, quiet. Yet her heart raced with each sudden snap and creak, sure she would soon be caught.

How much time elapsed before she reached the train depot, Angel didn't know. Her feet in her pumps hurt dreadfully, her legs, almost-numb, throbbed, and her stockings did little to keep out the chill night air. A late March wind blew sharp and cold beneath her calf-length skirt, and she pulled her coat closer beneath her chin as she approached the ticket window and took a place in line.

"A one-way ticket to Coventry, Connecticut, please," she informed the bespectacled man when her turn came, mentioning the town she'd seen on the envelope before Faye grabbed it.

"Certainly, miss. That'll be three dollars."

"So much?" she asked, her hopes plummeting. "I'm only going one way."

"That'll still be three dollars."

"Thank you, but. . .I—I've changed my mind."

Crestfallen, she moved away. The next gentleman in line quickly stepped up and took her place at the window before the idea surfaced to ask the stationmaster where two dollars and twenty-five cents would take her. Eyeing the line that had grown by half, Angel decided to continue down the platform. She should have taken a bus. She'd had no idea traveling by train would cost more than she possessed, the last of her earnings from working at the soda fountain before Mr. Hanson needed to dismiss her, unable to continue paying her wages. To her knowledge, which tonight had proven sadly deficient, she'd never taken a train; according to the picture in the album, she had. The photograph showed she had actually lived on one.

Too weary to walk even half a block more, she mulled over what to do. She couldn't return to her aunt's home and be forced to marry Benjamin Crane. Angel's life would then be over. . . .

The shrill call of a train whistle captured her absorbed attention. Without really giving the linked cars conscious thought, she stared at the long line of them on the nearest track.

"Mommy," she heard a little boy ask the woman holding his hand. "Is Coventry very far? How long till we get there? Will we be there soon?"

"Yes, Coventry is very far, Timmy, and we will get there when we get there. Hush now."

Angel watched mother and son move up the metal stairs of the car nearest her. A porter took their bulky case, helping the heavyset woman into the confined area. He looked toward Angel for a fearful heartbeat, and she wondered if he could read her mind. His eyes narrowed suspiciously. Her face went warm.

Quickly she averted her gaze down the length of the platform, pretending to look for someone. After a moment she allowed her attention to return and noted with relief the trio had disappeared inside the train. Through a line of filthy windows, Angel watched their progress down the aisle.

The train began to move. Each entrance glided past. Her heart began to race.

Did she dare?

An image of Nettie's disapproving features filled Angel's mind, but she was desperate. And besides, she didn't have that far to go.

Before the train trundled past, Angel threw her largest case up into one of the last entrances—grateful fate was at least kind enough that the case didn't rebound and spill onto the platform. Running to catch up, she barely jumped aboard herself, using one hand to grab the rail.

She made it!

She took a deep, shaky breath. Once she regained her equilibrium and her satchel, she approached the railcar on her right, wishing to get as far as possible from the shrewd porter and find somewhere to hide.

The door flew inward beneath her grip.

She inhaled a startled gasp as both the experience and the abrupt motion of the train's increasing speed made her stumble forward. A man's strong hand grabbed her arm to steady her, and for the second time that day, she dazedly blinked up into the enigmatic eyes of the tall, dark stranger who'd visited her aunt's home.

Chapter 2

Roland stared into a pair of bewitching eyes, as dark a blue gray as the Atlantic at dusk. It took him a moment to realize where he'd seen such eyes, and the jolt made him go stock-still.

"You," he said at the same moment her lips silently formed the word.

A brown hat was smashed down over thick, shoulder-length hair the color of sable, curly wisps blew into her face, and the ruffled edge of a scarf wrapped around her neck covered much of her jawline. But he couldn't mistake those rich, deep eyes.

"Did you follow me?" he asked in puzzled amusement. He assumed she hoped for either the opportunity of a handout or the prospect of a good time.

"F–follow you?" she spluttered. "Of course not! I wouldn't dream of doing such a thing."

"No need to go berserk. It was only a question."

The dame's icy courtesy and frosty smiles from that afternoon should have been enough to give him an account of her feelings for his company. She frowned, clearly unhappy to see him again. The cold air from the train in motion whipped through the opening between railcars. With his hand still closed around her arm, he pulled her inside and slammed the door shut behind them.

His intention of securing a newspaper no longer important, Roland turned to his unexpected guest. With a quick appraisal, he noted her tousled, windblown appearance and breathless manner, as if she'd run a long distance to make it to the train on time. Two spots of red colored high cheekbones belonging to a flawless face—what he could see of it—and she gripped the luggage handles in tight, gloved fists. A real doll, chinalike in appearance. But a hint of panic made her wide eyes even bigger, her full lips drawn and tense, and he wondered if she might lash out at him with her bags if he were to take a step closer.

He decided not to take the risk.

"The bends in the track can knock you off your feet. I'd advise you take a seat, Miss. . . ?"

Ignoring his hint to learn her name, she looked around, her manner distantly assured, as if she had every right to be there and he was the intruder.

Her brow wrinkled in confusion when she saw the small drawing room, containing dual leather benches with high backs, the length of twin settees. She moved to one and set her bags down with a muffled thump. Without a word, she sank to the padded seat nearest the dual windows and pulled away her scarf.

Curious about his new cabinmate, he took the seat opposite, farthest from where she sat and closest to the door. If he didn't know better, he might think her mute. Minute after taut minute stretched in silence.

"Something of a coincidence, bumping into you like this." He tried to initiate conversation, hoping it wouldn't crackle with tension like the quiet between them did.

"Yes." Her expression guarded, she afforded him the barest glance and pulled the fingers of each glove, one by one, removing the peeling leather. They, like the rest of her outerwear, appeared years old. With the nation in crisis, few had the luxury of buying a new winter coat, except for Roland, who could buy the train on which they sat if he wished, paid for with the dirty simoleons earned in others' blood.

He grimaced at the thought.

Her gaze remained fixed to the spotted window and the trees and buildings that hurried past in a dark, watercolor blur.

"Two strangers meeting twice in one day in the oddest of circumstances and on opposite sides of town—that's one for the books, isn't it? And now, here we are, sharing a car on the same train." He smiled. She didn't return the favor, behaving in a way similar to what she'd done at the house. Was it just him, or did all men provoke this sort of reaction?

She pulled a handkerchief from her handbag, put it to her nose, and sniffled. She didn't appear to be crying; her eyes were dry.

"Did you catch a chill?"

She shrugged one shoulder and looked back through the window.

"It's nasty weather to be out. I don't know about you, but I've had enough of this blustery cold and rain. I suppose we should be thankful it didn't rain today."

She gave him the barest inclination of her head in agreement.

"Are you visiting family in Connecticut?"

Her eyes cut to him, shocked, cautious. "Yes. Family." She sniffled again into her handkerchief. "Please, if you don't mind, I believe I have caught a chill. I really don't feel up to small talk."

"I can ask the steward to fetch you a hot toddy—"

"No." He barely got the suggestion out before she cut him off. "Thank you." Her words tried to be polite. She fidgeted in a clear attempt to get comfortable in her seat. "I'm fine."

Observing her clear distress, Roland doubted that but didn't insist. He grew silent and wished now he'd gotten that newspaper. Spoiled when it came to a social life, as the minutes ticked by with the clacking of train wheels marking each second, he felt restless. His aloof cabinmate had closed her eyes. Judging by the anxious frown wrinkling the pale skin between her eyebrows, he didn't think she was sleeping.

The door to the car swung open, and a Pullman porter appeared.

"Sorry, sir." He nodded to Roland.

The woman's eyes flew open. Dread inscribed her every feature as the dark-skinned man turned his attention on her and approached like a persistent fox cornering a frightened rabbit. With swift understanding Roland recognized the problem.

The porter looked between Roland and the woman, clearly noting the taut distance between them. "May I see your ticket, miss?" He held out his hand, palm up, a grim look entering his attentive eyes.

"My ticket?" Her words came raspy.

"Yes'm. Your ticket. The one you bought to board this train."

"I . . ." She pushed her shoulders into the seat, cowering within herself, the motion almost undetectable except that Roland intently watched her. "I'm afraid I didn't, th–that is, I don't—"

"The lady's with me." He captured their startled attention.

"With you, sir?" The man's attitude jumped a notch higher to deferential respect.

"I trust that's not a problem?"

"No, sir. Not at all." The porter literally backed up to the door. If Roland weren't so disgusted by his name and all it accomplished, he might have found the entire situation bizarrely amusing. "Sorry for the misunderstanding. Didn't realize you were traveling with a guest, sir."

Roland magnanimously waved him off, though his smile felt tight. "Don't concern yourself. I didn't mention it when I boarded."

"If there's anything I can get you, sir?"

"A newspaper would be nice."

"Yes, sir. Would a copy of the *New York Times* be all right, sir?"

"That's fine." He kept his voice pleasant. "And next time, if you would be kind enough to knock first rather than barge inside and scare the living daylights out of the lady, I'd appreciate it."

The steward's eyes grew larger. "Yes, sir. I—I only thought. . . . Yes, sir, of course, sir." He wiped his brow with a handkerchief, backed out, and shut the door.

Roland turned his attention to the woman. He leaned forward in friendly persuasion, keen for a little conversation. "Maybe now that that little matter has been taken care of, you'd care to relax, miss, and we can get to know one another better?" He hoped for a smile at the least. At the most, words of thanks and a thaw of her chilly personality.

At least she was no longer coldly distant.

Her smoky eyes sparked with a fire in danger of incinerating him. Resentment stiffened her shoulders, and he wondered what he'd said or done this time to earn such an unfavorable reaction.

"Thank you for taking care of 'that little matter,'" she said with lips pulled tight, sounding more as if she were telling him to get lost, "though I didn't ask for your help. And just so we're clear, I'm not some damsel in distress looking for a wandering knight to rush in and rescue me. I'll certainly never let you lure me into becoming your. . .your"—intense color heightened her cheeks—"your floozy!"

Entirely baffled by her response, he watched as in hot indignation she stood up, grabbed her bags, and whisked from his compartment.

❦

Angel had no idea of where she was headed. She only knew she must get away from the insufferable Casanova in the car behind her. Had she stayed, she might have blurted something she would dearly regret.

Juggling her cases to open the door, she went into the next car, finding it to be a sleeping car with curtains covering the berths. She quietly went through another, hearing snores, then another. As she moved through to the next car, she wondered if he tried to make moves on all lone female travelers or if she'd been his only hapless victim.

An attractive face didn't always go hand in hand with a pleasant disposition—a morsel of wisdom she'd learned while observing some of the dapper young fellows who visited the soda fountain. A good thing, too, that she knew better than to be captivated by his suave charisma and dashing smile. She understood the foolish danger of allowing herself to be taken in by such a rogue. In that single regard her aunt had not failed her, stressing to Angel that once the truth of her birthright surfaced no decent man would have her. And she didn't want a man who wasn't decent. She may have been conceived in sin and loathing, as Aunt Genevieve almost gleefully informed her, but she wouldn't succumb to a sordid life because of what had happened to her mother or the choices she had made, most of which Angel still didn't know in full or even if they were true.

The porter suddenly moved through the opposite door, *his* newspaper in hand. She tensed as the man noticed the luggage she carried. Rather than call her bluff, he offered a courteous if cool smile. "Is there a problem, miss?"

Still leery of him, she didn't answer right away. At least he didn't ask to see her ticket again, and she felt a niggling sense of guilt that she didn't have one.

He studied her as if she didn't belong there.

She swallowed hard. "Where can I buy a cup of coffee?"

His gaze again darted to her luggage, his eyes curious as they lifted to hers. "You'll be wanting the dining car, miss. Follow me." Before she could protest that she could find the car alone with his directions, he turned and walked back the way he had come. With no choice but to follow, she did, hoping she wasn't walking into a trap.

They reached the car, and he spoke to another man, a steward in a different white uniform. Instead of benches, small tables covered in white cloths lined both sides. She headed down the narrow aisle toward one then heard the steward clear his throat. When she looked, he shook his head for her to stop.

Her heart pounded. Had she been caught?

The porter left, and the steward motioned she should leave her luggage to the side, by the door. With such restricted space, she had little choice. He led her to a different table from what she would have chosen—far in the back, this one finer. A thin silver vase with a pink rose decorated its center.

She glanced at her first choice toward the front of the car and closer to her luggage. "I think I would prefer a table in the front—"

"I was told to seat you here." The man stood ramrod straight, unrelenting, his blue eyes refusing resistance. He held out a chair. Uneasy, she slid into it, feeling closed in as he scooted her closer. She shook off the crazy notion; the train encounter with the rogue stranger had definitely rattled her trust.

A black waiter soon appeared. After convincing him she wanted only coffee, knowing she must be stingy with her meager funds, he left. She took the peaceful opportunity to watch the few diners and figured it must be near closing time. Did the dining car close? A businessman sat alone, reading his newspaper. An elderly couple shared a meal. Two women with similar features, likely mother and daughter, chatted across a table in friendly conversation. Angel found herself studying them in wistful reflection, wondering if she might one day have as comfortable a relationship with her mother. . .if she could find her.

Engrossed in observing the two women, she took little notice that another passenger had entered the dining car. Not until the steward brought the newcomer to her table did she look up, dismayed to see the stranger. The third time to meet him by happenstance.

Wry amusement lit his dark eyes, but before she could protest to him about sharing her table, the steward moved away, almost bowing and scraping as he promised the man his "usual." The porter had also behaved like a serf eager to please the lord of the castle. Clearly the staff knew him well, and he was a man of means, accustomed to having his wishes obeyed.

Her observation brought back the feeling of being cornered.

"Well, well, what do you know?" He took the chair across from her, apparently unaware of her mounting apprehension. "We meet again. This is a surprise."

Angel noted the many empty tables he could have chosen.

"Is it?"

He narrowed his eyes cautiously. "I'm not sure I get your meaning."

"You accused me of following you. But maybe the shoe is on the other foot and you're the one following me." She tried to come across as cool and collected. "I'm afraid I might have given you the wrong impression. I'm not interested in any sort of. . .alliance. I'm not the sort of girl to engage in. . . casual acquaintances." Her face burned with embarrassment as she tried to express her standards in a delicate manner.

He lifted his hand to stop her. "Before you pursue that thought, miss, honest, all I came here for was a ham on rye and club soda."

"And you chose my table as the spot to eat your meal?" she scoffed with a little huff of breath. "It's one thing that we coincidentally found ourselves in the same car, but you purposely chose to sit here."

"Your table?" That irritating glint of amusement again danced in his eyes. "Then you really don't know. . . ."

"What should I know?" A mounting sense of dread made her slightly ill.

He settled back in his chair. "I've been remiss. We were never introduced, and I'm afraid there's been a misunderstanding."

"Oh, really?" She thought she'd read him well. Even now he studied her features from face to form, as far as the table edge allowed, as if he liked what he saw. She squirmed, her aunt's chilling words weighing on her mind. "When you said you wanted to get to know me better. . ."

"I meant just that. Getting to know you in what I hoped would be friendlier conversation than we've had so far. Nothing more. You might find this difficult to believe, but I'm not the sort to take advantage of casual acquaintances either."

He looked and sounded sincere, his dark eyes undemanding, his deep voice gentle. She relaxed a fraction, allowing him a small smile. Maybe she was overreacting; this evening had been traumatic. "I'll admit, my first impression of you was of a wealthy playboy or gigolo who makes the round of New York's finest speakeasies twice a weekend and lives on a diet of dry martinis and gin."

He fidgeted, glancing away. She guessed she'd hit the mark on one item, perhaps all of them.

"I take it dry martinis are your poison of preference?" he asked in a sociable manner.

"I don't drink. My aunt's a teetotaler—there's never been a drop of liquor in the cabinets. Even cooking sherry. And except for sipping a glass of white wine and finding it awfully bitter, I've never tasted alcohol. I mentioned gin and dry martinis because that seems to be what all the wealthy, disreputable playboys drink. Like Nick Charles."

"Ah." He smiled. "Good ole Nick. So, you're a gumshoe buff. I take it you've seen *The Thin Man*?"

"Since I lost my job, thanks to the economy, I don't go to the theater anymore. I like to read, and Dashiell Hammett wrote the mystery as a book before it became a motion picture, you know," she teased.

She couldn't believe how easily they were conversing, when minutes ago she'd done all she could to dodge his questions, to dodge him. He had a way about him, a strange charisma that made her relax while at the same time her pulse raced. She hadn't thought it possible to feel both calm and breathless at once.

"Is that what led you to travel?" he asked with that same quiet that invited a confidence. "Are you hoping to find work in another city?"

Angel blinked, surprised he so aptly read her dilemma. "Something like that."

"What I don't understand is why you would leave your family to look for work in another state. Are things that bad at home?"

Seeing the kindness in his eyes, she didn't take offense at his question.

"Let's just say I realized it was time I left my aunt's charity and found a way to make a living."

"So you took off in the night and stowed aboard a train. Don't worry," he quietly assured. "I won't tell a soul. Why do you think I spoke up for you?"

She glanced around nervously. "Why did you? I wasn't exactly nice." She drew her brows together in concern. "Is it so obvious? I mean—*what I did*?" She mouthed the last three words.

He studied her until a flush warmed her face. "The porter isn't going to care one way or the other as long as the fare is covered. Don't worry about that. As to why, let's just say I felt the urge to. . .help a damsel in distress." He grinned.

At the memory of her parting shot, she lowered her eyes and shook her head in embarrassment.

"Though I'm not sure anyone who knows me would call me a knight. Maybe a black knight. . ."

At his wry, amused response, she swiftly raised her head.

"No, don't look at me like that. Your virtue is safe. I have no intention of 'luring you to become my floozy,' I believe is how you put it?"

Rather than be insulted or injured by his light tone that gently teased, she found herself nervously laughing.

"I was a bit high-strung, but can you blame me? You pulled me into the car, one that had no other passengers, asked a lot of personal questions, told the steward to knock first, then told me you wanted to get to know me better. What's a girl supposed to think?"

He chuckled, a dimple she'd never noticed flashing in his cheek. "Okay, maybe I was overfriendly. But I couldn't get over the shock of running into you again in another strange twist of fate. It seemed. . .uncanny."

She nodded, deciding to trust him with part of her dilemma since he'd guessed the truth about the rest and hadn't turned her over to the authorities. "I've never done anything like this before. Sneaking aboard, I mean. I've never taken one red cent or even a stick of candy as a child. But tonight I acted before I thought."

"I believe you."

She studied him in confusion, having been sure she would need to persuade him. "Why? You don't know me."

"Let's just say I have a hunch you're the type of dame who'd never resort to such measures unless you were desperate. Again, don't worry about them finding out." He casually directed a thumb over his shoulder as he spoke. "Your secret's safe with me."

"I'll pay you back, of course." She didn't like being indebted to anyone, especially not this man whose name she still didn't know. "Give me an address where I should send the money, and I'll reimburse you as soon as I find work."

"There's no need. It was nothing. I have plenty." He grimaced, as if being wealthy actually displeased him.

"I insist." She vainly searched through her purse. Feeling silly, she looked up. "It seems I'll need to borrow a pen and something to write on, too."

He eyed her a long moment. She wished she knew what was running through his mind.

"Tell you what. Let's forget all about that, and let me try introducing myself again. We got off track the first time. Hopefully the conductor isn't as lousy at steering this train as I am at managing a conversation."

She smiled at his little joke.

"I'm Roland."

"Angel." He lifted his brows at her reply, and she added, "My name. A nickname I've grown used to. My full name is Angelica Mornay."

"It suits you. Pretty name for a pretty dame."

His casual compliment left her ill at ease, and she looked down, snapping her purse shut.

"Did I say something wrong?"

Before she could respond, the waiter returned to the table with their orders. "If there will be anything else, Mr. Piccoli, please do not hesitate to ask."

"Bring the lady a sandwich as well. I'm sure she must be hungry."

The shock of hearing his name struck Angel like an unexpected dousing of icy water; she couldn't think to respond or refuse. A kaleidoscope of startling facts twisted inside her mind, making her dizzy.

Roland Piccoli! Grandson of the notorious gangster Vittorio Piccoli. . .

who dispensed with his enemies as casually as she dispensed with a pair of damaged stockings. No wonder he seemed familiar when she saw him at her aunt's! His face had been plastered in the society pages a month ago, a blushing debutante on his arm, whom the article had said was his fiancée. And Angel had run across his path, not once but twice. . . .

Walking twice into the path of a killer.

He seemed not to notice her horror as he spoke with the waiter.

The curiosity she had shoved aside earlier raced to the forefront of her memory in a blaze of enlightenment: the cars, all of them crowded, full of smoke. The car she shared with him, empty of passengers, no smoke. Even decorated, she realized now, and differently than the others! She didn't know much about trains or fares or the cars in which passengers rode, but with sudden and certain knowledge, she knew she'd found her way into his private car.

Of all the foolish, dangerous moves she could make, this was the worst!

The Piccoli family owned gambling houses and nightclubs in all of New York City. At the soda fountain, she occasionally overheard the men she served talk with each other in awed, fear-filled conversation about the Piccolis' latest manner of doing "business" or "collecting" a debt. Those owing money suddenly disappeared or were found washed up by the river.

She couldn't imagine that this grandson of one of the worst crime bosses in the Big Apple, seated across from her and now staring at her with narrowed eyes, would lower himself to sit in a crowded, public dining car. The steward and all his entourage would probably fall over themselves in their readiness to please him by serving him dinner in his private car.

So why was he here?

The answer was obvious.

And now she, too, owed him a debt.

The car felt suddenly close, smothering her, and she desperately sucked in air. Hurriedly she stood, knocking into the table and spilling her coffee on the pristine cloth. Her chair almost flew backward, hitting the wall. The thought of the lifeblood his family just as easily spilled with horrifying regularity and without remorse made her scramble a step backward in retreat. Perhaps it wasn't her blood he would seek in payment for the favor of his silence, if she should refuse his wishes, or even her money as the reimbursement. But it didn't take her two guesses to figure out what he did want, despite his claim to the contrary. His gentle, sympathetic manner was all a seduction; once again in her life she'd been easy to deceive.

"Angel, what's wrong?"

"Nothing." Except that her voice sounded too high-pitched to convince him of that. "I. . .need to find the lavatory."

"I can't help you. I don't leave my family's private car often."

Of course he didn't.

"But I felt like company tonight and decided to eat at my table. Little did I know I'd entertain such charming company."

His table. Of course! Now she understood his earlier words.

Managing a flip response, though she had no idea what she said, she pretended nonchalance and walked away from his table, toward her luggage, toward the exit, toward freedom. . . .

She wanted to scream bloody murder and run.

Chapter 3

Angel darted a look over her shoulder. The immediate threat to her life still sat with his back to her. She grabbed her luggage and hurried out. At last, finding the lavatory, she managed to get both herself and the luggage inside the cramped area. She doused her face with water, trying to steady her nerves. Her fingers trembled as she let the cold liquid run through them, then patted her cheeks and turned off the faucet.

Of all the dumb luck. To find herself sharing a car and a table opposite a man with a family as dangerous as Al Capone. Not sharing a car. Sharing his car. His private car. And his table!

But what else could she expect? She had broken the law in stowing aboard, and Nettie's warning words of "*those who do evil, reap evil*" reverberated in her mind. She had entered the world of crime tonight; was it any wonder the first man to greet her would be a criminal?

If she believed in a God who cared, she would go to Him and plead for help out of this mess. Too long Angel had walked alone, learning from childhood that no one cared, except maybe one. "Nettie," she whispered, looking into the mirror, "I wish you were here with your wise advice." Her friend would probably quote scripture, but that usually comforted Angel rather than made her angry.

Once again the solution was up to her. And she had to think of something fast. She couldn't hole herself away forever.

Shutting her eyes to her pale image, she groaned. She must keep her distance, allow no more unforeseen meetings. But how? With little room to hide, if he pursued her, he would find her. He had the entire staff at his beck and call, whereas she had no one to give her aid.

A swift knock made her heart give a painful jump. *Relax, Angel, it's a public room after all.*

Breathing in deeply, she exited. The mother and child she'd seen on the platform stood in the corridor. The woman eyed Angel toting her luggage with a curious nod. The boy tugged on his mother's coat.

"Please, Mama. I wanna go to the cawnival. Can't we go to Grampa's later?"

"We can go to your grandfather's now, and if you're very good, perhaps I'll take you to the carnival when we return," the obviously harried mother replied.

"But what if it's not there anymore?"

"Hush, Timmy, and be a good boy. If we don't visit your grandfather first, we'll not have one thin dime to do anything."

"Will Grampa give us a dime?"

His mother smiled sadly. "I hope he'll give us more than that." She smiled at Angel, almost apologetically. "Would you mind keeping an eye on him?"

"I. . ." Angel swallowed, glancing at the boy and then in the direction of the dining car, several cars away.

"I won't be but a moment," the woman assured.

Angel nodded.

Once the woman closed the door behind her, Angel offered the child an uncertain smile. "Your name is Timmy?" He looked about four.

He nodded in an exaggerated motion, his big brown eyes wide under his tweed cap.

"Did you say something about a carnival, Timmy?"

Again he nodded, and her pasted smile grew genuine. He was such a sweet thing.

"The man said it's at the next stop." He pointed to the front of the train.

"Really? How fortunate. . ."

He cocked his head, wrinkling his nose in confusion. "Huh?"

She chuckled and tweaked his cap. "A grown-up word. It means that hope might just be around the corner."

He grinned. "You're pretty."

His adoring words made her a little sad. "Oh, Timmy. Pretty is nice, but it can bring a world of trouble. It's not so important how one looks, and trust me, pretty is a lot more pain than it's worth."

Again he looked at her strangely. She shook her head with a cheerless smile, realizing a boy his age wouldn't understand even if she did try to explain, so she offered a soft "Thank you" instead. It had taken a lifetime of informative and often painful experience to acknowledge what she had told Timmy. Only a person's character and heart made them beautiful, like Nettie, who was plain with buck teeth but possessed a warm heart and caring disposition that made her beautiful to Angel. Not for the first time since she'd been told of her existence, Angel wondered what type of heart her mother had.

It seemed that for once in her life, Fate or Providence or maybe even Nettie's God had offered a way of escape. And she might find the answers she so desperately craved.

The woman returned, and Angel continued on, finding herself in a coach car with benches on each side. She looked for a place to sit, feeling like a forlorn sparrow teetering on the edge of a cramped nest of sleek ravens. All these people, many of whom appeared to be businessmen in three-piece dark suits, knew exactly who they were and where they were headed. They each wore a confident look of self-assurance that their travels would take them where they wanted to be. She knew where she wanted to go but wasn't sure where her journey would end or what awaited her. A strange thought to flit through her mind while standing in an impossibly narrow aisle amid passengers seated in detached boredom. She found an empty aisle spot next to a gentleman who lay with his head back, his hat tipped over his face.

Now if the train would only get to the next stop before Deadly Enemy Number One went on the prowl and hunted her down.

⁂

"More coffee, Mr. Piccoli?"

"Excuse me?" Roland snapped from his musings. "Oh, coffee. No thanks." Before the waiter could leave, he added, "The lady who was with me. Have you seen her?"

"Not for some time, sir. She took her luggage, so my guess is she's getting off at the next stop." He glanced out the window as the train slowed. "Which we're coming to now."

Roland tried to process the information that Angel had taken her luggage with her to the lavatory.

"If there's nothing else, sir?"

"No, nothing. Thank you." Once the waiter left, Roland turned his attention to the window, deep in thought. The muted light from a lamppost flooded the station platform coming into view.

He'd felt drawn to Angel since she opened the door of the cottage and he witnessed her commendable patience with her family members as she attempted several times to give him directions. Here on the train, he had witnessed her fire and spirit but something more, something hidden surfacing for moments at a time. She retained a simple childlike innocence, no matter how daring she might appear. A girl, barely a woman, who would stow away in the night to escape. . .what?

She had been stunned and unnerved to learn his identity. He was accustomed to such a reaction, and he couldn't blame her for leaving his company. His family had amassed the worst of reputations. But still he wondered what had brought her to flee to this train in the first place, and he hoped for a second chance to ask.

The locomotive's short whistle pierced his thoughts. The train slowed and stopped. Passengers disembarked. A familiar navy coat and brown hat caught his eye, the colors faded in the weak light of the station's yellow bulb but leaving no doubt of whom they belonged to. She darted a furtive glance over her shoulder, as if uncertain where to go. Roland doubted anyone was coming to meet her, doubted, in fact, that Danbury was her stop.

As he watched, she approached a porter and spoke with him. He pointed to his right, and she turned to look. Roland also looked, seeing nothing but unlit buildings leading to a dark road fringed with dense trees. Through them, hundreds of incandescent lights flickered in the distance, but no buildings stood in sight. She nodded, picked up her luggage, and moved in that direction. His attention suddenly fixed upon three boys, up to no good from the looks of them, who detached themselves from the station's brick wall where they'd been casually leaning.

Roland jumped to his feet as the boys moved to follow Angel.

℘

Angel slowed her nervous pace, not wishing to turn her ankle on loose pebbles that made up the lane traveling into the distance, farther than she could see in the dark. At some point it then twisted to the right and led to a lit-up fairground. To her immediate right, through a gap in the trees, a field offered a shortcut to get there in half the time, without fences or other obstacles to bar her way. Hoping no snakes or mice inhabited the area or, at the very least, were in a deep sleep far beneath the earth, she chose the shortest route.

Her heels partially sank in the soil but not so badly she couldn't manage the walk. Halfway across, a rustling disturbed the grasses behind her. Worried that she had aroused some small nocturnal creature, she swung around in defense, clutching her luggage handles hard.

No vicious animal posed a threat, but three boys, the oldest at least three years her junior but almost as tall, closed in on her. The carnival lights lit up the taunting leers that marred their young faces.

"What do you want?" She backed up.

"The dame's a looker, boys, but dumb as dirt," the tall one said. "Whadda ya think we want, lady? Hand over your money and your jewelry."

Dazed, she gaped at them, unable to grasp what they wanted.

"Well? Whatcha waitin' for? Christmas?" he sneered.

"I—I haven't got much. Two dollars and spare change." At his menacing stare, she opened her purse and pulled out the bills. "See? B–b–but you can have it all. Here." She offered it to them with a shaking hand. "Just p–please. Go away."

He snatched up the money. "What about your jewelry?"

"I don't own any jewelry."

"All dames got some kinda jewels on 'em, 'specially those out so late at night. You want that we should show we're serious?" He threw a sidelong glance to his two cohorts. "Come on, boys. Let's show her how serious we can be."

They moved forward as a group.

"Leave me alone!" Frantic, she swung her heaviest case in a sideways arc, the momentum compromising her balance. She barely managed not to fall. The hoodlums jumped a step back and spread out, stalking her a second time. She swung both pieces of luggage, swinging herself around, gratified when she heard a smack as one case hit the nearest ruffian.

"Now you asked for it," he muttered, rubbing his bruised arm.

"I don't think so." A menacing baritone cut through the night.

Angel looked with shock behind her. She had been so intent on defending herself she hadn't heard his approach.

"Give the lady back her dough, and you boys beat it."

"Yeah? Who's gonna make me? You?" The leader of the bullies swung around in defiance. The boy's hand moved to his pocket. He pulled out a switchblade. "Maybe me and my pals here don't wanna go till we're good and ready. So who says we have to?"

Roland stood his ground, not looking the least bit daunted by the wicked blade that gleamed in the carnival lights. "I say."

"And just who are you, givin' out orders like you own the world? The president? The pope?" The lead hooligan snickered, and the other two joined him.

Roland's answering smile was grim. "Name's Piccoli. Roland Piccoli." He paused for effect. The boys darted anxious glances at one another. "I'm not an important leader, like those you mentioned. But my family eats runts like you for breakfast."

"H–h–how do we know you're not lyin' and aren't really one of the Piccoli mob?" the first boy stammered, though he tried to appear brave. "Them gangsters do their business in New York City."

"It's him, Johnny," one of the boys argued nervously. "I seen his picture in the newspaper. It's him, I tell ya!"

"Yes, it's me." Roland's words were quiet and sinister, like a loaded gun aimed in their direction. "So I suggest you boys take my advice and scram. I don't ever want to see your faces again."

"No harm done, mister. We wasn't gonna hurt her none." The leader threw the money at Roland's feet then looked at his friends. "Let's get outta here."

With mixed feelings, Angel watched the boys take off running. She worried she might now be in a more precarious situation, alone with a true gangster, and wondered if he carried a gun. She doubted a switchblade would be his weapon of choice. Warily she watched him pick up the money and turn his attention on her, the first time he'd looked at her since his stealthy arrival.

"I—I have to be going," she said quickly. "Thanks for stepping in once again. Good-bye."

She turned but should have known he wouldn't let her get away so easily.

"Don't you want your money?"

She hesitated and moved to take it, but he continued holding it.

"What do you think you're doing out here in the middle of nowhere?"

Annoyance put a sharp bite to his words. "Are you screwy or a complete dingbat?"

"My reasons don't concern you."

"Maybe not. But surely you've got more brains in that doll-like head than to walk alone in an empty field at night. In a place you don't even know!"

The reminder that his entire family were notorious criminals faded in the rise of her irritation.

"It's really none of your business." She walked away from him.

His steps followed. "I'm making it my business. If I hadn't come along when I did, those gangster pretenders could have robbed you, or worse."

"I was handling the situation."

He snorted in cynical amusement. "Oh really? How? By boxing with your luggage?"

She whirled to face him and stumbled on uneven ground. He grabbed her arms, letting go the moment she was steady.

"You can hardly keep yourself upright in those crazy things." With disdain he regarded her inadequate pumps. "This is nuts. You're nuts. Why'd you run from the safety of the train into the dark of night and nowhere? My guess is Danbury wasn't your original stop."

"Again, not your business, Mr. Piccoli," she seethed between her teeth. "I'm managing just fine."

"No, you're not, and if you'd stop behaving like an ungrateful brat and take a good look around while you reflect on the past few minutes, you'd realize it, too." His voice gentled. "Look, I'm not the threat here." He reached for her case, taking it before she could argue, and stuffed the bills in her hand. "They're scared off for now, but I don't trust those boys to keep their distance. Let's return to the road. With any luck, a car will drive by and we won't have to walk all the way to the station. I promise I'll leave you alone if you'll just get back on a train and out of harm's way."

"I'm not going back." She tried and failed to retrieve her case, blowing out a frustrated breath at his persistence. "I'm. . .looking for work. Like I told you."

"Where?" He dryly scanned the vast area. "As a tiller of the field? Were you going to ask the squirrels to hire you?"

"Funny man." She glared at him. "In case it's missed your notice, there's a carnival over there."

"Yeah, so?" He regarded her in stunned disbelief. "You're hoping to find work at the *carnival*? Wait a minute. . . ." His eyes narrowed. "Didn't you say earlier that you're visiting family? Next thing you'll tell me, they run the fair."

She fumed in silence at his mockery.

"So which is it, Miss Mornay? Out visiting family or looking to find work?"

"*Both*—not that it's any of your concern. Now if you'll please give me back my case."

"Not a chance. I'm not letting you out of my sight, not till I know you're safe."

His words almost made her laugh with skepticism. *Safe? In the company of a Piccoli?*

"I'll be all right."

"What if they don't hire you? What'll you do then?"

She hadn't thought beyond asking for work. Hadn't even planned to look for work at the carnival, until his bullheadedness forced her into the excuse. But it wasn't a bad idea. In fact it was perfect. She needed more than two dollars, and with any luck she could locate her mother.

"That's what I thought." He answered his own question. "You haven't a clue what you'll do. Obviously you don't have more than that"—he nodded to the bills in her hand—"or you wouldn't have stowed away in my car."

Two long whistles shrilled through the night.

"You'll miss your train."

"I can take another."

"But what about your things? You might lose your baggage!"

"The porter will take care of what little I brought till I send a wire telling them where to deliver it. My family owns an interest in the railroad."

The news didn't surprise her.

"You're not getting rid of me so easily, Miss Mornay. Until I'm sure that you're out of danger, I'm sticking beside you every step of the way. My conscience won't allow otherwise."

"'Out of danger,' he says," she grumbled beneath her breath, resuming her walk. "How'd a girl get to be so lucky?" And how could he talk about a conscience? His kind had none.

"I beg your pardon? I didn't hear you."

She gave him a sweet smile. "Since I can't shake your company, may we please continue, Mr. Piccoli? I'd like the opportunity to speak with the manager before they close."

"Of course, Miss Mornay." His smile was just as phony. He inclined his head. "For tonight, I'm your obedient servant. Please, lead the way."

She bit back a sharp retort. She was tired of arguing—her entire day had seemed composed of it—and if he truly meant her harm, he'd had ample opportunity to act before now. Even here, in a dark field with no one the wiser, he seemed to show nothing but consideration for her welfare.

Maybe, just maybe, she could be wrong about his motives in helping her. *Don't fall for his smooth ways*, logic warned.

Remembering the articles about his family, about him, she would indeed be foolish to think that a Piccoli entertained anything more than a selfish agenda. And she wouldn't be duped again.

❧

Roland had met plenty of dames by the time he'd turned twenty-three. Some smart, some dumb, a few falling a notch somewhere in between. But he had no idea what to make of this woman erroneously nicknamed Angel. Not that she wasn't as pretty as an angel; she was a real looker. And she could probably be sweet and pleasant if she tried. But she hadn't an ounce of sense in that sleek head of hers, and he felt more as if he'd taken on the role of her angel, her guardian angel.

He snorted at the preposterous thought of himself as an angel. Maybe a fallen one. She darted yet another wary and long-suffering glance his way, as if *he* were the chip on *her* shoulder.

He should just let her stumble her merry way through the field to the carnival, now that he'd diverted trouble for her a second time. But he couldn't bring himself to abandon the rash woman to whatever other dangers might await her recklessness. She reminded him of his sister, Gabriella—all spit and fire and independence, with no thought of where her hasty decisions could land her and no notion or experience of what to do when she got there.

He glanced at Angel's stiff profile. Perhaps he'd been too hard on her, calling her an ungrateful brat. He'd been relieved to spot her then alarmed to find her ringed in by a gang of street hoods, and he had allowed his exasperation with her to flame into ire once the danger had passed. His harsh words escaped before he thought twice; he didn't know her well enough to form opinions of her character. And she had thanked him, however curtly. Beneath the phony confidence she tried hard to exert, she was clearly alone and afraid. Grimly he plodded through the field of wild grass beside her.

"If we return to the station," he said again, "I'll buy you a ticket to wherever you want to go on the next train out of there. Only drop this screwy idea of joining the carnival. No telling what trouble you might find in a place like that."

"I appreciate the advice, but I've made up my mind."

"I've heard bad stories—"

"I'll be careful."

"I've yet to see that," he muttered beneath his breath.

"Listen!" She turned on her heel. "You don't have to hang around. No one's forcing you. By all means, go!"

"I already told you how I feel about leaving you out here all alone, so unless you're coming back to the station with me, you're stuck with my company, missy."

Drawing her mouth tight, she didn't answer. Roland reined in his frustration, realizing that talking to her like his kid sister wasn't helping. Finally they came to the fairgrounds. She asked a pretzel vendor where the owner was, and he pointed to a wooden ticket booth.

"Sorry, folks. We're closing for the night," the man said as they stepped up to it.

"Actually," Angel said, "I was hoping you might have a job available."

"You want a job?" The short, thin man with mustache and goatee beyond the brass grille window looked at Angel strangely, echoing Roland's thoughts. "At my carnival?" He looked from the luggage in her hand back to her face. "I can't pay much, with the nation's crisis being what it is."

"I don't need much."

"You running away from something, young lady?"

She hesitated, and Roland sensed it was because of his presence. "I'm looking for something," she said at last. "Something I think I can only find here."

The man, who reminded Roland of a dignified magician minus top hat and tails, raised neat eyebrows in surprise. "I'm not sure what you think you may find here, but my carnival isn't all fun and games. We take our work very seriously. If you haven't any intention of staying longer than a few weeks, it would be best for both of us if you'd just leave the way you came."

"Oh, I can be serious. Please, sir. I need the work."

He seemed to consider and held up a thick roll of tickets. "My ticket girl ran off two days ago, eloped with another one of my workers." He eyed her and Roland severely. "I can't have any funny business going on. I don't want to be left shorthanded again should you two not find the carnival to your liking and take it in your head to run off."

"Oh no! Y—you have it all wrong," she stuttered quickly. "I hardly know this man."

"Is that a fact?" He eyed her matching brown luggage still clutched in Roland's hand.

"Yes. We met on a train, and this. . .gentleman came to my aid." She hesitated with the word. "Please, give me a chance. I can sell your tickets. I'm good with managing money, and I get along well with people."

Roland held back a snort of disbelief.

"Well, you do have an enchanting smile," the owner drawled. "It helps to have beauty induce the tightfisted customers to loosen their wallets and buy more tickets." He looked her up and down. "But selling tickets won't be all that's required. Each carny helps raise and dismantle tents and engage in preparations at each destination where we entertain. Likewise we work together in daily chores. Can you cook?"

His words came fast, his question unexpected. She blinked, taken off guard. "A friend taught me how to do a number of things in the kitchen."

Roland wasn't sure why, but he had the feeling she exaggerated.

"Fifty cents a month comes out of your pay for board, another fifty for food. Like I said, I can't pay much. A dollar a week."

She winced but nodded. "That's not a problem."

"All right then, young lady, I'll give you that chance. The ticket girl who ran out on me was in charge of helping with breakfast. You'll also have that job. You can share a car with Cassandra. The living lot is the train at the back of the carnival. Her car is painted with a woman standing bareback on a white horse. Tell her Mr. Mahoney sent you. You start tomorrow, since this day is done." He locked up a small strongbox. "It'll be a relief to hand this job over to someone else and return to my office. If you need me, my car is at the head of the train."

"Thank you." Anxiety melted off her. "You won't regret this."

"Let's hope not."

She turned to Roland, looking a bit sheepish. "Thank you, too." She spoke under her breath so only he could hear. "I know I haven't been the best company, and I wasn't very nice when all you did was save me from that nasty situation earlier—both of them. But I'm not ungrateful. And I'm really not a brat." She gave him the first genuine smile he'd seen, stunning him, and reached for her large case, which he still held. "This time it really is good-bye. I hope you aren't late to wherever it is you were supposed to be." She nodded in farewell. Her luggage in hand, she walked down the midway toward the tents shielding the carnival train.

Flabbergasted by her change in attitude, Roland watched her go.

"Something more I can help you with, young fella? In case you forgot, we're closed for the night."

Roland came out of his semidazed trance and turned his attention to the owner.

Foolish. Crazy. Absurd. He could think of endless words to describe what he was about to do.

"You wouldn't happen to have another job for hire?"

Mr. Mahoney eyed the stylish cut of Roland's expensive silk shantung suit. "*You* need work? You're pulling my leg."

"Dead serious. I heard all you told Miss Mornay, about pay and board, and those numbers are fine with me."

The owner's sly smile warned Roland he wouldn't like what was coming. "Is that a fact?" the man drawled. "Well then, I might have just the sort of job for a strapping young fellow like yourself."

Chapter 4

Angel knocked on the railcar and stepped back to glance at the near-life-size mural of a slim blond standing atop a white horse. When no answer came, she set her luggage down and worked to slide back the door.

"Hey! What do you think you're doing?" A woman's irritated voice came from behind, and Angel turned to find the painted image in the flesh, rhinestone costume, feathered tiara, and all. "That's my car you're nosing around."

Angel picked up her luggage. "Mr. Mahoney said I was to sleep here."

The woman eyed Angel up and down. "You're my new bunk mate? Hmm." Her reply left Angel clueless as to whether or not she passed muster when suddenly a smile lit the woman's face. "All right then. Come on in, and I'll show you around. I'm Cassie, by the way. Horse trainer and bareback rider extraordinaire. What do you do for an act?"

"I'm Angel. I was hired to sell tickets."

"That can be an act in and of itself, so I heard from Germaine. She was my bunk mate, now happily married and away from this joint. Watch your step. Let me give you a hand with those."

Angel gratefully accepted help with the luggage and grabbed both sides of the car to hoist herself up inside. Her new living quarters were sparse and cramped with two cots anchored one atop the other. But a row of sparkling sequin costumes hung in one corner, a woven blue and brown rug covered the floor, and a colorful oil painting of wild horses helped make things cozier.

"You're not planning on eloping, too, I hope?" Cassie teased, setting Angel's large case next to a small, mirrored dressing table. "Seems I just get a bunk mate broken in, and she leaves."

Memory of Mr. Mahoney's stern caution to her and the handsome rogue rescuer flashed across Angel's mind. That made two people in the span of ten minutes suggesting she might elope.

"I never plan to marry."

At her declaration, Cassie lifted one perfectly arched sable brow. "A pretty thing like you? Is that what you're running from, honey? An unwanted engagement?"

Angel stared back in shock at her accurate guess. "Running?"

"Nobody joins a carnival unless they're running from something or they were born into it, like me." She gave a bright smile. "I'm part of 'The Magnificent Death-Defying Hollars.'" She quoted the words painted on her railcar. "An act my parents started long before I came into the world. You might have heard of us?"

"No, sorry. I never went to carnivals as a child—that is, not that I can remember."

"Really?" Cassie looked at her as if she were a strange new bug. "Hmm." "You've been with this carnival your entire life?"

"A good portion of it. My parents were part of a circus before the owners mismanaged it, and we came here."

Cassie's explanation led Angel to hope. "Then you know the sideshow acts?"

The pert blond laughed. "Honey, I'm well acquainted with all the carnies and showmen. From the vendor selling peanuts and pretzels, to the roustabouts, to the trainer of fleas." She blushed, making Angel wonder.

"Does a bearded lady work here?" Her question came out in a hopeful rush.

"A bearded lady?" Cassie tensed. "That's a rather odd question. You looking for one in particular?"

"Yes, as a matter of fact. She goes by the name of Lila. I'm. . ." She wondered how much to reveal and decided to be forthcoming. "I'm a relation."

Cassie regarded her with surprise. "Really?"

She didn't know it would be so difficult to say: "I'm. . .her daughter." The daughter she abandoned and wanted nothing to do with. Not for the first time, Angel wondered what compelled her to hope her mother's viewpoint might have changed.

"Her daughter," Cassie repeated softly, looking Angel over with curious shock before turning to the dressing table. Clearly she was amazed that Angel could descend from a woman with such an obvious flaw. Cassie sank to the stool. "I hate to disappoint you." She slipped off her feathered tiara, took a jar, opened it, and applied white cream to her thickly painted face. "No one like that works here now."

"Then she did before?"

"I wouldn't know." She moved her lower jaw to the side as she spoke, applying the cream, intent on her task.

Angel's expectations crumbled. "Perhaps she worked here years ago? I would have been with her. Fifteen or sixteen years ago maybe? I was only two, or three. . .I think. But she might have come back to join the carnival, though I'm not sure when. Maybe you might have seen her at some point these past few years?" Another ember of hope sparked. "Maybe she even told someone where she was going?"

Cassie busily set to work wiping off the cream with a cloth. "Sorry. I was just a little girl all those years ago. As for recently. . .sorry." She shrugged and set down the soiled cloth. "Other carnivals travel through the New England area, too. Maybe she's with one of them."

Devoid of the bold cosmetics, Cassie looked a great deal younger than Angel had first speculated, close to her own age. Maybe she really was too young to remember Angel's mother. Cassie swiveled around on the stool.

"Aw, don't look so glum." She smiled. "If it's meant to happen, you'll find her. That's what Mama Philena says. If things are meant to happen, they will. You'll meet Mama tomorrow. She was a gypsy fortune-teller when the carnival first started but gave that up several years ago and has become a helper wherever she's needed and a mother to us all."

She delicately slapped her palms to her thighs, seeming nervous. Angel assumed Cassie also felt unsure around her new bunk mate. "Now, let me fill you in on the goings-on of Mahoney's Traveling Carnival and who and what you'll find here." Cassie stepped behind a half screen beside the rack of costumes. All the while she spoke of the "family," rustles and bumps came from the opposite side. Her head popped up now and then, followed by one shiny article of clothing after another, slung across the top of the screen. Her white hand appeared and fluttered to reach and pull a distant garment from a hanger. Angel stepped forward and grabbed the cotton wrapper, handing it to her.

"Thanks." Cassie soon stepped out, tying the wrapper around her waist. She ran a brush through her hair, the curls just touching her shoulders. "Most of us retire early, once the customers have gone home and chores are done. We rise before dawn. It's fun working in a carnival, but a lot of hard work goes into it to make it as entertaining as can be."

Not wanting to make any mistakes her first night there, Angel followed Cassie's example and changed into her bed gown behind the screen. She brushed her teeth and hair then regarded the bunks with uncertainty. Cassie set down the brush and looked in the mirror at Angel's image.

"Yours is the lower one. I prefer the top. Helps me keep in shape for my act."

To Angel's astonishment, Cassie swished around, jumped up, and darted toward the cots. She leaped upward like a gazelle, using her hand as a brace, her body forming a graceful sideways arc as she landed with ease atop her mattress, light as a feather. She grinned down at Angel, who gaped at her. "I know. I'm a hopeless show-off. It's just in the performer's blood, I suppose, and both my parents are Class A acts. Do turn down the lamp, won't you?" She breezed her long, slender body beneath the blanket and laid her head on the pillow. "Good night, Angel. Don't let the train bugs bite."

Angel chuckled and doused the light. She liked her bunk mate and hoped they might become good friends. Maybe she could find happiness here. . . and peace.

"You can't find peace in the world, child, till you find peace in your heart."

Nettie's words of wisdom drifted into her mind. She still didn't understand how her friend could believe in an all-loving and caring God, with so much suffering going on in the world. Still, it was Nettie's wise words, some of them verses from her Bible, that Angel had found herself clinging to on the difficult days. The only thing she regretted about her hasty flight was not saying good-bye to her dear friend.

❧

Standing alone inside the huge tent, Roland stared with dismay at the stalls of animals, wondering how his life had come to this.

Before him stood four beautiful grays, though they were not his problem. Their owner had just made it very clear he or his family would tend to all care of the champion horses. Three black ponies, assorted barnyard animals, and a baby elephant completed the unusual menagerie—all of them in his charge.

"Is this a circus or a carnival?" Roland directed his question to the wrinkled gray beast that stood almost as tall as he did. How in the world did one take care of a baby elephant?

"At least you know there's a difference," came a jovial voice from behind. "That's a start. Not everyone outside the carnival world does."

Roland turned to see a short, barrel-chested man with a thin, waxed mustache and an infectious grin head his way. "I've been to both," Roland admitted.

"Impress me."

At the friendly challenge Roland took a guess. "A circus contains a variety of acts performed under a huge tent known as the big top. A carnival is a series of rides, games of chance, and sideshows along a midway, many of them rigged and containing acts of a far more sinister nature than anything one would find at a circus."

The newcomer raised his brows, not acting insulted by Roland's straight-forward explanation that made clear this wasn't his first choice as a place to be. He'd had enough of *sinister* to last a lifetime.

"Okay, so I'm impressed." The man extended his hand, and Roland shook it. "You must be the new carny Mahoney hired. Pleased to meetcha. The name's Chester."

"Roland." He purposely left off his surname, relieved that Chester did as well, which prevented the need for excuses as to the omission.

"Nice to have you aboard, Roland. Mahoney told me you'll be sharing my car. My last bunk mate eloped with one of the ticket girls. It was his job Mahoney gave you."

"I'm overjoyed," Roland said in a monotone.

Chester laughed. "Aw, it's not so bad. Jenny here is docile as a lamb and easy to take care of, aren't you, girl?" He reached out and smoothed his hand over the elephant's coarse trunk. Jenny curled it in a gray *U*, aiming her snout toward Chester. "You know me too well. And you're getting downright spoiled, little lady." He rolled his eyes when Jenny made a soft trumpeting noise. "All right then, find the peanut." The end of her trunk pressed over his shirtfront then into the side of his jacket, slipping into a pocket. She fished the peanut out, with her trunk tip curled around the morsel, and brought it to her mouth.

"Cute trick."

Chester eyed Roland's own suit. "That's some sharp duds you got there." He quirked his brow. "Just why did you say you needed the work?"

"I didn't." Roland took no offense at his genial probing. If he were in Chester's shoes and a stranger showed up to work at a carnival wearing an expensively tailored suit, he'd wonder, too. "Long story," he hedged. "I'd rather not go into it."

"There's a number of those up and down the midway. Most of them hard-luck stories, with a number of us carnies hiding pasts we'd like to forget. Some shady, some not so much. You're right about your description of carnivals, though this one is private owned and also has shows and games acceptable for the kiddos. I'll give you the lowdown on what to avoid. For the most part, the performers and other carnies are a good bunch; you'll know soon enough who's a shyster. Isn't that right, Jenny?" He stroked her gray wrinkled head.

"Is Jenny part of your act?"

"*My* act?" Chester laughed. "No. Jenny here is a recent addition Mahoney & Pearson acquired. Her owner's an Arab kid. Doesn't speak good English, but he's nice enough. One of the circuses split up a few years back, and some of the acts signed on here." He patted the elephant high on the trunk again. "Me, I deal in the tiniest of critters in the animal kingdom, if you could call it that. I own a flea circus."

"Fleas?" Roland repeated in surprise. "You mean real, jumping fleas?"

"Don't use nothin' else, only mine don't jump. I heard of flea circuses that use tricks with magnets and the like, but my fleas are real enough. Nothing rigged going on in my tent. Come by sometime, and I'll give you a free show." He grinned. "You're not asking, but I see the question in your eyes: Why fleas? Well, it's like this: I like things small, in detail, and I like insects. My grandfather, he owned a flea circus at the turn of the century and taught me all he knew. But not to worry. Taking care of my fleas won't be on your list of duties," he joked.

"That's a relief. I may know the difference between a carnival and a circus, but to be blunt, I know little about taking care of animals—though the horse owner came in here a few minutes before you did and informed me to keep away from his."

Chester nodded. "Stan Hollar. Very particular about his property and who comes in contact with it. Those beautiful grays are Andalusians, some of the best horses you can find, and one of the top acts the carnival can boast. A member of the family checks in a few times a day, usually Cassie. I guess you could say Mahoney & Pearson counted themselves lucky when the Hollars signed on. They're one of the star attractions of the carnival." The wistful note to his voice led Roland to believe Mahoney wasn't the only one counting himself lucky.

"You about finished here?" Chester asked.

"I have no idea where to start. Mahoney just said to bed the animals down for the night."

"I grew up on a farm, so I'll give you a hand. Mama Philena usually comes to help out. Been with the carnival over thirty years. Mahoney's mama and like a mama to us all. She'll turn up eventually and show you the ropes."

Roland worked alongside Chester, grateful for the man's help and company. He didn't have friends or, rather, those associates he would call friends: men and women who were honest, loyal, and honorable. Most of the moral class, once they learned his name, assumed his family reputation went along with the label, which couldn't be further from the truth. Rather than destroy a possible friendship before it had a chance to build, Roland chose to keep silent about his identity. Angel knew, but he didn't think he'd have a problem convincing her not to share what she'd discovered.

That was, if she would talk to him at all once she realized he was here.

Chapter 5

Angel woke up, found herself alone, and hurried to dress.

She met Cassie on the midway. "Sorry I overslept."

"That's okay," her bunk mate effusively greeted her. "Come on, I'll take you to the cookhouse tent." Soon they approached a structure composed of a canvas roof tied to poles. Two long tables stretched beneath, where the workers ate their meals.

"This is Angel," Cassie said in introduction to the few clusters of people who'd taken seats along the benches. "Say hi, fellow showmen and carnies, but you better be nice since she'll be preparing your breakfast in the future."

A sudden thumping shook a screen of canvas hanging beyond the tables as if a spoon had been whacked against it. "I'm still here, too, ya know!" came an unseen woman's grumpy voice.

A few of the men laughed. "As if we could forget," one of them muttered dryly. "Hello, Angel," more than several intoned, like a classroom of obedient schoolchildren.

"Hello," she said a bit shyly, darting a curious look toward the suspended canvas.

"Angel, my dear girl," a man said in a heavy British accent. "What a lovely name for a lovely face. As you are the latest connoisseur of food preparations, I should like to mention that I prefer my toast deeply browned and not blackened as the last girl chose to make it. I prefer the black to remain in my name."

A pretty, thickset woman with bleached hair and dark roots lightly slapped the wisecracking, balding man on the skull. "Be nice, Blackie. You heard Cassandra. She's new to the family." The woman turned a big, toothy grin Angel's way. "Hiya, honey. I'm Ruth, and this here's my ball and chain, Blackie Watson."

"Now there's a spectacular idea, Buttercup. Incorporating a ball and chain into the act. A balloon that looks like a cannon, perhaps? Yes? Or even better, one bigger than a cannon. I would carry it like a deadweight then throw it at the children and set them to squealing."

"Whatever you think, dear." Ruth shook her head in mock exasperation, holding her hand straight out beside her mouth as if in confidence to Angel but hardly whispering, "Anything sets him off. Be careful what you say." She

42

winked and lowered her hand. "We dress as clowns and perform up and down the midway, selling balloons to the kiddies."

Angel smiled in reply at the outgoing couple. Cassie took her beyond the sheet of hanging canvas that hid where food was being prepared. The delicious scent of warm oats she smelled upon arriving at the tent grew stronger.

"You're late!"

Angel winced, but Cassie smiled. "Millie, this is her first day. Be nice. Angel, meet Millie. Don't let her boss you around." She spoke to Angel with a teasing wink to Millie. "She's known for throwing her weight far and wide."

"You better just watch yourself, girlie." The grated tone belonging to the rail-thin woman didn't come across as amused. "Or you might find sand in your coffee 'stead of sugar."

Angel regarded the older woman with shock, but Cassie laughed. "We all joke with one another around here. You'll get used to us soon enough."

"Humph," the taciturn cook responded, but before Millie turned away, Angel thought she detected a smile on the worn brown face.

Cassie disappeared beyond the canvas. Angel wasn't sure what to say. She'd never lived in an environment that tossed around banter as a means to entertain and not hurt feelings. At her aunt's, she kept her thoughts to herself to avoid being criticized or having her feelings crushed. Still unsure of her footing in such a strange, new world, she kept silent, observing her fellow carnies.

Millie went back to work scooping creamy hot oats from a huge black pot and ladling the porridge into bowls. Angel was put in charge of making toast on a wire tray over the fire as Millie showed her. Since that was the sum total of food products Nettie had taught her to make, Angel felt relieved she wouldn't seem totally ignorant at her new job.

"We don't have a lot of the usual kitchen fare, as you can see, since you cain't very well pick up an oven and the pipes that go with it and move them 'round from place to place," Millie explained in her raspy voice. "There's a small stove on the train, but I do most of my cookin' over a slow fire. Like the rich flavor it brings. I can make any meal that goes in a pot. Cabbage stew. Potato soup. You name it; I can cook it. And when we have meat or poultry, they clamor for my pies." She beamed with pride as she poured coffee into tins that Angel then set on a tray to disperse among the carnies. As Angel worked, her initial nervousness dissipated, and she relaxed, enjoying her first morning there, even if she had yet to sit down and take her first bite.

She returned to the preparation area, tray empty, and refilled it with platters of toast, a rich golden brown, she noted with satisfaction. Concentrating on the success of her labors as she walked, she set the platter in the center of one end of the table.

"There you go, Blackie. Golden brown and not one speck of black, just the way you like it." She lifted her smiling gaze from the platter to where Blackie should be sitting. . .and inhaled so fast she thought she might choke, nearly swallowing her tongue.

The tall, dark stranger sat in Blackie's spot. Amusement danced in his rich dark eyes.

Blackie waved in acknowledgment to her from farther down the bench, where he'd taken another place at the table next to an extremely tall, bearded gentleman.

"Wh–what are you doing here?" she asked her persistent follower once she found her voice.

"And a good morning to you, Miss Mornay." Roland's straight white teeth flashed in a charming smile. "The toast looks delicious. Deep golden brown. And you're right—that's just the way I like it."

"I asked what you're doing here. This is where the workers eat. You shouldn't be here."

At her soft, insistent words, gritted through her teeth, those at that table quieted in curiosity.

"Actually, I should. I'm doing what every other carny is. Enjoying a hearty breakfast before taking on my duties."

"Your duties?" she gasped in mounting horror. For the first time she noticed his fine three-piece suit was missing. In its place he wore common clothes: a long-sleeved white cotton shirt, suspenders, and trousers like the other men, his lean, muscular build now apparent. But even with the change in clothing, he stood out from everyone else.

The gleam in his eyes was full of mischief. "Like you, Angel, I've joined the ranks of Mahoney & Pearson's traveling troupe. I'm a bona fide carny now."

❤

Roland watched without surprise as Angel made a quick excuse of being needed in the kitchen and hurried away as swiftly and gracefully as a kitten with a wolf in pursuit.

"She sure is jumpy," Chester observed from beside him. "You two have a history?"

"Not much of one and not like you mean it. A case of mistaken motives that started out in a series of awkward missteps. Truth is, I've known Miss Mornay less than twenty-four hours."

"You're joshing. With the way you two were staring at one another? No history whatsoever?"

"No history."

"Humph. Could've fooled me."

Roland decided it was high time to shift the focus off his life. "I happened to notice your eye wandering over to that pretty little blond sitting at the end of the bench." He glanced at the girl, who talked with another woman, similar to her in coloring and features, then looked back at his bunk mate.

Chester winced, and Roland noticed the flea man turn a shade red. "Cassandra Hollar. Part of the top act I was telling you about. That's her mother with her. And like her mom, Cassie's a bareback rider." His words grew wistful. "Best there is in all of New England, I imagine. All the world."

"I assume it's safe to say you two have a history together?"

"Nope. Her parents won't hear of it." Chester frowned, unusual to see on his effusive features. "They consider a flea trainer beneath them and unsuitable for their daughter."

"Tough break. She feel the same?"

"Hard to tell." Chester ducked his head, taking interest in his coffee. "Mahoney wants me to show you around after breakfast. Let you get a feel for the place."

"I'd like that." Roland looked toward the canvas, where Angel had disappeared. He thought she was taking a considerable amount of time to bring the next platter out and wondered if she was hiding from him.

❧

"This is ridiculous," Angel chastised beneath her breath. "You can't hide behind this curtain forever."

"You say something?" Millie wanted to know.

"No, nothing." She gave her instructor a bright smile to hide her embarrassment at being caught talking to herself.

"Humph. You gonna take them bowls of porridge out or what?"

Angel straightened her backbone. She had escaped being trapped in an unfortunate marriage, had fled the everyday cruelties of her severe aunt and cousins, and had jumped aboard a train bound for a destination unknown to her in the dark of night. Surely she could muster up enough courage to again confront the grandson of the legendary crime boss who ruled half of New York City.

She swallowed hard. Then again, when she thought of it that way. . .

"Those bowls ain't gonna sprout wings and fly to the tables."

Angel nodded, determined. "I'm on my way."

The next few minutes went unpredictably well. Every now and then she sensed Roland watching her, but she avoided looking in his direction overly much. She would have preferred not to notice him at all, but his deep laugh as he talked with a couple of the carnies was both appealing and distracting and caught her attention more than once.

"Why does he have to be so disgustingly handsome?" she muttered as she sneaked a glance at him while gathering empty bowls as Millie had told her.

"Were you talking to me?" Cassie asked from behind.

"What?" she gasped, nearly dropping the dishes in shock. "No. I'm afraid it's a bad habit I acquired. Talking to myself, that is."

"If that's your only bad habit, Angel, you're as good as your name around here." The blond laughed. "As soon as you finish with breakfast, I'll take you on a tour of the midway to help you get acquainted with your new home."

"I'd like that, but I don't want to interfere with your work. You've already helped me so much. And I imagine I should find my way to the ticket booth soon, whichever one Mahoney wants me at. I noticed there are a number of them all around."

"Oh, we have plenty of time. Relax. You need to eat, too."

Angel nodded and gathered her own food, taking a place far down the table from Roland and out of sight of him. Once she ate the bland but filling fare and the dishes and dining area were cleaned to Millie's satisfaction, Angel joined Cassie, who waited outside.

"Do you have anything casual to wear?" Angel's bunk mate asked.

"Will this not do?" She glanced at her navy skirt then at Cassandra's own denim trousers, knotted with a length of rope around her slender waist. "I don't own anything like that. My aunt wouldn't hear of it."

"I have a spare. I only wear them for manual labor—and you'll find there's a lot of that before the customers start arriving. Save your nice clothes for then."

"When is 'then'?"

"Early evening. Not much sense performing while the kiddos are in school and the parents at work, those lucky enough to have jobs. We spend the mornings and afternoons rehearsing and working on new acts. On weekends we open in the early afternoon. I've found that every circus or carnival is different, each employing their own set of rules. And about those men you'll be working for—Pearson's a bit of a stickler, but Mahoney's a peach." She grinned. "He can be all bark and bluster, but he's really a sweetheart once you know him."

Inside their railcar, Angel changed into the denim trousers Cassandra lent her. She rolled them up at the ankles and belted them around her waist with a rope. Cassandra also lent her a man's work shirt. "Father gives me his castoffs. No sons to bequeath them to." Cassie laughed, also tossing Angel a pair of flat-heeled shoes she had an extra pair of, which fit Angel surprisingly well.

As they left the railcar, Angel acknowledged the change felt better, warmer, and she didn't feel so out of place wearing men's clothes with Cassie dressed the same. Of course, had Aunt Genevieve seen her in anything other than a skirt or dress, she would have had a conniption fit. Angel smiled a little rebelliously at the thought, a smile that disappeared as both girls suddenly came face-to-face with Roland and a shorter man with laughing eyes.

Roland glanced at Angel's changed attire but didn't say a word. She wasn't sure if he approved or not, not that she cared.

"Hey, Cassie," the other man said. He stood as tall as she.

"Chester." Her greeting seemed shy.

"I was just taking Roland on a tour of the grounds."

"Funny. I was doing the same with Angel."

Barely glancing at Angel, he nodded in greeting. His eyes seemed hopeful as they again went to Cassie. "Well then, how about we go as a group? That way if one of us forgets something, the other can fill in."

Cassie darted a quick look around then nodded with an open smile. "Let's do that."

Angel's stomach dropped to her toes at this new arrangement. She couldn't exactly protest, since she did need to know the area and Cassie obviously wanted Chester to walk with them. During the next few minutes, however, the two leaders gravitated several feet ahead, walking together and leaving Roland and Angel to follow.

"I think they forgot about us," Roland said in amusement after minutes passed without either Cassie or Chester pointing out some attraction or sideshow tent along the midway, giving the new workers no more information.

"It does look that way." Her words came guarded.

He gave her a sideways glance. "I solemnly swear, on a stack of Bibles if you'd like, that I had nothing to do with this."

"No need to. This isn't a courtroom." She couldn't help but see the irony, though. No matter which direction she chose to run to rid herself of his company—a closed door, storming away, sneaking off a train—somehow she always ended up back in his path. "But you can't say the same about finding work here. You meant to choose this place."

He hesitated. "You're right. I did."

"Then you admit it. You *are* following me." She stopped walking and whirled to face him in accusation.

He gave a gentle tug to her elbow. "Come on. We don't want to get left behind. They'd never know we were missing." They resumed their walk, and he released his light hold.

"Well?" she insisted after a few steps.

"What do you want me to say, Angel?" He sounded frustrated. "I wanted to make sure you were safe, especially after seeing those young thugs go after you. I know I said all this before, and call it none of my business, but finding you in my car and alone on the train, somehow that made it my business."

"I don't need a bodyguard."

"I don't think you know what you need."

Offended, she glared at him. "That's an incredibly judgmental statement to make, since you hardly even know me."

"You're right. But if we're going to talk snap judgments, you've done your fair share. Don't judge my character just because of my name, Angel. I'm not the terrible, preying villain you've made me out to be."

"You sure don't mind throwing your last name around to achieve your purpose!" She felt a little ashamed when she realized he'd done so only to help her, but she couldn't seem to back down.

He sighed, pinching the bridge of his nose. "I'm glad you brought that up. I'd appreciate it if you wouldn't tell anyone who I am. I'm just Roland here."

"Then you intend to stay?" She couldn't hide her distress. "There's really no need. These people are nice. Cassie, Chester, Mahoney. I don't think I'll find trouble among this bunch, so don't feel obligated to remain on my account."

"Can we not argue, for once? We were coming close to getting along together on the train. Can we go back to that moment?"

"That was before you made me your personal mission." And before she learned he was a gangster. "I'm still not entirely sure of your motives."

"Okay." He released a weary sigh, throwing his hands up in defeat. "I confess. Joining the carnival did start out as a means to watch out for you, maybe even to get to know you better—"

"I knew it!"

"But that wasn't the sole reason. There's more to it than that."

She regarded him with skepticism. "How so?"

"I did a lot of thinking last night. You didn't ask what I was doing on the train, and I evaded your cousin's question about why I was in your home-town. Now I'll tell you, strictly in confidence, being as how only you know who I am and I'd like it to stay that way. But you must never tell anyone what I'm telling you. Do you understand, Angel? It's for your own good."

A sense of excitement mingled with dread at his overtly clandestine attitude made her nod slowly. She half-expected a car of gangsters to suddenly careen into view, tommy guns firing.

He remained silent for so long she thought at first he had changed his mind about telling her. Their pace slowed, until they were even farther behind their tour guides and well out of earshot.

When he looked at her again, his expression was somber.

"I went there to visit the family of one of my grandfather's victims. A man who once worked for him. I went to see his wife."

Her eyes grew wide. "Who?" She scoured her brain for all those in their small community who'd recently lost loved ones but struck a blank.

He shook his head slowly, his eyes grave, making it clear he wouldn't reveal that information. "For a long time I've wished to cut myself from the organization, from the family itself, but it's been nothing more than a hope-ful desire and empty words on my part. Grandfather never believed I would follow through, and he was right. I tried to break away before but made half-hearted attempts at best. The life I led, it's all I know." He frowned. "Lately, more and more, I've detested what my family stands for and faced some hard choices. Do I turn a blind eye to the horror they generate and embrace the organization as I've been trained? Or do I listen to what's in my heart, telling me that such loyalty holds too steep a price, amounting to no good and leading only to regret, sorrow. . .and death."

Angel listened, sensing his pain ran deep. For the first time since they'd met, she felt a strange connection to Roland, who also suffered through his family for being different, and she sympathized with what he must have undergone and was still going through.

"I was on the train because I was also running, but God only knows where I was going. I sure didn't. Without my family's knowledge, I'd just met the young widow of the man my grandfather had bumped off for money owed. The poor man had three kids with one on the way. He was a dope for getting involved with my grandfather in the first place, but his widow is the one suffering. The whole stinking affair made me question if I wanted to return and take my so-called rightful place in the organization, as has been expected of me since I was born."

Wetness shone in Roland's eyes, and he hastily averted his gaze, blinking furiously. Moments passed before he again spoke.

"Then I met you. Courageous, full of purpose, ready to take off alone in the night in a bold move to change what life threw your way. I may not agree with your methods, but I admire your spirit and independence, even envy it. You made a decision and were determined to follow through, no matter the obstacles. Watching you gave me courage to make my own getaway from family expectations, from the family itself."

She sensed him look at her. "I want to start over, Angel. To become my own man and somehow, if it's even possible, to redeem my family name. I never plan to spend another cent of their blood money, and that's one of two reasons I found a job here. I need the income, and they would never think to look for me at a carnival."

She snapped her focus his way. "You're in danger?" she whispered. "If they find you? Oh, but—surely your own family wouldn't harm you!"

His mouth tightened in a grim line. "My grandfather has a warped sense of right and wrong. A breach of loyalty to him and the organization is the same as treason to a king, even if it's morally the right thing to do. A cousin was rubbed out for having thought to be a squealer." His words grew vague, slow, as if he were speaking to himself and had forgotten her. She wondered if he'd ever aired his concerns to anyone before now. Somehow she doubted it and felt both honored and apprehensive that he confided in her.

He jerked out of his solemn musings and gave her a tight smile.

"Grandfather would never believe I'd be working with a traveling carnival heading in the opposite direction from where I last told him I was going. Besides, he and his men wouldn't be seen dead in a place like this. Operas are his form of amusement, and nightclubs are his men's."

"But what if the troupe heads to New York City and someone recognizes you there? What then?"

"According to Chester, the carnival is traveling north through Connecticut. But if that day ever comes, if the train heads for New York, I'll figure out a plan of action then."

She nodded, trying to sort through the startling weight of his disclosure.

"Hey." He stopped and pulled her around to face him, resting his hands lightly on her shoulders. "I didn't tell you any of this to upset or worry you. You're safe, even if they find me, which they won't. I only told you to set your mind at ease that I'm really not stalking you and do have a good reason for being here. Okay?"

She returned his faint smile. "I'm not sure. Does this mean you've finally quit your job as my guardian angel?"

He snorted in mild displeasure at the term, dropping his hands to his sides. "An angel? No. But you could do worse than have me for a bodyguard. I've been trained all my life to be alert and cautious, among other things." He didn't elaborate, and she decided she didn't want to know.

"I suppose then, it's okay," she said on a mock sigh. "But I really can take care of myself." She couldn't resist the reminder, and he laughed.

Shivers danced along her spine at the warm, spontaneous sound. For a reason she couldn't grasp, especially after such grim revelations, she felt buoyant as they caught up to their hosts. Chester and Cassie once again remembered they had company and turned to tell Roland and Angel about the next attraction.

Upon seeing the sideshow tent and the banner above it, Angel froze.

Chapter 6

Roland wondered what had happened. One minute they were finally talking on companionable terms, and the next, Angel seemed to have turned to stone.

"Are you all right?" he asked in confusion.

"Fine," she whispered, her eyes on the banner that hung high and spread from one end of the wide tent to the other. "Just. . .fine."

Roland looked up at the painted caricatures displaying all manner of human oddities lined up in a row, six of them, from a tattooed man covered in pictures and piercings to a pair of Siamese twins joined at the shoulder.

"The Human Freak Show," Chester read. "One of the carnival's main attractions. That and Cassie's act probably bring in the most money."

"More's the pity," Cassie intoned. "It's a shame to parade people around as if they were nothing more than animals."

Angel threw a swift look her way but didn't respond.

"I never noticed any of them at the cookhouse tent," Roland observed.

"They don't eat with the rest of us, except for Jim the Giant—the tall man who sat at our table," Chester explained. "He stands at near seven feet and sure is handy when I need something retrieved that's out of reach. I'm a tad on the short side, you might have noticed," he joked. "A likable fellow, Jim. Don't know the others. The man in charge of the sideshow keeps them hidden for the most part. He has a black soul, I'd wager, and doesn't treat them at all well."

"Then why do they stay?" Angel's words were hoarse. She stared at the tent.

"My guess is they have no other way to make a living. They're ridiculed by society and, especially in these hard times, wouldn't risk leaving a place that offers sure room and board. Back in the nineteenth century, things were worse. Their kind were thought of as monsters and put in cages. Some of them were even hunted down and killed."

Angel winced. "But some leave, don't they?" Her question seemed far from casual. "Some leave this carnival world and go on to lead normal lives?"

Chester scratched his head. "I suppose so."

"Do you know anyone from this carnival who did?"

"Can't say as I do. But I've only been with Mahoney & Pearson a little over a year."

"I'd like to meet them. . .the ones who work inside that tent."

Chester raised his brows in surprise. Even Roland looked at Angel oddly upon hearing the resolve that strengthened her melancholy words. Cassie's gaze went elsewhere, past the tent to the stationary Ferris wheel; she seemed to have detached herself from the conversation.

"I'm not sure that's possible," Chester said. "You'd need to talk to Tucker, the man in charge, and he's not a nice sort. Another thing, they might take offense to your asking them questions. For the act, they do as they're told, but for the most part, they keep to themselves and don't trust others. Can't say I blame 'em."

"I'd still like to try," Angel insisted softly.

"Just why are you so interested?" Chester asked.

Angel shrugged, but Roland sensed she was hiding something. "If they don't want me there, I'll go. I'd just like the chance to meet and talk with them. Not to. . .observe them."

"Tell you what I can do," Chester relented. "After my act some night, assuming you can find someone to man your ticket booth, I'll take you to the last show. Afterward, I'll talk with Tucker and pass along your request."

"Thank you, Chester. I'd appreciate that."

Roland felt Chester could be trusted but didn't like the idea of Angel going anywhere alone with the man. Judging by Cassie's slight frown, neither did she.

"We should be going," she urged. "There's more to see and do, and I have to get to work soon. I need plenty of practice if I want to try out my new act this weekend."

"Not the backward flip?" Chester didn't sound pleased.

"Exactly that."

"You almost got yourself killed last time!"

"I've been working on it. I have the timing down now."

The two moved toward the midway, quietly arguing.

Roland wondered what existed in women that their entire gender seemed to think they could face any risk and get away with it, as if supposing they could exercise complete control over its outcome. He'd never been dense enough to assume he had control over his life; his father and grandfather wielded supreme authority and rarely gave him the chance to think for himself. His little sister, on the other hand, possessed a streak of confident carelessness; Cassie obviously thought herself indestructible, and Angel foolishly entertained the same theory.

But it wasn't her string of reckless acts that concerned him at the moment. She continued to stare at the banner, her eyes full of horrified pity mingled with grief and. . .tears?

"Angel?" he quietly prodded.

She looked his way as if just coming out of a trance.

"Maybe we should catch up with the others?"

"Okay." She whisked away the moisture that beaded her lower lashes.

"Hey, what's wrong?" He hadn't expected the low blow to his gut that the sight of her tears caused him.

She shook her head as if she wouldn't answer then did. "Do you ever wonder where they come from?" she asked sadly. "About their families, and if they, if they. . .miss them?"

"Homesick?" he asked gently. "Wish now you'd never taken the train? You can still go back, you know."

"No." She gave one last somber glance to the banner. "I can never go back." Turning from him, she walked away.

Curious at her hollow words, Roland watched her a moment before moving to catch up to her. "Then it looks like there's nothing left but to make the best with the hand you've been dealt."

A slight grin tilted her mouth. "That sounds like something Nettie would say. Except for the gambling part. She abhorred it. Said it was the devil's game."

"Nettie?"

"My aunt's cook and a very dear friend. If she were here right now, she'd probably tell me that, in order to stay strong, I must face the day so that the shadows are behind me." At the puzzled lift of his brows, she clarified, "When you face the sunlight, shadows fall behind you. It was her way of saying not to live in the past or dwell on where you've been."

"Smart lady, your cook. Wish it were so simple."

"It's really not, is it? Sometimes the past leaves questions that need to be answered—"

"Hey, you two," Chester called back. "Are we talking to ourselves up here? I thought you wanted a tour."

"We're coming." Angel quickened her pace. Roland regretted that she'd had no chance to continue and hoped they might resume their conversation later.

The rest of the tour proved more peaceful. Angel didn't talk much, but she relaxed, laughing at Chester's jokes and giving Roland more than one of her pretty smiles in reply to something he said. He felt relieved that she obviously no longer resented or feared being in his company. The four parted ways at Chester's tent, with an invitation and promise to come view his act soon.

"Maybe we can talk again later?" Roland suggested to Angel once Cassie headed for the back of the lot, where the biggest attractions stood, and Chester disappeared inside his tent.

Peering up at him, she squinted, as if thinking it over. "Maybe we can."

She gave him an easy smile and walked in the direction opposite where the animals lodged.

Roland watched her go. And maybe. . .joining up with the carnival would offer bonuses he'd never dreamed of. He couldn't say if he desired Angel as a potential girlfriend, even as a date. That was thinking too far ahead, and his state of affairs was shaky at best, disastrous at worst. But he would like to know her better, and it seemed, for once, she agreed.

He found it a frightening prospect, but freeing as well, not having to answer to the immoral traditions of the Piccoli way of life. And this time he was determined to make it last.

❧

After hours of standing on her feet, Angel made her painful walk to the car she shared with Cassie. In the narrow ticket booth by the Ferris wheel, there hadn't been a stool on which to sit, though there was room for one. She enjoyed the lively music that rang through the evening, hour upon hour, and the children's happy laughter and squeals, but she envied those customers who sat in the little hanging cars. She would have been content to sit on the ground by the time she closed. At least the living lot wasn't far.

Once inside her railcar, she slipped off her pumps and wiggled her toes, lifting hot, swollen feet to the mattress where she half-reclined. Cassie wasn't there yet, and she took the opportunity to pull her valise from beneath the bunk, rummage for the album, and bring it to rest on her pillow. She found the photograph and ran inquisitive fingers over the faded image of the veiled face.

"Who were you, Mother?" she wistfully asked. "What did you feel. . . think? Why'd you give me away? Because of your face? Or did you even want me to begin with?"

A swift thump against the outside wall of the railcar startled her. She shut the book and sat up, almost banging her head on the bunk above. When the door didn't swing open, revealing Cassie, she grew curious and went to investigate.

Outside, a man with wild sandy brown hair leaned with one fist against their car. He looked her way, his hazel eyes snapping in anger.

"Whatta you want?" He pulled his hand from where he'd slammed it, making a clear effort to try to regain control over whatever upset him.

"I'm Angel. I live here." She hesitated then stepped down. "I heard a noise."

"Angel, is it? Yeah, I heard about you." He ignored her reference to his action. "I'm one of them who runs the gaming booths—Harvey's the name. My car's behind yours."

"Oh." She smiled politely. She knew the car ahead of theirs belonged to Cassie's parents, briefly wondered where Roland slept, then wondered why she should care.

"It's a pleasure to meet you," she said quickly, to cover up her flustered state over the thought of Roland so suddenly entering her mind.

Harvey's brows sailed up. "You might change your tune in time. I'm told I'm not easy to get along with." He shook his hand a bit. She noticed the knuckles were red and scraped.

"We all have our moments. Is your hand all right?"

He slipped the offended member into his jacket pocket. "Not a thing wrong with it."

His tone suggested she was prying, and she prepared to tell him good night, when the crunch of footsteps made her look behind. After all she had experienced with her rescuer rogue, it didn't surprise her to see her visitor.

Roland looked from Harvey to Angel. "Am I interrupting?"

"Just meeting my neighbor." Angel grew irritated. She'd thought after their last conversation he would stop snooping into her affairs, that they were on their way to relating on good terms. But he obviously hadn't quit his self-assigned role as her guard.

Roland looked the man up and down as if he'd like to eliminate him. "Name's Roland."

Harvey crossed his arms over his chest and narrowed his eyes. "You're the new fellow they got to look after the animals."

"I am." It sounded like a challenge.

"Don't like animals."

"How was your first day?" Angel asked quickly, hoping to defuse a potentially volatile situation.

Roland's taut features relaxed a bit as he looked her way. "For someone just learning the ropes, good, I suppose. Mama Philena was a big help. Have you met her yet?"

"I've heard about her."

"You'll like her. She's a character." He gave Harvey another once-over before again directing his attention to Angel. "How was your day?"

"Long, exhausting. I managed."

"Well, I'll just let you two get on with your little chitchat," Harvey said snidely. "I haven't the time." He moved toward his railcar without waiting for a reply.

"Nice fellow," Roland said dryly. "A new friend?"

His tone exasperated her. "What if he is? Are you going to disapprove and tell me I should stay away from him? That he's too dangerous?"

"Just asking."

She doubted it and tilted her head with suspicion. "Just why are you here, Roland?"

"Excuse me?"

"You must have come for some reason other than to reveal your displeasure with the company I keep." She wasn't really keeping Harvey's company but didn't bother to tell him that.

"Actually, I was heading to my car." He moved past her.

"Your car?"

Her stunned words stopped Roland in his tracks, and he turned to look. "You didn't think I was bedding down with the animals, did you? As a matter of fact, we're neighbors, too. My living quarters are next door to your new friend's." He tipped his hat. "Good night, Angel. I'll see you at breakfast."

She stood speechless, stunned that her curiosity had been so promptly satisfied. The train wasn't the longest she'd seen, but she didn't think he would be so close. It didn't irritate her, exactly, but it did unsettle her, making her stomach take a sudden sharp dip.

"Hi, Angel," Cassie's voice broke through her thoughts as Angel watched Roland retreat into the second car down from theirs. "What are you doing out here?"

"Talking to the neighbors." She noticed Cassie's puzzled scan of the now-empty area. "Did your stunt work?"

Cassie scowled. "Papa's being stubborn and won't let me try it out on the crowds yet. But I have half a mind to anyway. How was your first day?"

"Busy. Hardly got a chance to breathe."

"Not surprising. The rides are a huge draw." Cassie grew excited. "Say, I can ask Mahoney to let you work the ticket booth by our tent. That way you could slip in and watch me perform sometime."

"That would be great, only. . ."

"What?"

"Can I have a stool in the booth?"

Cassie laughed. "The ground not so soft on your poor pups?" She cast a glance down to Angel's stockinged feet as she opened the door of their railcar and swung up.

Angel followed. "That, and the heels of my pumps. It's muddy there. If it's all right with you, I'd like to wear the flats again."

"Sure. Keep them."

"Thanks." Angel slid the door on its track to close it but couldn't resist poking her head out one last time.

She didn't really expect Roland to be standing outside, did she?

Shaking off such silly thoughts and an even sillier twinge of disappointment, she firmly shut the door.

Chapter 7

As Roland worked, he thought about the grubbiness of his current task. Strange that as menial and dirty as his new job was, he felt cleaner than when he'd dressed to the nines and kept an account of his grandfather's books, which had been the nicest of his worst assignments.

"So when are you going to marry the girl?"

At Mama Philena's outrageous words, Roland almost dropped the long-handled brush he held. He looked inside the tent toward the nearest stall. "Excuse me?"

"You heard." She looked to where he stood outside with Jenny, giving her a bath. "It's obvious you're smitten and the two of you have something going on."

Somewhere in her sixties, Mama, as the carnies all called her, stood two feet shorter than Roland and had more brass than he'd seen in men twice her size. With her gray ringlets pulled back by a bright ribbon and wearing the most vibrant colors in clothing he'd seen—today's choice an eye-straining orange and violet—Mama was unique. She had a habit of squinting, as she did now, and Roland wondered if the woman needed corrective glasses as well as an alteration in judgment.

"I've known her three days."

"Could have fooled me. I can read people well, son. It's why I took a job as fortune-teller when I was young, when Mahoney's papa, my husband, ran the place. I knew nothing about looking into crystal balls and that sort of nonsense—didn't believe in it then; don't believe in it now. Just all for show. Gave the air of mystery the customers clamored for. But I could look into a person's eyes, watch their body language, and read their emotions easy. If they were sad. Happy. Nervous. Figuring out a fortune to match wasn't hard."

"Why'd you quit?"

"I got convicted."

"Convicted?" He stopped sweeping the brush along Jenny's hide.

Mama finished currying one of the Andalusians. Apparently the owners gave her free rein when it came to their beautiful beasts, unlike Roland, whom they watched as if he might suddenly set their horses' tails on fire. In the short time he'd been with the carnival, he'd learned that few crossed this feisty woman.

"A funny thing, that." She set the brush down on a sawhorse bench, growing pensive. "A few years back, a carny who worked here, she did the convicting. Told me about God and His love. Said a woman once came to see her act and witnessed to her—that was the word she used—'witnessed.' Funny word.

"Puts me in mind of someone being sworn in to tell the whole truth and nothing but at a trial. In a sense, I guess that's what it is. Plenty of people tend to act nervous and strange, like felons, when you tell them of God—much like they do in a courtroom, I expect. She said she wanted to spread His message and do for others what that woman had done for her. Sweet woman but so sad. And not just because of her appearance. . . ." Her words trailed off, as if she relived the moment or realized she'd said too much; Roland couldn't be sure. "Listen to me, carrying on when we have a full morning's work! How's Jenny's bath coming along?"

Roland's attention returned to the baby elephant that had begun to fan her ears and sway her immense body, a sign he'd come to understand as her becoming agitated. "It would help if Jabar was here. I think Jenny wants her master. She doesn't seem happy with me."

Mama let out a little huff of exasperation. "That boy can never seem to be anywhere on time, and having his arm in a sling doesn't help. Poor dear. We warned him not to climb on top of the train, but he just doesn't listen, or maybe it's that his English isn't good so he didn't understand. At least the fall only sprained his arm instead of breaking it—or his fool head."

Roland had been surprised to learn Jenny's owner was a ten-year-old Arab orphan whose parents died in a fire. What didn't surprise him was how Mama coddled him, a nurturing mother hen to an adopted lost chick.

"Hullo!" a boy's cheery voice called, and Roland turned to look. His heart jumped a sudden beat at the sight of the two approaching.

"Speak of the little devil," Mama murmured affectionately, exiting the tent.

"I brought pretty lady," the scamp continued, his black eyes twinkling merrily beneath his white turban at Roland. "She must see you."

Angel's skin flushed deep rose, her eyes flashing to Roland in embarrassment then settling on Mama. "Actually, he got that mixed up. I came to talk to you. Mr. Mahoney said he needs you. He also said you could tell me where to find a stool for the ticket booth."

"That boy of mine couldn't find an elephant in a pup tent," Mama quipped and patted Jenny's flank. "Isn't that right, Jenny?"

Jenny stood at attention, the snout of her trunk merrily roaming Jabar's front then curling around his slim hips. He fed her a peanut. "Up, Jenny! Up!" he commanded with a smile.

The elephant obeyed, lifting her agile owner, who couldn't have weighed more than Angel's satchel, high into the air and over her head, while the boy sat perched in the curve of her trunk. As Jenny loosened her trunk from around the boy, he stretched one skinny brown leg over the top of the elephant, nimbly swinging around to sit astride the animal.

Roland had watched but still couldn't figure out how the boy did it. Jabar beamed at the two new carnies staring up at him in awed disbelief. Roland shook his head and glanced at Angel. She looked his way, grinning, then shrugged.

"Jabar, you shouldn't be showing off any tricks with your arm in that sling," Mama reprimanded.

"Jenny not hurt Jabar. Jenny love Jabar." He leaned forward and patted the elephant's head.

"That may be, but that doesn't have anything to do with—oh, never mind," she finished in frustration when the boy quirked his head, puzzled, as if unable to follow her words. "Just be careful. We wouldn't want to put both your arms in slings, now would we?" She turned to Angel. "About that stool. Chester might have a spare. I remember seeing more than one in his tent. Roland, why don't you go along and carry it for her?"

"Oh really, that's not necessary—"

"I'd be happy to."

He looked at Angel as they both answered at once. "That is, if you don't mind the company."

Her lips lifted a fraction, and he felt relieved he had guessed right to give her the choice instead of choosing for her.

"I suppose not."

At her soft response, Mama chuckled and muttered, "Oh no, nothing going on there at all!"

Roland ignored her smug comment and brought his fingertips to Angel's elbow long enough to turn her toward Chester's tent and away from Mama's suggestive musings.

"What did she mean?" Angel gave him a sidelong glance as they walked down the midway.

"Did she say something?"

"Now Roland." Her voice took on the tone of an amused scolding. "You know she did."

"Sorry. Wasn't paying much attention, what with—"

"Hey! Watch out."

Startled to hear a childish shriek from near the ground, they looked down. But it wasn't a child who stood there, though the voice sounded as if it belonged to one. A dwarf woman in her twenties, the blue feather she wore in her hat half her approximate three feet of height, stared up with china blue eyes, her hands balled on her hips. Blond ringlets spilled from beneath her hat to her tiny shoulders.

"You can say that again—about not paying attention," she huffed. "You two trying to mow a person down?"

"Sorry!" Angel said. "We didn't see you. That is, I mean. . ." She blushed furiously at her thoughtless words, but the woman only chuckled and lowered her hands.

"That's all right, honey. I expect if I were ten feet tall, you wouldn't have seen me either, not with the way you two were staring at each other. So, you two are the new carnies I've been hearing so much about. Coming here together and pretending not to know one another?"

"Oh, but we didn't! It wasn't how it looked—"

"I got eyes." The woman interrupted Angel's flustered remark and winked. "My name's Posey." She struck up her hand. "As in pretty as a posy. That's what my sweetheart says." She smiled shyly, revealing two dimples.

"I'm Angel." She bent down to take the offered hand. The woman gave Angel's a swift shake then turned to Roland, doing the same as he introduced himself.

"Just don't let Mahoney know there's anything going on between you two, you being so new here and all. He's still upset Germaine and Lionel left him high and dry."

"But really, we're not together—"

Posey looked beyond them. "Oh, there's my sweetheart now!" She smiled. "Would you like to meet him?"

"Of course," Roland inserted, aware of Angel's distress over the misconception of their relationship.

A young man no taller than Posey, with dark red hair and blue eyes, came up beside her. "How's my darlin' Posey today?" he asked, an Irish lilt to his accent. He gave her a kiss on her dimpled cheek. Suddenly shy, she clutched her hand in her skirts and batted her lashes.

"Oh Darrin. These are the new carnies. Angel and Roland."

"You two married?" Darrin asked.

Angel gasped in outright shock, and again Roland answered. "Just friends." She didn't correct him, and he felt thankful that maybe he wasn't assuming too much to say so.

"That's how me and Darrin started off," Posey said, dreamily looking into his eyes. "We fought like cats and dogs at first, always snapping at each other, but one day something just clicked. We're getting married two weeks from now." She directed her happy gaze up to Angel. "You'll come to the wedding, won't you?"

Roland didn't miss Darrin's sharp look at Posey.

"I'd love to." Angel found her voice.

"I would, too." Roland felt Angel glance at him then away again.

"Oh good!" Posey beamed.

"But I'm surprised Mr. Mahoney will allow it," Angel said, "after all I've heard about his view on carnies getting involved."

"Mahoney knows a gold mine when he sees one. We're staying with the carnival. Our manager has already tagged us as 'The tiniest leprechaun couple to walk the face of the planet.'" She rolled her eyes. "As long as it snags the crowds, they don't mind what we do."

"Don't know the truth of that, us being the tiniest," Darrin added. "But let them have their fun, as long as they let us have ours. Right, Posey me love?"

She giggled like a besotted schoolgirl. "Right, my darling prince. We should be getting back to the tent. So nice meeting you both. Come on, honey." She took hold of Darrin's hand, pulling him away with her.

"Are you certain you should have invited them to our wedding?" Roland heard Darrin ask as the two walked away.

"Hush! They'll hear. And Mama was right. They're nice, not like some who joined up. I heard Angel's even been asking to speak with us—"

"More like gawk at us."

"You aren't used to that yet?" she scoffed. "Anyway, I like her. And she was gawking because you asked if they were married. Fine thing! She was all right before you did that. For whatever reason, they want to keep their little affair a secret, so let them. . . ."

Angel's eyes widened as she looked after the tiny couple, now out of earshot. *Affair?* she mouthed and swung her annoyed gaze to Roland's.

He wasn't sure whether to apologize or excuse himself and seek escape.

"This is your fault," she seethed. "You insisted on following me here, and now the entire carnival thinks we're headed for the altar or are already married and hiding it. I've been hearing remarks like that for days."

"And because I insisted on following me here," he responded levelly, "those young hooligans didn't try to come back and finish what they had started."

"They probably wouldn't have come back at all."

"You can't guarantee that. I know the type, remember."

"How could I forget?" she responded sweetly, her eyes filleting him where he stood.

"I wish you would."

At his quiet words, she clamped her lips tight, glancing away.

"Would it be so bad for them to think I happen to like you and want to see more of you?"

Her eyes snapped up to him again. "I told you once before, I'm not a loose woman, and I won't be thought of that way!"

"No one thinks that."

"An *affair?*" she reminded incredulously.

He winced at how vile she made the word sound. "Posey's colorful vocabulary. You met the woman. She'd probably call a dame blinking her eyes as being cast under a witch's spell."

"Could you please not use that word?"

Her unexpected switch caught him off guard. "What word? *Witch*?"

"*Dame*. I don't like it. It sounds. . .cheap."

Roland had never associated the word as meaning anything but a lady. Everyone he knew used the slang term, but he nodded. "If it'll make you happy, I'll stop."

His quick acquiescence mollified her. "I'm sorry I jumped on you. I suppose it really isn't your fault how they perceive us."

"You're upset. It's understandable. If I hadn't insisted on carrying your luggage, you're right, they wouldn't have immediately paired us off." Word of mouth obviously spread fast through the carny grapevine. "But again, is it really so bad for them to think we might happen to like each other?"

Her eyes widened. "Do you?"

"Like you? Yes."

She looked away as if suddenly at a loss, and he resisted the strong urge to ask if she returned the favor or at least no longer considered him the enemy.

"We're attracting attention." She released a weary breath, and he glanced around, noticing a few workers had stopped what they were doing to stare. "Let's walk. To Chester's tent, I believe it was?" She resumed moving down the midway.

Roland fell into step beside her, casting her sidelong glances. He wanted to know how his admission made her feel, but this was the worst possible time to broach the subject. If he tried, she might push him into the wall of the tent they now passed then run off as the whole thing came tumbling down on top of his head.

They arrived at Chester's tent just as Cassie rushed out of it. Dashing her fingers beneath her eyes shining with tears, she appeared more than a little upset.

"Cassie?" Angel asked in concern.

The blond shook her head, her face a picture of complete distress. "I don't want to talk about it." She hurried away.

Angel looked after Cassie, as if uncertain what to do, then glanced up at Roland. He shrugged and shook his head, defeated when it came to a woman's tears. He could barely figure out the woman with him, much less a near stranger. Even though the woman with him was almost that. So why, then, did he feel a connection to her, experience an urge to protect her, and battle an almost-constant desire to be with her?

Curbing a groan, he held the tent flap aside and allowed her to enter Chester's tent ahead of him.

Chester offered them both an abrupt nod in greeting, his jaw tense. Angel had never seen the affable man look so sullen. She considered asking if everything was all right between him and Cassie but decided not to interfere. She didn't know him well enough to invite confidences.

"Hope we aren't intruding," Roland said.

Chester shrugged, the smile he offered grim. "What can I do for you two?"

Angel told him about her need for a stool, and he readily complied.

"Sure, I can let one go." He moved to a wooden counter where three stools sat in front of what looked like a miniature circus, smaller than a dollhouse. Tiny striped tents and banners stood erected on a platform. A model of a Ferris wheel, half the size of her hand, stood to the side.

Fascinated, Angel drew near. "Did you make this?"

"Sure did." A bit of tension drained from his voice.

"It's very good. There's so much detail." She sensed Roland draw closer, though he maintained his distance.

"As long as you're both here, why don't I give you that free show? I haven't much else to do, so come see my little beauties." His manner undergoing a complete roundabout, Chester looked beyond Angel's shoulder with a grin. "Come on, Roland, my man. Step right up. Don't be shy." He moved to retrieve a cigar box and carefully slid back the lid.

Angel heard Roland's footsteps rustle nearer in the grass.

Chester put something from his hand onto the small carnival layout. He looked up again.

"You'll have to come closer. These human fleas are small. You'll need to look at them through the special Fresnel lens I have."

Angel inhaled softly as she felt Roland's warmth at her back, though no part of him touched her. She struggled to concentrate on what Chester said as he showed each of his fleas' amazing tricks. One appeared to lift a set of barbells, another to pull a wagon. A third to dance. Another flea moved the Ferris wheel by walking atop it.

"That is amazing," she said, genuinely impressed. "You called them names, but how do you tell them apart?"

"Waltzing Matilda is faster than the others. Slow Moe at the wheel, well, his name tells it all. Each of them has a different personality or characteristic."

She bent over the lens again. "They're so tiny! What do they eat?"

"They don't call them human fleas for nothing."

She straightened. "Wha—oh."

"Yeah, Cassie had that same horrified look in her eyes when she found out. Ever been bit by a mosquito? Dozens at once? Not much different, except I know my beauties haven't any diseases, since I take care of them. Sadly, their life span is short though. Doctors used to use leeches, and my little gems don't take anywhere near as much blood as one of those."

Unable to prevent a little shudder, Angel looked into the lens again. The sudden stirring of her hair by Roland's warm breath as he also leaned in to look had her jump as high as one of the fleas.

She straightened, knocking into him, and twisted around, startled to find him so close. His dark eyes stared into hers, only inches away. It took a moment for her mind to start functioning again.

"I imagine you want to see, too." She hastily stepped aside. "Please, take my place. I must be getting back. Thanks for the free show—and the stool." With a tense smile, she picked one up and escaped from the tent.

"She's got it bad," Chester said with an annoying chuckle.

"I don't think so."

"Then you're blind, deaf, *and* dumb." His words came calmly as he began putting away his flea family. "And I don't mean mute."

"Don't I get a look?"

"You're not going after her?"

"It's the last thing she wants."

"I wouldn't be so sure. Cassie behaved like Angel, too, at first."

Since he opened the topic, Roland pursued. "And now? She didn't look happy coming from your tent."

Chester's jovial features tightened into their earlier grimace. "Daddy problems. Someone told him they saw us together, and Cassie got a reprimand."

"I don't get it. She looks old enough to choose for herself and not have to worry about her parents doing it for her."

"Yeah, but she respects her father and his wishes. Crazy thing is, I actually admire that, as aggravated as it can make me. You, on the other hand, don't have a disapproving father to worry about. So get on out of here and find Angel."

"What about my free show?"

"I'm not going anywhere; neither are the fleas. But she is." Chester inclined his head toward the exit. "Go on." He resumed putting the fleas in the box.

"Fine."

Roland left Chester alone with his flea family. Angel was right. The whole blasted carnival seemed ready to pair them together, not that he minded. But he had more chance of riding atop an elephant and learning Jabar's tricks than he did of discovering the secret to talking with Angel on pleasant terms, and that's what infuriated him. The carnies' wisecracks and sly glances only added salt to the wound of Angel's indifference.

Roland had never classified himself as arrogant or conceited. Young women his family approved of had shown interest in him, his money, his name, but he never really took part in anything serious. He would be lying if he didn't admit that Angel's disinterest didn't sting a little—all right, more than a little. And maybe it was one part challenge and five parts concern that prodded him to find opportunities to share her company. But the most peculiar feeling had come over him, especially lately, that the reason for her frosty attitude had to do with more than Roland being a Piccoli. She was hiding something; he was sure of it.

Up ahead, he spotted her and held back, his muscles again going tense when he saw the carny from the night before with her. What was his name? Oh yes. *Harvey.*

Roland didn't want to behave like her shadow, stalking her, and he sure had no claim on her life or reason to be jealous. But when the crude man grabbed her elbow, once she moved away, he felt his hands curl into fists and just prevented himself from lunging forward. He waited, watching to see what she would do.

She glanced over her shoulder to where the louse held her, said something, then snapped her arm from his hold. Again she spoke then walked off, her head held high, leaving Harvey to stare after her, nudging his hat higher on his head as if befuddled.

Roland smiled grimly. She'd obviously put the man in his place. Remembering the sting of her words, he could almost feel sorry for the poor brute.

Maybe she didn't need someone watching out for her, but that didn't prevent him from worrying about her or wanting to get to know her better. The woman was constantly on his mind. Question was, how could he achieve what looked to be more impossible with each passing day?

Chapter 8

Angel clutched the bed frame in a death grip. It shook like what she imagined it would feel going through an earthquake or hurricane. The railcar walls vibrated with a metallic clunking noise as if they might suddenly disintegrate in a strong wind.

She didn't remember this awful feeling of being about to take her last breath on the train she took a week ago, though the accommodations were nicer in Roland's private car and the dining compartment. Angel could hardly believe she'd lived on a train like this as a child. The carnival was much different than she'd once imagined, and except for the present situation with the fear that at any moment she might be shaken apart, she'd found a sense of harmony she'd never known at her aunt's home. The carnies she'd met so far were all wonderful, making her feel as if she belonged. None of them ever belittled a remark she made, which helped her to relax and feel freer to join in their conversations.

"You'll get used to it," her cabin mate said from the cot above. "What's really bad is traveling this way when your head feels like it's splitting wide open."

Angel could imagine this kind of travel *giving* her a headache.

"I heard you've been asking about your mother. Any luck with that?"

"No." Angel gave a weary sigh. "No one remembers her."

"Mind my asking why you're so intent on finding her, especially since you don't remember her?" Cassie paused as Angel struggled. "If you'd rather not say, or if you tell me to mind my own business, I'll understand."

It was actually nice to have someone in whom to confide, a benefit she'd never shared with her waspish cousins. She'd been able to speak with Nettie only between her friend's chores. Strange how Angel's aunt lamented the difficulty of surviving the Depression but kept Nettie on, though she never did pay the woman her worth. Keeping up appearances was paramount to Aunt Genevieve.

Angel squashed further bitter thoughts.

"I never felt like I belonged at my aunt's. I. . .I suppose if I ever do find my mother, there's a strong possibility she might not wish to see me. But I'm willing to take the risk." The more she thought about it, taking into account the behavior of her aunt and cousins, she wouldn't put it past them to lie about the cause of Lila's disappearance.

66

Cassie's head suddenly popped down as she hung over the cot, startling Angel into jumping back a little. Her new friend gave a goofy smile. How she could balance herself in an oversize tin can that felt as if it might rattle apart at any moment, Angel couldn't begin to imagine.

"Don't you get dizzy like that?"

"I'm an acrobat; it's my nature. When I was little, I thought I'd be a tight-rope walker. But I prefer to do my daredevil stunts on things in motion—like my horses. Rattling train cars that zoom into the night work, too."

Angel grinned with admiration. If she tried doing what Cassie did, she would probably get herself killed.

"So if you find her, what then? Will you pretend like nothing's happened and ask her back into your life as a permanent fixture?"

"I suppose a lot depends on her. How you don't get sick to your stomach hanging like an opossum is beyond me."

"I'm tough." Cassie grinned. "Besides, I need the practice for my new act." She initiated a swift flip, holding to the edge of her bed while throwing her legs behind her and landing on the train floor, then threw her arms out with panache. "Ta-dah!"

Cassie's landing hadn't been solid, but Angel clapped, chuckling in awed disbelief. "Then you're going through with it?"

A determined look crossed her friend's pretty features. "Maybe if I show Papa I'm not a child anymore, he won't be so dead set against me seeing who I would like."

"Chester doesn't seem happy about the act either."

Cassie sighed. "Only because he doesn't think I'm ready. He has faith in me. That's one of the things I love about him." Her face grew rosy, and she quickly sank beside Angel on her cot. "What about you and Roland? I noticed you two haven't been getting along well lately."

"I wish people would stop pairing us off," Angel mumbled. "There's a lot you don't know about him. Things about his family. . ." She remembered her promise to keep his identity secret just in time. "They're not so nice."

"Well, I suppose if Chester let that stop him, we would never have gotten together. Not that we're together exactly," she added with haste.

"Cassie, it's okay. I won't tell. It's obvious you two are close."

Cassie sighed and nodded. "He wants to marry me."

"Cassie!"

"I told him no."

Angel thought back. "At the tent when Roland and I got there—"

"We were discussing it, yes. I can't go against Papa's wishes, but at the same time I don't want to live without Chester."

"Wouldn't Mahoney be upset if you two married?"

She scowled. "We can't live the entirety of our lives to suit our boss. I tried that, and I'm sick of it. After what Germaine did, running off with Lionel just because Mahoney didn't want them to marry. . . Truth is, I think he liked her. But Chester and I don't plan to leave the carnival, not that it matters. Not if I can't get Papa to change his mind."

"Doesn't it, um, bother you, how he takes care of his fleas?"

Cassie laughed, sounding relieved to change the subject. "I didn't like it one bit at first, let me tell you. But he's said it's safe; it's not like he could get a disease, since they aren't the type to bite animals." She shrugged. "I think when you love someone you just have to learn to take the fleas with the flowers." She grinned at her joke. "No one's perfect, Angel. You find that out pretty fast when working at a joint like this. Every man has his flaws or idiosyncrasies that you wish like everything you could change—and I'll bet the guys feel the same about us women. But if you love a person enough, you don't mind dealing with the problems or even ignoring them. Because there's so much more to appreciate. I love his laugh, the way he always tries to make others laugh, the way his eyes crinkle at the corners and. . ." She caught herself, embarrassed. "I just love being with him. And if living without a certain man is more difficult than living with him, imperfections and all, I think that's a basis for true love."

Cassie's words brought Roland to mind, which confused her. She didn't have feelings for him, and certainly, if she did, they would never include love. Still, she considered his main flaw: his mobster family. He couldn't change his origins, but he tried to change his future; she admired his perseverance in what she imagined couldn't be an easy challenge to undertake.

The train took a sudden sharp bend, throwing the girls against each other, and Angel again concentrated on striving to remain in one piece.

"Not to worry," Cassie assured her. "Won't be much longer. We should reach New Milford soon."

"I am so relieved to hear it!"

The girls looked at one another then giggled, and their conversation took on other directions as the train sped them to their destination.

❧

"How long did you say till we get there?" Roland didn't want to sound like a coward, but having never ridden in anything but his family's private car, he was getting a lesson in roughing it he would long remember. No one, but no one from the old life would imagine him in such a place. The thought pleased him.

With a maddening grin Chester eyed Roland's white-knuckled grip on the bedpost. "Track usually isn't so bad. Must have run into some rough. Winds are pretty high."

"You can say that again."

The train made another sharp rocking motion.

After endless minutes Roland heard the warning whistles and felt the train's momentum begin to slow.

"Don't look so smug yet. Now is where the fun really begins," Chester observed from where he sat on the floor, his back against the wall. "Once we pull in, we gotta get everything up and ready for tonight. Hope you got a good rest,'cause you're gonna need it."

At Chester's amused grin, Roland shot his new—and at the moment, questionable—friend a dirty look. Rest? The man had to be pulling his leg. The travel had been about as restful as racing pell-mell across New York City in a car with bad springs while being chased, like when Roland was a boy and his bodyguard grew a little too careless flirting with the lady friend of a dangerous mobster who happened to be one of Grandfather's worst enemies. After that incident, the bodyguard disappeared. Roland imagined his new locale was the bottom of the Hudson River.

Even riding on a train with a conductor who seemed to prefer the idea of flying by airplane to traveling by land and tried to push his locomotive to the limits of the airborne daredevils couldn't compare with the fear of that summer day. Living as a Piccoli, Roland had lost track of the times he'd been certain his life would end. Despite the hardship, he felt doubly thankful he had followed Angel what seemed longer than a mere week ago. He preferred living in this atmosphere, a world apart from his wealthy and dangerous roots. The carnies treated him with suspicion at first—he was a novice at menial labor and hadn't had an easy time of gaining their trust, something he still worked at—but at least they hadn't questioned him about his past, and for that, Roland was grateful.

Exiting the train, his legs still shaky, he noticed the glow of dawn filled the sky. The train had pulled off onto a sidetrack, away from the junction and out in the wilds, as before.

The roustabouts immediately began setting up the rides, and the meal tent was erected on the other side of the lot, breakfast administered rapidly. Afterward, with no idea what was expected of him, he searched out Mama Philena. She handed him a bucket of paste and a long-handled brush. "I'll take care of the animals. You go into town and hang flyers. On the sides of buildings, anywhere they'll fit."

He remained still when she turned to go. "Aren't you forgetting something?" He lifted the items he held in emphasis when she only stared. "The flyers?"

"Oh, I'm not forgetting anything, dearie. It's a two-man job. Your partner has them. Waiting over there for you, by Samson's railcar. Best hurry. It's a long walk into town."

Mama turned away, chuckling most wickedly, her shiny purple shirt seeming to echo her devious behavior, crackling with laughter at him as it rustled with her swift movements. He harbored no doubt about the identity of his partner. When he reached Angel waiting near the train, he went into surrender before she could pose an attack.

"I promise I had no part in this. If you want me to find someone else to help me, I will."

A grin, both amused and exasperated, lifted her mouth. "Oh don't be silly, Roland. I'm not mad. They do seem determined to put us together though, don't they? It's actually quite strange, when you consider it, since Mahoney's number-one rule for his carnival seems to be to discourage close rapport between male and female carnies." She shrugged in an offhand manner, further baffling him. "I don't mind working with you. Are you ready?"

Her eyes sparkled, as if she anticipated the outing.

Would he ever figure her out?

The walk to town was a few miles, but time seemed to pass quickly now that Angel had let down her guard and conversed on friendly terms. They talked of everything: the carnival; their experiences with it; the weather, sunny and clear. But they avoided the subject of their lives as if by unspoken agreement. Roland was almost sorry when they arrived in town, a pretty little community with the usual Victorian-style houses and stores, with a strip of short grass and blooming trees running along its center.

They chose a building with old, peeling posters as their first mark. While Angel held the carnival flyer against the wood, Roland executed a few swipes of paste over the paper with the brush until it rested flat against the building. Angel let out a little squeal when the bristles whisked over her hand.

"Sorry. This is my first experience doing this sort of thing."

"That's okay." She rubbed the back of her sticky hand on a leg of her denim trousers. "I imagine, with the life you've led, you're not accustomed to manual labor of any. . .regular sort."

Her words were cautious, her manner intent, and he recognized her desire to know more.

"You really don't want to know, Angel."

"Did you. . ." Her teeth pulled at her lip. "Did you kill anyone?"

Why did that always seem to be the first question the ladies asked? "No. But if I'd stuck around, my grandfather would have put me in a position to do so. He made that very clear at our last meeting."

She gave an abrupt nod. "Okay, so I guess we should find our next spot. Mama said fences or anywhere posters have been hanging and public buildings. They cleared it with those in charge, I would hope." She quickly moved away.

He followed her with brush and bucket. "I put that life behind me, Angel."

"I know."

"But it still scares you."

She hesitated. "Can you blame me? All I know about you Piccolis is what

I read in the papers. And what I've heard from others."

"We're not all cut from the same cloth. A cousin doesn't approve of the family business either. He's the quiet type though. Doesn't have the nerve to stand up against his father."

"What about your fiancée? How does she feel about it?"

"My *what*?" Stunned, he stopped walking. Her face was rosier, and he wondered if the exertion of the walk or the nature of the question had caused it.

"The papers said—"

"The papers. The society pages, no doubt." Roland grimaced at the reporters' tendency to get facts incorrect and spin their own web of tales to sell their blasted papers. "Well, they got it wrong. I'm not engaged."

"But—"

"I was almost engaged, for two weeks. We were thrown together by our families. Both of us realized it wouldn't work. She loves someone else, and I don't love her. End of story."

"Sorry. I didn't mean to be so nosy."

The tension left his muscles. "It's all right. No harm done."

"My aunt wanted me to marry someone, too. It's part of why I ran."

Taken aback, this time by her unexpected confidence, he shot her another look. He felt encouraged that she had relaxed with him enough to talk about her past and on her own initiative.

"Hey, mister!"

They turned to see a freckle-faced youngster, his brown hair uncombed and sticking out in tufts, his pants worn in the knees and a little too long. He looked around nine years of age.

"Whatcha carryin' a pail and brush for?"

"We're part of the carnival about three miles down the road."

The boy's eyes sparkled in excitement. "In Sutter's Field?"

"I. . .don't know. It's a field, near the depot."

"Shouldn't you be in school?" Angel gently chided.

The boy scowled. "Aw, book learning's for sissies."

"I'm no sissy, and I read books." Roland thought the boy's arrogant attitude toward education was much like his brother's. "An education will always benefit your mind and will keep working for you as you grow older." He felt Angel's stare and wondered if he was being too hard on the youngster.

The boy shrugged. "Can't go anyhow. Not since things got so bad. Mama needs me at home while Pa looks for work and Rex, too. That's my brother. I'm Sam. I'm runnin' an errand for Mama now."

Roland felt remorseful for his stiff words. After living a privileged lifestyle when it came to assets, it was too easy to forget the nation suffered a depression. "I'm sorry, son."

"How long will the carnival be here?"

"A couple of weeks, I imagine." Roland glanced at Angel, who shrugged. The flyers didn't say. He looked back at the boy. "I hope things go better for your family. We need to hang the rest of these posters now."

"Okay."

The boy dogged their steps up the road. He talked a mile a minute, and Roland thought a career as a carnival barker might be a strong prospect for his future. Their small, self-appointed guide pointed out buildings, talked about their owners, whether he did or didn't like them, and expressed a strong desire to visit the carnival. Roland wondered if Sam was forgetting his errand.

Together he and Angel pasted another flyer to a building, and the boy watched, engrossed. He followed them as they completed two more. Once they finished, he grinned.

"I gotta go now." He moved toward the druggist's, next door to the wall where they had hung the poster.

"If you come to the carnival, look me up," Roland said before Sam could disappear. "I'm a caretaker of the animals. We even have a live elephant."

"No foolin'? An elephant? Hot diggety dog! Wait'll I tell Joey. And he thought finding that turtle was so great!" He rushed into the building, and Roland smiled, remembering his own boyhood excitement and curiosities.

If only the warm feeling could have lasted.

Roland's blood froze as he caught sight of a thickset man wearing a three-piece, pin-striped suit and fedora five buildings away, near a lamppost. He slipped the bucket handle over his wrist, took the brush leaning against the building, and grabbed Angel's arm with his free hand, turning her quickly with him in the opposite direction.

"Hey!" She looked at him in confusion but didn't try to break his grip.

"Just keep walking."

He kept his voice low but couldn't mask his alarm. Her eyes widened, and she started to look over her shoulder.

"Don't look, Angel."

Quickly she focused ahead. Once they reached the corner of the next building and darted around it, he peered around the side, then he pressed his back against the wall and closed his eyes in a dizzying mix of anxiety not to be found and relief to have escaped.

"I should have known the conductor might say something about my sudden disappearance," he muttered. "My grandfather has close ties with the company."

All color drained from her face. "Your f–family? H–here?"

"He was too far away to make out, but a man back there looked like one of Grandfather's associates." Roland doubted many citizens of New

Milford wore such expensive suits or had the ox-like build Giuseppe did. And Grandfather's men traveled in pairs, which meant Giuseppe's partner, Lorenzo, wasn't far. "We need to get back to the carnival. Now."

She gave a jerky nod, her eyes round with the same apprehension he felt. "It's all right, Angel. He didn't see me. If we head around the back and circle the buildings, we should be safe. I won't let anyone hurt you." Again he clasped her arm, this time gently, his manner intense. He noticed her state of shock and gave her shoulder a shake to break her out of her daze.

"Are you with me?" He kept his tone calm but firm.

"Yes," she whispered.

He smiled to reassure her, though he felt just as anxious, and pulled her with him through the first phase of his plan. To his relief they found their way back to where they started, unobserved.

On the open road Roland felt like a sitting duck. He doubted Giuseppe would shoot; in all likelihood, his orders were to bring him back unharmed. But Giuseppe had no respect for women, those not connected with the family, and Roland dreaded the idea of him coming in contact with Angel, uncertain what the goon might do. The best-case scenario would be if he demanded she come with them; the worst-case. . .Roland didn't dare imagine the worst case.

Not once did he release his hold on Angel's arm, and he felt the tremors of fear that moved through her. She managed to keep up with his rapid gait but didn't say a word. Once the carnival tents came in sight, he felt her relax and heard her protracted sigh of relief.

"I'm really sorry about all this," he said grimly before they joined the others. He looked back at the road to make sure they weren't followed. "I guess you had the right idea all along about staying as far away from me as you could."

Instead of fleeing his company, as he was sure she would do once he released her, she whirled to face him, her eyes intense. "Are you in danger if he finds you?"

Shocked that she should care, it took him a moment to respond. "He probably only has orders to bring me home. But Angel. . ." He took a deep breath. "I told you once that you weren't in danger. With Giuseppe I can't make that promise. Of all the men my grandfather could have sent, he's the worst of the bunch."

She didn't ask him to explain, and he didn't care to.

"What will you do now?"

"I'll leave the carnival. I can't put anyone else in danger."

"But—where will you go? Won't you be in even more danger if you leave, since you said that here you can blend in and that your grandfather's men wouldn't be caught dead in a place like this?"

"I can't take that risk now."

She grabbed his arm, again startling him.

"You can't put yourself at risk either. You'll be easier to spot if you leave such a crowded place. And you said they could be ruthless, even to family."

"It's *my* family, Angel. I'm not going to let anyone here suffer because I had the luckless curse of being born a Piccoli."

"You can't leave," she insisted. "Talk to Mama; tell her about this. She'd be easier to talk to than Mahoney, and she *is* his mother. I'm sure she'd agree. And if you don't tell her, I will."

His mouth dropped open.

She nodded in emphasis. "She should know, Roland. She should know if there's a predator out there who might come to the carnival, in order to be prepared for whatever happens next. And she can tell her son if she feels there is a need."

He let out a harsh breath followed by a mild oath. "You're right. I'll tell her. Then I'll go."

"How? By train? They'll find you for sure. No, Roland. If you leave now, it could be the end of all you wanted. To break away from your family and what they stand for."

He looked at her curiously. "Why should you care? Ever since we met, all you've wanted is for me to steer clear of you. Now that opportunity has arrived, and you want me to stay? Why?"

She blinked, taken off guard, her gaze dropping to the ground. She seemed to realize she still held his arm and released it, her manner almost shy. "I. . . don't know." She looked up again, determined. "Yes, I do. I don't want to see you get hurt either. So I guess now the shoe's back on the other foot."

"You, playing my guardian angel?" he asked softly, still trying to grasp the sudden switch in her feelings.

"Yeah." She grinned. "If you want to call it that. Would you like me to go with you to talk to Mama?"

He cocked his brow. "Don't trust me to stick around?" Such words, delivered to Angel of all people, seemed incredible. He couldn't understand her change of heart. Thrown into the mix of danger, she hadn't pushed him away or fled.

"I just thought you might like some support."

Again she surprised him, and he realized he wanted her beside him more than anything. He managed a faint grin. "Yeah, I would."

For the time being he would honor her wishes. But their near escape made him realize that in order to do what he needed and become his own man while severing family ties, he would have to find a place where no one could locate him.

He withheld a groan, wondering if such asylum existed anywhere on the planet.

Chapter 9

Angel watched Mama Philena slowly nod, her eyes steady, not one change in her stolid expression as Roland finished informing her of the facts.

"You don't seem all that surprised." He regarded her with disbelief.

"With what? That you're a Piccoli? Or that your grandfather sent his men to hunt you down?"

"Either. Both." Huffing a confused breath, lifting his hands, he shook his head in bewilderment.

"I knew you were hiding something the moment I saw you. Remember"— she smiled and pointed to her temple—"I can read a person well. That said, I think you should stay."

"That's what I told him," Angel said, relieved, and Mama turned her smile on her.

"Maybe I didn't make clear to you the dangers," Roland explained patiently. "If I stay, my presence at your carnival could put everyone at risk."

"Maybe you don't understand the power of God," Mama responded just as tolerantly. "He brought you here; I'm sure of it now. And whatever His reasons, He can handle the situation."

Both Angel and Roland stared, speechless.

Mama chuckled. "Guess you two don't know much about Him, from the looks on your faces. That, too, can change." Her smile was secretive, the twinkle in her eyes somehow comforting.

"I have a friend, Nettie," Angel said. "She feels the same way you do and spoke to me about the Bible, though I never understood half of what she said. But she said the same thing—that I should trust God to work things out. That He always would."

Mama nodded. "It takes experience sometimes to understand the root of things people tell you. But once you've seen the Almighty at work—and by the way, He doesn't just have that name as an exaggerated hook to draw in the crowds, like some performers here do—you'll know what I say is genuine."

Roland cleared his throat. "I should talk this over with Mahoney and Pearson. Neither of you seem to understand the dangers. These are trained men. With guns. And without scruples."

"No reason to talk to the boys." Mama, for the first time since Angel met her, looked sheepish. "This is the time for confessions? Well, all right, I have one, too. The carnival is mine. I own it."

The resulting silence came brief but so thick Angel felt wrapped inside it.

"My husband left it to me," Mama continued, "but I let my son run things. It gave his life direction again. After his wife died, so young, he needed something to set his mind to, and I'm no good with figures and such, so it was the perfect arrangement. His partner is my nephew—it's all a family affair." She grinned. "I don't broadcast that I'm the true owner—only those few carnies who've been with us the longest know—but I have controlling interest and all important decisions go through me first. So, since this is my carnival, I say you stay. Now. . ."

She clapped her hands and stood, a sign that the urgent meeting Roland had requested was over. "We have work to do if we're going to have things up and running by tonight. Get busy. Roland, go help the other men raise the tents. Angel, you can help me."

Angel and Roland stared at each other. Clearly he was also at a loss at being so quickly reassured, dismissed, and assigned orders.

"Well, what are you waiting for?" Mama asked Roland. "The tents aren't going to erect themselves."

"Talk to you later?" He posed his soft question to Angel, and she nodded. He smiled. "All right then. Ladies." He tipped his hat to them both and left.

Angel watched him go.

Mama chuckled from behind, and Angel heard her mutter "Oh no. Not a thing going on there at all!"

Feeling heat flush her cheeks, Angel didn't dare face Mama.

Over the next few hours Angel found out what a strong support the woman was to the carnival. No job was beneath her. If she had the stamina, she did it, and Angel helped. They aided carnies in setting up the insides of their tents, fed the animals, scrubbed cutlery and dishes when Millie complained of feeling poorly, hoisted poles through metal rungs secured at the ends of banners to fly high overhead, set up tables and booths, shoveled in dirt to pack and flatten a dangerous pit that was part of the midway where a customer might fall—and when Angel was sure nothing was left to be done, Mama surprised her and took her on another round of odd and sundry chores. Angel was speechless with awe at Mama's tenacity mixed with a strength she never would have suspected in a petite, reed-thin woman in her sixties.

With her cheeks sore from blowing air into balloons for one of the game booths, Angel took a cooling drink of cream soda and observed how each of the carnies treated Mama with respect. Even those who wanted little to do with anyone else gave Mama a listening ear.

The afternoon's labor helped Angel forget the morning's fright. Having blown up the last of the colorful balloons and handed them to Fletcher, the agent for that booth, who pinned them to a board where darts would be thrown by paying customers, Angel found her hands suddenly unoccupied. Mama stood a short distance away, giving advice to one of the carnies who'd sought her out. And with irritating ease Angel's thoughts returned to her confusion over Roland.

He wasn't the only one flummoxed by her change of heart. She couldn't understand either what led to her desperation for him to stay. But when she suddenly ran smack into the dangers he had daily lived and realized he was ready to sacrifice all his hopes, perhaps even his life, to protect her and everyone there, the thought of something terrible happening to him made her blood run cold. She'd heard that expression before, but she'd never understood it until she shivered from the chill that raised gooseflesh on her skin when he told her he would leave and she'd never see him again.

At that bizarre moment his words she had long wished to hear became the dread she hoped never to face. She didn't want him to go; she wanted him to stay, though she restrained from delving too far into the reasons why.

Could life get any more insanely complicated?

"Finished with the balloons?" Mama approached, her face flushed rosy from work and sun. "You'd best get to Millie's tent and help with the food. With that stomach upset of hers, you might need to take over."

Angel hid a wince. She hoped that watching the cook through the past week would be enough to manage on her own. After one trial effort of Angel's work, Millie never asked her to prepare food again, except for the toast, which Angel did well.

"I enjoyed working with you today, Mama." Much more than sitting on a stool selling tickets. "It was fascinating to see how everything is done from all angles and be able to help those who needed it."

Mama tilted her head to the side. "I think you have a servant's heart, Angel. It's what I love most about my carnival, helping those who need a hand."

"We finished sooner than I expected. I understood it would take most of the day."

"Oh, there's still plenty of work to be done. Next I'll be headed to the Tent of Wonders to see if anyone needs a hand there. Don't like calling them freaks."

Angel's heart stopped beating. "Can I come with you? I'm really not a good cook." She hoped her confession would trigger the invitation she had long desired.

"Any specific reason you want to visit there?" Mama's expression grew guarded. "Even though Tucker thinks he owns them and displays them like cattle for money, I'm protective of all my family. They're people with souls, not creatures to be constantly gawked at. They get enough of that when the carnival is open to the public."

Angel had asked Cassie and other longtime workers about her mother but had lost hope of anyone knowing her on her fourth day there. She realized she'd never told Mama, since she rarely spent time in her company. "My mother was one of those so-called freaks." She winced at the word, also not liking it. "A bearded lady named Lila. I'm hoping one day to find her." The words, once so hard to say, now spilled off her tongue.

Mama stood frozen, but Angel was growing accustomed to this kind of reaction. Shock was better than the slight repulsion or blatant curiosity she'd also witnessed from those few carnies she'd told, whose gazes then intently scoured her jaw, as if searching for some sign of the imperfection her mother suffered.

"Is that a fact?" Mama breathed softly. "Well now, who would've guessed. . . ?"

"I've asked around but haven't had any luck. I'm still hoping to find someone who knew her or of her, maybe even worked where she did, since I discovered a lot of carnies here have come from other places."

"Yes. I've hired a number of performers who come from shows like mine." Mama stared at Angel as if making a decision. "All right then. Come with me. Jezebel," she said in passing to a young carny, "help Millie with supper. Let me know if she's feeling worse."

"Sure will, Aunt Philena." She nodded in curiosity to Angel before she took off running, her long black braids bouncing as she went.

"Jezzie is my nephew's daughter," Mama explained as they walked, and she threw Angel a sidelong smile. "Like I said, we're all one big family here. Those not by blood grafted in by the unique talents each has to offer."

Angel sucked in a nervous breath as Mama swept through the tent, then she followed. Seven people worked inside, one man looking less than pleased to see the newcomers.

"Everything's taken care of." A gruff-looking character with the stump of a cigar sticking out of his pudgy lips, he gave Angel the willies. "Don't need your services today."

"Speak for yourself, Tucker." A high girlish voice that Angel recognized came from her right. She watched Posey move eagerly forward and gave the woman a genuine smile, happy to see her again.

"Hi, Posey. How are plans for the wedding coming along?"

Mama looked from one to the other in surprise. "You two know each other?"

"You could say we ran into each other—almost," Angel joked, and Posey laughed.

"I'm having trouble with my gown." She held up her short, thick fingers.

"Can't hold a flimsy needle well, but I'm managing."

"I could help." Angel felt all eyes on her and blushed. "I'm somewhat handy with a needle. I've sewn my own dresses and my cousins', too."

"That would be swell!" Posey fairly bubbled. "Maybe you could help Rita and Rosa out, too—that is, if you wouldn't mind?"

"It's what I came for. To help." She glanced at Mama, and the woman smiled and nodded.

"Come along then, and meet the rest of the bunch." Posey took Angel's hand, pulling her toward the back of the large tent. "You've seen Jim at the cook tent, I'm sure." Angel smiled in greeting toward the giant, who tipped his hat and inclined his head in polite acknowledgment. "And that's Gunter." She motioned to a brown-skinned man covered in tattoos and piercings; even his eyelids had pictures on them. At her uncertain nod, he inclined his head slowly, unsmiling, his black eyes wary. "And you've met my darling prince."

"Hullo again." Darrin waved a casual, two-fingered salute from his brow.

"And this is Rita and Rosa."

Two pretty young women with bright green eyes and short black curls sat on chairs pressed close to each other. Angel blinked, realizing the women were joined at the shoulders.

"I'm Rita." The one on Angel's left offered her right hand.

"And I'm Rosa." She offered her left.

Angel shook each hand in turn, trying not to stare at the area that made them different.

"They're not seamstresses either," Posey explained. "And they've run into a problem for tonight's show."

"We tore our costume. See?" Rita sadly displayed a long tear in the shimmering crimson skirt.

"Speak for yourself, sister. If you'd not been so quick to move. . ."

"And if you'd not been so slothful to stay. . ."

"We would not be in this predicament," they finished together.

Posey tugged at Angel's skirt and grinned when she looked her way. "They're like this all the time. Don't pay any attention."

Angel smiled at Posey then directed her nervous gaze to the twins. "If you, um, have a needle and thread, I can sew it up."

"Would you?" Rita asked. "You're an angel!"

At that both Angel and Posey laughed, and Angel's tension drained away.

"Did I say something funny?" Rita looked at Rosa, who shrugged her free shoulder.

"Ladies, this *is* Angel," Posey explained. "The girl I told you about."

"Ooo—the one who came here with that handsome young man," Rosa exclaimed.

Angel didn't bother to correct her, weary of the undertaking.

"I hear you're looking for your mother," Rita said, enlightenment coming into her eyes. "Lila."

Angel's heartbeat quickened. "You know her?"

"Sorry, no."

"We joined Mahoney's carnival a little over a year ago."

"But another carny who once worked with us mentioned Bruce, a strongman who married a bearded lady named Lila, from another carnival. He mentioned she had a little girl. I'm guessing that was you."

Angel nodded, a twinge in her heart. "Do you know where I can find him? The other carny?"

Both girls shook their heads. "No, sorry," Rita said, "Abe left about the time we joined up."

Angel nodded and managed a smile, trying not to allow yet another sting of disappointment to wound her. If Abe knew them and he once worked here, there might be others who also did.

With quiet thanks, accepting the needle, thread, and a stool that Darrin brought her, Angel set to work, skillfully mending the rip. As the three women talked, she found herself easily entering into their conversation. She hadn't known how she would react upon meeting those who worked inside this tent. After having her desire met, at first she felt awkward, not wanting to be rude, but the curiosity of human nature caused her eyes to stray more than once to the differences that set them apart. But as the minutes passed, she relaxed, perhaps not able to ignore their oddities, as she would have wished, but able to accept these girls, just as she accepted and enjoyed their company. How strange that on such short acquaintance she felt closer to them than she'd ever felt with her cousins.

She would have liked to stay and chat longer, but Mama, having finished treating a boil on Gunter's leg, announced to Angel they had more work to do.

"It was a pleasure meeting all of you," Angel said to the group then turned her attention to the twins and Posey. "I'd love to be able to visit with you again."

"Yes. . ."

"We'd like that. . . . That is, if. . ."

Both girls turned nervous glances toward their manager. Tucker glared at the twins, Angel, and Posey, his arms crossed over his thickset chest.

"Why, I think that would be a lovely idea, Angel." Mama gave Tucker her own baleful stare. "They usually prefer to take their meals here, or outside at the back of the tent on nice days, except for Jim. So you can deliver them in my place."

Angel smiled her gratitude, ignoring Tucker. It was Mama's carnival after all.

"Thanks again, Angel, the dress looks wonderful—"

"Better than when we got it."

"What do you mean, 'we'? I'm the one who picked it out. . . ."

As the two sisters quietly bickered, Angel turned her attention to Posey. "Give me your gown, and I'll see what I can do."

"Oh, would you?" Posey practically squealed, clasping her hands beneath her chin. "Thank you, thank you, thank you! I'll be back in a flash." She whirled around and sped to a curtained area of the tent.

"You heard Mama!" Tucker bellowed. "There's work to be done here."

"Oh, I think a few minutes more for Posey to fetch her gown won't hurt anything," Mama answered sweetly.

Angel looked at the two, discerning the friction that seethed between them.

Minutes later, once Angel had Posey's gown in hand and they had left the tent, Mama addressed the matter of Tucker. "That man is as rough as sandpaper," she groused. "But with a good deal of prayer—and believe me, I've spent time on my knees for him, too—I suppose God can even take care of a man like Tucker and smooth out the grainy bits."

Angel thought a moment. "If I pray, do you think God might help me find my mother?"

Her hopeful words melted the stern look off Mama's features. "It's that important to you?"

"Yes. I—I never knew her." She didn't bother telling her she thought she was dead up until a few weeks before.

"Well, child. God can mend anything. With a little prayer. And sometimes it might take a lot, as in the case of Tucker." Mama slyly winked.

Angel thought about Mama's words all the rest of the afternoon and on through the evening as she sold tickets outside the tent with Cassie's act. Mama and Nettie thought a lot alike. Two people of different race, background, culture, and personality—but both retained the same strong beliefs in God and His power, and both were excited about it, making Angel wonder. She had attended Sunday morning services with Aunt Genevieve and her cousins but had never really listened to the elderly minister, whose quiet voice droned on and on, often making her sleepy or causing her mind to wander in countless directions.

"Hello!" a bright voice snapped Angel out of her musings. She counted change back into a customer's hand for the two ten-cent tickets he purchased and turned to the girl who hailed her.

"Jezebel?" Angel expressed surprise to see the girl, perhaps three years younger than herself.

"I was asked to take over your spot for a while."

"Take over?" Angel put the dollar into the strongbox. "Why?"

"Because I asked her to," a deep voice suddenly said from nearby, startling Angel and setting her pulse to pounding.

"Roland?"

"Cassie wants you to see her act."

She saw now that Chester stood behind him, his face tense. "I'm going in there and try to talk her out of it. Fool girl'll break her neck just to prove a point."

He hurried toward the tent, and Angel looked at Roland. "The new stunt?" she whispered.

He nodded, and quickly she joined him. Chester's words fed Angel's fear; he seemed to know Cassie better than anyone, and if he was worried. . .

Angel offered a silent prayer for her stubborn friend, hoping she formed her words right, though she wasn't on her knees, hoping God would hear her petition, hoping above all else that Cassie would be protected from danger.

Chapter 10

Inside the huge tent, spectators sat on benches in graduated levels and watched the center ring with the thrill of excitement. Only Angel and Roland viewed the unfolding events with absolute dread.

Cassie's mother stood with one foot atop each of two Andalusians running side by side, while a man in a matching flashy silver and gold costume stood in the center and held a prod. Roland scanned the right side of the tent and found the person they sought.

"There she is," he said to Angel, nodding to the closed-off area.

Beyond the gap of hanging tapestries, Roland spotted Chester, red in the face, looking as if he was giving his girl an earful. Cassie's expression was just as obstinate. Roland noticed her father catch sight of them as he turned in time with the horses then did a quick double take. But he continued with the act while his wife switched to one stallion and did a handstand amid a burst of applause. Once she'd traveled the ring and lowered herself to both feet again, in one move jumping down to straddle the horse and bring it to a slow stop, her husband announced a short intermission before the next act, saying his wife would answer any questions. She looked at him oddly, and Roland assumed this wasn't part of their show. But with an inviting smile she sat sideways on her horse and pointed to an eager youngster with his hand raised.

Her husband moved behind her to where Cassie now sat mounted while Chester firmly held the horse's bridle and looked up at her. By their stiff features, nothing had changed. Her father entered the fray. His displeasure at seeing Chester near his daughter soon turned toward Cassie as both men wore equal expressions of disapproval. Cassie's jaw remained set. She shook her blond ringlets tersely and proceeded, urging the horse to the ring and cutting off further questions from the audience to her mother.

Roland felt Angel's hands circle the muscle of his arm.

"She's really going to do it," she whispered in fear, and Roland grimly surmised the same thing. "Dear God, protect her." He barely heard the words leave her lips.

Cassie's mother rode out of the ring, clearly unaware of the tension or her daughter's decision as she dismounted and started another lively record on the phonograph. Chester and her father stood side by side with hands clenched on the wooden bar that separated the ring from spectators, their looks of anxious worry matched, while Cassie blithely waved to the crowd and performed her first act. Her movements were graceful, limber as she brought herself to stand atop the cantering horse, as nimble as its rider. Steps and movements led one into another, so fluidly she executed what looked like an acrobatic ballet as she took turns moving to sit and stand atop the horse.

Roland was impressed.

"She's really very good," Angel related his thoughts in awe. Her grip on his arm relaxed.

Cassie again stood straight on one leg and toed her foot before her. Her mother had joined her husband, clearly curious why he left the ring. He spoke, and she swung around as if to rush forward and try to stop Cassie. Her husband's hand on her arm stopped her.

Roland could almost tell how the young bareback rider judged her timing by the expression on her face, her smile not as bright, her features fixed as she stood, arms to the sides, and seemed to count.

"I can't watch." Angel turned her head into his shoulder. The feel of her nestled there brought a strong surge of warmth through his blood along with a desire to console. He cupped his hand to her head, her hair like silk beneath his touch.

Roland held his breath, also certain they would soon be carrying Cassie's broken body from the ring. A quick glance toward Chester showed his face, now pale, his eyes wide and intent on the woman he loved. Not sure he fully believed in the intervening power of God, Roland found himself muttering the same prayer Angel had for the stubborn girl's protection and for the trick to work.

Cassie suddenly vaulted into the air, bringing her legs up over her head in a graceful backward somersault. Her white and silver-sequined costume shimmered from the lights of many lanterns. In one breathless, heart-stopping moment it looked as if she might miss. . . .

The crowd gasped, echoing Roland's swift intake of breath.

She landed, finding solid footing near the back of the horse, and raised her arms high, her smile dazzling in her triumph.

The audience exploded with applause, many jumping to their feet. Chester whooped and threw his hat high. Her mother seemed to collapse against her husband, whose slow smile expressed grudging admiration for his daughter.

"She did it." Angel's words trembled, as if she might cry. "Oh Roland, she really did it!" She threw both her arms around his neck, hugging him fiercely.

Her soft warmth unexpectedly pressed against him knocked Roland's mental capabilities awry and didn't do much for his spiraling emotions either. He couldn't think of an answer to give, his tongue suddenly thick; if he did try to talk, he feared it would come out as gibberish.

She seemed to realize what she was doing and drew away, sending him a demure, embarrassed glance from beneath her lashes before turning her attention to the ring again. "She truly is a wonder."

Roland didn't want to talk or think about Cassie or the performance. He would rather focus on the woman who'd just held him so tightly, maybe even take her somewhere quiet and give in to his desire to discuss a potential relationship—though what he really wished to do, he realized in the moment she embraced him, was kiss her.

No opportunity presented itself for further conversation or a second daring demonstration on his part, for as Roland looked past the ring to the spectators, he caught sight of an oxlike man in a pin-striped suit, a smaller man dressed in a similar manner beside him. Neither seemed interested in the performance, both intently scanning the crowds.

"Angel," he said just loudly enough so she could hear above the frenzied clapping. "I want you to walk away from me now, turn around, and leave the tent."

"What? Why?" Instead of doing as he asked, she looked to where his gaze was fixed. She gasped, and he knew the moment she realized new danger, as she again grabbed both his arm and his hand, intent on pulling him with her.

⁂

"It's them, isn't it? You have to get out of here, too!" Whether it was Cassie's bold defiance to do what no one expected she could, or her earlier thoughts of this man that spurred Angel's own courage, she didn't know or care. But she wasn't about to flee two gangsters while leaving Roland to their doubtful mercy. "Come on!" She persistently tugged, refusing to let him go. He had no choice but to follow or bring attention their way by attempting to break contact.

"Angel, this is crazy," he muttered once she pulled him out of the tent.

"No crazier than you thinking you have to become a sacrifice for your family's sins! Let's tell Mama they're here. She'll know what to do."

He hesitated, and she thought she might have to pull him bodily down the midway. He was lean but hard and muscular, she'd learned during her spontaneous embrace, while she was slight of build but determined. "They might step outside any second. Do you really want to stand here and argue about this and risk them finding both of us?"

Her words snapped Roland out of his indecision. Grimly he nodded, and they hurried down the midway. They found Mama at Jabar's act and filled her in on the news.

"I see." Her usually merry eyes became grim. "Well then, we should teach those two that their type isn't welcome here. Jabar. . ." She turned to the boy who sat atop his elephant. "I think Jenny would like a walk."

He grinned and nodded.

Angel and Roland watched curiously.

"We'll make one stop at Corinthos's tent. I think that should be enough of a welcome committee, don't you?" Her smile was sly.

Angel couldn't help but grin. The Snake Man wore his pet boas around his shoulders, chest, and arms. Every time she saw him thus embellished, it gave her the jitters.

Roland caught on with a slow smile. "Come to think of it, I seem to remember Giuseppe has a fear of reptiles."

"Good. You two stay out of sight. No use letting them know you're here. Jenny and the snakes are just an. . .added precaution?" Mama smiled, though it didn't reach her eyes.

Once she left with Jabar and Jenny, Roland looked at Angel. "I've got to see this."

"You're not leaving me behind!" She grabbed his arm again, rather beginning to like the connection.

"No, I didn't think so. Let's go then. We can watch from a distance."

They followed, taking note of how quickly Corinthos agreed to Mama's request. He informed his audience he would return soon. Some of the crowd followed the foursome down the midway, curious to see an elephant with a small Arab boy in a turban perched atop, a silver-haired wraith of a woman in a sky blue satin dress leading the way like an aged warrior princess, and a tall, brawny man wrapped in snakes walking alongside the elephant.

Roland suddenly tensed beneath Angel's hold and brought his hand across her chest to grab her shoulder in warning, moving with her to a shielding tent. She caught sight of the gangsters, who stood out in the crowd. Their manner of doing business also garnered attention. The huge one had his meaty fist bunched around the shirt of one of the carnies, smaller by half, as he threatened him with his raised fist.

Mama calmly walked up to the men. "I don't allow any violence at my carnival." Her voice came out quiet, authoritative, and Angel admired her daring.

"Is that a fact? So, maybe we won't have to knock any heads together," the smaller man said. "Just tell us where to find Roland Piccoli."

Angel's shoulders stiffened at hearing his name, and she tightened her hold around his arm, afraid he might actually step forward and reveal himself if things grew too heated. His absentminded pats to her hand did little to comfort.

"Piccoli. . .Piccoli. . .Corinthos, you know anyone by the name of Piccoli?"

The Snake Man stepped out from beyond the elephant and into sudden view of the pair. The two gangsters jumped back, clearly disturbed at the sight of the spotted reptile that slowly moved in layers of coils around the man. Angel felt the quiver of Roland's chest as he quietly chuckled.

"No, Mama," Corinthos replied in an articulated accent, almost British like Blackie's but not quite that, either. His deep voice sounded both distinguished and sinister. His steady eyes settled on the gangsters. Even without the snakes, the dark-skinned man stood tall, formidable, and well muscled.

"Look here, we don't want no trouble," the bigger of the two gangsters said, his wide eyes never leaving the snakes.

"But we'll give it, if that's what it takes." The smaller man reached into his suit coat for what was undoubtedly a gun, and Angel saw the flash of metal. Roland hissed between his teeth, taking a quick step forward. Angel held his arm in a death grip, keeping him back.

"Jenny," Mama said quickly, pointing to the gangster, "find the peanut!"

Jenny's trunk eagerly swept up the man's shirtfront, and he let out a terrified howl. "Get that thing off me!" Jenny's trunk found his hand with the gun. As if realizing danger, she squeezed around his wrist. The man let out a yelp of pain, his weapon falling to the ground.

"Jenny, release." The elephant dropped her trunk away at Jabar's order. The man clutched his wrist. Jabar moved Jenny forward a step, and her foot, the size of a small tree trunk, stepped squarely on the weapon.

"You *gentlemen*"—Mama made the reference dryly—"will now leave my carnival. I don't take kindly to threats, and neither does my family. Should you decide to ignore my warning and return, I'll be sure to have Corinthos here aid you."

The Snake Man delivered a smile full of straight ivory teeth, and the manner in which he studied the gangsters was threatening, as if he was eager for the opportunity to meet them again. Angel knew it was all for show and what he, as a performer, did best. Corinthos was really most genial, even courteous, when Angel talked to him on occasion while serving him breakfast. But she shivered at the menacing picture he now presented.

"Get out." Mama's words were severe. "And don't come back. Corinthos will escort you to the entrance."

The Snake Man stepped in their direction. The two gangsters retreated awkwardly, almost stumbling over each other. "Come on, Giuseppe. That playboy wouldn't be caught dead in a dive like this. Don't know why you were thinking he might. Let's get outta here." Turning tail, they hurried away.

"Follow them," Mama told Corinthos.

He swept his head and shoulders down in a slight, gracious bow. "My pleasure, Mama."

The crowd who had followed and others who gathered burst into applause, obviously thinking it all an act for their entertainment. Mama didn't correct them. "Thank you, one and all!" She beamed. "There's plenty more to see and do. We appreciate your business. Be sure and come again—and tell your friends."

Once the crowd dispersed, Mama turned to the elephant. "Good girl, Jenny." She patted her above the trunk near her docile brown eyes. "You deserve a whole sack full of peanuts for that maneuver. Jabar, tell Simmons I said Jenny is to have a special treat."

"Yes, Mama!" The boy guided his elephant away to the peanut vendor.

Angel and Roland approached as Mama bent to pick up the compressed piece of steel that was once a deadly weapon. "That," she told them with a glow in her eyes, "is what my God can do for those who trust and rely on Him. I think it's safe to say you won't be hearing from those two ruffians around here again."

And with a smile directed to both Roland and Angel, she left.

They stared after her, mouths agape. He was the first to recover.

"I guess she told us."

Angel dazedly nodded. Becoming conscious that she still held his arm, she dropped her hand from his sleeve, also realizing she didn't want to let go.

"Angel. . ." He seemed intent, even somewhat nervous as he fully turned to her. "Is there any chance that. . ."

She moistened her lower lip anxiously as he spoke. He paused, his eyes dropping to her mouth.

". . .I could kiss you?"

His words came quiet, a quick exhalation of breath, stunning her, appearing to stun him, and she wondered if that was what he intended to say.

She felt her head nod as though it wasn't a part of her.

His eyes flicked a little wider in surprise and with something else she couldn't read, something that made her heart pound. His fingertips touched her jaw and chin, lifting it higher. Her breath stopped, and then he lowered his lips to hers. They were warm, gentle, and though he kept the contact brief, she wished his kiss could have gone on forever.

He pulled away to look into her eyes, seeming to read her wish there. But before he could fulfill it and their lips could meet a second time, a man called out, "Make way! Make way!"

Startled apart, they barely missed being run over by a Gilly Wagon full of prizes. Nor did Angel miss the smirk that the carny pushing the wagon delivered to them, and she realized, her face burning, that they still stood in the middle of the midway, with people walking by on each side. A few had stopped to watch, as if they were one of the acts.

"Maybe we should save this conversation for another time," Roland suggested.

"I think that would be wise."

They exchanged nervous smiles, and he took her lightly by the elbow, escorting her to her ticket booth.

After the evening's occurrences, she couldn't steady her thoughts to make sense of them, the sensation in her head and heart like emotional bumper cars crashing in one another. Friendship with Roland. That was all she wanted. All they could have. Wasn't it? She couldn't afford to get close! *Oh, but his kiss*. . . . No! It would be a mistake to get involved. A horrible mistake. Not only because of his family but because of hers. Like Romeo and Juliet, this could only end in tragedy because of their families: one, a warring family who murdered all who opposed them, and the other, a family with a mother who at one time in history anyone might have tried to murder. All because of fear. . .and being different. And then there was. . .the beast who sired Angel and made her into what she was.

If any two people were doomed from the start, it was she and Roland.

As she looked into his dark, mesmerizing eyes when he told her good night, she harshly reminded herself of those facts. But when he held her hand and kissed her fingers in farewell, her traitorous heart began to melt.

Chapter 11

"You're a ninny, Angel. A complete and utter fool."

Angel chastised herself as she sewed the last seam of Posey's wedding gown. From Mama she had acquired pretty seed pearls and white sequins and was eager to surprise her little friend with a delicate pattern of posies she would scatter along the bodice.

"Planning your wedding?" Cassie grinned as she stepped into the car.

"Funny."

"It wasn't intended to be. News flash, Angel—you may be the only one who doesn't realize it, but Roland is mad about you. And if you look in the mirror at your face every time his name is mentioned, you'll see he's not the only one whose head and heart are in a whirl."

That's what troubled her.

"You're doing it now! Your eyes are bright, and your cheeks are flushed."

Ignoring her friend's gentle teasing, Angel thought over the past few weeks. She had allowed too many walks with Roland, too many occasions of letting him escort her to work, and too many conversations shared after the show closed, when they stood beneath the moon in the living lot and spoke of their workdays and other areas of their lives. Sometimes she foolishly accepted his kiss good night. He never pushed her, never deepened the moment into something stronger, though she sensed he wanted to. But it failed to matter. Her emotions had spiraled into something she didn't recognize, her heart becoming entwined with his. And when he kissed her and held her, she felt as if she'd ceased to be a part of the carnival world and somehow shared a place all alone with him. She'd found a sense of purpose and peace during her time here with Roland. Having never known such feelings before, she didn't want them to end.

Frowning, she remembered Cassie's words about true love.

No. Surely not that. She was inexperienced in such matters. But surely. . . not that.

Yes, Roland was different from other men, despite his family roots. Unobserved, she had watched during their first week in New Milford and seen him dig deep into his pocket for coins to hand out to Sam, the poor boy they'd met in town, and his two friends, so that they could all enjoy the carnival. She'd watched him quietly lend aid to whoever needed it without

90

being asked, and though at first he clearly didn't fit in, he began to adapt to his surroundings—and appeared to enjoy the change—and gain others' trust. He didn't seem to mind getting his hands dirty or even miss the expensive silk suit he wore when she first met him.

But he was only a friend!

Who are you kidding? her heart taunted. *Friends don't kiss good night.*

You're a fool, Angel, her mind scolded. *You know why you shouldn't get involved. Are you insane?*

"Are you all right?"

"What?" Angel startled then realized what Cassie asked. "Fine. How are things between you and Chester?"

"Much better since the night I did my trick." Cassie regarded her oddly but didn't push. She seemed more animated than usual, fluttering around the railcar like a golden butterfly, and had yet to take a seat. "Papa now sees Chester can be serious and isn't just a funny man—they actually agreed on something, to disagree with me about doing my stunt. Can you believe it?" She laughed.

"Cleaning the horses' stalls for a month as punishment in going against Papa's orders, I didn't mind so much," Cassie pondered aloud. "Nor did I really mind him insisting I wait to do the stunt again until I perfect my timing—he's right. I need more practice, though I knew I could do it that night, despite what everyone said. And really, I'm glad I did. It made me feel stronger, like the woman I am. Not like the little girl I was, who couldn't make her own decisions and always needed Papa to tell her what to do. I think he's finally beginning to see that I've grown up. But that night did more than I believed possible. Since Papa agreed to let me see Chester, he got brave enough to ask Papa for his blessing. And Papa agreed." She glowed as she held out her left hand where a modest ring circled her finger. "See?"

"Cassie!" Angel squealed, setting aside Posey's gown to hug her friend, who sank down beside her. "Why didn't you tell me any of this before?"

"You don't know how much I wanted to! But Chester and I agreed to keep things secret, at least until we were sure how it would all turn out. We're getting married the week after Posey's wedding. I didn't want to steal from her day."

"So soon?"

"We've known each other forever, it seems, and have both wanted this for twice that long." Cassie giggled. "We'll be staying on, so Mahoney won't lose us as part of his meal ticket. And you and I will still be close." She grabbed Angel's hands. "Just think, I'm going to be Mrs. Chester Summerfield in two weeks' time!"

Angel felt thrilled for Cassie, but dismal in her own loss. Her two closest friends, Posey and Cassie, had found their true loves, and that made the bite of Angel's loneliness harder to swallow. . .though her heart again whispered it didn't have to be that way.

"It's getting late." She stood quickly. "I need to take this dress to Posey so she can try it on and I can make any alterations."

"You sure spend a lot of time over there." Cassie looked at her thoughtfully.

Angel shrugged. "They've become my friends. Though Gunter still gives me the willies."

Cassie laughed. "Gunter gives everyone the willies; it's just his nature."

"But I feel so sorry for him, how that gypsy carnival did all that to him when he was younger, inflicting all those tattoos and piercings against his will then caging him like an animal." She shuddered.

"That he even opened up to you was a giant step for the man. Harvey, too. He's always been a tough nut to crack, bitter and angry all the time, but even he seems different since you came."

"Well, he did get fresh with me my first week here. . . ." Angel remembered his dumbfounded look when she snubbed him. "I told him if he'd behave, I'd consider being a friend, but that if he didn't rein in his octopus arms, I'd smack him over the head with the stool I was carrying so fast he wouldn't know what hit him. He hasn't given me a problem since."

"You said that to him?" Cassie laughed. "I would have loved to hear that." Her eyes twinkled. "But really, Angel, being serious—you have a sweetness and sincerity mixed with a strength I never noticed when we became bunk mates. To be honest, I wasn't sure about you. I thought you were shy and maybe a little conceited, thinking you were better than any of us."

"Oh my!" Angel laughed. "That couldn't be further from the truth. I was nervous though."

"Maybe so. But I was wrong to judge you so quickly and harshly. You're none of what I thought."

"I am so glad I left my aunt's to come here. Meeting all of you has made such a difference in my life."

Cassie grew pensive. "Do you still think about finding your mother?"

At the leap to such a question, Angel regarded her oddly. "Why would you ask such a thing?"

"I just hoped that maybe, now that you've found a home with us, you were finally happy."

"I am, but—"

"Knock, knock." Chester's jovial voice came from outside the railcar.

Cassie lit up like she'd swallowed the sun and hurried to open the door. "Chester."

"Hey, honey bun. Thought I'd take my wifey-to-be out to lunch at a genuine restaurant."

"Only if you promise never to call me 'wifey' again." Her mock-stern features melted into a smile, and she allowed him to swing her down from the car, his hands at her waist. They shared a quick kiss, seeming to forget all about Angel.

She looked on, amazed to note the evident changes in their relationship, which they clearly no longer hid, and she grinned. "I hear congratulations are in order."

With Cassie's arms still wound around his neck, Chester glanced Angel's way, his face reddening. "You got that right." He looked into Cassie's eyes. "And I finally got my Cassie."

She sighed dreamily. "Now *that* you can call me till the end of time."

"We best hurry so we can get back, honey. Bye, Angel!"

They both waved to her and hurried away, hand in hand.

"Bye," she whispered, and for some foolish reason, she struggled with the insane urge to cry.

☙

Three nights later Roland stopped in front of Angel's ticket booth, with Chester beside him.

"Oh. . .hello?" Curiously she glanced from one to the other. Worry suddenly clouded her eyes. "Nothing bad about Cassie?"

"No," Chester assured her. "She's fine. Mama thought you'd like to see more of the carnival while it's in progress, and I'm here to take you and Roland on a tour."

"What about your own show?"

"I can close this one night. You two have been with us almost a month now, and it's time you saw the carnival as spectators, not workers. Jezzie's going to man your booth again."

"Hi, Angel!" As if on cue, the girl appeared, out of breath. She always seemed to be running to or from somewhere.

"Hi, Jezzie." Angel handed her the key to the strongbox from the pocket of her skirt. "Thanks for doing this."

"Oh, I don't mind. I love working the Hollars' booth. When there's a lull, I like to slip in and watch the show. I wish I could do what Cassie does. She's so good." It was evident Cassie had a doting fan.

Angel smiled at the girl and turned to Roland and Chester. "I'm ready."

"Then we're off!"

Roland held out his hand to her.

Angel looked at his open palm, indecision on her face. In that awkward moment Roland wasn't sure if he should drop his hand to his side or keep it held aloft and frozen like some ridiculous tailor's dummy. The seconds seemed endless. Just as he was about to pull away with some pithy wisecrack to cover his embarrassment, she slid her hand quietly into his.

There was absolutely no reason his heart should feel as if it had just risen to his throat and pounded there. At the touch of her soft, warm skin against his own, he felt as if he'd been given a prize far better than anything the carnival could offer.

Chester stood beside Roland, an annoyingly smug grin dancing on his face as they began strolling down the midway.

"Should I ask Cassie to make it a double wedding?" he whispered so Angel couldn't hear.

"Keep quiet, man." Roland darted a look at her face, just in case, relieved to see her interest wrapped up in one of the game booths.

The irritating grin did not leave his so-called friend's face as he began pointing out areas of interest. His previous words, however, lodged deep inside Roland's heart, and he found himself turning them over a number of times as they walked. *Marriage?* To *Angel?* Would she ever consider such a prospect? Did he want that?

Regardless of Chester's warning that many games were rigged to deflect the amount of winners, Angel exhibited a desire to visit the dart-throwing booth. "I blew up so many of those balloons I'd like the chance to try to deflate some," she explained with a grin.

"It's your nickel." Chester shrugged. "But I warn you, he uses darts with dull tips."

The agent behind the counter smiled widely to see Angel and greeted her with sincere preference. She didn't pop more than one balloon but clearly enjoyed herself in the attempt.

"For you," the agent said, handing her a small plush lion, one of the top prizes.

"But. . ." She looked at the toy in confusion. "I didn't win."

"If not for your help, I would have had to blow up all them confounded balloons myself. I may be full of hot air"—he winked—"but I don't have the lung power for that no more."

"Thanks, Fletcher." She awarded him with a sweet smile that made the agent beam.

If the man weren't at least two decades older than Angel, Roland might have been a little resentful of his focused attention. Who was he kidding? He was. And he had no right to be, which, for some reason, irritated him further.

"The carnival is certainly different from what I expected," Angel said as they walked away. "My aunt led me to believe it was quite horrifying."

"The perverse acts you might have associated with carnivals are in the bygone days of its glory," Chester replied like a true tour guide. "Ever since it's become more of a family event, things are kept pretty clean. Though you still have your shysters to avoid." He nodded back to the game booths.

They ate hot dogs and pretzels and popcorn until no one had room for more.

"Want to try the rides?" Chester motioned to the lot where the Ferris wheel stood. Angel's attention fixed on a covered musical dais with gilded horses.

"I love the carousel," she said wistfully then laughed, placing a hand to her flat stomach. "But right now I don't think I could stand anything in motion."

They continued down the midway and ran into Blackie and Ruth selling balloons. Blackie gave Angel a blue one, refusing to take her penny, and the clownish duo went into one of their performances, drawing a crowd. Angel laughed so hard Roland noted tears coming out of her eyes. Afterward Blackie passed around a hat that several threw coins into, and Roland did as well. It had been worth the dime, and more, to see Angel happy.

A trip to the crazy house of mirrors and a sack of peanuts shared rounded out their fun, when suddenly Angel stopped, as though frozen.

"Angel?"

She stared, and Roland followed her line of vision. His heart clenched as he recalled the day they had stood before this tent and she'd behaved in the same manner. THE HUMAN FREAK SHOW, the banner above proclaimed.

The whole spectacle disgusted him. The way these people were treated reminded him of his grandfather's cold manipulation over others and their inability to break free, acting as marionettes to his callous whims. Roland knew Angel had befriended the people there, and he put a hand to her elbow.

"Come on, Angel. We don't have to see this."

"No." A determined expression crossed her face. "I need to."

Chapter 12

Angel knew her reply surprised Roland, but she had to see, had to know. She couldn't understand her desire, but neither could she quench it.

"Step right up, and see the most amazing creatures to walk the face of the planet. That's right, folks, we're going to bring them out here, all for free, just to let you get a peek. Watch the entranceway for the amazing Siamese Twins, the Leprechaun Couple, the Illustrated Man, and that's not all. . . ." The barker paced the stage, his energy and ballyhoo swiftly bringing in a crowd.

"That's Tucker." Chester's voice became grim. "A seedy fellow. I've had dealings with that man. Trust me when I say to steer clear of him."

Angel had also had dealings with Tucker, none of them pleasant. When she brought Posey and the others their meals, he had tried to rush her off. The first time, she submitted. But his maltreatment of her friends ignited a righteous anger that burned deep, and the next time, she refused to leave, ignoring the ill-mannered beast to stay and talk with the other women and help, usually by stitching up tears or sewing on buttons for any of the performers who needed it. Tucker soon realized she wasn't the hindrance he thought and allowed her to stay. Angel would have done so without his gruff permission.

"Why do they let him do that to them?" she asked sadly as he spun his thoroughly demeaning ballyhoo for Rita and Rosa, making them sound more like monsters than people, and the two women stepped out of the tent on cue. "*Why*? It's just not right!"

Chester shook his head; he had no answer. Roland's eyes filled with sympathetic concern as he regarded Angel. His hand still at her elbow, his thumb caressed her arm through her sleeve. His gesture warmed her, and she sensed he understood her heartache. Yet even he couldn't begin to comprehend the extent of it.

Was this how her mother had been treated? Forced to stand on a platform as a "peculiar specimen of nature" and made to endure belittling remarks from a crass talker, who poked and prodded, while an insensitive crowd gawked as if she were something less than human? How could she have borne such humiliation, night after night?

Angel's eyes brimmed with hot tears.

She'd known the sting of scorn and embarrassment from her aunt and cousins, but this was much worse. Perhaps at times her rebellious tendencies invited their nasty behavior. But these people, these friends, had done nothing to warrant such ridicule! Rita and Rosa had been born into a life of poverty. Their parents, had they wanted the twins, couldn't have afforded an operation to separate them. Why were life and people so cruel? How could Mama allow such a thing to go on at her carnival? How could her own mama have had any spirit left to go on living, especially after her attacker defiled her in the most vicious of ways. . . .

"Angel?"

A tear followed by another rolled down her cheek. She heard Roland's sharp intake of breath and felt him gather her close, his strong arm around her shoulders, protective and warm. Grateful as she was for his consideration, she felt numb and frozen.

How easily she might have been one of them, up on that platform, raped of all self-worth in the cruel and careless spiel of a barker's belittling words. And yet, she *was* one of them. Her face and form may have escaped physical imperfection, but in her soul she'd struggled with the contempt of others her entire life. By the bond of blood in being her mother's child, she identified with Rosa and Rita and others like them more than she did with those who stood on the opposite side and rudely gaped. She felt so utterly alone.

"That's called building the tip—the crowd," Chester said solemnly. "Next, he'll turn the tip, with a ballyhoo to send them running to buy tickets to see more."

"Let's get out of here." Roland moved to draw her away, his arm still around her, but she resisted his gentle pull.

She needed to remain through all of this until the crowd went inside for more, needed to experience what her mother had lived. In that way she hoped to begin to understand the heart of the woman who'd given away her child.

"I'm staying." She glanced up. In Roland's eyes she spotted the strength and support she so desperately craved. Not once in his expression had she seen any sign of curious revulsion, apparent on every other face looking toward that awful tent platform.

"Please stay with me?" Her soft request was unnecessary; she knew he wouldn't leave her. But she needed to hear his answer.

"I'm not going anywhere." His firm response warmed her cold insides, while making her shiver with uncertainty, for it implied so much more than the here and now, something she wasn't sure she could ever handle. "I'm here for you, Angel."

She nodded in gratitude, casting aside all doubt and logic, and her heart clung to his promise.

ᴵ♥

In one night everything changed.

Roland wasn't sure what to make of the changes in Angel, but he hoped they would last. Aside from the few kisses he'd been unable to refrain from, he'd made no overtures to a close relationship. And though her nervousness when near him didn't vanish completely, she was nowhere near as jumpy as she'd been their first week together.

But that wasn't what amazed him.

Over the weeks that followed their little carnival participation with Chester, Roland had watched Angel begin to blossom, seeming to find peace within. The carnies all loved her, women and men both, to his chagrin. With selfish gratitude he watched her gently turn down interest after romantic interest, and his heart surged with hope when she didn't refuse his own tender advances of affection. Inwardly that affection grew in strength each day.

Though the two recent weddings sparked a desire he'd never had, the sparkle left her eyes and sadness settled there after first Posey then Cassie tied the knot with their fellows. He assumed Angel missed her bunk mate and felt lonely for companionship. Roland was only too happy to act as a stand-in.

He had never seriously considered marriage until Chester's wisecrack. Since then it seemed to be all he thought about. Regardless of the fact that he was hiding from his mobster family and trying to carve a new life, one in which he'd found, to his surprise, satisfaction and the same peace Angel had, he'd never planned to live out the rest of his days in bachelorhood. When the time was right and he felt assured he could keep her safe, he wanted a wife. And he was fairly certain he knew her identity.

During a night in Kent, once the fairgrounds closed to visitors and the nightly chores were done, Roland approached Angel at the ticket booth.

"Take a walk with me?"

Angel's face brightened. She closed up the strongbox, locking it. "I just need to drop this off at Pearson's car first."

They took the night's earnings to the disgruntled man, who never once looked up from his account book and barely paid them a moment's notice, mumbling something that could have been *good night* or *get lost* to their parting words.

Roland shrugged as they walked away, and she giggled. He took her hand in his as he'd done often lately, since the night of "the change." She offered no resistance.

"You look like you had a good day." He appreciated how the silver moonlight brought out a cool sheen to her hair when they weren't walking near the incandescent yellow bulbs of carnival lights, which conversely brought out touches of silky red warmth.

"I did. Cassie went with me at lunchtime when I delivered meals to Posey and the others. We all had a lovely talk." She grew pensive as she focused on something in the distance. "I finally had the chance to talk to Mama again, in private. I asked her why she had such a degrading show at her carnival. Even if all the other carnivals have them, it still didn't seem like she would, as caring and sensitive as she is."

When it didn't appear as if she would continue, Roland prodded, "What did she say?"

"She doesn't like it either. But she said at least here she can visit them, treat them with kindness and respect, help them out—something they might not get with another carnival. Tucker doesn't care about them, to see to their needs." Angel frowned at that. "She did tell me it was their choice to be in the show; apparently she asked each of them in private when they first joined the carnival, telling Tucker she would never condone any form of slavery if he held them against their will. Sadly they were all here because of choice, feeling that's all life has to offer them. Mama says she hopes by giving her friendship and prayers she can help make a difference. She has a very soft spot in her heart for those who work in that tent. One of the previous performers was a woman who led her down the path to find God, and she owes everything to that woman."

Roland nodded, recalling when Mama had told him the same thing.

"How do you feel about them? You never did say."

Her question came quiet, but Roland got the distinct impression a lot hinged on his response. "I never really gave it much thought. You're asking, what? Do I think them freaks of nature? Am I disgusted by their appearance?"

She tentatively nodded.

"The answer is no. Especially not after getting to know Jim, probably one of the smartest men I've ever met. His knowledge of the classic literary works is incredible. Did you know he's memorized every work of Shakespeare? Still, I can't help but feel curious about how they got that way and pity them for how they're treated."

His sincerity brought a faint smile from her. "Jim and I were discussing *Romeo and Juliet* several weeks ago. He recited parts of it for me."

At her odd words and the even odder note in her voice, he looked at her. "Oh?"

"It's a very sad story." She sighed. "Two people in love but with everything going against them."

They approached the carousel. The horses no longer revolved, the customers gone for the day, but bright lights from within the dais bounced off its huge, mirrored column. Lively calliope music played from a door within.

She looked at the gilded horses, her face alight with wonder. "I've always loved the merry-go-round. . . ." She stopped suddenly, focused.

"Angel?" His fingers went to her chin, bringing her eyes to meet his.

"It's nothing. A memory that's gone before it even begins." She gave a nervous laugh and shrugged. "So what's your favorite thing about the carnival?"

Wishing to erase every hurtful memory she'd ever suffered, he looked into her beautiful wide eyes that shone like blue midnight in the dark evening. The feelings he'd cautiously pushed aside for weeks rose to fill his heart.

"You."

At his whisper, her lips parted in surprise, and he leaned in to her, his mouth taking in their soft warmth. He cupped her face, slowly brushing his lips over hers more than once, unable to resist her sweetness. Her arms wrapped around his neck, and she breathed a sigh of delight, which enticed him to press closer and deepen the kiss, giving in to his desire to love her. . . .

Her legs soon gave way. He lowered his arms around her back, pulling her firmly against his body to steady her. It took every bit of willpower for him to finally break free from her delicious mouth and let her go.

She wobbled a step. His hands reached out to support her. She blinked up at him, unfocused, her breathing as rapid as his. He had not meant to take their kiss so far, and he winced at the trace of anxiety he saw beneath the longing in her eyes.

"Angel, you must know you mean the world to me." He brushed her hair from her temple. "I want this—us—to have a relationship like Chester and Cassie have. Like Posey and Darrin—"

"M–m–marriage?"

He saw the thought terrified her and dropped his hands away from her, working to get his emotions under control. What was wrong with him? He was rushing this, ruining everything.

"One day maybe. If you want it." He swallowed hard, fighting the impulse to kiss her again, gently this time, to hold her close to his heart and eliminate whatever doubts were running through her lovely head. "I want us to be more than friends," he finished lamely.

Her eyes, if wide before, grew enormous. She backed up a step.

"Th–this is so s–sudden. I. . .have to go. I need time to. . .to think."

"Angel. . ."

"No, don't." She shook her head, backing up another step. "Please, Roland. Not right now. I. . ." With a pained expression, she whirled around and hurried away.

✍❤

Not right now. Not *ever*!

She moved without really seeing, anxious to reach her railcar.

"Angel?"

Blinking hot moisture from her eyes, she noticed Cassie and Chester strolling arm in arm. She couldn't form a greeting, afraid it would come out as a sob.

"Angel, what's wrong?"

She shook her head and walked faster. Within moments she felt Cassie's arm around her waist—glad for the support, wishing to be alone, wondering why Roland didn't follow, relieved and disappointed he hadn't.

Heaven help her, she was a mess.

He had never, *never* kissed her like that! And while her heart had raced with the desire for more, was still racing, her mind callously scolded her for letting it come to this.

Once he found out the truth, once he knew. . .

He could never know.

"There now," Cassie said as she stepped up with Angel into the railcar, "tell me what happened. Did you have a fight with Roland?"

Angel laughed without humor. So far from a vocal fight yet a powerful confrontation that destroyed all hope. She looked at her dear friend, wishing she could tell her everything but feeling unable to. She cried harder.

Cassie pulled her close, holding and rocking her as if she were a child. Angel brushed her tears away with resolve. She never cried. But then, little in her life had mattered so much.

"I have to leave the carnival."

"What?" Cassie's eyes rounded in distress. "Why?"

"I can't explain. I just. . . I have to go." She gulped down another sob. "I'll go back to searching for my mother. It was one of the reasons I left my aunt's in the first place."

A calm but determined expression crossed Cassie's face.

"Angel, about that. . ."

"I've earned enough so I won't have to do what I did before. Did I tell you?" She forced a laugh. "I stowed aboard a train. That's how R–Roland and I met." She couldn't even say his name without stumbling over it.

"Angel. . ."

"It's for the best. I know it is." It had to be.

"Angel, I know where your mother is."

Chapter 13

Angel stared, unseeing. Her mind went numb with shock.

Cassie's skin flooded with shamed color. "I didn't tell you at first, because. . .well, honestly, I didn't know if I could trust you. Lila's been hurt by so many. And I thought you were one of them who hurt her before."

Angel remembered to breathe. "She *worked* here?"

Cassie nodded. "I didn't know her well, but she was so sweet, and I. . ." Her gaze shifted to her lap. "I'm sorry. When it seemed you'd found happiness with us, I thought it best just to leave things be. But I know you now. You really care. You don't like seeing them hurt. I was only trying to protect her from that possibility."

Angel's initial anger at her friend's deception faded in the glow of hope that she knew her mother. "Where is she?"

"I don't know. I'm sorry, I really don't."

"But I thought you said—"

"I don't, but Mama does."

For the third time that night, Angel felt as if she'd been struck.

Mama knew? All this time?

"Please don't be angry. Please forgive me. . . ."

Angel nodded absentmindedly, her thoughts rushing ahead. "We'll talk. Later. I have to find Mama now."

Her battered emotions in a precarious tailspin, Angel left Cassie and ran to the front of the train and Mama's car.

The woman often helped others, and Angel worried she might not be there. She had waited what seemed her entire lifetime for this moment, but a matter of minutes she didn't think she could bear. Thankfully a light shone from the crack, and Angel pounded on the door.

"Angel?" Mama said in surprise as she opened it.

Out of breath, Angel strived for control. "I want to know where my mother is. And I know you can help me."

Mama remained composed. "I've been expecting you."

That was the last thing Angel thought to hear.

"Come in, child." Mama opened the door wider, and Angel woodenly stepped inside. "I assume you spoke to Cassie? I spoke with her earlier about telling you. That it was time. And I imagine you're feeling very betrayed right now. But I want you to consider this: Your mother lived with that emotion daily, and I couldn't allow her to be hurt again. You see"—and here Mama smiled gently, smoothing her hand against Angel's hair like she was a little girl—"your mother was the one who led me to the Lord."

Angel sank to a nearby chair, her legs suddenly useless. "My mother did?" Her voice came whispersoft.

"Yes. And especially after hearing her story, I owed it to Lila to protect her interests."

Her story? "Tell me. Please. I know so little about her. Only what my aunt told me." Which was all suspect.

Mama seemed to consider then shook her head. "It's not my place. It's your mother's."

"Then you'll tell me where she is?" Angel pleaded.

"Now that I've received her permission to, yes."

Stunned, Angel inhaled a shaky breath. "Sh–sh–she knows I'm l–looking for her?"

"I called her from town. Told her about you. Asked what she wanted to be done."

"And?"

Mama picked up a piece of paper from a table. "This is where you can find her."

Angel took the slip as if it were the most fragile, expensive china. Here. . . now. . .the answer she'd been praying for! Dread and anticipation fought for control in her heart.

"I guess it's safe to assume you'll be leaving us?" Mama asked as Angel continued staring at the address. At Angel's nod, Mama sighed. "I can't say I won't be sorry to see you go, but I know it's the right thing. It's high time the past was fixed."

Angel didn't ask what she meant, only stared at the worn face and merry eyes of the slight woman who'd been an inspiration.

"Thank you, Mama. For. . .everything. And. . .I. . .I do understand." For the most part, she did. Mama and Cassie had only been trying to protect Lila, just as she had wished to shield Posey, Rita, and Rosa from others' cruelty. That they thought Angel could bear such malice toward her own mother stung a little, but then Angel herself hadn't known how she would feel around those considered different.

Now, in knowing, she no longer feared how she would react to her mother's appearance. It was how she would respond to her explanations that chilled her.

Mama Philena held out her arms in understanding, and Angel numbly walked into them, hugging her close.

Unable to sleep, Roland stood at the door of his boxcar, a cool breeze hitting his face. Angel wasn't the only one to lose a bunkmate, and though Roland missed his wisecracking friend, he felt grateful for these quiet moments to think.

He had never wanted for anything, though he hated the ruthless methods his family used to obtain wealth. Yet Angel, deprived of most worldly possessions, had shown Roland that for all his affluence, he'd had nothing. Here, at this rinky-dink carnival, he had discovered a measure of happiness, found out who he was, and learned what truly mattered. Who would have believed it? Angel was everything to him, and he didn't want to live without her. No matter how slow he must take things, he would. He had no intention of scaring her away ever again.

A sudden rectangle of yellow light glowing on the ground brought his attention to the left. His eyes widened in disbelief.

Angel had descended from her boxcar, set down her suitcases, and turned to give Cassie a long hug.

"What the. . ." He blinked. She was *leaving*?

His initial shock gave way to anger. Again, in the dead of night, she was sneaking away into the countryside she knew nothing about and putting herself at risk. Was ever such a reckless woman created?

With a growl of frustration, he tied on his shoes, slipped his silk jacket over his carny work clothes, and pulled on his hat. His manner of dress was bizarre, but there was no time to change. Besides the clothes on his back, he took nothing but the wages he'd earned. Compared to his former weekly allowance, it was a pittance, yet it was also a king's ransom, due to the burden lifted off his soul for not spending blood money.

He followed her at a distance, watching her move toward the boxcar where Posey and her husband slept. She knocked and spoke to the tiny blond who opened the door. Suddenly she, too, was wrapped in Angel's hug, which Posey returned just as fiercely. The same ritual happened at Rita and Rosa's car, leaving Roland no doubt as to Angel's intent.

"You going after her?"

Mama's quiet voice coming from near the tree he stood behind startled him. "I can't let her go off by herself."

"I wouldn't expect so. Your feelings are plain to see. Always have been." She patted his arm. "A word of advice. She's had a bad shock so she might be touchy. Handle her with care. . .and with caution."

He wondered if Angel's shock was due to his earlier lapse of self-control; he also wondered if Angel had told Mama about it and felt a twinge of guilt. "I don't like leaving you in the lurch like this. Mahoney isn't going to like it either."

"Don't you worry about my son. I own the carnival, remember?" She winked and patted his cheek. "You just go and do what needs doing. Take care of her, Roland. She's a dear, but I don't need to tell you that."

He nodded, and they watched Angel move away. After a farewell hug and thanks to Mama, Roland followed.

He trailed his misguided Angel to the train depot before she suddenly whirled around, her angry eyes pinning him to the spot.

✎❤

Angel had sensed him earlier but had written the feeling off as nerves. Yet there he stood, not twenty feet away, dark, handsome, and oh so dangerous. . . .

Not to her life but to her heart.

He approached her. "Nice night for a walk."

His tendency to initiate conversation with the understated would have made her laugh if she hadn't felt so hollow.

"What are you doing here? Please tell me that you're not following me again."

"I could ask you the same." His eyes glimmered with frustration and hurt. "You don't have to run away, Angel. It was only a kiss. I promise I'll behave if you'll just come back."

She didn't know whether to laugh or cry. His explanation of *only a kiss* and his vow to behave brought an irrational pang to her heart. He thought his kiss sent her packing? Though it had shaken her to her core, making her feel things no decent girl should, she would never admit that to him. Perhaps her aunt was right, and she wasn't decent at all.

"It's not about. . .the kiss." Even saying the words made her breathless, and she condemned her awkward tongue. "I'm not that childish. It's just. . . something came up. And I would appreciate it if you'd just. . .go back to the carnival. You're safer there than out here in the open—especially on a train, since your family owns an interest in the railroad!"

Concern touched his rich brown eyes. "Angel, what's wrong?"

She forced a calm she didn't feel, knowing he would never go if he suspected her pain. This man had been her friend, though she felt much more for him. But that wasn't his fault either, and he didn't deserve her antagonism.

She softened her tone. "I'm sorry I gave you a hard time, Roland. I—I hope you find a happy life and the peace you deserve. I'm fine. Really." She smiled, hoping to convince him. "The, um, family I told you about months ago? I've decided to visit. So you needn't worry any longer. I'll be fine." Before she could curb her instinct, she stepped forward and raised herself on her toes to press a kiss to his cheek.

Startled at what she'd done, she backed away, seeing the shock reflected in his eyes.

"G—good-bye."

Her heart pounding like a drum, she whirled away, almost running for the ticket window.

Brilliant, Angel, she chastised herself as she paid for the fare. *Well done. If anything, you just aroused his suspicion.*

She chanced a fleeting glance over her shoulder. Relief and despair vied for top billing when she saw he was gone.

It's what you wanted, she tried to convince herself as she thanked the ticket seller and moved down the platform to a bench to wait. Despite the heavy beating her emotions had taken, once she sat immobile, she grew sleepy. She jerked awake several times but couldn't keep her eyes open.

"Miss!"

She jolted awake to see a man shaking her shoulder.

"I think this is your train."

"Oh." She straightened and put a hand to her hat, her ticket still clutched in her other hand with the location visible. That must be how he'd known. "Thank you."

He smiled, tipped his hat, and walked away.

Once aboard, Angel grew restless. She found a seat beside a genial, older gentleman who talked about his grandchildren for quite some time. She displayed the right amount of interest, but his words made her sad. She would never have grandchildren, never have children. She couldn't. No decent man would have her.

That led her to think of Roland. Months ago, upon first meeting him, she would have labeled him as far from decent. But the truth was, he was nothing like his family, everything a girl could want, and all that Angel wished a man to be.

Dear God. . . . She had taken to praying in her head often since meeting Mama. *Can You please help me forget him? And to forget that I l–love him. . . .*

Her eyes opened wide in horror at the truthful plea of her heart.

Love him!

She sucked in a deep breath, feeling the sudden need for oxygen.

Yes. Love him, her heart confirmed. *What did you think these feelings were that you've been having?*

No, no, no! She couldn't love him! Because of what she was, because of who he'd been. A gangster's son. A Piccoli. But. . .but he had changed. She had seen him change.

Yet that didn't erase the cold, hard fact that she never could.

"Are you all right, my dear?" the kind gentleman asked in fatherly concern. "You look a mite piqued."

She offered an unsteady smile. "Y–yes. I. . .I haven't eaten. I think I'll check what the dining car has to offer."

"Of course." He stood for her to get by.

This time, at least, she didn't have to worry about luggage, since she was a paying customer and a porter had taken care of her things before she boarded. Asking for directions from a steward, she felt grateful she had every right to be there and again determined to refund the fare Roland had paid on her behalf.

Roland, Roland. . .again, Roland.

I have to stop thinking about him!

Yet as Angel entered the dining car and stood frozen in the doorway, she realized with breathless shock her wish would not be granted.

Roland Piccoli sat inside a booth, his gaze lifting from the newspaper he held and melding with hers.

Chapter 14

Roland watched Angel stand in the doorway as if she might turn and run. A wealth of expressions swept across her face—shock, disbelief, anger, uncertainty, acceptance, fear. But one he hadn't expected to see—relief and even, dare he think it, happiness—made him take in a stunned breath. He clung to those last two expressions as she stiffly approached.

"I told you not to follow me," she accused in a hoarse whisper.

He motioned across the table. "Won't you take a seat?"

She ignored him. "But here you are."

"Here I am."

"Why?"

He folded his newspaper. "Because I care."

"I told you I can take care of myself!"

"Yes, and through the past months I've seen that, more and more."

She blinked. "Then why did you follow me?"

"I told you when we were last together at the carnival." Her cheeks flushed as if she also thought of their kiss. "I care about you, Angel. *You.* I want to be with you. And I think you want the same thing."

Her gaze fell to the table. "I can't be your m—mistress." Her face flooded with color.

He stared, at a loss. "Did I ask you to be? Do you still have such a low opinion of me that you think I would? This isn't a movie, Angel." His tone was sober. "Despite what they show about gangsters, just because I come from a family of them doesn't mean I woo every pretty dame—lady," he corrected, remembering how she disliked the former word, "and take her to my bed." Her face flushed darker at his frank words. "Don't you get it?" He leaned across the table, his eyes never leaving hers as he reached for her hand. "I care, Angel, because I love you."

Her reaction wasn't what he expected.

Her face lost all the color that had rushed into it earlier, her eyes went huge, and she snatched her hand away.

"You can't love me," she choked out.

"Too bad. Because I do."

"No, you don't understand. . . ." She backed up a step. "You can't! Just—just leave me be, Roland. Please!"

She hurried out of the dining car.

He blinked, confused, then went after her. For the first time he noticed they'd drawn the interest of every patron there, but he didn't care. Something troubled her, and he wanted to know what it was.

Sneaking a peek at the destination on her ticket while she'd been dozing on the platform bench had been a cinch. Suggesting to a fellow passenger that the lady there might miss her train had produced the required results, as Roland watched from a safe distance and the man had roused her. But trying to get Angel to see the facts would take every ounce of reason and persuasion he possessed, along with help from above, if Mama was right and God did listen.

He never doubted God's existence. It just seemed hypocritical for his grandfather to attend mass in the morning and order some poor sucker's death in the afternoon, at times brought about by his father's own hand. With that kind of upbringing, Roland had quickly been jaded. But Mama Philena was a different story, living her belief, showing it in her actions. And even Angel, in her confused way, had been enlightening, admitting her own ignorance in matters of faith but sharing Nettie's verses and inspirational sayings, which seemed to help her.

He caught sight of Angel in the aisle of the second coach. She turned at his step, a plea in her eyes. "Please, Roland, don't do this."

"You can't keep running from life, Angel. At some point you have to stop." He gently took her elbow, guiding her past her seat and to an empty row a short distance away. He couldn't help but notice her tremble.

If he'd not been positive Angel shared his feelings, he might never have admitted his own. But he had seen the tenderness returned in her eyes more than once, had noticed her face light up when he would approach at the carnival. He had known since he first met her in his private car that she was hiding something, something she was afraid would now upset him, and he resolved to remain calm no matter what she revealed.

Not wanting her to feel closed in, he took the seat near the window, shifting his hold from her elbow to her hand, and pulling her into the row with him. She sank to the seat, her body stiff.

"Tell me what's got you so upset."

She shook her head, her eyes squeezing shut.

"Angel, darling. . .I want to help. Don't clam up on me."

"Why, Roland?" she bit out softly, her eyes still shut. "Why did you have to fall in love with me? Why'd I have to—I. . .I can't do this, don't you see? It's too hard."

"What's so hard about it? Love is a beautiful thing, so I've heard."

Her eyes flew open, and she glared at him. "You can't love me because of what I am."

"An angel in the flesh?" he gently teased in his confusion.

She didn't laugh. Pain flickered in her eyes, making him wish he could erase the last few seconds. "Angel, I'm sorry. I didn't mean to sound flip."

"It doesn't matter. Oh Roland, can't you please just walk away and pretend you never knew me?"

"Can you?"

His low, deep response brought tears swimming to her eyes.

"This wasn't supposed to happen," she sobbed softly.

He noticed the passengers staring across the aisle. He cursed public cars and wished for a private car, but to get one, he would have to reveal his identity, and he could never do that.

"Angel, whatever it is can't be that bad. It won't change my feelings for you—"

"Won't it?" She cut him off, a hysterical edge to her words. "You're so sure, but you don't know. My aunt said no decent man would have me, and she's right! You could never want me."

That she now classified him as decent cheered him, but her self-condemning words gave him pain. "Well, your aunt's wrong. Why would she say such cruel things to you?"

"You want to know why?" Her voice raised a notch. "Because she's right. She hates me. Hates what my mother is. What if I were to tell you that my mother was one of the freaks at the carnival—what then, Roland? Would you be so quick to tell me you still love me? You tolerated their presence, even accepted them, when so many couldn't, but could you really accept me and still love me if I told you that my mother was once a bearded lady at the carnival? Could you?"

She jumped to her feet. "Because she was," she whispered. "And she is. And that's who I'm going to see. My mother, who abandoned me as a baby because my aunt said she didn't want me anymore. And heaven only knows why I'm visiting her now, because I sure don't!"

Stunned speechless, he could only stare. A pained look of acceptance hardened her features, and she straightened, almost regal.

"I thought so. I imagine I won't be seeing you again, Roland. Have a nice life."

She turned and swept back in the direction of the dining car, ignoring the shocked passengers who watched her retreat, many of whom then sneaked glances back at Roland.

Still dumbfounded, he couldn't move as her condemning words played repeatedly in his mind. His eyes fell shut.

Oh Angel.

❧

Twisting her napkin in knots, Angel ignored her Danish and coffee. What seemed like hours had passed, and still she replayed their words.

She should never have told him those things. What would he have done if she'd told him everything? About being nameless. Illegitimate. Trash.

He probably would have run to the farthest coach from hers, she thought with a hoarse laugh that was more of a sob. She, who never once cried in what amounted to years, now always seemed to burst into waterworks like a fountain. If she'd had a better grip on her emotions, this wouldn't have happened. With a disgusted sigh she looked out the window, watching the miles rush past in the blur of the lush countryside.

At last the whistle sounded. The train slowed. A porter made his rounds, calling out the location.

Coventry. Her destination.

Her eagerness in her quest began to dissolve. She twisted the napkin tighter. This was a mistake. She shouldn't have come. What would she find? What would she learn? That her aunt was right? That no one cared about her and no one ever had?

Someone came to stand beside her. Expecting the waiter with the bill, she looked up... And she froze, all words lodging inside her throat.

Roland looked at her limp hands and took the mangled napkin from them, laying it on the table. "I believe this is where you and I get off."

"Roland?" she said dumbly, as if staring at a ghost.

He gave her a faint smile.

"But..." She tried to think. "You... Why?"

"What you said changes nothing." He took her hand, helping her from the table. "I just thought you needed some time alone."

She moved without thinking, without feeling, letting him guide her through the train. By the time he collected her luggage, she had recuperated enough to speak.

"You don't have to go with me."

"No, but I want to. If you'll let me."

She nodded, a powerful relief surging through her. She didn't want to confront her mother alone, feared the very thought, and craved his support.

They moved toward a waiting taxi. Suddenly she stopped. He looked at her, curious.

"I forgot to pay for my food!"

"I took care of it."

"Roland, thank you, but..." Her cheeks warmed. "I still haven't paid you back for the first time."

"As if I would let you," he growled with a smile that quickened her breath. "You don't owe me a thing, Angel. Not now. Not ever."

With that enigmatic reply, he helped her into the cab.

The drive tested every one of her frayed nerves. The countryside was beautiful with its pretty farms and trees in bloom, but with each mile she knew she was getting nearer to the encounter she had longed for and equally dreaded.

Feeling Roland's warm hand cover hers, she began to relax, then turned her hand in his and gripped it like a vise when the cab pulled into a dirt lane. A small red farmhouse with maples and pines beyond and a cornfield off to one side came into view.

They had arrived.

Chapter 15

Angel still had not let go of Roland's hand when the cab stopped in front of the farmhouse.

"It'll be all right," he said, trying to reassure her.

Will it? she thought when she caught sight of a slender woman in the doorway, a veil covering the lower part of her face. Angel didn't need anyone to tell her who this was: the same woman in the faded photograph of the album in her luggage. Lila.

Roland helped her from the cab. Angel stood motionless at the end of the walk and stared at the woman, who didn't move either. *I have her same curly, dark hair,* Angel thought distantly, followed by another thought, even more startling. *Why, she's beautiful.* Her eyes were huge and dark, her nose and brow above the veil, delicate and creamy white.

"You are Angel."

The vision spoke, and Angel gave a terse nod, noting how she didn't address her as Angelica. Had she first given her the nickname Angel preferred?

Lila held out a slim hand that trembled. Only then did Angel see how nervous the woman also was. "Please, won't you come inside?" Her voice was quiet and husky. "And your friend as well." She offered Roland the briefest of glances before looking at Angel again.

They followed her into a comfortable parlor. An elderly man with white whiskers sat in a chair. He looked up, an expectant but uncertain gleam in his eyes. Eyes the color of Angel's.

"This is my father. . .your grandfather."

"It's a pleasure, my dear." He took her hand in greeting.

Angel managed a reply, and the woman—her *mother,* though she still had a hard time thinking of her as such—excused herself to pour coffee. The man who was her grandfather talked amiably with Roland about the farm. When Lila returned, he invited Roland outside to see the land. Recognizing the polite maneuver to give them privacy, Angel smiled in reassurance at Roland, wordlessly assuring him that she would be fine when he cast a questioning glance her way.

"You must have many questions." Lila stirred her coffee once the men left.

Angel watched her, wondering if she would remove the opaque veil to drink, but she only lifted it slightly, making room for the cup.

"Why did you abandon me?" she asked tonelessly and without preamble. "I thought you were dead."

Lila's cup clinked to the saucer. "Th–that can't be true. Why would you think that?"

"You *didn't* abandon me?"

Lila winced. "Yes. I. . .I thought it best. Please, forgive me. I loved Bruce very much, and when he died of a brain hemorrhage, I was devastated. His sister—your aunt—despised me. We lived with her then, and she made it clear she didn't want me there any longer. She hated me for marrying her brother, and—and I knew the carnival would take me."

She gave a regretful sigh when Angel remained silent. "She convinced me it would be in your best interest to leave you with her. I think now she did it just knowing it would hurt me. And in remembering the difficulties and fear I had for you growing up at the carnival, I realized she was right. You did need a good home. Believe me, Angel, it was very hard to let you go." She began to reach for her hand but drew back. "I. . .I wanted to breach the gap between us, to try to right the wrong I'd done. You were twelve when I first wrote. But when I heard nothing, I assumed you found a happier life without me in it. But why would you think I was dead? Because I stopped writing?"

Angel's blood went cold in shock then began to simmer with fury. "You wrote to me?" she whispered.

"Of course. Once a month. Up until three years ago, when your aunt wrote back, telling me. . .that you wanted nothing more to do with me. . .and to stop. . ." She gasped. "You never got the letters!" Her words came out hoarse in troubled realization.

"Aunt Genevieve told me you died when I was three." Angel's angry shock reverberated in her words. Her aunt had purposely kept them apart! Knowing that, and after what her mother now shared, Angel grew bold. "She was wrong. So were you. That's why I'm here."

Her mother's eyes swam with tears. She sat frozen in disbelief. "And now. . .now that you know. . .a–and see what I am? A sideshow freak?"

Angel's heart ached for her pain, and she answered with a question. "Do you wear that thing all the time?"

Her mother blinked in confusion. "The veil? No. I wanted to make you less uncomfortable. I—I have a deathly fear of razors, you understand, because of a bad accident with one as a child. I wear this when it's not just Father and me. He used to spurn me, too, but when I learned he was ill, I left the carnival to care for him, and God mended our relationship. Father doesn't mind me like this anymore." Her words rambled nervously.

Angel slipped out of the chair and knelt before her mother. Looking steadily into her eyes a moment, she reached up and gently pulled down the veil. Her mother tensed as Angel took in the short, curly beard then gasped as she curiously put her fingertips to it. It was soft and silky like everything about her. Angel's tears fell as her mother's did, and she lifted her eyes to the beautiful dark ones that regarded her with both dread and hope.

"I don't care what you look like either. Ever since I can remember, I've dreamed of you. Of you holding me and singing me to sleep. It was the only memory I had, and I thought it would be the only one I'd ever know."

Her mother tentatively cradled her face. "You would never close your eyes unless I sang to you. You were my Angel, my one bright light, and when I walked away that morning, the sunshine left, too."

"M—mama?" Angel whispered on a childlike sob, the years, the hurt, the anger all falling away.

Her mother swiftly embraced her, and memory sharpened to reality. Angel clutched her hard, crying in earnest, while her mother rocked her, holding her head to her breast. At the pure, sweet sound of the first lines to the lullaby from her dreams, Angel smiled through her tears, knowing no matter what the future held she would never be alone again.

❧

Roland would never forget the stunned look of hopeful confusion on Angel's face when he told her he was staying, too, thanks to her grandfather's invitation. His own need to find work and hide somewhere secluded—and Birch Grove Farm, nestled in the middle of a small community, was about as secluded as you could get—coupled with his desire to help the aging minister aided his decision. Pastor Everett never had fully recovered his robust health after fighting pneumonia, so Roland was more than happy to help. Of course, being near Angel had been the main reason he stayed. So much of her previous behavior now made sense, and the only regret he had was that she hadn't trusted him sooner, though he couldn't blame her. He supposed if their situations had been switched, an ex-gangster wouldn't be his first choice as a confidant either.

Lila had dispensed with the veil, and Roland was amazed, intrigued, and impressed that a woman who'd gone through so much suffering could have so stalwart a faith. To her soft-spoken question regarding the absence of her veil and his feelings on the matter, he casually assured her if they could tolerate his being a Piccoli, he could handle her beard, since his misfortune was the greater of the two. At his clear acceptance, any remaining tension dissolved, and Lila even laughed.

Everett expressed his faith with almost every sentence, opening up the Bible after suppertime and reading aloud then opening discussion. And Roland had a lot of questions.

"God is the Author of second chances," Everett told Roland one afternoon. "He gave one to me and my daughter, gave one to Lila and her daughter, and he's given you a second chance, too, son."

Roland couldn't argue with that. After his association with Mama, with his Angel, and now with her family, it wasn't long before one Sunday morning Roland made his decision.

He walked alone outside, his heart full with all he'd learned, and fell to his knees. The sun had just risen over the horizon, beaming hope. "I surrender all," he whispered, shaken. "All the pain and bitterness, all the anger. I choose to follow in Your footsteps, Lord. Please cleanse me of my many sins, wash me in Your blood. . .make me whole."

Caught up in a cushion of peace, what could have been minutes or hours later, he rose from the ground and felt as if a burden had literally dropped from his shoulders.

Mama was right. God did answer prayer.

With each week that passed, Angel felt more at ease around her mother, whom she'd come to regard as a friend, and her grandfather, who became to her a wise teacher. His words inspired her to open her heart, to forgive her aunt and cousins, and not to judge herself harshly for things she couldn't help.

Her mother's story shocked and saddened her, and it was with great care they delved into the question buried but always dominant in Angel's mind. Her father. Her mother admitted she never knew the identity of her attacker: The night had been dark, and she'd never seen his face. But she assured Angel that she was very much wanted and always had been.

"You were my lifeline, Angel. My reason to carry on. And such joy you gave me! Everyone at the carnival loved you. . . ." The more she spoke of Angel's early years, the more embers of memories faintly stirred: snippets of when her mother took her on her first ride on the carousel, after all pleasure seekers went home for the day and the operator gave in to the request of the man Angel had called Uncle Bruce before her mama married him.

Her grandfather was her counselor, her mother her inspiration, and Roland. . . She took in a deep breath as she envisioned the man who took up the greater portion of her thoughts. To her he meant the world. A friend, a protector, a confidant. Her reasoning finally gave in to her heart, admitting if only to herself that she was madly in love with him. She still hadn't told him her dark secret. With her mother's example, she came to accept what could never be changed. But would he feel the same about her once he knew? Of one thing Angel was now sure.

"Mama," she said late one Sunday afternoon, "I want what you and Grandfather have. What my friend Nettie and Mama Philena have." She smiled softly. "She said it was thanks to your influence that she found God. Will you show me how?"

Overjoyed, her mother prayed with her, and Angel added words of her own. "Thank You, dear Lord, for bringing me to this moment, for helping me find my mother, for Nettie, and for all those at the carnival who helped me understand what true beauty is. Please help my aunt and cousins to learn. And thank You for becoming the Father I never had."

Her mother squeezed her hands, her eyes teary, and Angel hugged her, feeling as light inside as goose down.

"It's amazing," her mother said, "how the stubborn doings of one woman who came to visit the freak show that night long ago and wouldn't take no for an answer"—here she laughed—"could have initiated all this. God truly is a miracle worker, and just you wait and see, Angel, the plans He has for you!"

Thrilled and eager to share her news with Roland, Angel kissed her mother and hurried outdoors. She caught sight of his tall form, his back to her, his hands on his hips as he surveyed the land. Weeks of hard labor had strengthened his already lean, muscular frame, and her heart pounded in shy admiration at the sight of him.

Taking a shaky breath, she walked his way.

Chapter 16

Roland?"

He turned, clearly lost in thought, but his eyes sharpened as they went to her face.

"Marry me, Angel," he whispered, his request as intense as his gaze.

"Wh–what?" She blinked, and all coherent thought vanished.

"Marry me." He gently grasped her shoulders. "You're all I think about, all I dream of. I want to share a life with you—this life. I want you to be my wife and the mother to my children." He looked at her lips that had parted in bewildered shock. "Angel. . ."

Her name came as a hoarse groan that warmed her lips as his mouth brushed hers. She yielded to him, pressing closer, having missed his touch so much. . . .

Then she remembered.

"No." At the flinch of pain in his eyes when she pushed him away, she quickly explained, "There's something I never told you." *Oh dear God, please. Please help me.* She didn't want to tell him, not like this. But she no longer had a choice. She loved this man. He had to know.

"I–it's about my parentage."

Roland relaxed. "Angel, Lila's condition doesn't bother me. I think she's a wonderful lady—"

His words brought some relief, but she shook her head to silence him. "It's about my father—my. . .lack of one."

She was going about this badly. There was no alternative but to blurt out the whole nasty truth and hope she wouldn't disgust him, hope he would at the very least remain her friend. Somehow she could learn to live with just that, as long as he didn't leave her life completely.

"So now you see," she said, as she finished her brusque retelling, "I'm nameless. Illegitimate. I can never change what I am, like you could change your circumstances. I don't have that choice."

To her absolute surprise, he moved forward and crushed her to him.

She'd thought she had no more tears left to cry.

He held her close, stroking her hair. "What you are is an angel."

At his gentle words, she pulled back to look at him. Sincerity shone in his eyes.

"You are what influenced me to change my life and escape the bonds of my family. Your grandfather told me that only God could bring something beautiful out of what was meant to be hurtful and wicked. And He did, Angel. He brought you." He smiled tenderly, and with his thumb he brushed away her fresh tears. "I consider myself fortunate to have been on the train the night you stumbled aboard. And I struggled over asking you to marry me for some time. I'm not exactly considered a great catch," he joked, bringing from her a soft smile. "The name Piccoli has struck fear into the hearts of many."

"You're nothing like your family!" she argued. "Any woman would be lucky to have you for a husband."

"Including you, Angel?" His fingertips brushed over her lips, causing her to tremble with new emotion. "Would you consider yourself lucky to be joined for life to someone like me? I think we're safe now. Your grandfather's faith has rubbed off on me; I trust that God will take care of us. But could you consider such a thing?"

"You're sure, after all I told you, that you still want me—"

Her words were cut off by his passionate kiss. A long time later he lifted his head, his dark eyes softened. "Does that answer your question?"

She nodded in breathless wonder, unable to speak.

"The truth is, my darling, I have never stopped wanting you."

They were married a week later, with her grandfather officiating and her mother acting as witness, along with a shy neighbor named Rose, whom Angel had met the previous week and welcomed to share in her joy. The private ceremony was all Angel desired, and she and Roland pledged unrehearsed vows, giving God the glory for the bizarre coincidences that had brought them together—events that perhaps were not coincidences at all—and for their blessed union, promising always to love, honor, and protect. Their vows were possibly unconventional, Angel thought, as she moved eagerly into her husband's arms for his kiss. . . .

But then, her dear family including herself, could hardly be considered typical.

Nor could her new husband who, in his delight to hear Angel pronounced his wife, firmly embraced her, lifting her off her feet and kissing her most soundly. Remembering the others, he abashedly broke the kiss and thanked them for their help, while letting Angel slide, breathless, back to the ground. Amid amused chuckles, the trio moved to the next room, to give them a moment's privacy. Eager to continue where they'd left off, Angel cradled Roland's head, lifting herself on her toes to press her mouth to his.

His arms fastened around her back, lifting her against his solid form, and she decided that *typical* was highly overrated. She wanted Roland Piccoli no other way.

Epilogue

R oland!"
Angel waved a letter and ran toward her husband as he walked home from the field. She threw herself into his arms, and he held her against him.

"What has you so excited, darling?"

"Cassie and Chester are coming! Oh, can you believe it? We'll get to see them again! The carnival train is coming east—to our town!" She pulled away and laughed, waving the letter. "If they can, I'd like them to come here to the farm and visit, but I do so want to go see them. To see everyone! Mama and Posey and Rita—and, oh, everyone!"

"Of course." He grinned at her exuberance.

"I cannot wait for the day to arrive!"

"I would never have guessed it."

"Oh you!" She slapped his shoulder then reached up to kiss him.

One afternoon later that week her mother received her own guest, sharpening Angel's curiosity when they immediately shut themselves up in her bedroom. She had yet to meet the woman from New York, and when Roland and her grandfather came in for supper, Mama and her guest were still behind the closed door. Angel knocked but found it locked. Her mother announced she wouldn't be coming to dinner, a strange note in her voice.

Concerned, Angel joined Roland and her grandfather for their meal of corn and bread with milk. Afterward her grandfather excused himself to do some reading.

"Roland, I'm worried." She cleared the dishes from the table. "Mama's been acting odd lately."

"How so?"

"Anxious. . .distant."

He pulled her willingly into his lap, his arms linking around her waist. "You think it has something to do with her visitor?"

"That or the carnival. She hasn't seen them for years, and though only Mama, Cassie, and Chester will be coming, I'm sure it brings back bad memories."

His fingertips went beneath her chin. "What was it Nettie told you in her last letter? Not to borrow worry because there's more than enough to go around?"

120

"As if someone would actually want it?"

He chuckled and kissed her. Her heart so in love with this man, Angel pressed her hand to his cheek, eagerly deepening their kiss.

The sound of the door creaking open vaguely reached her ears.

"Angel? Roland? Could you come here a moment, please?"

Startled, Angel moved away, and Roland lifted her off his lap. She took his hand, and he squeezed it, helping to steady her nerves as they went to her mother's door.

✒

They looked in shock at the visitor, and then at Lila, whose jaw, delicate as the rest of her bone structure, was now clean-shaven. A faint white scar the length of a few inches lay visible on her jaw line; despite the flaw, she was easily one of the most beautiful women Roland had ever seen. He saw the lingering fear in her eyes and knew the process had been an ordeal.

"Why, Mama?" Angel didn't sound pleased. "Why'd you do it?"

"I didn't want to embarrass you. For myself I don't care. I've learned to accept this cross."

"Oh, Mama." Angel moved forward to give her a hug. "I don't care either! Don't feel you have to change for me. But Mama Philena and Cassie have seen you, right? I still don't understand."

"Faye hasn't."

"Faye?" Angel squeaked. "Why should Faye come here?"

"She wrote a letter of apology, though I don't think her mother knows. She said she feels horrible for what her family did to you and me. Of course she was just a child then, and I certainly don't blame her. She's coming for a visit this weekend. Strangely the letter came the same day my friend from New York did." Lila smiled up at the woman who stood by her chair.

"But. . .I still don't understand. Although. . ." Angel grew pensive. "I remember she didn't approve of Rosemary's decision to tell me the truth. She tried to stop it." She sighed. "I always thought that maybe without Rosemary's influence Faye could have been a better person. Of all of them she's the nicest. Still. . ." Her eyes grew fierce with loyalty. "If she can't accept you as you are, she shouldn't be welcome here."

Roland silently agreed. He thought about what Lila had said regarding crosses. They each had one to bear—Angel's being her harsh upbringing and knowledge of her conception; Roland, his gangster family and the blood he could never eradicate; and Lila's cross was living with a man's beard. Oddly enough he realized that, through those crosses, they each had found their strength.

"See there, what did I tell you?" the stranger exclaimed, her accent British with a slight twang. Laugh lines graced her mouth and the corners of her eyes, which were a dark blue and twinkled as they regarded Lila. "You had no cause to fret so."

She set down the foamy straight razor she held, wiped her hand on her skirt, and struck it out toward Angel. "Name's Darcy. Darcy Thomas. And you're Angel." Her smile was as effusive and outgoing as her manner. "I took care of you when you were just a babe in nappies."

Angel laughed at this, shaking the woman's hand. "This is my husband, Roland."

"A pleasure." Darcy shook Roland's hand.

"Likewise."

"Darcy is my oldest and dearest friend," Lila explained. "She gave me a home when I first left the carnival, when Angel was still a baby, and she helped me find my way to God."

"You're the one?" Angel's eyes widened.

"Aye, luv, that I am."

"Oh, we must talk! I have so much I want to know. About Lyons' Refuge that Mother told me so much about, and about how you and she met. . . ."

The gathering moved to the parlor. Over the next hour the women excitedly conversed.

Roland excused himself to take refuge on the porch—women's talk was too hard to follow with their fluttering changes into home, children, husbands, fashion, church, the economy, and whatever else existed under the sun. . .although he never got tired of conversing with Angel.

As the sun set beyond a fringe of distant beech trees, he entered the house for a glass of water. A protesting cry came from the bedroom.

"Oh, that's our boy. Wait till you see him, Darcy!" Angel hurried past Roland with a gentle brush of her hand along his arm, and Darcy beckoned him farther inside.

"You have that hunted animal look my Brent gets when the women sit down for a nice cozy chat." She chuckled in understanding and patted the cushion beside her. "Come, don't be shy. I won't bite. Tell me about the farm and what you do here."

Roland warmed to Darcy's carefree, no-nonsense manner. In a way, she reminded him of Mama Philena, and he found himself opening to her. While he assumed Angel fed the baby, he spoke of his worries—the farm was failing, what with the Depression, and Everett couldn't handle the workload, though he insisted on it. Lila sadly agreed. Roland felt concerned about the health of the man he'd come to consider as both a father and grandfather. "I do all I can, but things are bad. We want to try and keep the farm and not give up on it, as so many other farmers have done. But if we're ever going to manage, we need another hand." He shook his head helplessly.

Darcy got a pensive gleam in her eye. "Well now, guvner, I might be able to help at that. There's a boy at the refuge—well, a man now—been there since I came. Tommy's got a wanderer's spirit, but his clubfoot keeps him homebound. What he doesn't have in stride, he makes up for elsewhere. The boy's as strong as an ox with sturdy arms and build. What would you say if I talked to him and see if he'd be interested in helpin' out?"

"I'd say that would be swell, but I'd have to talk it over with Everett. And. . ." Roland hesitated. "We couldn't pay him. Not with the way things are right now."

"Oh, I imagine he'd be happy enough just for the change of scenery. His two best friends have moved on—Herbert now lives here in Connecticut— that's why I'm here. I was visiting. The other, Joel, well, we've lost track of him I'm afraid, and Tommy's become somewhat restless."

"We have that back storage room we could make up for him," Lila said. "Do ask him, Darcy. I remember Tommy—such a nice boy."

"Now he's a man." Darcy sighed. "Time flies away so fast."

"And here's our little man," Angel announced from behind. "May I introduce you to Everett Roland Piccoli."

She bounced their son in her arms and approached Darcy, who clucked over him. Everett gurgled in contentment, allowing Darcy to hold him.

"Oh, he looks just like his daddy!" Darcy cooed. "What a peach!"

Angel grinned and moved to stand beside Roland's chair; out of habit he slipped his arm about her waist. They shared a look of loving contentment, and Roland wished the room were empty so he could pull her onto his lap and kiss her like he wanted. Their earlier embrace had only whetted his appetite for more.

By the time Darcy left, she and Angel were fast friends. Excited about the prospect of Tommy soon joining them, Lila excused herself to talk to her father. The baby again slept in his bassinet, and Roland did what he'd wanted to do for hours.

He cornered Angel in the kitchen, advancing toward her until he had her back pressed to the wall and his hands around her waist. She gave a soft intake of breath at the unexpected move and wrapped her arms loosely around his neck.

"Roland?"

He kissed her long and thoroughly, amazed that after more than a year of marriage, she still affected his senses as if it was their first time. She clung to him as if she might fall if she were to let go.

He broke away to look into her eyes.

"I don't suppose you really want me to put the coffeepot on?" she whispered.

He smiled at the hopeful note in her voice, his every nerve ending awakened. "I think we should skip that tonight and retire early."

She reached up to brush her lips against his. "I like the way you think, Mr. Piccoli."

"I love everything about you, Mrs. Piccoli."

She gave a contented sigh. "Roland, darling, you can shadow me forever."

He chuckled at her reference to their first days together and kissed her again, thanking God above that his Angel had finally stopped running.

IN SEARCH OF
A DREAM

Dedication

A huge thank-you to my critique partners, Theo and Mom.
And to my Lord, who removed the scales from my eyes
so that I could see truth, I owe everything.

Prologue

C lemmie Lyons toiled over her letter, her mind elsewhere, her heart
playing betrayer with thoughts of. . .
   Him. . .
Her dream. . .
A dream no longer. . .
"Stop it," she chastised herself. "It's been more than three years. He has his
own life, a different life."

He had a life all right; one that evidently didn't include acknowledgment
of her or her parents, who had practically raised him on their farm. They'd
received not one call, not one letter or lousy word that he was still living and
breathing. She knew he must be; they would have heard otherwise, since the
navy informed next of kin. His mother died giving him life; his father died in
jail. He had no living relatives. Was he even still in the armed forces? It had
been more than seven years since he entered them.

Clemmie blew out a frustrated breath and put pen to paper:

   Really, Hannah, your offer for me to come visit couldn't have come at a
   better time.

At least with such a diversion, Clemmie would be away from Lyons' Refuge and all the persistent memories that nagged at her. She shook her head
and went back to writing her letter:

   Things aren't hopeless here, despite the depression, since Grandfather
   didn't invest in stocks, but I look forward to a change of scenery, regardless.
   It's very gracious of your great-uncle to allow me to visit his estate for the
   rest of the summer. How fortunate that he also protected his investments
   and didn't lose everything on that horrible Black Friday.

And maybe, if she did go to Connecticut, *his* face wouldn't haunt her from
every corner of the house!

Did I tell you we received a letter from Angel? She and her husband are well, as is little Everett. I remember when I learned that Roland was Vittorio Piccoli's grandson I questioned Angel's logic and sanity! But after visiting with them last summer, I can see why Angel is infatuated. He's very nice. I'm sure I don't need to tell you what a monster his grandfather is, since he was the mastermind in the tragedy that befell your parents, with the loss of their first child and almost killing your mother! How terrible those days must have been for them!

But I digress; Tommy went to live at their farm two years ago, to help out—I think I told you? However, that's not all—he's fallen in love! Can you believe it? Our little Tommy? Strangely enough, it's with Angel's cousin, Faye, who's been a frequent visitor to the farm. They were married last month. We only learned news of it when Angel thought to write us. I'm so thankful she did! Tommy was always such a horrible letter writer, much like Father.

And very much like Joel Litton.

Clemmie curbed the desire to throw her fountain pen across the room. Her behavior really was absurd. She'd barely thought of him these past years—well, not as often as in her childhood anyway. She'd been all of ten when he entered the navy. And on his last visit home, near her fifteenth birthday, he'd had a girl hanging on his arm. Clemmie scrunched up her nose in distaste at the memory, but a faint smile soon tilted her lips.

Despite his being twelve years older and quite obviously the man about town—a true heartbreaker, from all the unattached young women she'd seen panting after him—Joel always had made time for Clemmie. He treated her as a kid sister, and his annoying habit of calling her "Carrottop" rankled, the older she grew. But even if he did tease, she tolerated such behavior to be near him. All the boys had teased her, but Joel had also shown kindness. He'd acted as if he enjoyed her sole company, what little of it she scrounged from his clinging female companions, and had treated her as if she mattered. Was it any wonder that she had developed a hopeless fascination for him as a child?

He'd been a true scoundrel and the original ringmaster of troublemakers at Lyons' Refuge when her father first started the reform school. Joel had been a trial and a terror, in direct opposition to his angelic looks. Perhaps, in part, it was his wildness and devil-may-care attitude that had been the attraction for her then. Added to that, his princely features and heavenly blue eyes. . .

"Stop it, Clemmie! This is getting you nowhere fast!"

She threw the closed pen on the coverlet, congratulating herself that she didn't send it smacking into the wall. Such half-buried memories wouldn't be torturing her if she hadn't run across a box of Joel's things while looking through her trunk for items to pack. He'd entrusted her with his box of boyhood trinkets before he went into the service, in an effort to stem her tears at his departure.

"There, there, Clemmie," he'd soothed, his hand going under her chin, his other wiping her eyes with his handkerchief. "It's not like I'll be gone forever, sweetheart. I'll be back soon enough."

But not to stay.

And obviously those few paltry furloughs home were to be the sum total of his appearances, thus ending his life and time at the refuge.

Yes, a summer in Connecticut was looking better and better.

"You look rather like a dog in the manger."

Clemmie started at the teasing voice that also held a note of concern. She realized she'd left her door ajar and turned to look at the dear woman who cooked for everyone at Lyons' Refuge. She wasn't her aunt by relation, but Clemmie regarded the sprightly woman as close to being one and addressed her as such.

"Aunt Darcy." Clemmie wondered what she'd heard of her little outburst and how long she'd been standing there. "I didn't hear you come up."

Darcy moved into the room, worry lines marking her usually smooth brow. Youth could no longer claim her, but the only evidence of age were the silvering hairs among the dark ones crowning her temple. "What's got you so upset, luv?"

She sat next to Clemmie, her gaze taking in the unfinished letter then straying to the cigar box Clemmie had beside her. No one at the refuge smoked; it wasn't allowed, and Clemmie wondered where Joel had found the box. Probably from her grandfather who did smoke, to Mama's consternation. Clemmie prevented her hand from straying to the box, hoping Darcy wouldn't realize whose items it contained.

"I'm just in a melancholy mood. Late spring fever in the early summer, perhaps." She tried for an offhand smile.

Darcy cocked her brow. "It wouldn't have anything to do with you leaving, would it? You don't have to go. Things aren't so bad we can't manage. With your grandfather's aid and other supporters, we do quite well, I daresay." Her smile lit the room, chasing away the clouds that had settled on Clemmie's spirit.

"I know. But I *want* to see Hannah. We were closest in age, and I miss her. It's been years. But. . .well, it's my first time to step foot away from home. Ever." Even during the outings her parents sometimes took with Darcy to New York City, the children always were left behind under the watchful eye of Brent—Darcy's husband and the schoolmaster.

"A bit nervous, luv?" Darcy put a hand to Clemmie's chin. "You're a big girl now. Aye—more'n that. A young lady! Coo! I never thought I'd see the day.

And I think it's a good thing for you to see a bit of the world."

"I feel guilty leaving when I know Mama depends on my help with the smaller children."

"You shouldn't feel the blame—none at all! You're long overdue for a treat, and there's plenty living here at the farm to help out."

"I agree with Darcy."

Clemmie turned toward the doorway and smiled at the woman whose looks she favored. She only hoped her hair darkened to the beautiful auburn of her mother's, now sprinkled with gray. Strange how while she favored her beautiful mother, Clemmie felt so plain.

"Don't feel that you should stay, dear." Her mother moved the cigar box and took the space on the other side of Clemmie. "If you don't want to go, that's one thing, and you mustn't feel obligated. But it would be a golden opportunity for you to spread your wings. I fear, with you being my firstborn, I've coddled you severely. Your father would agree."

Clemmie wrapped her arm around her mother's waist. "I don't mind, Mama."

"Would you like to go see Hannah?"

Clemmie nodded.

"Then go with my blessing."

A stampede of running footsteps clambered upstairs, making all three women face the door, where Darcy's two youngest sons came to a sudden awkward stop, bumping into one another and almost falling.

"Mama! Aunt Charleigh! Come quick," Roger blurted out. "That new boy is making trouble again. They're outside fighting!"

"He gave Adam a bloody nose," young Matthew piped up, almost gleefully.

"And Adam gave him a black eye."

"The other boys are taking bets on who'll win this time."

Her mother and Darcy exchanged long-suffering glances and quickly rose. "Go tell your father and Uncle Stewart."

"Yes, Aunt Charleigh!"

"And don't you dare be gettin' in on the gamble!"

"Yes, Mama!"

The two boys disappeared.

"He's a terror, that one," Darcy mused.

"Quentin is no worse than any other boys we've handled. Do you recall the fistfights Joel and Herbert used to get into?" At the mention of Joel, a brief, worried silence ensued as it so often did. "And then there was Clint and anyone who looked at him cross-eyed, be it boy or girl," her mother added quickly. "I still think it a wonder that he and Miranda are now married."

"Aye," Darcy said on a laugh mixed with a groan. "Those were days unforgettable. And you, Charleigh, always ready to tackle the impossible."

Her mother laughed. "You're one to talk! You were and still are the first into the fray—to jump at any unconventional new idea. Remember your initial endeavors to bring order to the refuge? The fence painting contest and the trip to the carnival?"

"I suppose I'm a bit gung ho at that. Brent tells me the same. . .though it didn't turn out all bad. I wound up getting him in the bargain." Darcy winked, and both women chuckled. "Time's a wastin', and I'm for certain both our men'll need help issuing order among that brood, once they take care of those two rapscallions."

"We'll talk more about your visit after dinner," her mother assured Clemmie.

Watching them go, Clemmie shook her head and smiled in wistful contemplation.

Just another crazy, mixed-up day at the refuge.

She would miss her home and family, even miss the daily chaos that went hand in hand with keeping, raising, and reforming young hoodlums, as strange as that seemed. But Mother was right. And after hearing Joel's name mentioned, she realized that if she was ever to embark on her own life, she needed to get as far away from memories of him as possible. At least for a little while.

For Clemmie, the time had come to grow up and put childish dreams far behind her.

Chapter 1

Clemmie stepped off the train, holding in a nervous breath. With wide eyes, she scanned the crowded platform of lively passengers, eager to spot a familiar face. She'd rarely left the farm in her entire life, and then no farther than a few miles' drive—to church, to her grandfather's estate, to the central hub of their small town. The hustle and bustle of passengers leaving from and coming to this strange station unsettled her, much as it had in Ithaca, only there she'd had her parents' company before her train departed.

Here, she was all alone.

She almost bit a hole through her lip before she caught sight of Hannah Thomas's shining black hair and piercing blue-gray eyes. As pretty as ever, her friend waved and ran forward to greet her. The girls met halfway in a warm hug.

"I thought your train would never get here! You know me—so impatient." Hannah laughed and hugged her again. "Oh, it's so good to see you, Clemmie! It's been ages and ages. I enjoy your letters, but togetherness is so much nicer, don't you agree? I see your hair has gotten darker—you were right. And I think your freckles faded, too. Me, I can't tolerate the sun, though Mama's half-Polynesian. But I inherited my fair skin from Papa's side of the family. Still it's nothing like Bette Davis's. I have photographs of her and other movie stars in my photo box—I'll show you when we get home. Some of them are even signed! Oh, but listen to me carrying on! How's everyone at the refuge? Are they well? I can't believe it's been *years* since I've seen most of them!"

In her excitement, Hannah bounced from one subject to another like a runaway ball, and Clemmie smiled. It was nice to see some things never changed.

"Everyone's well. They send their love. And you have the prettiest skin I've ever seen, so don't complain." And Hannah did. Flawless, without a freckle to mar it. Hannah also blushed prettily, like a pink rose, unlike Clemmie, who resembled something less attractive, like a tomato.

"You're sweet to say so." Hannah gave her a dimpled smile. "Oh look, there's Papa! I was too excited to wait and ran ahead." She grabbed Clemmie's arm, pulling her along toward Bill Thomas, Brent's brother. Clemmie marveled how the two men looked as if they could be twins, though Hannah's father looked more like an outdoorsman, solid in physique with stronger, defined features.

"Wait," Clemmie said with a laugh. "My luggage!"

"Oh—sorry!" Hannah giggled. "I'm just so excited to finally have you with us."

Hannah's father met them at the baggage car with a warm welcome for Clemmie and retrieved her luggage. Trailing her father, who toted both bags, Hannah filled Clemmie in on as much as she could in the short distance they had to walk.

". . .Mama has a picnic planned after church Sunday. Everyone will be there. You might see Herbert, too. He and his wife go to our church and—"

"Wait—what?" Clemmie stopped midstep and turned to Hannah.

"Herbert Miller. From the refuge."

"Herbert and his wife live in Cedarbrook?" she asked in amazement.

"I thought you knew. When he quit working for my father and got that job at the paper, he met Thea. They had planned to move to where her family now lives—in Maine."

"That much I knew. They decided to stay?"

"Yes. Since the house is bought and paid for, it gives them a sure place to live. It's small, but they seem to like it. I think it once belonged to a member of her family. I heard the story but can't remember details." Hannah gave an unconcerned toss of her head. "They don't live far from my uncle's. Within cycling distance. You could pay her a call if you like. She must be lonely since she has only her two little girls to talk to all day while Herbert's at work."

Clemmie didn't ask why Hannah never visited Thea. Her fifteen-year-old cousin, sweet as she could be, had a touch of snobbishness, though she wasn't unkind. Her few faults aside, Hannah made a good friend, and Clemmie had her own batch of shortcomings so knew better than to judge anyone.

Once the chauffeur pulled the Rolls Royce into the winding drive of the estate, Clemmie's eyes widened theatrically. Having the chauffeur waiting at the car and opening the doors for them had been bizarre enough. She'd never had a stranger wait on her before. But this. . .she felt almost like a princess or maybe a pauper coming to abide at a fairy-tale castle.

Lyons' Refuge was big—it had to be with all the children her parents housed—but this home was majestic, a haven for the wealthy, bigger than her grandfather's manor. Round turrets flanked both ends of the pale stone dwelling, the architectural design of the house medieval. Pink roses and ivy climbed the walls. The arched window above the double front doors was composed of so many different shades of glass that in the sunlight, it glowed with iridescence.

"My great-uncle has a thing for the late Middle Ages and the Renaissance.

He had the house designed. Wait till you see the inside!"

The inside of the monolith reflected its exterior grandeur. Clemmie's mouth dropped open in amazement, and Hannah giggled. "He isn't home much, what with his canned tuna business and constant business trips. He isn't home now. Just Mama and the rest of the family."

A beautiful woman with glossy black hair and exotic features glided into the foyer. Her skin was still incredibly smooth, her hair not silvered one iota. She looked like she could be Hannah's sister, though Clemmie knew this was Sarah, her mother. She wore a common, blue cotton dress, seeming out of place in so fine a home, but her manner was regal.

"Clemmie," she said, smiling and moving forward to hug her. "It's so nice to have you come stay with us."

"Thank you for inviting me, Mrs. Thomas."

She smiled. "And your family? They are well?"

"Yes, they send their love."

The remainder of the evening passed smoothly. Hannah's brothers and sisters were quiet, nowhere near as boisterous as the children at the refuge, including Clemmie's own siblings. She wondered if they were on their best behavior or if they always acted docile and well behaved. After supper she went upstairs to the room she'd been given. Her friend appeared at the door, just as Clemmie put the last of her things away.

"Oh, Clemmie." Hannah dropped to the bed in a foul temper. "I forgot I promised Mama I'd help her catalog items for the bazaar. She just reminded me. It's such a bore, and I don't want to burden you by asking you to come along on your first real day here. But I hate to leave you alone. I'll be gone at least four hours every afternoon. It's dreadfully tedious work. So many donations." She sighed. "But I promised."

Clemmie was awful at itemizing and categorizing. She feared that if she did offer her aid, she'd be more hindrance than help. "I don't mind having some time to myself." She pondered an idea. "If you give me directions to Thea's, perhaps I can visit while you're at the bazaar."

"That's a marvelous idea! Then I know you'll be entertained. It's easy to find their house. They live a few miles from here. I'll loan you my bicycle."

Clemmie thought about her uncoordinated lower limbs. "I prefer to walk."

"Walk?" Hannah regarded her as if the word were foreign to her vocabulary.

Clemmie laughed. "It's okay. On the farm I do a lot of it."

So mentally armed with directions and eager for a chat with Herbert's wife, Clemmie set out the next day for a visit. The air felt bracing though tolerable, the neighborhood opulent. The farther she walked, the more crowded and less flagrant the houses appeared, more like she felt real homes ought to look.

Coming upon a quaint house beyond a short picket fence, Clemmie reasoned this must be Herbert's residence since it was the only blue-shuttered house on the street. An abandoned pile of wooden blocks sat to one side of the porch, waiting for their small owner's return. Somewhere a dog barked, and bees hummed from nearby hydrangea bushes.

Clemmie straightened her hair, her blouse, and her skirt then rang the bell. She ought to have called first, but Hannah didn't know the number or if the Millers even owned a phone. That seemed strange to Clemmie; her father had installed a telephone at Lyons' Refuge when they first were made available to residential homes, though since they ran a children's reformatory, the expense had been not only helpful but also necessary.

The door opened. A short, pretty, brown-haired woman with a weary smile and welcoming eyes looked at her.

"Hello?"

"Hi, Thea. You might not remember me, but I was at your wedding. I'm Clemmie Lyons, Charleigh and Stewart's daughter. From the refuge."

Thea's eyes grew wide. At first Clemmie thought she saw alarm but decided it must have been from her eyes adjusting to the bright sunlight, since Thea then smiled.

"Of course I remember you. Herbert talks about his days there all the time." She hesitated. "Do come in. He's at work at the newspaper office, and it's just me and Loretta. Bethany's at school."

"Hello there." Clemmie smiled at the little girl, who peered shyly up behind her mother's skirts. "What a pretty dolly you have."

Loretta smiled bashfully. Clemmie at once felt a bond with Loretta, seeing the little girl's head of bright copper red hair.

Thea led Clemmie inside, to the back of the house and the kitchen. Their home was cheery, not neat as a pin like the mansion she'd just left, what with bits of evidence here and there that this place housed two little girls. But it was inviting and warm, like the refuge. Only Thea's manner seemed distant, as she darted an anxious glance out a window facing the backyard.

"Would you like some refreshment? I'll make coffee." Thea stopped suddenly, her hand on the scoop in the coffee grounds. "You do like coffee?"

"Coffee sounds wonderful." Clemmie felt awkward. "Did I come at a bad time? I could return later."

"What. . . ?" Thea looked at her again, distracted. "No. Now is fine. It's nearing noon, and Herbert should be home for lunch unless things at the paper are busy. But you're welcome to stay."

Her words were gracious, only her tone didn't sound welcoming. The sudden reverberations of a bell proved that Herbert did own a phone. "I'll just be a minute." Thea hurried from the sideboard and disappeared into the hall.

Loretta watched from the doorway, creeping closer to Clemmie. The girl's bashfulness dissolved into delight as she glanced at the window.

"Kitty!" she pointed, with a sunny smile at Clemmie, then darted for the door.

Clemmie had a glimpse of orange fur shooting away from the pane before Loretta flung open the door and raced outside.

Clemmie paused only a moment before going after her. The child, she knew, was only three and too young to be left outside on her own. Clemmie's lifetime of experience looking after her brothers and sisters told her that much.

"See my kitty?" Loretta asked Clemmie with delight. An orange tabby evaded Loretta's small, chubby hands as the child pounced. The kitten scampered toward a shed a short distance away, or rather what looked like a shed at first glance. Clemmie noticed a chair sitting on boards that formed a short porch under an overhang, all of it enclosed by a railing. A few abandoned toys lay near the wall. Perhaps it was the children's playhouse, though it seemed too big for that.

All interest in the whereabouts of the cat forgotten, Clemmie watched the door to the small dwelling open and a man step into the shadow of the overhang. She squinted through the glare of the sun, trying to get a good look at him as she drew close. His hair was fair, not red, so it couldn't be Herbert, and he stood tall and slender, not short like Thea's husband. He stepped out farther, crossing the line of shadow into sunlight.

Clemmie's heart seemed to stop beating. She felt dizzy, as if she might swoon, and experienced a rush of energy at the same time.

"Loretta? Is that you?" His piercing blue eyes looked in Clemmie's direction, staring at her as if reaching deep into her soul. She stood rooted to the spot, unable to move if a brush fire started beneath her feet. "Tell me that blasted cat isn't on the loose and under my feet again, ready to trip me."

Joel!

There was no mistaking his identity; his face, though slightly altered with time and bearing a scruffy mustache and beard, had been imprinted on her memory for years, aided by yearly photographs her mother had organized for those who lived at the refuge. The man from whom she had yearned even one word of communication or the barest glimpse now stood before her in the flesh, with only the length of several grassy feet between them.

She curbed the immediate impulse to fly into his arms and wrap hers tightly around his neck in exuberant relief, as she'd done at his arrival to the farm three years before, during his last visit home.

Something wasn't right.

He moved closer to the porch edge, while all the time she felt as if she were living in a bizarre dream. He stared straight at her but didn't seem to know her. Had she changed so much? She'd grown taller, her body more curvaceous and womanly, her hair almost auburn; but her face hadn't altered so greatly that he should look at her as if she were a complete stranger. He appeared similar to the last photograph she'd seen, though his unkempt hair had grown roguishly long, to brush the tops of his shoulders. And then there was that beard. She noticed he was as slim and well built as ever, with broad shoulders and a narrow waist. She pulled her brows together in concern. On deeper study he seemed too slender, as if he'd not been eating lately. . .or eating well.

That she should quietly ponder such things while her heart had awakened and was hammering cartwheels against her ribs amazed her.

"Who are you?" His body tensed as he wrapped his hand around the post, using it to step down. "Who's there. . . ? I *know* you're there. Speak up! I can hear your clothes rustle in the wind."

Her vocal cords as frozen as the rest of her, Clemmie drew in a sharp audible breath, pain crushing her heart and filming her eyes with tears. He jerked his head as if he'd heard her bare inhalation of air.

Oh, God, no. . .please no. . .don't let it be true. . . .

But the longer she watched him, the more she realized her incoherent prayer came in vain. Joel frowned, an anxious expression momentarily touching his eyes. . .his remarkable, crystalline eyes. Heavenly blue eyes that always had and still did make her heart shift in beats. Eyes that now looked straight through her. . .

Because they couldn't see her.

Her dear sweet Joel was blind.

Chapter 2

How?

How had such a horrible tragedy happened to such a handsome young man who'd had everything going for him, who had once been brimming over with vitality and life? Joel was still beautiful, his features like that of a Raphaelite angel—or at least what Clemmie could see above his beard. As he slowly drew near, she could see faint lines never there before, and his skin had become a shade sallow, as though he didn't go outdoors as often as he once had.

She wanted to weep bitterly, wanted to turn on her heel and run back the way she had come, far and fast. At the same time, she wanted to run to him and hold him tightly in a strange mix of relief and despair. But she knew he would scorn any show of pity. So she stood, silent and dumb as a scarecrow, while he continued to draw closer.

"Why won't you speak?" he snapped. "You never see a blind man before?" He snorted in impatience. "You can't pretend you're not there. I'm not fooled by your silence, even if my eyes can be."

His voice lacked any real emotion, except to snap with sarcasm. This was a Joel she didn't know. His surliness both unnerved and saddened her.

He took in a long, deep breath through his nostrils. "I can smell your scent. Thea doesn't grow lilacs. I know you're there—so speak up, confound you!"

He came to a stop, only a foot away. She couldn't take her eyes off his flawless features, his beautiful, clear, useless eyes. She brushed away the tears that dripped down her cheeks.

"Loretta left the house while Thea was on the phone—" She blundered the reply, barely aware of what she said. Her voice had grown huskier over the years, was hoarse now, and she suddenly felt grateful he wouldn't recognize it. "I didn't think she should be left unattended."

"Yes, I hear her giggling. And that darn cat yowling. But that doesn't explain why *you're* here."

"I'm—I'm an acquaintance of Thea's." Clemmie wasn't sure why she gave that explanation, so she rambled aimlessly on. "I came to—to see about. . ." She stopped, realizing she couldn't air her key reason for her visit—to discover if Herbert or Thea knew of Joel's whereabouts. Clearly they did.

"To see about. . .a job as a nanny?" he filled in when she didn't continue, his manner curt. "Or maybe you're a curiosity seeker from the neighborhood, eager to learn what terrible secret Thea's been hiding in her backyard?" With that flair Joel still possessed, he swept his hand before his person from collarbone to thigh. "So, had your fill of gawking yet?"

The sudden slam of the kitchen door alerted Clemmie to Thea's presence. A rapid glance showed the woman hurrying their way, alarm in her eyes. Clemmie forestalled her before she could speak, her mind instantly jumping into gear.

"I'm not any such thing. My name's Marielle." She gave her middle name before Thea could introduce them. She sensed Thea gape at her. "I've come for a visit. I didn't mean to intrude."

"That's *exactly* what you're doing." Joel didn't curb his caustic words. "Now if you'll excuse me, I'm done providing entertainment for the day." He whipped around before she could respond and stomped back to the porch as though he'd trod the course often and had it memorized.

He entered the shed-like building. The slam of the door shot through the air like the report of a shotgun. Neither woman spoke. At last Clemmie looked at Thea, who appeared almost remorseful.

"We need to talk," she said quietly, and Thea nodded, leading the way back to the kitchen.

Clemmie sat down at the table, feeling like an invisible puppeteer must have control of her limbs; she didn't understand how she could be moving them. She stared into the cup of coffee Thea set before her, not even thinking to add her usual lump of sugar. Right now she needed it black. Black and strong.

She took a sip, wincing as the liquid scalded her tongue. A thousand questions flew through her mind, and she grabbed one at random. "I'm assuming he lives here?"

"Yes."

"How long?"

Thea exhaled deeply. "He didn't want anyone to know."

"That's obvious. But now I do. So you no longer have any reason to conceal such information."

Thea reluctantly nodded. "Herbert found him over a year ago."

"Found him?"

"In a hospital. He'd been searching. Joel usually kept contact, but then all correspondence abruptly ended. The reporter in Herbert investigated and found him."

Clemmie wasn't sure she wanted to hear the rest, but she needed to know. "How did it happen?"

"He was better than you see him now, when Herbert found him. Well, physically, that is. Emotionally he was a wreck, much like he is today. Only he's grown more bitter. At first Joel took a job with Herbert at the newspaper. Shortly after that he started complaining of headaches and began losing his vision a little at a time. One day he couldn't see at all."

"But *how?*"

"An accident. He'd been out of the navy for a while. From what I understand, he was with friends when it happened. One of them was driving and lost control. The driver was killed, and Joel was badly hurt—thrown from the car. Strangely there were no signs of blindness then. It took about a month. I don't remember the medical reasons Herbert gave, but Joel's been walking around like half a man ever since. Hiding here. Becoming a recluse. We tried to get him to move in with us, into the house, but he refused. Herbert almost had to twist his arm to get him to accept our help—and you know what best friends those two have always been. We finally convinced him to stay, but he was resolute about keeping his distance. He insisted on living in the shed, and Herbert finally agreed, making the necessary adjustments. It was the only way he could keep an eye on Joel. Herbert has been very concerned about him; we both have."

Each stabbing word inflicted a wound in Clemmie's heart. Now she understood why he'd made no contact, and that hurt almost as much.

"He wouldn't even contact my parents to tell them?"

"He didn't want handouts."

"*Handouts?*" Upset, Clemmie repeated the word forcefully.

Thea lightly grazed her teeth along her lip, as if uncertain she should answer.

"There's more, isn't there? Please, tell me."

Thea searched her face then nodded. "There's an operation that could relieve the pressure of whatever is pushing against his optic nerve, but it costs a great deal of money."

When she paused, Clemmie filled in the rest, her anger at Joel's muleheadedness rising to the fore. "So he decided it was better to stay blind than to tell my parents what happened and ask for a loan? The fool man," she muttered under her breath.

"I take care of him as much as I'm able," Thea continued. "Doing his laundry, straightening up after him, bringing him meals. That sort of thing."

"It must be difficult, taking care of your family and your home, too."

Thea glanced into her coffee, her solemn expression making it clear.

"Let me help."

"What?" Thea's head jerked up in shock.

"I can do all those things. I have some free time on my hands, and that would give you a needed break."

Thea smiled, uncertain. "You're kind to offer."

"Nothing kind about it. Actually I'm selfish. Joel needs someone not just to tidy up after him and feed him, but to. . .be there." She had difficulty explaining her feelings when even she didn't understand them. "I want to do whatever I can to help him."

"He's changed, Clemmie."

"We've all changed."

"No, you don't understand." Thea fidgeted. "He's. . .different. Hard. Angry at the world. At God most of all."

The news didn't surprise Clemmie, though it did distress her.

"He takes it out on anyone within reach of his voice. He can be cruel."

"Violent?" Clemmie whispered in dismay. "He hasn't struck you?" Joel often had been the mastermind behind pranks at the refuge when he was a boy, but she'd never known him to initiate physical violence. At least not that she remembered.

"No no. It's just that he's so. . .caustic. With his words."

Clemmie exhaled in relief. "If you're worried about me—don't be. I'm not afraid of anything Joel might dish out. I really want to do this."

"Don't you think he'll feel threatened and angry when you tell him who you are? That someone from his past has learned the truth of the misfortune he's tried so hard to hide?"

"You're right." Clemmie heaved a sigh. "Knowing him—at least based on what I once knew of him—he'd be furious."

"He hasn't changed in that regard."

Clemmie frowned, again not surprised. His foolish pride had prevented him from contacting those who loved him, who would have cared for him. After hearing Joel's story from Thea, Clemmie knew him well enough to be certain that if she were to reveal her identity, it would end her plan to help him.

"And he won't be mad at just you. He'll blame Herbert and me as well."

"All right. So. . ." Clemmie carelessly shrugged one shoulder. "We won't tell him."

"What?" Thea looked at her as if she'd suggested they take a torch to his walls and burn down his home. "You can't be serious."

"Marielle *is* my middle name. He'd never remember that, even if he did once know it. Which I doubt anyone told him. Mama wasn't in the habit of speaking it. Only when she was really upset with me. And if Joel ever did overhear, I highly doubt he would connect the two. Not like he would if I introduced myself as Clemmie."

"Tell me you're not actually going to pretend to be someone else."

"Only for a little while. Just until Joel feels comfortable having me around. I'll tell him eventually."

Thea frowned in disapproval. "I don't know. . . ."

"You said your hands are full. This will give you extra time to take care of your family. I'll take full blame should he find out. But there's no reason he should. I've changed over the last three years, my voice included. I was little more than a child when he last saw me."

Now that the shock of finding him—and in such a tragic state—had partially worn off, Clemmie wasn't sure why it felt so important to try to reconnect with Joel again. But at least this way she could share in his life without being considered the intrusion he might think her if he knew the truth.

She was pathetic.

She was walking a thin line, and she knew it.

But this was Joel. Not some stranger. And he was in clear need of help, help she was only too willing to give.

"I'll talk it over with Herbert tonight," Thea said at last. "I can't give my consent without him knowing the facts."

"Fair enough. Ring me at Hannah's when you reach a decision."

Whatever the two decided, Clemmie grew firm in her resolve to remain in Joel's life, somehow. Now that she'd found him, she wasn't about to lose him again.

Chapter 3

The air blew cold, moist. It would rain. Again. The skies for him were always dark, but so was the earth and everything in it. Only in strong sunlight could Joel discern vague shadows—all of them a darker shade of gray than the black that continually filled his world.

Day.

Night.

It was all the same to him. The same void, the same darkness.

All that was left of his life.

With a grimace he stepped out onto the porch and wondered for the umpteenth time why he bothered. Why leave his four walls to visit the outdoors when he couldn't see the grass or the skies or the hydrangea bushes that rimmed Herbert's home? Where his eyes failed him, his other senses had sharpened, and before he found his way to his chair, he picked up an aroma different from the fresh soil near his porch that Loretta had dug up in her play or the clean scent of rain coating the air.

The scent of lilacs.

He scowled, crossing his arms over his chest, and turned toward the whisper of footsteps he heard over the breeze.

"You again. What do you want this time? Didn't get enough entertainment ogling the blind man the other day?"

"How did you know. . . ?"

Her voice, quiet and lovely with a throaty huskiness, trailed off in shocked confusion.

His lips curled into a hard smile. "I told you. I may be blind, but I'm no fool."

"I never said you were. But I could have been anyone. How did you know it was me?"

He decided not to answer. "You haven't stated your business for coming here again. Does the term trespassing mean nothing to you?"

"My business?" A hint of amusement laced her tone. "I suppose you could call it that. But for your information, I'm hardly trespassing."

He didn't like this sudden turn, as if she had the upper hand. It made him feel even more vulnerable and at a loss than he already was. To bring things back to his control, he relied on his acerbic behavior. His jaw hardened.

"State it, then beat it. I don't want you here."

"Well, Joel, that's just too bad. Because here is where I'll be staying."

Her casual use of his name and stubborn response threw him for a moment.

"That's 'Mr. Litton' to you. And no, you're not. Not anywhere near here. Go back to the house and visit Thea, since you're her friend. Or if you'd like, I could bodily remove you from these premises."

Silence answered, and he could tell he'd addled her. He smirked in his victory, small though it was.

"Very well, Mr. Litton. If you prefer such a silly formality in title, so be it. There's no need to be so rude. And you may call me Marielle."

Irate, he unclasped his folded arms and took a swift step toward her. "I won't call you anything! Except gone from my home. Now! Scram!"

"My, we did wake up in a grumpy mood this morning, didn't we?"

Joel blinked with shock at her wry words and heard her approach. He took an involuntary step back. The thud of her steps hit the planking, the smell of lilacs assaulting him. He felt the air stir as she breezed past—then heard the door he'd left ajar swing fully open.

"Whatta ya think you're doing?" he demanded, moving her way. He just prevented himself from following through with his threat of reaching out to find and grab her arm and throw her off his porch. "Don't you know a direct order to go when you hear one? I haven't given you any invitation to invade my privacy."

"Oh, I'm sorry. Didn't Thea tell you?" Her tone shifted from utter brashness to mild chagrin. "I'm your new housekeeper and cook."

"My *what*?" The breath escaped his lungs as if he'd been punched in the stomach.

"I'm going to take care of you."

Over his dead body! Her words rankled, stiffening his pride. "I don't need anyone looking after—"

"Thea looks after you."

"Yes, but it's her place to—" To what? Wait on him hand and foot? It wasn't her place. But this irritating woman's logic stymied him, and his words came out jumbled. "What I mean to say is, it's her home."

"And I offered to help. She's looking a bit peaked, and I thought it would ease her workload, since I have plenty of time on my hands."

The news that Thea wasn't well concerned him, though he didn't show it. Was taking care of him as well as her family such a trial? It must be. He certainly hadn't made her task any easier. Before he had time to think up a reply, he heard the woman intruder's footsteps move away and realized she'd entered his home.

Grimacing, he followed but remained on the threshold.

"This isn't necessary."

"I think it's very necessary. *Tsk,* you quite obviously need help keeping order around this place."

"Maybe I like it sloppy. It's not like I can see to know the difference."

"Well, I can. And it's just not healthy to live in such disorder."

"Put those down!"

She gave a shocked gasp at the same time he heard the buckles of his suspenders hit the planks and the rumple of his slacks follow. It unnerved him for her to touch his personal items.

"H–how did you know I was holding anything?"

"I have very acute hearing. There's nothing you can get by me."

"I wasn't trying to." She released a tired little sigh. "Look, can we at least try to give this a go?"

"I didn't ask you to come here or invite you inside. You're not here by mutual agreement." Remembering what she'd said about Thea being exhausted, he gave in with a grumble. "Trial basis. One day. If I'm not happy with your work here, you promise to leave and never come back."

"One week. And if you're pleased with my work, you agree to keep me on the rest of the summer."

He smiled wide, showing his teeth, sure he'd found the winning hand. The clinks of the dishes and silver she was gathering abruptly stilled, and all went silent, except for her slightest indrawn breath. He wondered what had happened; apparently something had occurred to make her react with such shock. Had she seen a mouse? He'd heard the rodents scuttling over the floor at night when he couldn't sleep.

"I can't pay you." He tossed his trump card at her. "Not one red cent. I haven't got the money."

"Th–that's all right. I don't need wages."

Irritated that she'd pulled an ace from her sleeve, he scowled. "Ridiculous! What kind of woman are you that you'd want a job and not get paid for it? Especially in these hard times."

"I only want to help," she practically whispered.

"I don't need your pity!"

"I'm not giving it. I mean I want to help Thea."

He couldn't argue with that logic, which made him all the more disgusted. "I still don't like the idea. And I don't take charity."

"All right. How about this: I'll think up a way you can pay me back."

He scoffed a laugh. "Sorry, not able to do much manual labor these days."

"Doesn't matter. I'll think up something you can do for me, if you're so insistent not to let me volunteer. Something to which you'll be agreeable and which won't make you feel you're taking charity. Is it a deal?"

He thought her proposition over, wondering what she might come up with as substitute payment. He probably wouldn't have to worry; he doubted she would last two days.

"Okay, one week. First rule: hands off my private things. Second rule: Leave me alone. Got it?"

"Yes."

"Swell." With nothing more to say, Joel walked back outside.

His shed had never felt so confining.

✒

Clemmie blew out a long breath, as if she'd just escaped being the unwitting target of a firing squad or, better to describe her situation, fought hand-to-hand combat with cutting vocabulary. His tongue was as sharp as Thea had warned, but Clemmie had been raised at the refuge and had learned to spar with words while growing up among young scalawags or risk getting sliced to smithereens. Joel would find himself matched to a worthy opponent.

She chuckled at how her mind compared their conversation to battle. And in this, their first skirmish, she had come out the victor.

"Be prepared, Joel Litton," she whispered, looking at the door he'd left ajar. "You've met your match this day. I'm not about to let you wallow in that pit of self-despair you've dug for yourself. Clemmie Lyons has come to town."

She smiled at her private declaration.

Just like Christian in her favorite allegory, Clemmie felt like a pilgrim about to embark on a journey. A masked pilgrim, in withholding her identity, which made her goal to get through to Joel trickier, but as Darcy always said, "Where there's a river too wide, somewhere there's bound to be a bridge, and if not, it's up to you to make one." She'd proven that when a person's will was strong, success ultimately followed. What Uncle Brent coined as her "harebrained schemes" always worked out in the end. So why couldn't Clemmie do the same and cross her own devised bridge to reach Joel?

She set down the cleaning tools she'd brought and planted her hands on her hips. In the dim light from the doorway she took quick inventory of what still looked very much like a shed. Next time she would need to bring a lantern to see well.

The area was less than half the size of the bedroom she'd been given at Hannah's. A single cot sat in the corner, a table and chair stood at the foot, and an old-fashioned, big-bellied, small cookstove took up the opposite corner, most likely to provide heat in winter. Two shelves were mounted to a wall. They bore odd and sundry items, including one single place setting of dishes and silverware. There were no windows, and ugly dark siding of some coarse nature covered the walls. She assumed it was put there to insulate the room in colder months. Not one decorative embellishment cheered the place, not a picture, not a colorful rug, not even a small memento.

Not that Joel would be able to see them if they were there.

Her vision swam, the room going wavy as her eyes watered. The first night she had returned to Hannah's, she'd enclosed herself in her room and thrown herself across the bed, bawling like a baby over Joel's tragic circumstances.

Not this time.

She pulled her lips in a thin line. She *would not* pity him. Joel could have chosen to have that operation, to call her parents and get a loan, though she knew they would never ask for recompense, but his stubborn pride had gotten in the way. Infuriating! Nor could she bring up the subject without revealing her identity, and that would guarantee he'd throw her bodily from his home and slam the door in her face. No questions asked; no explanations allowed.

"Drat it all!" She whisked the dish towel with unnecessary force along the table she'd cleared, scattering a shower of crumbs to the floor.

Her endeavor to help would most likely try her patience to a worn frazzle, but as she'd told Herbert on the phone when he finally rang Hannah's two nights after her initial visit, she not only wanted to do this for Joel, she needed to. As a youngster he had championed her when he didn't tease, and she wished to return the favor of being a friend to him.

The thought of not seeing Joel again was unacceptable. After she rang off with Herbert, she emphatically assured a concerned Hannah that she was long over her schoolgirl infatuation. Hannah had been sympathetic and encouraging, relieved after hearing Clemmie's plan, since she had her hands full for the next month helping her mother prepare things for the bazaar.

"Maybe God had a hand in this all along," her friend had surmised, sounding much like her wise mother, before she had giggled like the fifteen-year-old she was. "Well, of course He did. Silly me. He always does have a plan, doesn't He?"

Clemmie glumly reminded herself of that nugget of encouragement as she fetched the broom she'd brought and took out her frustrations with vicious swipes along the boards.

One thing could be said about trapped irritation—it made cleaning go by a great deal faster.

With her work done, she gathered her supplies and walked outdoors. Joel sat rigid in his chair, in profile to her and facing the woods. The small orange tabby of the other day wove a loving arc around his ankles. Joel didn't acknowledge Clemmie's presence, but she did see him flinch the moment she walked out the door.

"I did what I could," she began, "but that floor could use a good scrubbing. I'll bring the items tomorrow and do it then."

"That's not necessary."

She ignored his curt response.

"Also, just so you know it, I took your clothes to be laundered."

His hand gripped his knees hard, his knuckles whitening.

147

"I told you not to touch my personal things."

"Unless you plan on becoming a poster child for 'bum of the century,' I found that gathering your soiled laundry was even more essential than cleaning the floors, which, by the way, are also darkly spotted. Now, if you'll excuse me, I'll be seeing to your lunch."

He clenched his lips into a white line, as if withholding another negative response. But he couldn't very well tell her not to cook him a meal since he had to eat or starve to death. Eyeing his lean frame, she wondered if he had tried doing that.

Biting off words she knew would not be appreciated, she marched off his porch and crossed the yard to Thea's. Inside the cheery yellow kitchen Clemmie let her facade drop—not that Joel could have seen her distress in any case, but he sensed things so strongly he might have felt it.

"Things not go so well, I take it?" Thea greeted, glancing at her and tapping the spoon against a bowl she used to mix batter.

"I wasn't expecting it to." Clemmie set the cleaning basket on the floor with a sigh. "And I received my full expectation."

Thea tsked and went back to her chore.

"I appreciate you letting me use your things."

Thea waved aside her thanks. "I'd never expect you to bring your own supplies on your walk here every afternoon. Just leave them there. I'll put them away."

"I'd like to help with the meals. I feel bad about infringing on your generosity."

"Are you kidding?" Thea looked at her in shock. "You've been such a big help to me! The least I can do is to provide you with lunch every day. I've cooked for all of us for so long I don't mind. It's become a habit. Hope you don't mind pancakes?" Thea looked up from dropping a dollop of batter onto the hot pan.

"I've never had them for anything but breakfast, but I do like them. And I wouldn't mind contributing in the kitchen some days. I'm a very good cook, and that's not bragging. Darcy taught me everything I know."

"High praise indeed!" Thea smiled. "In that case I'll take you up on your offer. And that makes me think of something." Her expression became contrite. "I'm sorry our car isn't in working order for Herbert to give you a lift home. It's a blessing his job is only a fifteen-minute walk from here and that he's kept it. So many are out of work right now. But I guess where there is life, there is always news, and the public wants to stay informed."

Clemmie had to smile. As a boy at the refuge, Herbert sometimes squealed on his pals and got them in trouble. She was glad his tendency to broadcast events had matured to an acceptable position as a reporter for *The Cedarbrook Herald*. Joel had been the ringleader of the close-knit bunch of boys, his chums always looking to him for answers. Now he'd closed himself off from the entire world, except from his best buddy, Herbert.

"At least Joel turned to someone," she aired her thoughts aloud, only just realizing they had nothing to do with the present conversation.

Thea looked at her closely. "Hmm." She flipped a pancake. "Well, Herbert gave him no choice. Once Joel lost his sight, he was a fish out of water and had to rely heavily on Herbert, hating every second of it." She shook her head. "Men and their pride. I understand that during their childhood, Herbert had his eyes bandaged for weeks after Joel got whitewash in them during one of their spats. The two forgave each other, and Herbert then relied on Joel. That's the sole reason Joel agreed to let us help him, I think. Herbert brought the incident up and told him he wanted to pay him back—even though Joel was the one who painted Herbert's face with the whitewash."

Clemmie hadn't yet been born during that time, though over the years she'd heard about the alarming results of Darcy's first whitewash contest.

At the sound of the front door opening, both women turned their heads.

"Thea? I'm home."

Her face bright with pleasure, Thea set down the spoon and hurried to greet her husband. Soon she returned, Herbert behind her.

"Well now, aren't you a sight for sore eyes? You're quite the grown-up lady!" He held out his arms to Clemmie, and she grinned as they exchanged hugs. Clemmie stepped back to do her own survey. Still of medium height and build, still a little on the stout side, his hair the same shade of russet, Herbert was easily recognizable.

"I see you haven't changed," Clemmie returned.

"Oh, I wouldn't say that. We've all changed. But look at you! Last I saw, you were just a squirt with bright orange braids."

"Hmph." She crossed her arms. "Not that bright."

"Should you two be talking so loudly?" Thea interrupted with a glance toward the open kitchen window.

"It wouldn't matter." Herbert shook his head. "He rarely steps foot off that porch, and we're not exactly shouting for our words to carry that far. How's he doing today?"

"The same."

Herbert and Thea exchanged a long, telling look. Clemmie didn't add her own opinion of Joel's irascible behavior. Herbert looked at her.

"Are you sure you want to do this? It's not too late to back out."

"Yes. And no, I don't want to back out."

She didn't hesitate with her answer, and Herbert chuckled wryly. "I should have known you'd say that. I'm still not comfortable with the idea of keeping the truth of who you are from him though."

"If I tell him, I'll never get through to him." She unwittingly aired her core reason for going through with her ruse.

He peered at her sharply, making her want to squirm. "Tell me again that you're over your girlhood infatuation, that this desire to help is all in friendship."

"It is." She laughed. "Like you said, we've all grown up and changed, Herbert. I know the way I used to behave was quite silly. I'm beyond that."

"Good." He gave a pleased nod. "I wouldn't want you hurt. And, Clemmie, keeping the truth from him could wind up putting you in quite a pickle."

She smiled upon hearing the echo of Darcy's admonishments when doling out advice to wayward young hooligans. It was amazing how, no matter their differences, children picked up sayings from the adults by whom they'd been taught. She even found herself speaking some of Uncle Brent's professorial words now and then.

"I promise I'll tell him. When the time is right."

Herbert twisted his mouth in uncertainty, mulling over the prospect. "Well, nothing else has worked. If you really think you can reach him, then you have my support. But I have to warn you, Clemmie—"

"You'd better start calling me by my middle name—Marielle."

He sighed. "Once Joel finds out, he's not going to be one bit happy to learn he was hoodwinked."

"That's why he can't find out. Not until I tell him."

Clemmie didn't want to think about that disturbing day to come.

Chapter 4

"I f you've come to offer advice, Herbert, you can just stop right there, turn around, and go back the way you came."

The rustling in the grass reached a sudden halt.

"How'd you know. . ."

"That it was you?" Joel laughed bitterly at the surprise in Herbert's voice. "That you should even need to ask such a question by now baffles me. I smelled you."

"I took a bath."

Joel grunted in disdain. "Good to know."

"Unlike some people I could mention."

"The odor of ink from the printing press gives you away. It sticks to your clothes."

"Are you planning to adopt the Bohemian look, ole pal? You could do with a haircut, too. And a shave."

"And your steps are faster. Brisker than the women's."

"Ah, the women. Speaking of, how's the new girl working out for you? I'll bet she'd give you a shave if you asked."

"There's also a trace of odor from those cheap cigars your boss smokes. It seeps into your clothes, and all of it carries to me on the breeze."

"Are we going to dance around this subject all night?"

"Is that a question that requires an answer?"

Herbert snorted in exasperation. "The new girl. Marielle. What do you think of her?"

Joel fidgeted, uneasy to be put on the spot. "She annoys me."

Annoy wasn't exactly the word to describe the emotion he felt with regard to the woman. His notice of her fell somewhere between irritation and intrigue. He hadn't been able to get her out of his mind since she stepped foot on the property a few days before and challenged him. Now that she worked for him and they had shared in more lengthy conversations than Joel's usual—"Get out!"—something about her niggled at the back of his mind. He couldn't put his finger on what it was, which put him in an even grouchier mood, since feeling clueless about a situation made him feel more vulnerable.

It was bad enough he'd lost his sight. He wouldn't let her scramble his mind.

"Not thinking happy thoughts, I take it." Herbert's referral to his daughter's trite saying carried an undercurrent of amusement and triggered Joel's defensive response.

"Tell me just what I have to be happy about? That the sun never gets in my eyes? That I'm spared having to stare at my drab walls? Or that I don't have to see your ugly mug every day?" He shifted in his chair in mock deliberation. "Come to think of it, that is cause for celebration."

"You can be happy you have a roof over your head and three meals a day. Entire families are starving, what with the state of things in our nation. You aren't the only one suffering."

"Spare me the lectures."

"Don't worry. I won't bother. It's useless anyway. All you can think about is yourself."

Joel clutched his hands around his thighs, rubbing them to his knees in aggravated silence. Uncomfortable to have his behavior criticized, whether he deserved it or not, he offered no reply. His old friend had been nothing but helpful, offering him room and board, and Joel was helpless to repay him. That stung worse than anything—having to be a useless sponge that soaked up others' generosity. Finding work these days for a sighted man was near impossible; for a blind man it was laughable. He hated being dependent on others and often found himself taking out his frustrations on the ones who made him feel that way.

"It's been over a year, and you still act as if it were yesterday," Herbert said.

"I wonder if you'd be half as glib if the roles were switched," Joel shot back darkly. "It's easy to tell me how to behave when you're not the one who was once living life, happy as a clam, and in the blink of an eye—pardon the expression—had everything ripped away from him."

"You haven't lost everything," Herbert responded with weary patience.

"I might as well have! I can't do anything but sit here day after lousy, stinking day—and for what? Why did I survive? Tell me! Did God decide I needed some special punishment because things were going so right for me during that all-too-brief period in my life?"

"Right for you? You were out of a job before the accident."

"So is at least a quarter of the nation as you pointed out. But at least I was a whole man before I got struck down from on high."

"God's not like that. You know it."

"No I don't. Didn't Saul get struck blind on the road to Damascus?"

"I'm surprised you remember anything from our studies at the refuge."

Joel scoffed, but Herbert continued. "Anyway, that was different. It was temporary and for a reason. If you remember, Jesus healed the blind. He didn't make them that way."

"Well, He did a fine job with me! But you're right. I'm being punished for thinking only of myself. I deserve this."

Herbert blew out an exasperated sigh. "I didn't mean any such thing, and I'm not going to stand here and listen to you wallow in self-pity. It's a handicap, Joel. Not the end of the world. Learn to make the most of it, since you chose to live with it. It's about time you did."

"It's so easy for you, isn't it?" Joel's voice was deceptively polite. "Doling out advice like you've actually lived through the situation."

"I have."

"Not the same. You got your sight back."

"But at the time I didn't know if I ever would."

"And as I recall, you were a titanic pest, ordering everyone at the refuge to wait on you hand and foot and manipulating Darcy into reading all of that blasted pirate book to you in under a week's time."

Herbert chuckled. "True. But the fact remains, I know what it's like to suddenly be without sight and have to rely on others for just about everything. I know what you're going through."

"You were eleven when it happened. You had no life."

"You think age has anything to do with feeling scared or helpless?"

Joel gripped his knees more tightly, not wanting to continue with the conversation. "Tell Thea to find someone else."

"What?"

"That girl—Marilou. I have a sneaking suspicion she won't work out."

"Her name's Marielle. And you promised her a week's trial."

"She told you?" Joel groused, wondering if the woman was trying to manipulate Herbert behind Joel's back in order to keep her position.

"Just why don't you think she'll work out? She seems efficient, skilled, willing to do whatever is asked. Just the type of help you need."

"She's too bossy, too nosy, and speaks her mind without being asked."

"Like I said," Herbert drawled. "Just what you need."

Joel didn't miss the laughter in Herbert's voice.

"And speaking of the wise lady, she's headed this way."

Joel straightened his back in irritation. Following Herbert's lighthearted declaration, he heard the whisper of footsteps rustle across the yard, steadily growing louder, accompanied by the rich scent of meat loaf and potatoes.

"Hello." Her voice came cheery. "I brought supper."

"I'm not hungry," Joel replied petulantly, angry at his stomach for its eager lurch at the aroma of delicious food.

"Well, that's just too bad, because you're going to eat."

"No. I'm not." His reply came just as obstinate.

"Yes. You are. I just spent the past two hours helping Thea and slaving over a hot stove, and you most certainly will eat every morsel I brought you, Mr. Joel Litton."

Before he could counter her verbal attack, he heard her swift footsteps march with determination inside his house. He turned to where Herbert quietly chuckled.

"You see what I mean? She's impossible! There's no way I'm putting up with her insolence for one solid week."

"What I think I see is Thea at the window. Yup, there she is. It's my suppertime, too. And that meat loaf smells absolutely scrumptious."

"You're going to just go and leave things like they are?"

"Leave things like what?"

"Her," he growled between clenched teeth. "This situation. I was hoping you might side with me in getting her to leave me alone for good and go back to wherever it is she came from."

"Aren't you the one always telling me you can do fine on your own and don't need any mollycoddling? After all, you're bigger than she is. And she's a girl."

"Aw, go chase yourself," Joel snapped, in no mood to put up with his tormentor's jests.

"I'll drop by after supper."

"Don't bother."

Joel grimaced when his so-called friend laughed again as he headed for his house.

"Mr. Litton?" came his new tormentor's voice from inside.

Crossing his arms over his chest, Joel determined to ignore her presence and never give in to the intrusive dame.

⁓

Clemmie threw open the door to her room and flung her purse on the bed.

"Imbecile!"

Her hat followed.

"Ignoramus!"

She ripped apart the buttons of her cardigan and tore it from one side, flinging her arm and flapping it around to rid herself of the rest of her sweater. "Mule-headed. . .pigheaded. . .dimwitted. . .obstinate!" She muttered each insult with each flap of her arm. Her cardigan at last gave way and with one final wave shot to the bed.

"I didn't know you could be a mule and a pig at the same time." Hannah's amused voice came from the doorway.

Clemmie swung around to face her. "When your name is Joel Litton, you can! He is such a, such a. . ." She sought for appropriate words.

"Cantankerous idiot?"

"Exactly!"

Clemmie whirled around again, falling to a sitting position on the bed. She crossed her arms over her chest, feeling as if she could spit nails.

"So I take it working for the 'master of mischief' wasn't smooth sailing today?"

"Ha!" Clemmie grunted the exclamation in disdain. "Not only would he *not* eat the perfectly lovely meal I brought him at the end of the day, but he threw the plate at the wall when I insisted he eat it, and he missed me by bare inches!"

"He didn't!" Hannah's eyes grew wide as she drew closer. She worked not to smile.

"He did. And it's not funny, Hannah. They eat meat only twice a week. And just look at my skirt." She groaned, lifting the brown cotton splotched with smears from the flying mashed potatoes and gravy.

"It'll wash."

"Oh, I know that." Clemmie sighed, thinking of the hardened food she would have to scrub from the wall, baseboards, and floor tomorrow. Joel had cursed her, ordering her out and yelling the directive in cruel, shocking words that she would never tell Hannah, much less say aloud to anyone, and she hadn't dared stay longer and clean up the mess.

"Are you going back?"

"Of course."

At Clemmie's emphatic and quick reply, Hannah couldn't hold back the laughter any longer. She wrapped her arms around herself, her enthusiasm growing as she toppled to her side on the counterpane.

"Stop it. It's not funny." Clemmie felt her lips turn up at the corners. "Stop it, I said, or you're likely to cast a kitten!" Her smile grew.

Hannah's glee became infectious, and Clemmie was soon laughing as well, the two girls holding each other until they got a grip on sobriety again.

"He can be a terror and a trial," Clemmie mused once she'd calmed. "I can't say I wasn't warned. But I'm no quitter."

"I admire that about you. Me, I often give up too easily or worry what other people might say or think."

"Well, I'm not worried about that, either."

"Except when it comes to Joel finding out who you are."

The girls grew quiet.

"Do you also think I'm wrong to keep it from him?" Clemmie eyed her friend. She had earlier told her that Thea shared such reservations, and so, apparently, did Herbert. "I'm only keeping quiet for his own good. If he knew who I was at this rocky moment in our all-too-brief association, anything positive I want to accomplish would be lost, and he'd remain in his pathetic little pit of despair forever."

Hannah grinned. "Like *Pilgrim's Progress*. I read that for a book report."

"Exactly."

Hannah lowered her gaze, growing introspective. "I'm not exactly sure

Mama would agree with your methods. She would say deceit is deceit, plain and simple, but your heart's in the right place, I think." She peered intently at Clemmie as if she could see through her. "What do you hope to gain by all this? You're not still all gaga over him, are you?"

"Of course not. I told you. I'm not a child any longer."

"I know that, silly. But, well, you're a woman. And he's a man."

Her words brought the strangest tingle to Clemmie's skin. "I only want to help him. That is, if he'd put his armor and weapons down long enough to let me."

"Weapons?"

"The tongue can be a powerful weapon."

"Oh, right."

"And his throwing arm isn't half-bad either."

They both giggled.

"Well, like I told you when you first brought it up, I'll support you however I can. With this bazaar Mother's partly in charge of, I find my days occupied. I'm just glad you found something to do—but still sorry I'm not here much of the day."

"It's not as if we don't spend any time together. We're talking now."

"That's true." Hannah's smile again brightened. "So, what's your first plan of attack in 'Operation Save Joel'?"

" 'Operation Save Joel'—I like that! I do often feel as if I'm in a war zone when I'm around him." Clemmie dropped her chin to her hand, deep in thought. Suddenly she smiled.

"Is that offer to help immediately available?"

"Sure. What do you have in mind?"

"I need you to take me to your grocer's. I have money from what Grandfather gave me. And both Father and Uncle Brent slipped me some, all without any of them knowing." She laughed with affection at the antics of her male relatives, each of whom had tried to evade notice when giving her "a little cash" before she left for the train. "Aunt Darcy always said the way to a man's heart is through his stomach, though what I really want is to get through to his brain. But maybe that's the best route to get there."

"Are you sure just a small, teensy part of you wouldn't like to get through to his heart as well?" Hannah teased, holding her thumb and forefinger a slight distance apart. "Are you absolutely sure you're as immune to him as you say?"

Hannah's eyes were much too sharp. Mumbling an offhand "Of course," Clemmie rose from the bed and shrugged back into her sweater.

The bitter, cantankerous Joel she now contended with was far removed from the easygoing boy and pleasant young man she once knew. Strangely, however, that didn't deflect her desire to keep him in her life. She didn't elaborate on her feelings to Hannah, not wanting to admit there might be more than a grain of truth to her statement.

She was beyond schoolgirl obsessions, for pity's sake. But then, she was no longer a schoolgirl, as Hannah had pointed out. She was a woman. And blind or not, Joel was every bit as much a man as before, the same man who could still make her heart beat triple time or come to a sudden, breathtaking stop.

When he wasn't being impossible.

"To the grocer's then?" Clemmie asked cheerily, tamping down any spiraling thoughts that might resurrect the old dream.

"This late?"

"If they're still open, I'd like to get an early start tomorrow and do a few things while your uncle's cook isn't in the kitchen. Think she'll mind me using it?"

"Annie? No, she's gone home to her family for the night. And Mr. Carter does keep late hours on weekends, hoping for more business. So his shop would be open, I would think."

"Perfect."

"I'll ask Father to drive us."

"It's too far to walk?"

"Unlike you, I don't walk." Hannah gave a little shiver. "Not when there are four perfectly good wheels and an engine begging to be used."

Clemmie giggled at the silliness of her pampered friend, feeling ten times better than when she had arrived that evening. She just hoped the feeling would last through tomorrow, when she faced the temperamental lion in his confined den once again.

Chapter 5

Joel sat on his porch chair, the warmth of the sun acting as a rebel to his belligerent mood. He waited for the inevitable footsteps in the grass. When they finally came, he sat so rigid they could have made a springboard to a pool out of him.

"Good morning. I brought back your clean laundry."

He grunted in reply.

"Is there anywhere special you keep it?"

"In the latrine," he bit out.

"Fine, if you're going to be that way about it." Her voice maintained a calm cheeriness, rasping against his nerves like a cheese grater. "I'll find a place to put these myself then."

Her light steps disappeared inside his shed, and with a groan he got up to follow. The last thing he wanted was her nosing through every one of his personal things.

"In that trunk," he grumbled. "At the foot of the bed."

He heard the lid creak as she raised it, the rustle of cloth as she put the articles away, and the muted thud and click as she closed the trunk.

An eternity of silence passed, though his fine-tuned ears could hear her breathing and noticed it had picked up a notch. He sensed her eyes on him.

She approached.

On involuntary impulse he backed up a step, to the porch.

Her steps halted.

His mouth thinned.

Ridiculous! He was not afraid of a girl as Herbert had implied. Especially not this girl.

With resolve Joel moved forward more than the single step back he'd taken, until he came close enough to feel the warmth of her body and to be awash in the scent of lilacs, though no part of him touched her.

She gave a sudden and soft intake of breath.

"Was there anything else?" he asked, striving to sound polite, though he would rather toss her over his shoulder and carry her from his home.

"I. . ." She gulped and swallowed loud enough for him to hear. "H–how did you. . ." He felt the stir of air as she moved past him, toward the wall. The brush of her fingertips smoothed over the oilcloth.

"I may be blind, lady, but my hands weren't amputated."

"O—of course not. I only meant. . ." She sighed. "You cleaned this?"

"No, the elves slipped in while I was asleep."

"Well, at least you never lost that charming sense of humor," she mumbled.

"What?" He grew alert at her strange choice of words and swiftly turned his head her way.

"I—that is, Herbert told me you once were quite. . .funny." Her words trailed off weakly into an explanation.

"Yeah, that's me," he quipped derisively. "Funny man Joel. Take a seat, and let me entertain you. Slapstick is my specialty. Especially if you leave my pathway cluttered."

She blew out a harsh, disgusted breath, not in the least amused, which adversely brought his first genuine smile.

"I'll just leave you to practice your act then, shall I? Though with me around, I defy you to find one thing out of place, on your floor or otherwise." To his surprised relief, he heard her retreat to the door. "I'll be back later with your supper." She hesitated, retraced her steps to the table, where he heard the silverware she scraped together, then marched out once again.

At last he was left alone. Alone, that is, except for the trace of her scent lingering in the air, surrounding him. The warm, clean smell of sunshine on skin and hair, mixed with lilacs. It stirred his traitorous thoughts into reliving the past moments.

Again that niggling sense of something not being right prickled at his mind, something he couldn't place his finger on. That, more than anything else, was what he didn't like about this new cleaning woman and cook Thea had hired. The girl unbalanced his sense of reality, setting him on an uneven keel, which made living ten times worse when all he saw was darkness.

Four more days, as he'd promised her—or rather, as she'd manipulated out of him—and then he would demand she leave. At least with the wait he couldn't be accused of not trying, as Herbert had said. Or of being intimidated by a slip of a girl.

❧

Chop!

Clemmie let loose with a cleaver, neatly slicing a potato in half. *Chop!* Off went the head of the onion.

Chop! Chop! Chop!

The long, lean carrots became history.

"You seem to be taking more pleasure in that task than it should involve," Thea remarked in amusement as she watched her. She picked up the saucer holding a slab of creamy yellow butter. "And real butter? You're spoiling him."

Clemmie hated the butter substitute of oleo that so many people were forced to use in these hard times, what Darcy also used at the refuge. For what she had in mind, oleo wouldn't suffice, and it had been worth the extra money to procure the genuine article. She knew it would make a huge difference in flavor, too. Just this one time, and one time was all she needed for the hoped-for breakthrough.

"He needs a little spoiling. Maybe that's part of his problem." She stopped chopping long enough to cast Thea an embarrassed glance. "Oh! I didn't mean that you haven't been doing a good job of things."

Thea laughed her off. "I know. Don't worry. You're being very tolerant toward him after his ill behavior. Herbert told me," she explained at Clemmie's curious glance. "And I also know what daily interaction with Joel can entail!"

"So why do you put up with it?" Clemmie knew her own reasons, but she wondered what motivated Thea to beard the beast in his self-made cage every day.

Thea shrugged. "He's Herbert's oldest and dearest friend. Before he went blind, he really was quite the debonair fella." She sighed. "I'm also hoping that by showing him people care about what happens to him, maybe he'll draw close to God again. And that God will use me somehow to reach him. That reminder is the only thing that keeps me patient when he's in one of his moods."

"Then he really has turned from his faith?" The news distressed Clemmie.

Thea wasn't quick to answer. "He's very bitter and confused. Even before he went blind, he was getting to that point."

"Oh? But why. . ."

"He didn't actually come to Connecticut of his own free will. Did I tell you? Herbert pushed him into it, worried about the trouble Joel was getting into—or rather had gotten himself into."

"Trouble? What tr—"

A horrendous shriek followed by loud wailing cut off Clemmie's words.

"Oh dear. Loretta must have fallen. I do hope this is just a clumsy phase she's going through!" Thea hurried from the room, leaving Clemmie to deliberate her thoughts.

What had happened before his blindness to set Joel on the path of turning from God? Though she wouldn't have called him a strong Christian when he was at the refuge—not like her parents—he was no heathen. His father's long incarceration in jail had at first been the stimulus for the young Joel to become a hoodlum, but later the penalty of his father's crimes, along with the knowledge that he'd died in his cell, had made Joel want to repent and not become like the man who sired him. He'd told Clemmie on several occasions that he thought of her father as his own. So what had happened to change all that? What kind of "trouble" could Thea be referring to?

The questions revolved inside her mind. Throughout the rest of her meal preparations, she tried to come up with answers. Thea didn't return, and once all was ready, Clemmie resolved she would ask her friend at the next available opportunity. Taking a deep breath, she picked up the plate she'd prepared and a glass of water and set them on a tray.

"All right," she muttered, building up nerve. "Prepare for round two, Joel Litton, and this time I'm coming out the winner."

Loaded with her delicious weapon that with any luck would break through his barricade, she made her way to his shed. He wasn't sitting outside as she expected, and she pulled at her lip with her teeth, hesitating, before she balanced the tray with one hand and knocked.

"Get lost."

"It's me. Cl—Marielle." She caught herself just in time.

"I know who it is."

She gritted her teeth. "That knock was a courtesy, not a request. If you don't open the door to me in the next three seconds or give me a legitimate reason why I can't enter, I'm coming inside." When he didn't respond, she put her hand to the latch in resolve, her shoulder to the wood. It wouldn't budge.

He'd barricaded himself inside!

"Joel Litton, if you don't open this door right now, I'll go and get Herbert to break it down. You know me well enough by now to know I mean it!"

Silence.

"All right then, till the count of three. One. . .two. . ." Maybe she should have given him to the count of five—or perhaps ten—and wondered if it was harder for him to navigate without his vision, even in familiar areas.

"Thr—"

The barricade he'd used made a scraping sound, and the door swung open. Joel's blue eyes blazed down at her. Strange that they could see nothing, as vibrant as they were. Like living blue coals.

"What do you want?" he growled.

She tamped down a fleeting moment's nervousness. "I brought dinner."

"I'm not hungry."

"Nonsense." She managed to brush past, knocking him aside without upsetting the tray, and heard his grunt of surprise. "You have to eat. You didn't eat last night, and Thea mentioned you had no breakfast or lunch. You can't keep this up, or you'll starve to death."

"Maybe that'd be best."

She set the tray on the table with a little slam and whirled to face him. "Joel Litton, don't you dare talk that way! Shame on you! There are plenty of people suffering in this world—not just you. If everyone gave up on living, where would this nation be, I ask? We'd all be history!"

He took two steps toward her. "Don't give me any lectures, lady! You can't possibly know what it's like."

"To be blind? No. But I do know about suffering. I know what it means to hurt."

He narrowed his eyes. "What pain has a little thing like you suffered in this world? You seem disgustingly cheery most of the time."

His tense but flippant words were like blows, since he'd been the crux of much of her pain. "Oh, I've suffered. The loss of a family member. The ache of rejection. The desolation of loneliness. But I've learned to put my faith in God, even when I don't understand why those things happened. He knows all and always has an answer if I'm quiet enough to listen. Sometimes He gives no answer, just a feeling of peace."

Hardness carved his face into a mask of stone. "Don't talk to me about God! Where was God when my friend's car went over an embankment? Where was God when I had to tell his ailing mother that her only son had died and attend his funeral and two others—but by some twist of insanity I alone survived? Where was God when his fiancée tried to overdose a week later, after learning she was pregnant with his kid?"

Shock ran cold throughout Clemmie, freezing her anger, which then melted into horrified compassion. Without thought she reached out to him. "Joel, I'm so sorry. . . ."

He knocked her hand away from his arm. "Spare me your pity. I don't need it, and I sure don't deserve it."

"Don't deserve it?"

He turned his back on her, his head lowered.

Confused by his belittling words but realizing that to extend the conversation might result in getting her thrown out a second time, she changed the subject. "Please eat. I spent a lot of time preparing this meal. I was told it's your favorite."

Joel's shoulders jerked, his stance becoming rigid again. After what seemed endless seconds, while Clemmie held her breath, he slowly took a seat at the table.

He stared down at the plate as if he could see it. Often she had to remind herself he couldn't. He seemed so familiar with everything, rarely fumbling in his actions, which came steady and sure.

"Roast. . .potatoes. . .carrots. . .onions. . ." He quietly ticked off the food groups. The aroma of the meal permeated the cabin, which is how he must have known each one.

"Yes and a special surprise for dessert."

"Oh?" His tone wasn't exactly inviting, but neither did it condemn.

"Strawberry shortcake! With real cream."

She had hoped her declaration would at least bring a smile.

Instead he became very still and frowned.

"Why would you think that was my favorite?"

"It's not?"

"I never told Thea. As a matter of fact, I never told her any of it. Or Herbert."

Clemmie sucked in a breath. They'd taken care of him for over a year and didn't know his favorite foods? "I—but—h–he mentioned he grew up with you. A–at the refuge. He probably remembered from that." She swallowed, her conscience uneasy at her little deceit. But Joel couldn't find out her identity yet. Things were still so rocky between them. She forced her tone to achieve calm and not stutter. "If those aren't your favorites, I apologize. It's still delicious food."

He grunted something in reply and, to her relief, picked up the fork. His other hand searched the other side of his plate, brushed over a spoon, then came to rest on the table in a loose fist. Intently she watched him spear a piece of roast, scowl, and take a bite.

"I'm not an invalid or a baby," he said.

"Excuse me?"

"You don't have to cut up my food for me. I'm perfectly capable of using a knife. You don't have to keep them out of my reach."

"Oh." Her face warmed. "I wasn't trying to do any such thing. I—I was only trying to help."

He expelled a low breath and gave a reluctant nod.

After his first few bites, the revolutions of his fork from plate to mouth steadily increased until he was practically shoveling food inside. Happy just to stand and watch him now that the lion was calm for once, her eyes feasting on his person after having been deprived so long, she waited until he finished with dessert. Silently she congratulated herself that for a man who claimed he wasn't hungry, he'd just managed to consume his meal in under five minutes.

She gathered the empty dishes. "I might be a little late tomorrow. I'm shopping with a friend."

He didn't respond but, for once, didn't tell her not to bother returning.

Clemmie smiled. It wasn't much, but it was a start.

Chapter 6

Clemmie turned the page, her mind absorbed in the fictional and fantastical world of angels and monsters.

"Must you be so loud with that?"

Startled into the present, she looked across the table where Joel sat, brooding.

"Must you be so dour all the time?" she shot back. "If you knew how to use that tongue in your head to converse instead of just snap at people, maybe we could have a decent conversation for once, and I wouldn't have to resort to keeping my mind occupied with reading."

He growled in disgust and crossed his arms over his chest, turning his head away.

Earlier in the week she'd brought another chair from Thea's house so she could sit, too. At the moment, however, she was sorely tempted to vacate the chair and his dismal company and escape to pleasant surroundings. Only the rain prevented her departure. What had begun fifteen minutes ago in a sudden downpour effectively trapped her inside his cage. Usually she left the door open when she visited his shed, for fresh air and better lighting than what the lamp could give; today she'd needed to close the door to block out the torrential downpour.

She also felt like growling.

During the past week, relations between them had been stormy but did have calmer moments. Moments when he didn't yell at her or throw things but accepted her presence as a master begins to accept a new servant hired without his approval or knowledge. After days of working for Joel and talking with Thea, Clemmie had learned such erratic mood swings and fits of temper were normal patterns for Joel. The doctor who'd attended him warned to expect such behavior because of whatever caused the pressure to his brain. He never physically harmed her, though. Even when he threw things her way, he always missed, and she wondered if his misses were intentional, meant only to frighten her away, since he always seemed shockingly on target with every other action. His acerbic words, however, found their mark and stung only because Joel said them.

Yet she had formed an invisible armor long ago at the refuge, with the many young hoodlums the judge ordered there, most of them coming from

164

living off the street and impolite society, so she managed to let his insults bounce off her, too—when she wasn't snapping back at him. A fault of hers, responding in kind. Because of their shared history, of which he was still unaware, Joel had the ability to hit the nerve that controlled her cross nature every time.

She had passed the one-week trial period, and much to her surprise, he hadn't terminated her employment as he'd threatened. She didn't ask why, not wanting to tamper with a good thing and possibly cause the tide to turn against her favor. Right now, however, she would give her classic book collection in exchange for the sun to return so she could retreat from his maddening company.

The day had not started well. One thing after another went wrong, and she'd been late to arrive, to find Thea also out of sorts, not wanting to talk, and the children both crying. Clemmie's mood had already been topping the red zone of her emotional thermometer. Add to that, Joel had been the epitome of churlish disdain from the moment she walked inside.

Out of sheer spite, she turned the page, making sure to rustle it loudly. She turned another. And another. . .

"Just what kind of book are you reading?" Joel groused after the sixth turn. "A child's primer?"

Confused by such a question, she stopped mid-page rustle. "What do you mean?"

"There must be only one paragraph on a page for you to turn them so constantly."

She wasn't sure why, but she laughed. Her mood lightened a bit—surprisingly thanks to Joel's dry words—and she felt a twinge of guilt for acting so childishly. "I'm reading a book my mother gave me. *The Pilgrim's Progress.*"

"That sounds familiar."

She told him a little of what it was about, and he cut her off mid-sentence, sounding almost civil. "I remember that one."

"You read it?"

"Don't sound so surprised. I do—or at least did—read." His tone came out wry again.

She thought of asking why he'd never tried Braille or even suggesting he start but decided against it, not wanting him to slip back into a brooding silence. "Was it for a school assignment?" She asked the first thing that came to mind.

"No. I did read but not that one. I heard someone else read it. The lady who ran the refuge. She had a friend, a viscountess who visited from England one year, shortly after I came home on furlough. Strange thing that. . ." His voice trailed off. "They weren't always chums, more like enemies. At least I know they weren't friendly with one another when they sailed on the *Titanic.*"

Clemmie held her breath during his explanation, realizing he was talking about her mother. "Oh?"

"Interesting story. Mrs. Lyons—only she wasn't married then—robbed the viscountess of a family heirloom. In the end she got it back and forgave Mrs. Lyons. Later she donated the necklace to help in funding the refuge. They became good friends after that. She gave Mrs. Lyons a copy of that book when she visited the States. Mrs. Lyons had developed a habit of reading classics to the children once a week, and I joined in a few nights to listen. Not that I remember much. I heard maybe three chapters before my leave was up." He shrugged.

Clemmie caressed the cover of the old book, realizing this must be the same copy Lady Annabelle had given her mother. She'd been twelve at the time and had greatly admired the soft-spoken, regal woman who braved her fear of sinking ships to cross an ocean again with her husband, Lord Caldwell.

"Would you like me to read to you?" The words were out of her mouth before she could hold them back. Worried he might take her offer wrong, she fumbled to add, "to help pass the time. Since you never heard the rest of the story."

When he didn't speak, she closed the book. "It was only a suggestion. Forget I mentioned it. I just thought it might—"

"Okay."

"What?"

His brow went up. "Have you forgotten your question so soon?"

"Of course not. Do you mean you *would* like me to read to you? Or to forget it?"

"Is that the question you asked?"

She hissed a breath through her teeth. "Must you always make things so difficult, Joel Litton? Can't you just give me a straight answer?"

His mouth twitched in what she thought might become a smile. "All right. Read to me, Marielle."

She blinked. "Is that an order?"

"Did it sound like one?"

"Doesn't it always?"

Joel laughed, and Clemmie forgot to breathe.

It was the first time she'd heard him laugh since their days together at the refuge, and the deep, rich sound of his spontaneous laughter warmed her spirit, soothing away all the previous hurt and angst he'd caused.

"*Please* read to me." His tone slightly mocked, but his voice came soft and silken, his entreaty matching his expression.

Clemmie hoped she could make her vocal cords work, and if they did, she prayed her voice would sound normal. She felt suddenly flushed and out of kilter. How could the room at once feel so hot when the clouds were pouring chilled water outside?

She opened the book to the first chapter.

Joel tucked his hands beneath his armpits, tilting his head back to rest his neck on the tall chair rim as her quiet, husky voice washed over him. She had a beautiful voice. . .warm, gentle when she wasn't upset with him, and Joel was reminded of the place where he grew up and the people there.

In the week and a half she had worked for him, the manner in which he heard her say a few words or trite phrases of Darcy's or Brent's or Charleigh's, the same words that he and Herbert also unintentionally adopted, reminded him of his past at the farm. That must be how she knew such sayings, being around Thea and Herbert. Or maybe they were more popular than he realized.

While she spoke of the quest of a man named Pilgrim and the descriptions of the strange beings he encountered, he found himself wondering what she looked like. If one could match voice to appearance, she was tall for a woman with a self-assured poise. Dark hair. Darker eyes. Deep brown and mysterious, ones that could see right through to a person's soul and not let him get away with anything. He was surprised he could remember color; so much else had faded from his memory.

"Are you even listening?"

Startled out of his thoughts, he gave an involuntary jump.

"What?"

"You're not listening," she gently accused. "Were you sleeping? Your eyes were closed."

He heard her little gasp of remorseful awareness and grinned bitterly. "Not that it matters either way, but no, I wasn't sleeping."

"I'm sorry."

He brushed aside her weak apology, not wanting to dwell on the reason for it. "That's enough reading for one day."

"But I haven't finished the second chapter!"

"It's stopped raining. I'm sure you want to get out of here while you can."

"Would you rather I did?"

"Isn't that what you want?"

"I'd like to stay."

Her quiet admission confused him. "Why? I'm not what you could call good company."

"I like being with you. When you're nice."

He snorted a laugh. "If you were to tally up the occurrences of me being 'nice' over the past week and a half, the scales wouldn't exactly tip in my favor."

She exhaled in exasperation. "That's your choice. You can be nice when you choose to be. And when you are, you're pleasant to be around."

He scoffed. "Why care so much?"

"Pardon?" A sudden hitch tightened her voice.

"Why do you care what the blind man feels? Why do you even want to be around me?"

For a moment he didn't think she would answer. When she did, her words snapped with exasperation, and he sensed she held back the extent of her anger. "That's your problem in a nutshell, Joel Litton. You have this crazy idea that your condition makes you some sort of leper of the human race. And that's so far from the truth, as east is from the west. The only handicap putting up barriers to people wanting to be around you is your constant boorish attitude and spiteful behavior."

"Is that so?"

"Yes, that's so."

He could picture her crossing her arms in belligerence, not willing to back down. Rather than spar further he decided he'd had enough.

"You can go now."

"You're kicking me out?"

"If you want to call it that, fine." Her silence prodded him to add, "It's getting late. You shouldn't walk home in the dark."

He heard her sudden intake of breath. "It's nice of you to care."

Her words came out uncertain, almost a whisper, and for some reason they rubbed him the wrong way. "If you got mugged or worse, it'd be hard on Thea. She'd blame herself."

"Well, at least you care about *someone's* feelings."

He couldn't help but smile at her dry remark. He listened to the rustles and clinks of her gathering her things and the dishes from his meal. Her footsteps tapped to the door. "All right. I'll go. We wouldn't want Thea to feel any unnecessary guilt should anything happen to me." The door creaked open.

"Marielle?"

A few seconds elapsed before she answered. "Yes?"

"Bring that book when you come tomorrow."

Chapter 7

Seven little words, but they had the power to boost Clemmie's outlook on Operation Save Joel. For the first time in almost two weeks, she glimpsed an elusive ray of hope. Not only had he not ordered her out, he'd almost given his consent for her return by stating she would come and had expressed a desire for her to read to him again. It wasn't much, but it was progress.

Yet while the situation had mellowed between her and Joel and they had achieved workable boundaries, if not a friendship, one irritating factor dampened this new turn of events. Thea broached it before Clemmie had a chance to leave the following evening.

"You still haven't told him who you are, have you?" Thea shook her head, answering her own question. "Of course you haven't. If you had, things wouldn't be so quiet around here. Joel would have gotten in a lather by now."

"Is that what you want?" Clemmie regarded her, unflinching. "For Joel to get upset? Because that's what'll happen. And then I'd never be able to talk him into it."

"Into what? The operation?"

"Yes. No. . .maybe." Clemmie spread her hands, in an attempt to explain. "It's about so much more than an operation. It's about getting on with living again. Joel has given up, and I want to know why. I think this goes deeper than just bitterness over his physical condition."

"And you don't think asking him as Clemmie would be the same?"

"Asking him as Clemmie will get me the bum's rush, booted out the door."

Thea took a seat at the table. "Then let me ask you this: What makes the future any different? What makes you think it wouldn't be even worse?"

"Pardon?"

"He'll know at some point. You can't go on lying to him forever. And then he'll feel betrayed."

Clemmie flinched at the word *lying*, and her heart dropped at *betrayed*. She knew speaking falsely was wrong, but in extenuating circumstances, some deceit could be helpful, couldn't it? Her own mother had assumed another identity after being rescued from the *Titanic*, in order to evade the man who'd almost killed her. If she'd given her real name for the survivors' list instead of the name of one of many who had drowned that night, would she be alive today?

"It's complicated."

Thea threw her hands up in exasperation. "It's going to be a whole lot more complicated if you continue with this ruse. Joel may be a lot of things right now, but he's not dumb. Have you thought of this: What if he finds out before you can tell him?"

A piercing scream came from nearby, followed by a wail of pain. Clemmie jumped in her chair, and Thea was up and down the hallway in a flash.

Soon Thea reappeared with her youngest, leading her by the hand. A knotted kerchief hung loosely around Loretta's neck as if it had been a blindfold. Fresh blood trickled from a minor cut on her knee. Thea set her trembling daughter on a kitchen chair and went to wet a towel.

"What happened, sweetheart?" She knelt in front of her and pressed the compress to her knee. "You've been having so many accidents lately."

The child sniffled, wincing as Thea cleaned the cut. "I—I wanted to see what it'd be like."

"What what would be like?"

"To be Uncle Joel."

Clemmie drew in a sharp breath and exchanged a look with Thea.

"I thought I could do better and not fall down. But I can't remember where everything is. I fell on my blocks. They hurted and poked my knee."

The doorbell rang.

"You've got your hands full." Feeling suddenly flustered, Clemmie offered, "I'll get that."

Hannah stood outside the front door like a godsend. "Mother and I finished with things at the bazaar early this evening and thought you might need a lift." Clemmie noticed the chauffeur sitting outside in the Rolls.

"Yes, let me grab my things."

Inside the kitchen she said a quick farewell to Thea.

"Remember what we talked about," Thea said somberly, glancing up at Clemmie.

"How could I forget? Bye, Loretta." She forced a smile. "I hope you feel better soon."

Farewells made, Clemmie hurried to the car. All during the drive, while listening to Hannah's bubbly conversation, her mind revolved around what Loretta had said as she tried to block out Thea's more sobering words. Three conversations, two of them silent, made it difficult to concentrate, and she asked Hannah to repeat herself more than once.

At dinner that night, Clemmie tried to participate in the conversation with Hannah's family and share in their excitement about the upcoming fair, but she could barely follow the discussion. Her mind was still back in Thea's kitchen.

"Is everything all right, dear?" Hannah's mother asked. "You seem not quite yourself this evening."

Clemmie managed a reassuring smile. "I'm just tired."

"I understand you've been hard at work helping Thea during this summer break. A sweet thing to do, but not very restful. Why not turn in early, and I can send you up some hot tea?"

"Thank you. That sounds lovely." Clemmie's gaze dropped to the table. She felt a little remorseful for swearing Hannah to secrecy regarding Joel. Hannah's mother still had no idea he lived a few miles away.

Once Clemmie had returned to her bedroom, she closed the door, leaving the light off. Moonlight seeped through the thin curtains while she remained in shadow. Remembering little Loretta, she grabbed her scarf from a dresser drawer, tying it around her eyes.

Darkness swallowed her, entombing her within a strange, empty well of silence that affected all her senses. She put her hands out, carefully edged forward on the rug then stopped.

Trying to remember the room's layout, she turned toward the window, where the scantest amount of moonlight could be seen through the scarf folds. Thea had told her Joel could differentiate between degrees of shadow, so he did see some variation of light, just not a lot. Slowly Clemmie edged that way.

The toe of her pump snagged on something—the fringe end of the rug?— and she lost her balance. Her palms slapped against hardwood, saving her face from taking the brunt of the fall. Her heart beating fast and erratic, she resisted the impulse to tear away the scarf so she could see. Instead she gathered her wits, letting her breathing calm down.

An anxious sort of vulnerability descended on her as she got to her stinging hands and throbbing knees, struggling to stand. Once upright she slipped out of her pumps and inched forward again, her hands reaching out in front of her. Her fingers met with the bedpost, and she curled them around the carved wood like an anchor, relieved to find something familiar, to gain an idea of where she stood.

The wood beneath her stockings was cool and smooth, and she resisted the impulse to slide her feet along the floor. Any confidence that returned swiftly disintegrated when something sharp pricked the sole of her foot.

"Ow!" she cried out, bending down and raising her foot to grab it. The motion unsteadied her again, and she landed with a thump on her rear.

The sound of the door swinging open preceded the flash of illumination beyond the scarf as the wall sconce flashed on.

"Clemmie?" Hannah asked in surprise. "Are you okay? I heard you yell out...." A dull *clink* followed as Hannah set what Clemmie guessed was her tea on the bedside table. Her footsteps drew close. "What on earth are you doing? Playing blindman's bluff solo?"

Clemmie pulled the scarf away, her expression grave as she looked up at her friend. "We have to help him, Hannah."

"Him?" Hannah knelt down. "You mean Joel?" Her gaze lowered. "What happened to your foot?"

Clemmie inspected her sole, pulling out a tiny splinter. She ran her palm along that area of the floor, finding it rough. Of all the places on the smooth planks, she'd found the one area that was eroding. Hannah noticed it, too.

"I'll tell Uncle about that. This place is old. Sorry you got hurt."

"I'm all right. It's Joel I'm worried about." Clemmie had battled with fear, uncertainty, and vulnerability for mere minutes; Joel dealt with this every second of his life. Knowing that, she could begin to understand him a little better. At the refuge, he'd been the leader and all the boys had idealized him, looking up to him. To have all control ripped from him must have been devastating.

Hannah's eyes were sympathetic. "When you first told me about finding him and wanting to help, I told you I was in favor of the idea and would do what I could. I meant that. I don't know, maybe God really is behind this and I'm not the only one who wanted you to visit Connecticut. I think He wanted you here, too. For Joel's sake."

"Then you don't think I'm wrong to conceal my identity in order to help him?"

"I didn't say that. But Clemmie—and don't get sore." Hannah hesitated. "If you have to keep asking and always trying to get affirmation from others, maybe it's you who doesn't believe it's the right thing to do. And maybe you don't need to be told the answer by anyone else after all."

Clemmie didn't want to hear or acknowledge such sound advice. She wished she could phone her mother and seek her counsel, but she didn't want to breach any slim and grudging trust Joel had given by telling others his location; that was his responsibility. Or maybe—God help her, and she prayed for His guidance each night—maybe the true reason she chose not to ring home was the worry over what her mother might say about Clemmie's ruse. She hoped she wasn't making a royal mess of things.

❧

Joel settled back in his chair and closed his eyes. It didn't matter if he did or didn't close them, as far as blocking out the world went, but it did help him relax. Marielle's voice also relaxed him when she wasn't scolding him. To be fair, she only snapped back when he initiated the arguments, which this past week had been sporadic, to his surprise and hers.

He hadn't thought he could feel comfortable around anyone again, but something about Marielle reminded him of the only home he'd known. Maybe that's why he hadn't refused her staying the extra hours after her family expressed concern over her walking home near dark every evening and told her to wait for someone to come and collect her. She hadn't wanted to get in the way of supper and other family doings once Herbert arrived home from work, so she'd stayed at Joel's shed of a home, even sharing his meals. He had demanded solitude for mealtimes in the past, so to have a dinner guest was disconcerting at first, but he'd grown accustomed to her company. To pass the time, she read to herself or to him from her book, as she did now.

Joel's mind, however, had strayed far from the wanderings of Pilgrim. Not for the first time he wondered about his storyteller.

"You're not listening." She heaved a sigh. "Have you had enough for today?"

"Tell me," he mused aloud, "what do you look like?"

She gasped, and he could imagine her shock. He'd never posed any personal question to her, though she'd shown no hesitation to grill him.

"Does it matter?" She hedged in giving a straight answer, which puzzled him.

"Maybe not, but fair is fair. You can see me. Why shouldn't I at least be allowed to draw a picture of you in my mind?"

"I guess I see your point."

He grinned at her reluctance. "I never would have thought you were shy."

"I'm not. I just don't like talking about myself."

"Humor me this once."

"Oh very well." The leather binding creaked as she closed the book. Her skirt rustled as she fidgeted in her chair. "What do you want to know?"

"Let's start with hair and eye color," he suggested drolly.

"My hair is a sort of light brownish, sort of reddish. My eyes are a greenish sort of grayish."

"Sounds colorful," he drawled at her unenthusiastic admission. "Any freckles?"

"What?" Her question came sharp. "Why do you ask?"

"The few redheads I've known have them." He wondered if she was as sensitive about her freckles as those girls were.

"Can we talk about something else, please?"

"You really don't like talking about yourself, do you?" He might not be able to see her, but he could sense her apprehension.

"I'm not that interesting."

"I disagree." He deliberated. "I'd place you at about five foot five. Am I close?"

She gasped again, and he assumed his guess was correct.

"How could you possibly know? I mean, w—we've never. . . touched. Or—or anything." Her voice came soft, nervous.

"When you stand in front of me, I not only hear your voice, I feel the level of it. It comes to just below my collarbone."

"Oh."

At her quiet reply he added, "I told you before, my other senses have kicked in and sharpened since the accident that got me this way. I sense a lot of things about you."

"Speaking of sharpened, you could really use a haircut," she squeaked out quickly. "And a shave."

"Changing the subject?"

"Stating a fact. Unless your plan was to imitate a Viking? Or maybe a bum? That's quite a beard you've grown. It's the only thing saving you from others mistaking you for a girl, with how long your hair has gotten."

Instead of riling him, it made him laugh. "Why should I care how I look? I'm not going anywhere."

"Maybe you should. It's not healthy to stay cooped up in this shed or to limit your excursions to your sliver of a porch."

He folded his arms across his chest. "Nice try. But this conversation isn't about me. I just realized that in the four weeks since you've invaded my privacy, I've learned very little about you."

She cleared her throat. "Well, I like the great outdoors. Speaking of, did you know the county fair is starting up next weekend? The weekend before the bazaar my friend is working at."

"If that was a ploy to get my mind off track, it didn't work. Where are you from, Marielle? Where do you go after you leave here?"

"Is it so important?"

Five minutes ago he might not have cared. But with her evasive responses, Joel realized just how badly he wanted to know. "Yes."

He waited, as rigid and determined as she was silent. She let out a surrendering breath.

"Okay, fine. I'll make a deal with you. Let me trim your hair and give you a shave, and I'll tell you anything you want to know."

"You have got to be joking."

"No, I'm quite serious."

Surprised she would be so adamant about his grooming, he narrowed his eyes in sudden distrust. "And you've done such a thing before? Used a straight razor?"

"Worried?" Her words held an undercurrent of amusement. "Don't be. You're perfectly safe. You wouldn't be the first man I've shaved. And I've cut hair before, too."

"Are you married? Widowed? Divorced?"

"No answers to any more personal questions unless and until you agree to my terms."

He let out a rasping breath of a laugh. "Fine." He didn't care one way or the other how he looked. Neither Thea nor Herbert ever offered to groom him, and he never asked. He bathed regularly so he wouldn't "stink to high heaven," as Darcy used to say, and that was about the sum total of his grooming habits.

Why would he so suddenly think of Darcy and Lyons' Refuge?

"Swell!" He heard his guest hurry to the door and open it. "I'll just get the things I need. I'll be back in two shakes."

Before he could change his mind or stop her, he heard her footsteps whisk outside and hit the porch.

Joel wryly wondered what he'd gotten himself into.

Chapter 8

Procuring Herbert's razor and other implements wasn't a problem. But evading Thea's string of questions about Clemmie's intentions took up the entire five minutes she waited in the kitchen for Herbert to retrieve his shaving tools. Thea put her hand to Clemmie's arm before she could whisk back outside.

"Tell him."

"I will. Soon. Just not yet."

"I don't like this, Clemmie. I hope you know what you're doing."

She ignored her conscience agreeing with Thea's assessment and hurried back to Joel, to find him in a brooding mood. No longer dryly amused, he seemed quiet, suspicious. He allowed her to tie a tablecloth around his neck and waited while she whipped up shaving foam. But before she could bring the coated bristles to his face, he grabbed her wrist. She gasped in surprise.

"First things first. How do I know that you know what you're doing?"

"I—I was taught. My uncle doesn't have a steady hand, and my aunt sprained her wrist once," she explained, speaking of Brent and Darcy. "She shaved him before, and when I said I would help, she walked me through the motions. Due to his profession, he needs to keep a clean-cut appearance and felt whiskers made him look too scruffy for an important meeting."

"You lived with your aunt and uncle?"

"They live with us."

He nodded, as if taking it all in. "So you've done this once before."

"Actually, five times."

"There are no barbers left in town for your uncle to run to?"

"I suppose. I—I don't know. Or why he chose not to go to one of them. Look, I do know what I'm doing."

"But you've never shaved a full beard before, am I right?"

"Well, no. . ."

"So maybe you should cut it first."

She smiled wide. "That's an excellent idea! Must be why Herbert included the shears."

At her enlightened enthusiasm, he pushed her wrist away. "Maybe this isn't such a good idea. . . ."

"No. You're stuck with me now, Joel Litton." Determined again, she pushed against his chest when he moved forward to rise then picked up the shears. "No sudden moves, or I won't be held responsible." She made cutting noises, pumping the handles to stress her point. He grew as still as a block of wood.

Amused to suddenly have the lion as docile as a kitten, she snipped at the light brown curls covering his jaw, careful not to graze his skin. She didn't even sense him breathing and was surprised she herself didn't tremble. This was the closest she'd been to Joel since their days at the refuge. But she'd learned from her mother to keep focused on a task, despite any distractions, and see it through to the end. She imagined that's what helped her concentrate on playing barber and not think too much about being so close to him, actually touching him. . . .

Focus, Clemmie, focus!

Once the beard was manageable, she lathered up his jaw.

"When do you fulfill your end of the bargain?" He softly spit out lather that had gotten in his mouth when he opened it to speak.

"Do you really want me to concentrate on answering personal questions when I've got a razor at your throat?"

"Good point. I'll wait. But before you start, I've got one question, and it won't wait."

"Okay," she said uneasily.

"Why is this so important to you? Why do you even care?"

"Maybe I just want to see what you look like beneath that lion's mane you've been hiding behind."

He snorted a laugh. "Not the answer I expected."

"But it'll do?" she asked hopefully.

His eyes were intense, like clear blue crystals. They seemed to see through her, and she reminded herself yet again that he was blind and couldn't pick up on the anxiety in her eyes or how she nervously bit her lip, afraid he would discover all her secrets.

"For now." He settled back, leaning the nape of his neck against the chair rim. "So if you're going to do this thing, let's get it over with."

"Your wish is my command, good sir." Slowly, so slowly, she made her first swipe with the razor.

He was the epitome of cooperation, remaining so still she wondered if he'd fallen asleep. She didn't rush through the task, fearful of leaving even the tiniest nick, and felt thankful he hadn't asked if she'd ever cut Brent.

At last she slid the razor along his jaw one final time, set it down near the bowl of warm water, wiped his face with a dry towel, and observed the entirety of her handiwork. She couldn't help the gasp that escaped her lips— she'd forgotten just how handsome he was. With his hair still touching his shoulders, he looked more like a warrior angel than ever before, every feature of his face appearing as if it were sculpted by the finest artisan.

"What is it?" he asked tersely. "What's the matter?"

"N—nothing."

His winged brows drew together. "You don't sound like it's nothing. What have you done to me?"

"I told you, nothing. You're fine. Not a scratch on you. I—I just realized I forgot a hot towel. I—I was supposed to put that on your face first, I think, though I did wet it." Her heart pounding from nerves, she took a hasty step in retreat, but he reached out and grabbed her arm, hauling her forward as though she might run for the door. The abruptness of his move unbalanced her and caused her to topple to his lap.

Shocked motionless, neither of them spoke or moved for endless seconds. She didn't breathe. And he didn't let her go. His other strong arm moved around her middle, trapping her in a rigid embrace.

"You're not going anywhere until you answer some questions."

His voice rumbled against the palm she'd pressed to his chest when she fell. She snatched it away. "I—I. . ." She worked to keep her voice low and even. "What is it you want to know?"

He tilted his head, his blank eyes on her. "Why are you so nervous if you didn't do anything wrong?"

Her lips parted in disbelief. He really needed to ask? Did he feel nothing of the same surge of emotions from holding her against him? She'd never been this close to a man who wasn't a relative and felt the blood rush to her head, warming her entire body.

"If I had made a mistake and slipped, don't you think you would be feeling the pain by now?"

He seemed to consider. "Okay, I'll give you that." But he didn't let her go. She fidgeted a little to remind him of her predicament. Her action had the opposite effect as his arm tightened around her.

"I told you. You're not going anywhere till I get answers."

Her heart pounded harder, if that were possible. "Answers to what?"

"For starters, where do you live?"

She gave an almost hysterical breath of laughter. Did he not trust her enough to keep her end of the bargain, feeling he had to hold her prisoner to answer such questions?

"A few miles from here."

"And about what I asked before. Are you married?"

"No."

"Widowed? Divorced?"

"No and no."

She felt the tension drain from him slightly. His hold on her relaxed, but still he didn't release her.

"How old are you, anyway?"

"It's not polite to ask a lady her age."

He snorted. "Since when did I come across as being polite? Well?" he insisted when she didn't speak. "It's hardly fair since I can't see you to make my own guess."

"Nearing eighteen."

"You're just a baby!"

"No, I'm a woman," she said stiffly.

"And I'm an old bachelor nearing thirty. What do you think of that?"

What did she think of that? She'd only kept a record of his birthday every year since she'd been old enough to mark the date on the calendar. "Thirty's not old."

He grunted as if not pleased with her response. "So, you live with your family?"

"Yes."

"And what do they think of their daughter walking across town every day to tend to a blind recluse?"

"Everyone I've told supports me."

"Everyone you've told?" His brow lifted.

"Yes." She fidgeted again, trying not to tell a lie, though the deceit of her ruse made it difficult.

"In other words, your parents don't know."

"I didn't say that."

"Do they?"

"Does it matter? I'm old enough to make my own decisions. I don't need their permission. And besides, I'm not doing anything wrong."

"You sure about that? I think maybe you're hiding something."

His words came laced with suspicion and prickled at her conscience.

"Seriously? You think I'm hiding some terrible dark secret? That I have a skeleton in my closet?" She tried to make her voice sound light and confused, humorous even, but it came out strained. "Why? What have I ever done to make you feel that way?"

But as she said the false words, they only made her feel worse. This was all wrong. Hannah was right. Thea was right. One lie begat another, and she was tired of always needing to cover her tracks. She must confess, hope he would forgive her, and pray he wouldn't shut her out of his life. She opened her mouth to try to find the right words to explain, but his fingers tentatively touched her lips before she could.

"No. Don't. You're right. You've been nothing but helpful, even when I was a real jerk, and I'm sorry. You don't have to answer any more questions. And you sure shouldn't have to defend yourself to me. I'm the last person to act as judge and jury."

She wondered what he meant by that remark but couldn't think straight as, featherlight, his fingertips trailed her bottom lip in the act of slowly pulling them away. "I just hope I'm not wrong about you."

The mood between them changed, her every sensation intensely felt as she teetered high on an emotional seesaw.

"I"—she breathed against his fingertips—"don't know what you want me to say."

"Say nothing." And then his lips covered hers, stealing any words and every breath.

She had often wondered what it would be like to receive Joel's kiss, ever since she was a young girl. The reality of her dream shook her to the core of her soul.

The lime scent and taste from the specks of remaining shaving cream mingled with the heat of his mouth on hers, all of it making her lightheaded and strangely warm inside and out. She clung to his shoulders as if she might fall, when suddenly he pushed her away and leaned back, holding her far from him.

"I shouldn't have done that." He momentarily remained frozen then practically shoved her from his lap. She forced her wobbly legs to stand. "This was wrong." He shook his head, clearly angry. With her, with himself, she didn't know. "Look, I think it would be better if you just left and didn't come ba—"

"I'm not upset," she hurried to say before he could finish and throw her out for good. "And—and I want you to know. I've decided how you can pay me back."

"What?" Confused, he shook his head at her abrupt change of topic. "What do you mean, pay you back?"

"When I first started working for you, you said you didn't feel right about not giving me wages." She was surprised she could speak rationally, as addled as she felt by the memory of his touch and kiss, both of which she could still feel traces, and she had to hold to the table's rim to remain steady. "I know exactly how you can pay me."

❦

"Well?" Joel asked when she didn't elaborate. "I'm waiting."

"Take me to the county fair."

Her preposterous words at first didn't connect. When they did, he snorted in disbelief that she would suggest such a thing. "Are you off your nut? That's impossible!"

"Why?"

"Why? *Why*!" He worked to get his temper in check. "In case you've forgotten, I'm blind."

"You have two good legs, don't you? Use your cane."

"No." He winced at the thought of the blind man's stick that stood unused in the corner.

"Why not? You're the one being impossible."

"How can you say such a thing to me? Do you know what it's like to live like this? It's not your eyes that were struck blind. Do you know what it's like to step off a stair and walk into the unknown? To be literally in the dark? To have people stop and stare at the pathetic wretch, wondering if he'll trip and fall?"

"How do you know they're staring if you can't see them?" Her voice had gone quiet and subdued. "From what I understand, you were never one to care what strangers think about you. And if you're really all that concerned, I can be your eyes."

"I said no!" He flung his hand sideways in an arc. Without meaning to, he felt it connect with the bowl. It crashed to the floor. "See what mistakes a blind man can make? Now beat it before I get really upset."

Her footsteps were steady as she did the opposite, moving toward him. He heard the bowl scrape wood as she picked up the shattered pieces.

"Leave it."

"I can't just leave this on the floor for you to step on."

"I'll take care of it. You could cut your hand."

"Nice of you to care, but I've had to clean up worse messes than this when my younger brothers had one of their little tantrums."

He pulled his lips in a tight line. "So, you think I'm throwing a tantrum?"

"Yes I do. You're so full of self-pity, it's a wonder you don't drown in it."

He snorted in exasperation. "Will you just get out of here?"

"We're not finished. I haven't cut your hair."

"I've had enough of your help for one night."

She paused. "Fine. We'll resume tomorrow, and I'm not taking no for an answer." Her steps moved to the door, paused, then turned around and came back. "Before I go, there's one thing I don't understand."

"What's that?" he bit out through clenched teeth.

"If you're so unhappy with the way things have been and so dissatisfied with life as it is now, why don't you agree to the operation?"

Incredulous anger made his face burn hot. "Thea had no right to tell you about that!"

"Don't blame Thea. I got curious and asked. I guess you could say I almost forced the information from her."

He slammed his fist on the table. "Well, stay out of my affairs! It's none of your business!"

"I understand there's an element of risk involved," she persisted, "but you were never the type of man to run from danger. Even as a boy, you never retreated from a challenge. Even life-threatening ones, though I understand this doesn't qualify. In fact, you were usually the first one to jump into trouble, feet first."

He narrowed his eyes at her correct assessment of his character, though she had the logistics of the doctor's findings wrong. "How do you know so much about me or what I'm like?"

"Herbert talks about the old days quite often."

He snorted in derision. "Another person who should keep his big trap shut and his opinions to himself."

"And I've built my own evaluation of your character in the month that I've been here." She continued as if she'd not heard him. "One thing you're not is a coward. So why didn't you go through with the operation, if there's a chance you could see again? Why don't you go through with it now? You're clearly not happy."

"Thanks for the psychoanalysis, doc, but for the last time, mind your own potatoes and keep out of my business."

"Is it that you have no one to help you financially? No friends or family?"

"I'm not a charity case!"

"There are such things as loans."

"In these hard times? Look, just leave it—and me—alone."

"You asked me questions. Don't I have the right to do the same?"

She wasn't backing down, and rather than argue further, he felt weary of the whole subject. "Go home, Marielle. I'm tired and want to turn in for the night."

"A shave exhausted you so much?"

He heard the skepticism in her voice.

"Having a veritable stranger hold a razor to your throat does tend to wear on a man's nerves," he countered dryly.

"That's all I still am to you then? A stranger?"

He couldn't mistake the sadness in her words. But that was all she could ever be to him. He couldn't afford to get involved, no matter how phenomenal it had felt to hold and kiss her. It had been well over a year since he'd been so close to a woman, but she had a rare quality he couldn't pinpoint that separated her from the rest.

Even so, he had nothing to offer, and she had no reason to want to give him an opportunity. He was only a curiosity to her. A charity case upon whom she wished to dole out her good deeds and brandish compassion. Even if she was interested in more, once the novelty wore off, she certainly wouldn't want to find herself trapped in a relationship with a man who couldn't see and would always need some sort of guidance.

She'd been accurate in most of her assumptions regarding his character, but she was wrong about one thing. He didn't pity himself for his condition. He deserved no man's pity. But he did warrant all the blame.

"Go home, Marielle," he said tiredly.

"Then you agree?"

"No, but you can't spend the night here, and I'm going to bed."

"Fine." He heard her huff of exasperation. "But this isn't over, Joel Litton."

He ignored her declaration. "As long as you insist on using both my names all the time, you might as well save yourself the trouble and just use the one."

"Litton?"

He couldn't help the faint smile that quirked his mouth at her teasing. "Joel."

"All right." Pleasure softened her voice. "Good night, Joel."

He laid his head back without answering and closed his eyes. At the soft click of the door, he knew he was again alone.

"Good night, pixie angel. I don't know whether to call you a menace or a saint. Just who are you, Marielle?"

It was then he realized he didn't even know her last name.

Chapter 9

I t took four visits to convince Joel to change his mind. For every reason he gave that he couldn't go to the fair, Clemmie offered a solution showing that the outing was not impossible for him—as he claimed— but probable, even preferable. He needed to get out of the house and into the world.

Thea offered her support, and Herbert announced they would make it a family outing. Hannah talked to her mother, both of them overburdened with work for the upcoming bazaar, and Hannah's mother gladly relinquished the chauffeur for a day, eager to help when Clemmie broke down and told her of Joel's presence in town. Sworn to secrecy, Hannah's mother also expressed concern that Clemmie was keeping her identity from Joel, but Clemmie assured her hostess she would tell him soon. And at last, with no further arguments, Joel curtly agreed to attend the fair, though his mood grew dour the rest of that afternoon.

She hadn't realized it would be so difficult. Not just to conceal her identity but to continue in her plan to help him. Some days everything proceeded smoothly, and she felt the heavens smiled upon her—that God, indeed, had orchestrated her arrival to Connecticut, and she was following through with His plans. She'd even begun to hope for her girlhood dream to come true, realizing she'd never gotten over wanting to be more than Joel's friend, no matter how hard she tried to convince herself and everyone else she was long over her infatuation. Only this didn't feel like the old silly schoolgirl fascination.

His unexpected kiss had brought her buried feelings back into glaring relief; she had to stop lying to herself and especially to him. Still, every time she considered how to tell him she was Clemmie, her mind played out the scenario of what would ensue. No matter how many ways she imagined it, the ending always remained the same—they both wound up hurt and losers. She had mired herself in this web of deceit too deeply and didn't know how to gracefully extract herself without breaking the fragile cords of trust that slowly had begun bonding them—and causing her pain.

Those were the days she wondered if she could or should continue the charade, feeling sadly inadequate to help Joel who bore a secret burden he wouldn't share, no matter how she tried to get him to open up to her. But she wasn't a coward, and that's what she would be if she never returned, giving no confession or explanation except for whatever Thea might offer Joel should Clemmie suddenly quit working for him.

And if she did conclude all association with him, wouldn't he feel rejected and betrayed despite his demands that she go, which had been coming less frequently?

When asked, she continued to read her novel to him. One afternoon after they'd both eaten, he was in one of his sullen moods and ordered her to resume their reading. She did—from the book she had open. She'd brought along a Bible, intrigued to find symbolism that was in the allegory of the novel and the verses relating to it. When she started reading where she'd left off, he'd shown surprise not to hear her speak of Pilgrim's progress to the Celestial City. He hadn't ordered her to stop, but his expression had grown hard and shuttered, making his feelings clear with regard to her choice of reading material.

Each evening she shared her frustrations of the day and concerns for Joel's spiritual health with Hannah. And when she retired, she offered supplications to the Lord, asking Him to intervene and bring the lost lamb that Joel had become, however black, back to God's fold. She hurt for him but refused to show pity, knowing it would only make things worse. Instead her pillow bore the brunt of her heartache as, alone in her room, she shed any tears she'd held at bay while in his company.

But this day held no place for tears. The morning shone sunny and bright, full of promise. And Joel, much to her surprise, seemed in a pleasant mood, though he showed some stubbornness in his refusal to use his cane, even just for the walk to the waiting car. She clung to his arm, both to aid him and for the closeness such an action afforded.

Inside the Rolls, despite its roomy nature, the seats were crowded. Any closer and she would have been sitting on his lap. The memory of that moment and what followed made her face go hot, something that Herbert, who sat directly across from her, didn't fail to miss.

"What did you say to Marielle?" he teased Joel from the seat opposite, where Thea and Loretta also sat. "You should see her face—as red as a peony. Almost matches her hair."

"Thanks a bundle for that trite and unnecessary information." Clemmie modulated her voice gently while staring daggers at her old childhood torturer. "But I'll have you know my hair is not that red. It's almost auburn."

"Dream on, little girl."

Thea sharply elbowed him in the ribs, though she couldn't know the extent of damage her husband may have done. Clemmie's heart skipped a beat at the words he often used to say to her when they'd lived at the refuge. She hoped Joel hadn't caught on and gave him a swift glance.

His perfect features, no longer half hidden by facial hair, were a mask, his blue eyes indifferent. She couldn't read his emotions no matter how hard she tried. Herbert realized his error by the deer-struck look on his face and mouthed, "Sorry."

"Well, old man, at least your hair no longer resembles a caveman who hadn't yet invented a comb," he said too robustly. Clemmie rolled her eyes heavenward at his lame tactic to save the moment, and Thea elbowed him again. "What? What did I say? She did a good job is all I meant."

"Enough talk about hair," Thea inserted. "Tell me about this bazaar your friend's mother is holding. I ran across some things yesterday if it's not too late to make a donation."

"I would think the ladies on the committee would be thrilled." Clemmie mouthed a thank-you. "I'll ask about it tonight."

"Mommy," Loretta interrupted, "will there be animals at the fair?"

"I think so, sweetheart. If I remember, fairs have them."

"Have you been to the fair?"

Thea laughed. "It's been many years."

"What about you, Uncle Joel?" Bethany asked.

All eyes turned his way, and Clemmie uneasily thought again how silent he'd become since the drive began. Of all things, this morning he had shocked her speechless when he'd asked her last name! She had literally been saved by the cat when it chose that moment to run between them, and Loretta had given chase.

"When I was a boy, I went to a carnival." His reply came quietly.

"Is a carnival like a fair?"

His grin to Bethany was halfhearted. "Something like it, I guess. I've never been to a county fair."

"What did you do at the carnival?"

"Look, Bethany, see those tents ahead," Herbert pointed out. "We're almost there."

"Yippee!" Loretta bounced on the seat, clapping her hands and earning her mother's admonition to sit still like her big sister.

Clemmie knew about that carnival and understood Herbert's eagerness to change the subject. As an adventurous boy of twelve, Joel had run away from his chaperones and into the path of a dangerous criminal, getting into some of the worst trouble he'd ever been in and also deceiving her parents. Thinking of her own deceit she squirmed almost as much as Loretta.

Joel's hand suddenly clamped down on her knee, startling her into sucking in a huge lungful of air—one she found difficult to release.

⁂

The feel of her leg tensing beneath his hand made Joel realize what he'd done. He had initiated his reflexive action to keep her still, but at her shock he quickly withdrew his hand.

"Stop fidgeting," he explained, "or you're going to bruise me black-and-blue." The admonition was extreme. Though they sat with their sides touching, she could hardly bruise him from wriggling around. But he felt every movement she made, even sensed those he didn't physically experience, and to have her so close was doing strange things to his mental faculties, bringing back thoughts of her sitting on his lap and their kiss.

And she had kissed him back that night, though it took days for him to acknowledge it. Did she kiss him out of pity? Curiosity? If for neither of those reasons, what was her motive?

What was his?

His motivation to understand her, to know her, clashed with his reluctance to have anything to do with her, all of his feelings becoming increasingly blurred as the weeks elapsed. Lately she reminded him of someone, though he couldn't place her, and he wondered if he'd met her at a party or an acquaintance's house.

Such a likelihood seemed improbable, because he didn't remember meeting anyone in the month before he went blind who fit Marielle's description. Besides, if they had met before, wouldn't she have mentioned it?

He thought about asking her but was cut off by Loretta's excited squeal, just as he'd been interrupted by the cat's yowl earlier when he'd tried to get Marielle's full name.

"We're here! We're here!"

At the cry that their destination had been reached, Joel's fears resurfaced. Herbert opened the door on his side while the chauffeur helped the women out the other side. Herbert's hand touched his sleeve, but Joel hung back.

"Come on, old man. Don't dillydally. Need help getting out?"

Joel recognized the teasing the two of them had shared since boyhood, but right now he felt far from joking. "I'm only one year older than you—and don't patronize me!" He whipped his arm away from Herbert's touch. "I should never have agreed to this! It was a mistake."

"Mama." He heard Loretta whisper. "What's wrong with Uncle Joel?"

Suddenly the scent of lilacs strongly assaulted his senses as the woman who'd been both tormentor and savior approached his side. Her fingertips were gentle upon his shoulder.

"You promised to be my escort," she reminded. "Please don't back out now."

Marielle's soft voice calmed him where nothing else could. He offered a curt nod—shocked to feel her arm slip through his once he was standing—but didn't protest.

At first the cane seemed awkward in his hand; he felt vulnerable walking over uneven ground he didn't know and couldn't see. But despite his peevish edginess, she didn't abandon his side or chastise him for his disagreeable behavior.

"Tell me," he said, hearing people hush or talk in undertones as they walked past. "Are they all staring?"

"I assume you mean the ladies?"

Marielle's answer and the tightness in her voice took him aback. "What?"

"You heard me. The ladies." She made as if to move her arm away, but he tightened his grasp, not willing to let her escape without explanation.

"What do you mean by that?"

"I. . ." Her breath hitched as if she were now uneasy. "I understand you were quite a ladies' man."

"And that was your first thought when I asked if anyone was staring?"

"Yes." Her admission came reluctantly.

With a disbelieving laugh he scoffed at her. "Trust me. I'm no longer the object of any woman's admiration. I'm surprised you'd even think it."

"Are you really so stupid?"

The anger in her voice hid the barest trace of tears, and the way her fingers tensed around his sleeve perplexed him.

"Are you all right?"

"Swell." Her voice came steadier. "But since you ask, why do you care if anyone stares? Let's just try and enjoy the day."

He exhaled a frustrated breath. She was right, he supposed. He couldn't see anyone's reactions, and he'd never cared about what people thought before. So why had it become so all-fired important now?

"All right. On one condition."

"You're making a condition to enjoying the day?"

He couldn't help but grin at her amusement.

"You don't baby me or treat me like an invalid, and I won't reconsider hunting down that chauffeur of your friend's to get me out of here."

"All right. It's a deal." She slipped her arm from his, but he grabbed her hand and looped it back where it had been. He sensed her surprise in the sudden trembling of her hand, which he kept under his.

"That I'll allow."

"Oh really?" she asked with a soft laugh.

He smiled.

Chapter 10

Joel's bright smile and persistent hold on her arm gave Clemmie a much-needed boost of confidence. She hadn't been jealous, not really, but the curious yet clearly interested looks from young women walking in the opposite direction made her recall the old days, when Joel had only to give one of his engaging boyish grins for the ladies to take notice and nearly swoon where they stood.

For herself, she didn't read more into his action to keep her close than what she assumed it meant. His pride wouldn't allow him to admit he needed help, and clearly he felt nervous without her holding his arm as they strolled over the unfamiliar ground and through the crowds. For him, she would be whatever he needed, though she wished to be so much more.

Relieved the atmosphere had eased between them again, she surveyed her surroundings. Though the fair wasn't much different than the annual one near home, the day seemed brighter, the crowds friendlier, the amusements more interesting, and she felt sure it was because she walked with Joel.

Tents and booths stood scattered in no real order, as if a giant hand had tossed them to land where they may. A fringe of trees provided a backdrop against a sky so blue it almost hurt to look at it. The nearby woods shielded the morning sun, which peeked in scattered rays between thick foliage. Everywhere, she saw smiles and heard laughter, and she silently thanked God again that she'd been able to convince Joel to come, certain such a fun climate would be good medicine for his wounded soul.

She described everything she saw, remembering to be his eyes, and warned him of anything his cane might miss in an offhand manner, so he wouldn't accuse her of coddling him.

Some passersby did openly stare as he searched the ground with his cane for obstacles that might trip him. But she ignored their curiosity, happy that Joel was finally away from his stifling shed and out among the populace again.

"Do I smell hot dogs?"

Clemmie laughed at his sudden boyish enthusiasm and scouted the myriad booths and tents ahead. Far in the distance she spotted a hot dog vendor.

"Can I have a hot dog, Daddy?" Bethany wanted to know.

"We just got here, cupcake!"

"Aw, let the kid have a hot dog if she wants one."

"You're just saying that because you want one," Herbert accused Joel.

"What can I say? Blame my stomach."

"You mean that bottomless pit below your chest?"

"Funny man. I seem to remember you couldn't get enough pies in your day. A habit you never outgrew. Tell me that you don't plan on visiting the pie-eating booth for a contest."

"How'd you know about that, Uncle Joel, if you've never been to a fair?" Bethany interrupted the men's banter. "I don't see any booths with pies."

"I know because your daddy told me there'd be one. Don't worry. If it's there, he'll find it. He has a nose for such things. And a mouth."

The adults chuckled and moved toward the booth. Five minutes later the happy vendor pocketed his change and the group moved away loaded with steaming hot dogs slathered in mustard. A rare treat in such hard times.

"Mmm." Joel angled the end of the bun and meat into his mouth. "This isn't half bad. Almost reminds me of the old picnics at the refuge."

Herbert laughed. "Nowhere near as good as Darcy's cooking though."

"Or her baking. She made some of the best pies while we were growing up."

"Yes, her pies are contest winners," Clemmie mused aloud.

Uneasy silence descended. Joel's arm tensed beneath her hand.

"Or so you've said," she hastily amended. "Right?" She shot a pleading look at Thea and Herbert, who appeared just as apprehensive as they looked between Joel and Clemmie. She also glanced his way. Nothing on his face gave a hint that he'd noticed her slip, and she exhaled in relief.

"My Herbie's always filling us in on tales of your days together at the refuge," Thea answered. "He goes into such vivid detail we feel we've actually lived it. He mentioned that famous fence-painting contest for a pie more than once."

Both men groaned then chuckled, and again the mood eased. But Clemmie noticed the disapproval in Thea's eyes as she glanced her way.

Thea didn't lie, but Clemmie saw her unease at covering over the comment about Darcy's pies. Thea shouldn't have to. Clemmie's well-intentioned ruse had gone on long enough; Joel deserved the truth. They'd grown close enough that perhaps he wouldn't toss her out on her ear once he learned she was "clumsy little Clemmie" as he'd affectionately teased while tweaking her nose or ruffling her hair in her awkward years. She'd grown out of her clumsiness—except when it came to untangling herself from the sticky web of half-truths she'd created.

How could she tell him? Certainly she couldn't do it today. She wasn't about to spoil any memory of his first outing since he'd gone blind.

Confessions of the soul must wait. They had to!

"Ewww," Bethany squealed, appalled. "What are they doing?" She pointed to a booth in the distance. A young blond leaned over the booth's rim to plant a kiss on the cheek of a boy at least five years younger. He walked away grinning, his fingers rubbing the red lipstick imprint she'd left on his skin.

Clemmie grinned as Thea covered Loretta's eyes with her hand when an older man pecked the woman on the lips.

"That's called a kissing booth," Herbert said. "And those dandies in line are paying the lady to receive her kiss."

"Ixnay," Thea reproved. "The children."

"It's all for a good cause, dear. Most of the proceeds of the fair are going to help the homeless. I help write the news, remember? Perhaps I should contribute."

Thea grabbed his arm as he teasingly moved in the direction of the booth. "Don't you dare take one step farther, Herbert Miller, or you'll find yourself out in the shed with Joel tonight."

"Aw, honey, you know you're the only gal for me. But maybe Joel would like a turn." He looked at his friend. "Whatta ya say, ole pal? I've never known you to refuse such a worthy cause."

Clemmie waited tensely for Joel's answer.

"I think I'll pass."

"You've got to be joshing me—you pass up a smooch from an attractive dame?"

Thea elbowed Herbert in the ribs, doing what Clemmie wished to do.

"Yeah. Those days are history."

Clemmie didn't know whether to cheer with relief that he wouldn't undertake Herbert's challenge to kiss a stranger or sigh with wretchedness that he now thought himself unfit for a woman to love.

Oh, how she wished to show him differently!

"Yuck." Bethany wrinkled her nose at the kissing booth and looked up at her father. "Can we go find the animals?"

"Sure, cupcake. Whatever you want."

The morning passed into afternoon, both little girls bubbling over with excitement at the fun they shared, especially petting a black baby goat a farmer had brought for children to befriend, along with his prize animals competing for the winning blue ribbons. They laughed when the little kid ate a tin can, and Joel remarked that the animal not only had a bottomless stomach but an ironclad one and that he'd "give Herbert a run for his money on the pies."

Of course then Herbert took up Joel's challenge, much like when they were boys, and entered the contest. They all stood on the sidelines and cheered him on. Bethany giggled.

"What's so funny?" Joel asked.

"They tied Daddy's hands behind him so he'll have to eat the pie just like our cat drinks milk from her bowl!"

Joel grinned. "Now that I'd love to see."

Thus encouraged, amid gales of laughter, Bethany told Joel every detail of the messy endeavor once the contest bell rang.

"I can't see!" Loretta complained from Joel's other side. "I wanna see, too!"

Joel handed Clemmie his cane and reached down, lifting the little girl onto his side so she could witness the messy event above the heads of the adults in front of them.

"Ooo, there's Daddy!" she squealed, pointing and giggling, bouncing up and down on Joel's hip. "His face is all blue with berries!"

Clemmie smiled to watch Joel with the children. They clearly had a fondness for him, and he didn't appear to dislike them as she'd once thought.

Herbert finished his pie in record time. Thea wiped berry juice from his cheeks and chin, chiding the girls who crowded close to their father that they should not take a lesson from Daddy, while Herbert proudly pinned his blue ribbon to his lapel for all to see.

Clemmie felt exuberant with how marvelously the outing had gone, and in her glee she squeezed Joel's arm. "I can't tell you when I've had such a delightful day," she said as they walked among the booths again. "Being here with you as my escort has been the highlight of my week, no, make that my year!"

He lifted his eyebrows in surprise. "You must lead a very dull life."

She couldn't help the laugh that escaped. "Hardly dull—"

"Joel Litton, is that you?" a woman's voice exclaimed in surprise.

Clemmie felt her balloon of mirth deflate and her heart drop to her stomach as a young woman with light brown hair and sea green eyes, as beautiful as any movie star in Hannah's memorabilia photo box, glided their way. She reminded Clemmie of a cross between Jennifer Jones and Lana Turner, with both an exotic innocence and cool sophistication.

Instantly Clemmie didn't like her.

"It's Paisley Wallace," the woman said to Joel. "We met at my sister's party when you first moved to Connecticut. My great-uncle owns the newspaper where Herbert works."

"Oh yes. How are you, Paisley?"

"I'm fine. I—I hope you're well," she said, clearly not knowing what to say.

Joel motioned with his cane. "As you can see. . ."

The girl's classic features softened in sorrow. "No, I—I didn't know. We didn't even know you were back in town. Sheridan will be pleased to learn of it. You just so suddenly disappeared. . . ."

"Perhaps, under the circumstances, it would be best not to tell her."

"Oh. Of course." Paisley glanced toward Clemmie, noticing her arm linked around Joel's. Clearly flustered, she made a few trite comments about the fair and the weather before excusing herself, while Clemmie jealously wondered who Sheridan was and what kind of hold she'd had on Joel.

"Shall we continue?" Joel suggested, his voice losing its earlier spark.

The rest of the day passed with an uncomfortable wall of reserve between them, which resulted in the adults trying to force the ease they'd earlier enjoyed. Their attempts made the atmosphere more taut. The children continued to frolic along the fairgrounds like excited puppies, oblivious to the changes.

"So," Joel said when they were alone, once Herbert and Thea excused themselves to take both girls to enjoy a nearby attraction of a pony ride. "Tell me your last name."

Chapter 11

Wh–what?"

He noticed how her voice trembled.

"Your last name. We were interrupted before."

"My name?" Her voice rose higher in pitch, but that could have been because of a noisy crowd of children who ran past. "Is it so important?"

Why was she evading the subject? "I'd like to know."

"I'm not sure why—"

"Are you going to make me guess?" he asked incredulously.

"If you like."

He shook his head, flabbergasted that she should take his joking seriously. A previous thought occurred to him.

"If we'd met somewhere before, you'd tell me, right?"

Another pause. "Of course." Her voice seemed tight, and he wondered if his question offended her.

"So is this a tale similar to Rumpelstiltskin, with you making me have to guess your name?"

She laughed in delight. "Oh, I haven't heard that tale in ages! It was in a book my mother read to me as a child. My favorite story was 'Rapunzel.' She was locked up in a stone tower by a cruel man so that her true love couldn't reach her. But he always found a way to her side by climbing her thick rope of hair. I used to envy her beautiful, long, golden hair. . . ."

What's the matter, Carrottop?

Stop it, Joel! I hate my hair! Why'd I have to have ugly orange hair anyway? I wish I could be Rapunzel and have her pretty, long, golden hair.

Aw, don't feel so bad. It's not that orange. . . .

"Joel. . . ? Are you all right?"

Marielle's concern shook him from an old memory of a girl who'd been like a kid sister to him at the farm. "Yeah, fine. But you're changing the subject."

"Can't we have this discussion later?"

Again he shook his head in baffled surprise. "It's just a name, for crying out loud. Not your entire history."

"But that comes next, right?"

He couldn't understand her strange defensiveness and reluctance to talk about herself. "Okay, I'll admit I am interested in knowing more about you. But for now I just want a name."

"And I told you, I'll tell you that and everything else—later. Right now I just want to enjoy the rest of this day."

He tightened his hand around her arm to stop her from walking farther. "You're upset. Why? Is the prospect of telling me your full name so earthshaking? Are you a fugitive hiding from the law?"

"No, of course not. I just. . . Who's Sheridan?"

"Sheridan?" His mouth parted in surprise that she would ask such a question. "A woman I took out a few times. Why?"

"I just wondered."

This entire conversation perplexed him. This woman perplexed him.

He remembered a conversation he and Herbert once had. His friend had just had an argument with his wife, and he and Joel discussed women and their bizarre mood swings that made little sense—they were so hard to figure out!

But with each day that passed, Joel found himself wanting to figure out this woman and very badly. To focus on another person after a year of thinking only of himself was oddly. . .freeing. He'd been selfish; he knew that. At the time he hadn't cared, had been able to concentrate only on his bitterness and anger. But today he'd not only stepped out of the safe box of his home into the big, bad, wide world, but out of the cage that had enclosed his heart from feeling. To feel had been too painful. It was still painful. But now he had reason to try.

She was that reason.

It was foolish, it was crazy, perhaps even impossible as he'd told her before. But she hadn't pulled away from him every time he told her she should, instead always reaching out to him. And as unbelievable as it seemed, she sounded jealous when speaking of Sheridan. He resolved to test his theory at the next available moment when they were alone.

Soon, but not soon enough for Joel, the children complained of being tired. As the sun dipped low—the coolness of the air a testimony to evening's arrival—they decided to call it a day.

The drive back was quiet. Marielle's body relaxed against his, and he wondered if she had dozed off. His assumption proved correct when her silky hair brushed his jaw as her head slowly nodded off until it dropped to his shoulder. An unexpected surge of protection shot through him along with the sudden desire to hold her, but he resisted the temptation. She jerked awake, her warmth immediately absent as she quickly lifted her head. He heard her hands rapidly smooth her skirts, as if flustered, but neither of them spoke until they reached Herbert's home.

"Come talk to me?" he asked.

He sensed her sudden tension. "Can it wait? I'm really very tired and don't feel much like talking."

"It won't take long."

"Joel. . ."

"I'm not asking for personal disclosures. Not tonight anyway. Please?" He hadn't used that word in ages, not without sarcasm, and recognized her surprise in the shaky breath she inhaled.

"All right."

Marielle asked the chauffeur to wait and walked with Joel toward his shed. Though she didn't take his arm and he didn't take hers now that he was on familiar territory, he could sense her mounting anxiety.

"Relax," he murmured when they reached his porch. "I just have a favor to ask."

"I can't guarantee anything. It depends on the favor."

He turned to face her. "I want to see you, Marielle. Will you let me do that?"

"See me?" she asked, clearly puzzled. "How?"

"Like this."

And he lifted his hands, gently pressing his fingertips to her smooth jaw.

❤

Clemmie trembled at his unexpected touch. Any lethargy she felt disappeared in an instant as her blood pounded like a living thing, making her head swim.

"Do you mind?" he whispered, not taking his hands away.

She couldn't speak, only shook her head the barest fraction in consent.

His fingertips continued along her jawline, warm and gentle. He moved his hands higher, his fingers flush against her cheeks, their tips learning her cheekbones. Higher still, against her nose, and she closed her eyes as his touch ghosted along her lashes and eyelids, gently swept her brows and temples, and trailed upward to brush her forehead. He moved them into her thick hair, weaving through the strands, and then his large hands cupped her scalp and swept down over her ears, to the ends of her wavy hair, down to her shoulders . . .sweeping above her collar to brush slowly upward again. . .along her neck . . .beneath her chin.

Clemmie shivered strongly but not from chill. Warmth rushed through her when his fingertips slowly drifted feather light across her lips.

"What. . .what are you doing to me?" he whispered, his breath suddenly warm against her mouth. "Don't you know this isn't possible?"

"No, no I don't—"

And suddenly his lips covered her own, cutting off her adamant whisper.

Being kissed once by Joel had been an unattainable dream come true, a momentary wish fulfilled that just as soon ended.

Being kissed twice brought the dream into startling reality, no longer unattainable, this kiss no fleeting reminder.

Just as his hands learned her face, his mouth took time making its own discoveries. Barely able to stand, she wound her arms around his neck, soon returning his kiss with eagerness.

After a long moment of bliss, he drew back and pressed his forehead to hers. She felt so lightheaded she continued to cling to him for support. Gradually her eyes fluttered open, looking into his beautiful, unseeing ones, taking in his perfect features and stunned expression as they both caught their breath.

"I. . .I should go," she whispered at last.

"Yes." His agreement came quiet.

"I'll come back tomorrow," she said needlessly, pulling her arms away from him and stepping back, contrary to what she truly wanted: to wrap her arms tightly around him again, melt in his warm embrace, and share in another heart-escalating kiss.

If things were complicated before, they'd just reached a point of total insanity.

She hugged herself, feeling suddenly chilled as she hurried from his porch and toward the house. Before she entered Thea's kitchen, she glanced over her shoulder and noticed Joel hadn't changed position or moved from his spot.

She burst inside, finding Thea at the stove, and fell into the closest chair.

"Dear God in heaven, help me," she whispered in a plea, her elbows on the table, her face in her hands. "I love him. I've never stopped—"

"I know."

"You *know*?" Clemmie peeked up through her fingers.

"Everyone who has eyes does. It's been as clear as a summer's day."

Clemmie realized she'd only fooled herself into believing otherwise. "This isn't some girlhood crush anymore, Thea. It's escalated into something much stronger, much dearer. He means everything to me! I can't imagine a day without him. I think my heart would drain empty because he has everything inside. . . . Oh, what am I going to do? I have to tell him the truth, I have no choice anymore. He's starting to question me. At the fair I evaded him, but I think he might suspect something's amiss with my crazy answers and the way I avoided giving him the answer he wanted. When he finds out who I am, what if he's not angry? What if he's disappointed—to learn it's me? The clumsy little carrottop he once knew? That's what he called me, you know. I can't hold a candle to the beauties he's been involved with. And I can't bear his rejection, which is sure to come."

"You don't give yourself enough credit. You have many fine qualities."

"You mean besides deception and fraud?" she wryly asked. "Oh, I should have never done this. You were right. I've made such a mess of things."

Thea came to her side and put a hand on her shoulder to calm her. "It's impossible to second-guess what'll happen once Joel knows. But whatever does happen, please remember I'm here if you need me. And, Clemmie? You must tell him soon. Tomorrow. Better yet, go back there and tell him now."

"Now? No! I can't. N—not after. . ." She trailed off, thinking of his kiss, that wondrous moment she wasn't willing to share. "Tomorrow?" The prospect made her heart race. "It's too soon. I—I need more time."

"You've had more than enough time. I watched you two together today. You've gained his trust, and things are finally on an even keel between you. There's no longer any reason to hold back in telling him who you are."

There were plenty of reasons! Had Thea not heard anything Clemmie told her?

Feeling as if she were suffocating and in need of air, she shot up from the chair. "I—I have to go now. I'm sorry."

"Wait!" Thea called after her.

But she was already out the door and hurrying to the waiting chauffeur.

"Henley, please take me home."

He nodded, shutting the car door behind her, and hurried to resume his place at the wheel. All through the drive back to the mansion, the knowledge of what she must do haunted Clemmie. Upon arriving, she found no one home, and relieved she hurried to her room. But simply closing the door couldn't block out what must be done.

She had to tell him the next time she saw him. . . .

Tomorrow.

The word crashed like a brass gong, booming out a sentence of judgment in her mind.

Chapter 12

Clemmie took a deep breath and knocked, equipped with her sweet peace offering that she hoped would make the bitter pill of what Joel must soon swallow easier to bear.

"It's open."

His voice sounded grim, and once she stepped inside, she noticed his expression matched his tone. Wonderful. He was in one of his dark, brooding moods. Perhaps it would be best to wait with personal declarations of guilt. . . .

Relieved that she had evaded her unwanted mission for one more day, she moved to stand before him where he sat in a chair.

"I brought you a treat," she said cheerily, hoping to dispel his gloom. "I baked it fresh this morning. That's why I'm late."

"Really."

"Yes." She set the pan down and removed the towel cover. "I think you'll like it."

"Because you know so much about me."

"Well, yes. I'm learning."

"From all those stories Herbert had to tell."

Uneasy, she studied his expression. He may as well have been wearing a mask; his face gave nothing away.

"Well, that, too. But I feel I've gotten to know you for myself."

"And that's important, isn't it? Getting to know me."

Clemmie swallowed hard, his pointed questions making her nervous.

"It helps."

"Yet I know nothing about you."

"I told you I'll tell you all you want to know soon."

"Soon. Right." He laughed harshly then frowned. "Forget soon. Tell me now."

She cut a hunk of the bread. "Not when you're like this. Later."

"It's always later with you, isn't it?"

She handed him a slice. "Here. Maybe this will help sweeten that nasty disposition of yours."

He snatched the bread from her hand with a frown and took a bite. His scowl grew darker. To her shock, he threw the rest of the bread on the table.

His eyes were blind, but they sparked with blue flames as they snapped her way.

Wishing only to escape, she retreated a step. "I—I think I left something at Thea's. I'll be back shortly."

His hand flew to her arm, securing her. "You're not going anywhere. . . Clemmie."

At his mocking twist on her name and the knowledge that he knew it, she felt faint. She pressed her other palm flat to the table to steady herself.

"W–why did you call me that?" she whispered.

"Do you deny it's your name?"

She didn't answer, wishing for escape and knowing there wasn't any.

"You really must take me for a fool. There were so many pieces that didn't add up. Your refusal to talk about yourself, some of the bizarre things you said, your vague description of your appearance. But this—" The hand not clamped around her arm found the bread he'd tossed and raised it. "This was the dead giveaway. You should have been more careful, Clemmie. Darcy's date nut bread is one of a kind, like no one else's."

"S–so it was the bread?" she nervously asked. "That recipe could belong to anyone. Maybe Darcy gave it to Thea, and she gave it to me."

"Still trying to deny it?" he bit out. "Don't bother. I heard the tail end of the conversation you had with Thea last night. Through the kitchen window. I actually left my porch to find Herbert and got the unpleasant shock that you were withholding your identity from me. Adding it all together, it didn't take long to figure out, *Clementine Lyons*."

"All right"—she gave in, almost shouting the words—"all right, Joel. You caught me. And you may not believe this, but I'm really sorry it had to be this way. You don't know how sorry! But you gave me no choice." Her own temper rising, Clemmie wrenched her arm from Joel's hold. "If you hadn't concealed your whereabouts—if you'd only called or written us one time in these past three years—I wouldn't have felt the need to deceive you!"

He blinked in surprise, clearly not expecting an attack. "You're not actually turning this around on me, are you?"

"You're just as much to blame as I am! Yes, I was wrong to keep my identity secret—I admit it. All I wanted to do—all I ever wanted to do—was help you! But your pride is too big for your fool head. Otherwise you might have realized there are those who care about you and support you and would have helped if only you'd asked. But no, you didn't stop to consider that we might be concerned by your sudden disappearance, with no explanations, no word, not even one lousy letter. And heaven help me, I have no idea why we care so much, but we do. My parents love you. I love you. And—"

Clemmie broke off her spiel when she realized what she'd just admitted. Her mouth dropped open at her slip, her face flaming with humiliation. She whirled around and fled out the door.

In shock, she heard his steps pound behind her, closing in on her, right before he grabbed her waist. His other hand then found her arm, and he spun her around to face him. "Oh no, Clemmie. You're not getting away that easy." He grabbed both her arms, and she thought he might shake her. "I want some answers. And I won't take 'later' or 'soon' this time!"

He towered over her, so close that on the overcast day she could see within his sky blue eyes the fascinating kaleidoscope of darker blue that rimmed his irises. How had he moved, even over familiar territory, so swiftly and accurately, like a wildcat pouncing on its prey? He'd lost none of his agility, none of his enthralling power that made her go weak every time he was near. If anything, those traits had become enhanced through his adversity.

Breathless, she stared up at him, feeling as lightheaded as she'd been when he kissed her. And she wanted that, wanted desperately to feel his lips claim hers and his strong arms enfold her against him. Something painful twisted inside her heart when she realized that would never happen again.

"You want answers, Joel? All right." She forced her voice to calm. "I would never have felt the need to deceive you had you behaved like a civilized human being instead of some rude, unmannerly, uncouth beast when I first came here. I didn't know you were here, not originally. I came to visit Hannah Thomas for the summer and paid Thea a visit. It was all a matter of happenstance that we met. But I knew if I told you who I was, you wouldn't have listened to a word I had to say. You would have just been angry that I'd found you and learned your secret. Tell me that's not true."

He didn't bother denying it.

"I thought so. Perhaps my methods were wrong, but my motive was pure. I wanted to show you that you weren't alone in this world and try to help you find a reason to live again. I had hoped I might convince you to have the operation, to call my parents—"

His mouth thinning, he released her and in so doing pushed her back.

"And that's the problem right there! You keep pushing away the people who care about you. As Clemmie, I wouldn't have had a chance, but as Marielle, a stranger working for you, you might have listened to me. You *did* listen to me."

Tears of angry frustration clouded her vision and leaked down her cheeks. "No one thinks you're your father's son. You're not a con artist anymore or a thief. Sometimes a person needs help, and I know my parents would gladly pay for any operation you need. They're proud of you and think of you as their own flesh and blood, their son. They love all the boys at the refuge, but you've always had a special place in their hearts because you're one of the originals, because you've come so far. Mother told me so. They would dearly love to help if you would only ask them."

"Leave it alone, Clemmie," he said gruffly, taking a brisk step from her. "Just go back home and leave me alone."

"There. There it is. Now you have your reason. And you've just proven every word I said is true." She kept her head held high, though she wanted to sink to the ground in misery. "Maybe what I did was wrong, but at least before you knew I was Clemmie and rejected me—as I knew you would, as you've just done—at least for a short time you emerged from this box of a home you've turned into a prison. At least you had one small taste of what it felt like to really live again. And it's up to you now if you're going to live on that little taste from this day forward or if you're going to take another step away from your cage and decide one small taste just wasn't enough. I really hope you make the right choice."

Her heart aching, she left him standing there. As Clemmie approached the back porch, Thea opened the screen door, her expression sympathetic. Inside the kitchen, Clemmie allowed her trembling bravado to splinter, and she collapsed in tears against her friend.

"He knows," she whispered between shaking sobs. "A–and he hates me. I've ruined everything. Oh God, help me. H–him. Us. Please help us." She whispered the prayer against Thea's shoulder. "What have I done?"

❧

Joel stomped back to the shed, the path so familiar he didn't need to count steps, though even with all the noise Clemmie made when running from him, he was surprised he'd caught her so easily, as if attuned to her every movement, even if he couldn't see them.

Moving through the door he'd left open, he frowned at the thought of entombing himself within these four walls another day. Blast the girl, she had made what he once regarded his sanctuary feel like the prison she'd called it. It didn't help that a trace of her lilac scent always lingered in the air, no matter how many hours since she'd left or how long he kept the door open to try to remove the reminder of her. The second chair at his table also bore silent testimony to her frequent presence in his home, as if she belonged there.

Strangely, without her presence, his home didn't feel. . .complete.

With a grimace, he thought about removing the chair to the porch, but as he let his fingers trail the table to guide him, they bumped against two books she'd left behind in her haste. The smaller one on top was undoubtedly the novel she'd been reading to him, and the thick, larger one beneath with the thin, rough leather cover. . .it didn't take two guesses to know its identity.

Nor could he ignore the dull ache in his chest that never went away, the need to reach out again to a God who couldn't want anything to do with him any longer. Not after his long record of mistake after mistake, each worse than the last. He was serving the penalty for his crimes, he knew that.

At times he railed at God—when the pain and despair threatened to choke him—but deep down, Joel knew he was solely to blame.

He'd been resigned to living out his purgatory on earth, but then she had come charging into his life—with her broom, dusters, and maddening doggedness.

Joel growled, shoving the books away. When he first realized her deception, he'd been furious and impatient to confront her. Now, after challenging his saintly tormentor, her words exasperated him no end.

Granted, he was wrong to have kept news of his whereabouts from the couple who'd raised him. It seemed like the best idea at the time, but he hadn't realized they'd be worried. They had so many children to look after, all with checkered pasts, he didn't think once he left their home to strike out on his own they would give him more than a fleeting thought.

And then there was Clemmie. . . .

He still worked to reconcile the woman he'd known as Marielle with the young girl he'd last seen at the refuge. There had been hints in the past weeks; he could see that now: the British phrases she sometimes used, so much like her mother's and Darcy's; her favorite story; even her familiarity with him from the start and her bossiness that daily combated a sweet nature. . . Yes, he could see Clemmie now in everything she'd done. But he could also see the woman she'd become, because it was that woman he had come to know.

And she had told him she loved him.

It hadn't been difficult to see her infatuation with him when she was a child, and he wondered if she still felt that same little-girl adoration. But how could she? He had been worse than an ogre, had rarely said one kind thing to her since she'd found him. A childish fascination would have quickly crumbled in the reality of all the cruel things he'd said and done.

He was still angry with her, but as the minutes passed, he grew calmer, remembering all she'd said to him, the reasons she'd given for her ruse. And she'd been correct; he would have sent her packing the moment he learned the truth.

But something had happened since then. . . .

She had felt familiar to him from the start, soon making him feel at ease where no other woman had, especially since the accident. As a child, she'd done the same. A bond of friendship had formed between them, despite their age difference, and he didn't have to pretend to be someone he wasn't around her. His chums at the refuge had looked up to him, making it impossible to confide in them when he felt in the doldrums, since they'd regarded him as a leader who couldn't fail. And that was part of the problem. His accursed pride made it impossible to contact anyone at the farm with news of what he'd become. A blind sinner. Clemmie may have hero-worshipped him as a little girl. . .but she'd also been genuine, letting him be who he truly was.

And she had not changed as a young woman.

The walk to Herbert's house wasn't familiar to Joel, so he counted steps, knowing Herbert kept the level ground free of debris. As long as that wretched cat didn't run across his path, he would have no problems.

He heard the women's voices through the kitchen window Thea had left open and felt reassured he wasn't too late. He knocked twice in warning then opened the kitchen door. A hush settled over the room, Clemmie's subdued sniffling the only sound.

"I'll just go check in on Loretta," Thea said, her steps hurrying from the room.

Joel appreciated her effort to give them privacy but didn't want to risk any chance of being overheard. "You and I need to talk."

"Look. . . ." Clemmie's voice trembled. "I know I was wrong, and I'm sorry. A thousand times over, I'm sorry. I'm not sure what else you want me to say, except I hope one day you can forgive me for—"

He put up a hand to silence her.

"Will you come outside with me?" He sensed her hesitation. "You had your turn to speak. Now there's something I need to say."

He thought she might never answer. "A–all right."

He heard the rustle of her skirt and the slight skid of the chair on the floor. He waited until she approached then stepped aside to let her precede him.

Chapter 13

There should be an apple tree beyond the shed. With a tire swing for the girls. Herbert told me about it."

Clemmie blinked in stunned amazement. Talk of apple trees was the last thing she'd expected Joel to say. "Yes?"

"Guide me there."

She swallowed hard, grateful he couldn't see her damp cheeks. Was Joel actually asking for assistance? Gingerly taking his arm, she walked with him to the tree, not far from the edge of the woods. His hand went to the trunk, familiarizing himself with where he was, and he sank to the ground.

Clemmie remained standing and stared, openmouthed.

"Won't you join me? I seem to remember you had a fondness for the outdoors and didn't mind getting your clothes dirty."

"I didn't, when I was a little girl." Regardless, she sank beside him on the dry grass, sitting on her legs. "Joel, what's this about?"

His sightless blue eyes seemed to stare at the horizon, his expression undergoing a swift change. He looked very sad, and Clemmie held her breath.

"When I was in the service, I made friends with another sailor in my unit whose term ended the same time as mine. His father owned a lumber company, and he convinced me to get a job with him when our time was up."

Clemmie listened, her eyes wide. Joel was talking to her? Did this mean he'd forgiven her?

"Things went well for a while; then his father lost the company. In that time, I'd. . .well, I met up with some people—friends of Jim's—and got into some trouble." He sighed. "I'm not going about this very well, am I? I've never told anyone all of it, not even Herbert."

Clemmie's amazement grew. He'd chosen to *confide* in her?

"I started gambling. Heavily. Drinking. Carousing in town with the fellows. Used up most of my income. Jim did, too. He met a girl he fell hard for, wanted to marry her and live the honest life—and I kept pushing him to go on our wild binges. The accident was my fault. The weekend before his wedding, I convinced him to do one more night on the town. She didn't want him to. He held back, but I persisted till he gave in. Him and two of our pals. . ." His words came bitter, low. Tears filmed his eyes. "I wish to God that He would let me live that night over! That I could go back and change everything. . ."

Clemmie held her hand hard in an effort not to touch him in comfort. She sensed he needed physical distance in order to say what had been burdening his heart for over a year.

"I had cracked a joke—you know me, funny man Joel—and he looked away from the road. At me. I still remember him laughing. A deer ran in front of the car. One of the guys cried out a warning. Jim swerved and went over an embankment. That's the last I remember seeing any of them. I woke up in a hospital and learned my friends all died in the crash. I got thrown from the car but have no idea how I survived."

Clemmie's heart felt ripped in two by his pain. Something occurred to her. "Oh, but Joel, you know it wasn't your fault, don't you—"

He put up a hand to silence her.

"After I was released from the hospital, I visited his mother to express my regrets. I learned his fiancée tried to overdose. It seems she was pregnant with his kid. They admitted her to a mental facility to get help. She lost the baby."

Clemmie could scarcely breathe from the painful pressure in her chest. Oh, so much made sense now! So much. . .

"That's why you didn't go through with the operation," she whispered. "It wasn't just about money, about asking my parents for help. You didn't feel you deserved it."

"All of it, Clemmie—all of it was my fault. From the start. I didn't want your parents to know what kind of man I'd become and be ashamed and sorry they ever knew me. I've failed so much in life—I didn't want them to know I'd done it again. I felt this was God's punishment. That's a big part of why I didn't pursue an operation. I felt I didn't have the right to see when others had died. So now you know. And now you can understand why I can't do it."

Glad he couldn't see the tears that ran down her cheeks, she worked to keep her voice even. "Joel, that's not God's way. He wouldn't hurt you like that. You're not to blame! You can't help it that a deer ran across the road or that your friend wasn't paying attention at that precise moment. No more than my mother could help it when she found herself trapped in a relationship with an abusive con man who forced her to assist him in taking Lady Annabelle's necklace on the *Titanic*. No more than Darcy could help it when she was a lost little girl fending for herself in London's streets and doing anything she could to survive, even if that meant stealing."

"Ah, but there's a difference, Clemmie." His tone came wry. "They didn't know better. I did. And your mother was trying to protect her life."

"I still say, God isn't like that. He doesn't want you to suffer, to make your own penance by living in a box, refusing the chance to see again. You're repentant for your actions. God can and will and does forgive you, Joel—but will you forgive yourself?"

"What right do I have to see, when Jim's mother will never have her son back?"

"Does she blame you for the accident?"

He grew quiet. "No."

"Then why should you?"

At her soft words, he heaved a weary sigh. "There were others—"

"Grown men with the ability to make their own choices. And the woman, his fiancée. . .if she would try something so horrible as that, who's to say she didn't already have considerable problems?"

The slightest smile tugged the corners of his mouth. "You sound like your mother."

"Is that a bad thing?"

"I'll get back to you on that."

She smiled through her tears. Not exactly a reassurance but his old teasing manner suggested there would be future encounters between them, allowing the light of her dream to flicker again.

However it had happened, whatever his reasons, Joel had reconciled with her.

She wouldn't ask for explanations; she would thank God for His merciful hand that had once again intervened to mend the outcome of her own foolish mistakes.

❧

"Out twice in one week?" Herbert's voice shocked Joel who'd been so absorbed in trying to fasten his tie he hadn't heard his steps creak on the porch. "That's one for Guinness, isn't it?"

"Will you just help me tie this blasted thing?" Joel whipped the ends from the mangled mess of the knot he could feel with his fingertips. He hadn't worn a tie in over a year. Even with sight, he'd been lousy in the art of knotting one.

"I'm not much better, but I'll give it a go." Herbert's steps came closer. He took the ends from Joel's hands and began the intricate steps of the accursed rite that polite society demanded. "So what's the occasion for the glad rags? I'd forgotten you owned anything so nifty."

"The bazaar." Joel said the words as if it was an execution chamber.

"Oh that. You're going?"

"You're not?"

"Duty calls, old boy. I must head to the newspaper office. I was just coming by to see if you needed anything." He tugged the tie sharply, pushing the knot up to Joel's neck. "Clemmie talk you into it?"

"I can't believe she did. Again."

Herbert chuckled. "You're just putty in her hands."

Joel shoved Herbert's hands away and made the final adjustment himself. "That's not funny."

"Oh, so you're not?" Herbert made a disbelieving sound in his throat. "That gal has had you wound around her little finger ever since she was old enough to say your name—before that even. Now it's worse."

"You're all wet," Joel grumbled. "You have no idea what you're gabbing about."

"No? All of us were sure you'd shoot through the roof once you learned the truth. Not only did you not barricade yourself inside and refuse to see her again—you did the exact opposite. Actually left your porch, went off somewhere with her for a good half hour, and came back as friends. Don't get me wrong—I think it's great you recovered so fast. But it's not what we expected."

"I was angry at first, sure. Who wouldn't be? But to realize it was Clemmie, that someone from the past cared enough to do something like that. . . It didn't bother me like I thought it might. Besides, what right do I have to hold a grudge after all the grief I've caused others?"

"My, my," Herbert said in awe. "Clemmie must be a miracle worker for you to talk like that. Joel Litton: sinner turned saint."

Joel grunted. "Will you knock it off? I'm hardly a saint."

"Hmm. Offer still stands, you know. The one I've issued again and again. Now that you're out and about and have no excuses, come with us to church Sunday."

"Clemmie asked me, too." Joel grew somber. "I can't see how God would want me in His house after all this time."

"Well, that's where *you're* all wet."

"Yeah, maybe, but not in the way you mean. I burned my bridges when I turned my back on Him."

"Did you? Turned your back completely? I don't think so. There's a sadness in your voice when you say that, Joel. . . Remember what Darcy used to tell us: 'There isn't a bridge God can't rebuild, if you'll let Him be the carpenter.'"

"Actually she said 'ain't a bridge.'"

"And Brent winced every time she used bad grammar or her cockney accent."

Herbert's reminder caused Joel to crack a smile. "They did make an odd sort of couple."

"Speaking of couples. . ."

"Don't say it," Joel warned, sensing what was coming.

"You two make a nifty one."

Joel sighed. "I'm blind."

"Whether you can or can't see doesn't seem to make one bit of difference in Clemmie wanting to be with you."

"There is the age difference. Twelve years."

"She's not a kid anymore. Unless age is a problem for you."

"Just drop it." It wasn't a problem; he'd known her age when he first kissed her—just not that she was Clemmie. At first it felt odd to realize the girl he'd considered a kid sister was the young woman he'd kissed and who had made him feel emotions deeper than he'd known before. But because of all his present obstacles, Joel had not given much thought to developing a romantic relationship. He held his arms out to the sides. "Will I pass?"

"Hmm. Well, if the fashionable new look for society is one brown sock and one black, you look swell."

"Funny." Joel didn't take him seriously, since he owned only one color.

A light step on the porch followed by the sudden aroma of lilacs alerted him to her presence.

"Joel. . . ?"

Strange that his breath should come short and his heart so suddenly clench at the sound of her soft, husky voice, when he'd heard it for weeks.

He turned to face her, and she gave a little gasp.

Chapter 14

"Is something wrong?" Joel asked.

"Wrong?" Clemmie worked to keep her voice natural. The sudden sight of him always took her breath away, but she really had to get a grip on her emotions. "Nothing's wrong. I came a little early. I hope that's all right. I can wait on the porch."

"No need. We're done here." Joel's face gave nothing away, and she wondered what the two men had been discussing. She had the oddest feeling the subject had been her.

Herbert smiled. "I need to get to work. Have fun at the bazaar."

"Hannah's mother lent her chauffeur again if you'd like us to give you a lift."

"I enjoy the walk. Helps clear my head. Thanks all the same, Clemmie."

Once Herbert left, her footsteps moved farther into the shed. "You look very nice."

Joel's answering smile was grim. "I wish I could offer you the same compliment."

Oh no! He isn't in another of his black moods again, is he?

Quickly she closed the distance. "I brought you something. Take a seat."

"Is there time?"

"I told you I came a little early." She pushed the cigar box into his hands. "Do you remember this?"

A puzzled expression crossed his handsome features. He lifted the wooden lid, his fingertips warily searching the interior. A delighted smile suddenly flashed across his face, causing Clemmie to haul in another swift intake of breath at the pleasant change it made to his entire being.

"My boyhood treasures!" He withdrew an iridescent blue black feather of a jay, his forefinger tracing its soft edge. "You kept it all this time?" His tone came wondering.

"Of course. You asked me to keep it safe before you left for the service. Since you know who I am now, I thought you should have it back."

His smile faded into gentle melancholy. "Thank you, Clemmie. I don't know what to say."

She stared in wonder, noting moisture filmed his eyes. Never had she thought her return of his trinkets would affect him so deeply. She wished now she'd brought them earlier in the week, at a time when she and Joel didn't have to be anywhere and he could spend as much time reminiscing as he liked. But she'd promised Hannah she would attend and didn't want to disappoint her friend either.

"We should probably leave soon," she said reluctantly.

"Of course." His smile disappeared as he set the box on the table. "You really don't want to do this, do you?"

"Can you blame me?"

"You survived the fair. Even enjoyed it."

"Yes, among strangers and those who already knew—of this." He motioned to his eyes with an impatient jerk of his hand.

"Hannah knows. And her mother. They don't think any less of you."

"They haven't seen me yet. It's bound to be awkward."

Clemmie hissed an annoyed breath. Talk about awkward! Sometimes he could be so difficult.

"If your present condition bothers you so much, you should have the operation."

"I told you why I can't."

"And I told you why that's rubbish. God doesn't want you to suffer, no more than any of us want you to suffer."

He shook his head in skepticism.

"Remember the thief on the cross? The one crucified next to Jesus? That thief deserved punishment and suffering. But when he asked Jesus to remember him when He went to paradise, Jesus told the thief that he would be with Him that day. You've suffered, too, Joel. A great deal. And if you're bound and determined to believe that you deserve to carry out some crazy penance for what happened to your friends, well then, I should think that penance is long over and you've paid your debt in full. Now it's time to forget the past and turn back to God. He's never forgotten you."

Unable to bear another negative response, she moved out onto the porch to wait. No more than a minute passed before he joined her. He remained silent, his face a tense mask. But he took her arm, and together they went to the waiting car.

The ride remained silent, scrambling Clemmie's nerves, but she didn't dare speak. She didn't want further discord, and clearly Joel was upset with her.

The bazaar was crowded, held inside a huge room of a civic building Hannah's mother had rented, and Clemmie marveled that not one foot of unused space appeared visible. Everywhere—against the walls, in the center of the great room—stood antiques, knickknacks, useful and decorative objects, and some modern items as well. All of them were itemized, along with a description of their use neatly printed on each attached yellow tag—very helpful on some of the more unusual antiques, which at first glance had no purpose Clemmie could identify.

To a passing stranger, she and Joel might look like a couple in love, as close as they walked, but Clemmie knew better. For whatever reason, Joel had decided not to bring his cane, and he stuck to Clemmie like glue, holding her arm tightly. She made sure to point out each step or problem in the path that could hamper him.

They stopped walking with the crowd so Clemmie could inspect a cuckoo clock, something for which Darcy had often expressed a fondness, thinking the little bird that popped out "quite a corker."

"Clemmie!" Hannah practically squealed. "I thought you'd never come. Joel, hi." Her tone went shy and girlish as she looked his way. "You may not remember me, but I'm Hannah from the refuge. Bill and Sarah's daughter."

"Of course I remember you." He gave her a kind smile. "Though you were just a little thing before I left. Seems you've grown up, too."

Hannah giggled. If Joel could see the manner in which the cute brunette prettily blushed, Clemmie felt sure he wouldn't worry so about how others perceived him. Blind or with sight, Joel still had the ability to turn every young woman's head and make them act like little more than besotted schoolgirls. Had she been that bad as a child? With a flush of warmth, she realized she'd been worse, though she'd also been able to talk to him on a sensible level, not chattering away nervously as Hannah now did. Of course Hannah always had been a chatterbox.

"Mother will be so pleased to see you. What a surprise to learn you've lived here all this time. And, oh, you simply must come to the church picnic. They're holding it by the lake, and there will be croquet and plenty to eat and boating. . . ."

Sensing Joel withdraw at the mention of *church* just by the tensing of his muscles beneath her fingers, Clemmie was half-tempted to cover her free hand over her young friend's mouth. Instead she widened her eyes and raised her brows as a signal to stop. Hannah got the message.

"Oh, but just listen to me carrying on. I really should get back to work. Were you thinking of buying that cuckoo clock?"

"Yes. For Darcy. Her birthday is in two months. But I haven't decided. . . ." With regard to the benefit's good cause and the condition of the piece, the asked-for five dollars wasn't steep, but Clemmie didn't have much money left, not after buying the ingredients for Joel's special dinner, as well as a new hat and gloves for herself to wear to church. Her old ones had worn dreadfully, something sweet-but-blunt Hannah had pointed out her first Sunday when she'd dressed for the church meeting.

"If it's for Darcy, I'm sure Mama would agree to knocking off a dollar or two. Darcy's always been such a lamb to us, and she helped Mama and Papa plenty when they first came from the island all those years ago."

"You're certain?"

"If there's a problem, I'll chip in the difference."

"Thank you, Hannah. You're a dear." Clemmie unsnapped her purse and pulled out three bills, which Hannah took with another smile at Joel then Clemmie, as if she approved.

Once Hannah left, Joel spoke. "Is there anything else you wanted to see?" To her surprise, he took the clock from her and tucked it under his free arm. Clearly he wanted to leave. Her mission accomplished, she longed for some place more quiet as well.

"No. We can go now."

His nod clearly relieved, they moved together toward the exit.

"Joel Litton, as I live and breathe," a sweet feminine voice said. A classy blond moved before him and put a light hand to his sleeve. He jerked, and Clemmie's gratitude that he hadn't dropped the clock barely eclipsed a surge of jealousy.

"Sheridan?"

She laughed brightly. "Yes, it's me. I'm glad you remember." She glanced at Clemmie, not one ounce of jealousy in her eyes, though Clemmie couldn't say the same for her own. "Hello, I'm Sheridan Wallace. An old friend of Joel's." She again looked at him. "Who's been a very naughty boy for not letting anyone know he was in town. Paisley told me, and when she did, I couldn't believe it. But here you are."

"Yes, here I am." Joel's voice sounded grim. "Did she also tell you I'm blind?"

Clemmie realized his condition might not be apparent, since he carried no cane.

No shock crossed Sheridan's elegant features. "She did." Her manner became quiet and concerned. "And I'm very sorry to hear that happened to you, so very sorry. But tell me, where are you staying? Paisley mentioned you were with Herbert and his family. Surely you're not living there?"

She moved into the subject with such skill, making it clear she didn't consider his blindness a flaw. Clemmie wanted to hate her, just because of what the woman had once been to Joel, but found she couldn't bear such an immature grudge.

"Actually, I am." Joel's expression eased, and he smiled. "In his shed, if you can believe that."

Sheridan's big baby blues grew wider. "Oh, Joel, tell me you're not serious? Doesn't he have enough rooms in his house? I hate to think of you all alone in a cold shed with the spiders and rats—"

Joel laughed. "No rats. There are mice." His voice teased. "But it was my choice."

"But why? That's simply ridiculous."

Clemmie looked back and forth between them, feeling like an outsider watching a Ping-Pong match as they conversed. She thought Sheridan would never go away.

"I would love to stand here chatting all afternoon and catch up, but I have to get back. I've been on a break."

"You're working at the bazaar?" Clemmie asked in surprise.

"My mother is on the women's committee. Do you know Sarah Thomas? She runs it."

"She's my friend Hannah's mother. I'm staying with them for the summer."

"Really? My mother and her mother are best friends."

"Really?" Clemmie's tone lacked Sheridan's enthusiasm. "Small world."

"Isn't it? Listen, we simply must all get together sometime soon. Are you going to the church picnic next Sunday?"

"You go to their church, too?" Clemmie's heart dropped another level. "I've never seen you."

"We sit in the balcony."

"Oh."

"Well, if you'll be at the picnic, we must talk more then. I really have to go."

"I look forward to catching up," Joel said with a smile.

Clemmie gave him a sharp look, one which, of course, he couldn't see and she couldn't help. She practically bit her tongue in two so she wouldn't spout anything that might make her seem green-eyed with envy. Because, she realized with a grimace of self-loathing, that's exactly what she was.

❧

Clemmie remained quiet the entire drive back, and Joel wondered what bothered her. To try lightening the atmosphere, since he knew he'd brought about enough dark moods, he decided to share with her a decision he'd reached.

"Next Sunday, I'd like to go to church with you. Would you mind?"

She gasped. "Of course not, but after the way you acted before the bazaar, I, well. . .I must say I'm surprised. What changed your mind?"

He expected that question but not the tightness in her voice. Wasn't she pleased? She'd been bugging him for weeks to attend. "Between you and Herbert, I've been getting an earful. I guess something sank in. It doesn't mean I've changed my mind about everything, but I've been around crowds twice now and survived."

Actually those who knew him hadn't treated him much differently at all. Maybe at first he'd noticed a slight awkwardness and uncertainty about how to proceed because, he assumed, no one wanted to injure his feelings. On both occasions the discomfort had faded, if not disappeared altogether. And those he didn't know, well, he didn't really care what they thought. Clemmie had been right about that, too.

"Maybe I'm ready to take that next step," he added when she didn't respond.

"Then I'm honestly happy to hear it." Her tone became softer. "I'm sure you'll find it a lovely place. Since I've been there, I've found the people to be kind and caring. But we don't have to go to that picnic afterward if you don't want to."

"Would you rather we didn't?"

"No. It's just. . .I understand if you don't want to."

"I'll think about it."

He had hoped his answer would have eased the tension; instead, the resulting silence felt thicker than before.

Chapter 15

I'm a terrible person, Hannah."

Her friend moved into view behind Clemmie, who stared soulfully at her image, trying to tame her wild waves with a comb. She gave up, dropping her arms to her sides.

"Why would you say such a thing?" Hannah's eyes were curious.

"Because it's true?" Clemmie slumped in the vanity chair. "This last week, Operation Save Joel has undergone significant improvement. He doesn't always give negative comebacks when I talk about his condition or suggest that he can enjoy life again. He's become more positive, nicer to be around."

"I must admit I agree from the little I saw of him. He's a real sheik! That man and the man you described to me after your first day there are poles apart! Still, I couldn't believe it when you told me he wanted to go to the church picnic. You've made remarkable progress!"

"Yes."

"So why so glum? You should be dancing for joy."

Clemmie gave a wry grin. "I question his motives for his sudden change of heart. Instead of accepting it at face value and being happy, I wonder if it's because of his old girlfriend. That's what makes me horrible."

Hannah put a hand to Clemmie's shoulder, looking at her in the mirror. "It doesn't make you horrible. It makes you human."

"If only she were mean and nasty, I wouldn't feel so bad."

"But she's not?"

"You tell me. You probably know her. Sheridan Wallace. Her mother is a friend of your mother's."

Hannah's eyes went huge. "Sheridan is Joel's old girlfriend?" A sympathetic frown creased her brow. "Oh, yes. I can see your problem. She's tops. Very nice to everyone."

"Great," Clemmie said unenthusiastically. "You're a fan, too."

"Has Joel expressed. . .feelings for you?"

Clemmie hesitated. She couldn't tell her young friend about the kisses; they were too special to share, even with Hannah. "Nothing untoward or meaningful." On his part anyway.

"Oh good." Hannah's relief was evident. "Then I think you should just reflect on your reason for starting this whole endeavor. To help Joel learn to live again, which is exactly what you're doing."

Clemmie sighed. "You're right. I need to stop being selfish and do whatever I can to support and encourage him. Thank you for reminding me what truly matters. You're a real friend by keeping me in line. Don't take this wrong, but sometimes you seem so mature for your age."

"Mother would disagree. She doesn't like the girls I've been keeping company with, before you came. She says they're a bad influence and make me do childish things."

As Clemmie fastened her hat to her head, lowering the netting that covered the upper portion of her face, she wondered why she hadn't met them but didn't ask. She had enough to ponder.

Half an hour later, when she arrived at Herbert's, she found Joel in a pleasant mood, even offering cordial conversation to Hannah and her mother. Herbert had managed to get his car running, and he and his family followed in their Ford.

In church, Clemmie could feel Joel's tension—his body strained from where it touched hers in the crowded pew. Whether he got anything out of the message on releasing one's burdens to the Lord, she didn't know, but she felt it appropriate for his situation. They didn't spend time mingling afterward, instead driving straight to the picnic area.

"It's a beautiful day, isn't it?" he questioned almost sadly as they strolled, arm in arm, to a shady copse of trees. Today he'd brought his cane, but he still held fast to Clemmie's arm. "I can feel the warmth of the sun and smell the grass and flowers and even the water."

"You can smell water?" She knew his senses were sharpened but hadn't realized water had a smell.

"It's a cool, brisk scent. The grass is earthy but fresh. And the flowers. . ." He looked almost remorseful. "I wish I had paid more attention to the different kinds of wildflowers there are. I never cared much for them when I had my sight. They were all the same to me, except in color and shape of course. But a flower was a flower."

"Just as a rose is a rose by any other name."

An awkward silence ensued. Reminded of her duplicity, Clemmie hurried to add, "The ones we're walking among now are white and yellow. Some sort of daisies, perhaps?"

"I know the scent of roses," he answered her previous statement. "And lilacs. That's your scent. Soft and fresh. Brisk but soothing. . ."

Clemmie held her breath. Just what was he saying? Or was she reading too much into his low words?

"Joel!"

The breathless moment was disrupted as a newly familiar voice called his name. Clemmie turned to watch Sheridan's graceful approach. Even over uneven ground, she seemed to float.

"It's so wonderful to see you! I wasn't sure you were coming when we talked at the bazaar."

"I have persuasive friends."

"Oh?" Sheridan laughed and glanced at Clemmie. "Well, good for you! He can be so stubborn, can't he? Sometimes it takes a bulldozer to move him."

"Yes, he can be a cross between mule-headed and pigheaded."

"I'm here, too, ya know."

Clemmie smiled, ignoring his mock affront. "He's always been like that. We go far back. We were both children at the refuge. My parents ran the place."

"Oh! So you must be little Clemmie!" Sheridan's voice sounded pleased. "Joel told me all about you and growing up on the farm."

"Yes," she murmured, not thrilled to be referred to in such a manner.

"Clemmie and I have always been good friends."

She felt as if a weight dropped to her shoulders. By Joel's reply, of course Sheridan would understand they weren't dating. And they weren't, she reminded herself. So if he wanted to resume whatever relationship he had with the woman, Clemmie shouldn't feel betrayed.

She reminded herself of that all through the luncheon. Clemmie could barely eat the thin slice of pork—the pig donated by a wealthy church member—or the brown beans as she fought despondency. Sheridan stayed close to Joel, and given the manner in which they reminisced of past occurrences, Clemmie felt like a third wheel.

When Sheridan offered to get Joel a slab of peach pie, something else Clemmie knew he enjoyed, she gritted her teeth at the smile he gave the pretty blond, wishing his effusive thanks could have been for her instead. Indeed, he seemed quite in his element, his old gregarious nature for which he'd been greatly admired back in full strength.

Stop it, Clemmie! You're acting like a green-eyed witch, and you have no right. Just be happy he's happy. It's what you wanted.

Sheridan seemed not to notice Clemmie's tart responses to her questions or the little glares that she immediately tried to curb, and Clemmie did her best to improve her disposition, knowing it wasn't fair to either of them. But she couldn't help wishing more than once that Sheridan were a vindictive shrew and not the pleasant young woman who shared their company.

It was with great relief that Clemmie realized the picnic was coming to an end, as members of the congregation stacked dirty dishes in crates. Soon the blessed moment arrived when they made their farewells.

"It's been wonderful being with you today, Joel." Sheridan put her hand to his arm. "We really must do this again sometime. Do you still have my number?"

Clemmie wondered if her face had turned flame red due to the fire of jealousy building hotter inside.

"Not anymore, no."

"I'll give it to you."

"Won't do me much good. Can't read it, you know."

"Oh, but someone surely can read it to you if you ask. It would be better than me relying on that faulty memory of yours."

He laughed, and she joined in. Only Clemmie remained sober.

Equipped with Sheridan's number, which he'd stuffed inside his pocket, Joel walked with Clemmie to the waiting car. All through the drive back, Hannah happily chattered about a boy she'd met, but Clemmie wished for silence. Once the Rolls pulled into Herbert's drive, Joel took her hand, surprising her.

"Come with me inside Herbert's house. I have something I need to talk with you about."

"Oh, but. . ." Clemmie glanced at Hannah's mother, uncertain.

"We can send the chauffeur again," the woman assured. "Just give us a ring."

"Or Herbert could take her home, now that he has his car running," Joel assured. "Either way, you'll have a ride."

"All right."

She said a quick good-bye, sensing Joel wanted to speak before Herbert and his family returned. He'd taken them out for an ice cream soda to top off the day, a rare treat judging by the manner in which the girls had jumped up and down, squealing, when they heard his plan.

Joel used his cane to find the door and opened it for Clemmie. She preceded him inside, wondering what he had to say. She followed him to the sofa and sank beside him.

"Tell me before I burst, Joel. You're so mysterious. . . ."

"I guess I got that lesson from you," he teased.

"Joel. . . ," she warned.

"I've decided to have the operation."

Chapter 16

Clemmie grew so silent Joel could barely hear her breathe. He had thought she might squeal, like the girls often did, or display some other sign of enthusiasm since she'd been urging him for weeks to put the past behind him. Today at church, no, even before that with Clemmie, he'd begun to consider seriously the subject he'd chosen never to think of since his initial consultation with the doctor.

"Clemmie, did you hear me?" He twisted around and slid his hand on the cushion, leaning in her direction. The tips of his fingers suddenly met her hand, and she jerked back a little, as if scalded. He frowned, wondering why she acted so jumpy.

"Joel. . .I—I don't know what to say." Her voice trembled. "I'm so pleased you made this decision. Th–that you found something worthwhile to live for. . ."

Her words trailed off in a wistful fashion, and he drew his eyebrows together, confused. He moved his hand purposefully along the cushion until he found hers and covered it with his. "I wouldn't be where I am right now if it wasn't for you, Clemmie. You kept at me and wouldn't take no for an answer."

"Sometimes a stubborn will can be a blessing if you look hard enough. But only sometimes, Joel."

He chuckled. "That first part sounds like something Darcy might say."

"Actually, she did."

He heard the smile in her voice and laughed outright.

"And the last was a warning to me, hmm?"

"If you like." There was no mistaking the amusement in her voice.

He felt better now that the mysterious tension had eased but still found the next subject difficult to introduce. "Clemmie. . .about what you said regarding your parents and your grandfather. . .and. . .and helping me out—"

"Oh, they'd consider it a privilege!"

"What with these tough times we live in? And running the reformatory?"

"Grandfather's money is tied up in banks in England. My family wasn't affected like so many, and the refuge survives on the patronage of its investors. So you needn't worry, Joel."

She seemed so assured and confident Joel couldn't help but feel a spark of that same hope. "Well then, it seems I have a call to make. Would you mind getting things started?"

She gasped. "Oh—I'd love to. Are you sure Herbert won't mind?"

"He won't, and Clemmie, well, the charges will have to be reversed. I doubt Herbert could pay for the call, and I sure can't—"

Clemmie squealed as she jumped up from the sofa, keeping Joel's hand in hers and tugging him. "Oh that's no problem, I'm quite certain. Come on then! My parents will be thrilled to hear from you. I can't wait to tell them the good news—that you're here and alive. At times we did wonder. . . ."

Joel felt a niggling of guilt, again shocked that any of those at the refuge had given him more than a fleeting thought. He'd been such a trouble-maker during the majority of his time there; he'd have thought they would feel relieved to have him out of their lives for good.

She led him down the hallway to where the phone was. He heard her connect with the operator and give the number of the refuge, asking to reverse the charges. It took awhile to get through, Clemmie's toe tapping almost wearing a hole through Joel's nerves, but at last she gave a delighted laugh.

"Aunt Darcy? Is that you? . . .Yes, it's me. I have some huge news to share, but you best be sitting down. . .no—no, nothing bad. Honest. . . Well, guess who's standing here beside me?" She took his hand in hers and gave it a squeeze. "It's Joel! He's here at Herbert's. . . . Yes, yes. . .all right."

Joel felt her prod him with the receiver. "She wants to talk with you."

Joel swallowed hard, fighting down the ridiculous impulse to cower or run. He felt like a boy reprimanded and sent to his guardian's office.

"Uh, hullo."

"Joel, bless me soul! As I live and breathe, it is you. What have you been doin' with yourself all these years, ye naughty boy? Why give us such a scare?"

Through the static it felt strangely good to hear Darcy's no-nonsense words chastise him in her distinctive British accent.

"It's a long story. I, uh, was hoping to speak with Mr. Lyons."

"Not before you explain yourself, young man. Where have you been?"

"Darcy, cease with all your fluttering and let the boy talk to Stewart." Even over the static, Joel heard Brent admonish his wife. Apparently they were both listening in.

"Uh, hi, Mr. Thomas." Nearly thirty years old, Joel still felt like a school-boy talking with his teacher.

"Are you conducting yourself in an appropriate manner, Joel? You haven't blocked off any more pipes, have you?"

He laughed. Trust his old schoolmaster to say such a thing. And to remember when Joel had been the culprit behind climbing the roof and stuffing rags in the pipe of the old wood-burning stove, in the hope of getting a day free from schooling.

"No, sir. I've steered clear of all pipes."

"Good lad."

"Are you eating well?" Darcy wanted to know. "Are you getting enough to eat?"

Joel reassured her his health was fine; yes, his eating habits were normal, and yes, he really was alive and kicking. Soon Clemmie's mom came onto the line, demanding to know all of what Darcy had already asked. Finally the phone was handed to Clemmie's father.

"Hello, sir." Joel squelched the emotion that coated his throat at the familiarity of hearing so many special voices from the past. "I actually called because I have a favor to ask."

His hand still in Clemmie's, he felt her give him an encouraging squeeze. As briefly as possible, he told his former guardian the basics of what had occurred and the reason for his call.

"Whatever you need, son," he said once Joel finished. "Just say the word. Do you remember when I first met you living in the streets, trying to con me by snagging my interest in that rigged shell game? Then that gentleman had you arrested for stealing from him, and I got the judge's permission to take you with me as one of my first boys to help at the refuge?"

Joel remembered; he'd been almost nine. He couldn't help the moisture that stung his eyes and closed them.

"I told you then that I didn't want you to think of me as just your guardian. That I wanted to be a father to you and would always be there when you needed me. You had only to ask."

"Yes, sir." The evidence of tears coated his voice, making it gruff.

"I meant it then, and I mean it now. Anything, Joel. We're family. You'll always be a son to me."

If he didn't get off this phone soon, he would humiliate himself by breaking down into a binge of weeping. He couldn't remember when he had last cried. "Yes, sir. Thank you, sir. This is only a loan. I'll pay back every penny."

"I know you will, though it's not necessary."

But it was to Joel. To clear his name of the criminal lifestyle his father had passed down to him, he was determined to stand on his own two feet, to prove that he could, and to never take another penny of charity.

Clemmie's father asked for details, and Joel answered as best he could, explaining he hadn't yet been to see the doctor. The line filled with more static, the words fading out now and then and getting difficult to understand.

"Before we lose connection completely, put Clemmie on, would you, son?"

Joel gratefully handed the earpiece her way, needing a moment alone. "He wants to talk to you."

Once she took the phone, he moved back to the sofa and took a seat. He pulled his handkerchief from his suit pocket and wiped his damp lashes. Incredible. After all he'd done, after the lousy way he'd treated those at the refuge, they still held their arms out to him and called him family.

He realized then how much he had missed that. . .missed them.

He wondered if part of the reason Clemmie was able to get through to him had to do with the familiarity he'd felt toward her before knowing she was Clemmie. Had he sensed the feeling of home in her presence? His "box of a home" didn't feel the same without her there, and he knew if it weren't for his pixie angel he would be in the same dark rut. He still had areas in which he wasn't ready to move forward, still felt issues in resuming his former connection to God and issues all his own that stemmed from guilt. But he had come far in the past week alone, and Clemmie was responsible for the majority of his changed attitude.

Once she ended the call and came back to sit beside him, he spoke.

"I'd like to ask a favor of you."

"Of course, Joel. Anything. You know that." She sounded like her father, and again he felt overwhelmed by the Lyonses' generosity. As a boy he'd never appreciated it, but as a man he could see the many sacrifices her father had made and the good heart that led him to those decisions.

"Without you I wouldn't be doing this, Clemmie. It's a lot to ask, but I'd like you to go with me to the doc and"—he shrugged—"just be around through whatever happens."

"I wouldn't dream of leaving your side at a time like this."

Her fervent admission encouraged him, but he shook his head. "There's no telling how long this'll take. I know your stay here is nearing an end. You mentioned you were only staying through the summer, and summer's almost over."

"I. . .um. . ." She sounded nervous with the way she hedged. "Fact is, I already asked and received my parents' permission to stay as long as you need me here, in case it came to that. I was, um, hoping you might ask."

He smiled at her shy admission and again reached for her hand. "Clemmie, you're a true gem. I don't know what I'd do without you."

"I'll always be here for you, Joel."

✍♥

Clemmie rushed for the exit door, feeling as if a clamp squeezed her lungs; she couldn't breathe. Her excuse for needed air had been flimsy; she was sure Joel had seen through her guise and knew so when she heard the hospital door open and the taps of his cane.

With unbelievable precision, he found her where she leaned against the brick wall of the building and put his hand to her arm. "I'm sorry. I should have told you."

She wasn't sure if she was angrier with him for keeping such a dangerous fact hidden or for refusing to get help when he knew it was crucial.

She whipped around to face him. "I can't believe you, Joel. The doctor said you could have lost your life, that every day death is a possibility if something goes wrong. That whatever is causing this awful pressure to your cranium and optic nerve could push a little the wrong way and do severe damage—likely kill you. And you knew. All this time, *you knew*? Why didn't you go through the surgery before now? Why?"

She felt frustrated with both him and the doctor, who'd so matter-of-factly stated that the medical profession still remained in the dark when it came to head traumas such as Joel had suffered. At the same time, he confirmed to Joel that his erratic mood swings and severe headaches were likely related to his condition but that the operation itself was extremely risky. He could die either way. It had been the first time she realized Joel still suffered any type of headache, though he'd told the doctor he hadn't had one in over a month.

"I told you." Joel's voice was grim and quiet. "That's all I wanted at the time. To die."

Hearing him speak the words she'd just thought, Clemmie shuddered. She simply couldn't believe it. Oh, she'd heard him say it before, but she'd never believed he would go to such extremes, to neglect the value of life and refuse the surgery. She had been under the mistaken impression that the operation was a recommendation to regain his sight, not a necessity to prevent probable death. Based on what the doctor had said during the lengthy consultation, Joel was extremely lucky to be alive.

"Hey. . ." He slid his hand down her arm and found her hand, squeezing it. "If this is too much for you and you want to pull out, I'll understand."

She blinked in disbelief, staring into his eyes, which were soft with remorse. Here he'd been told that his life was at risk with every day, every minute that passed, and *he* felt bad for *her*? Of course, he'd had over a year to deal with the doctor's grim prognosis.

"Just try and get rid of me, Joel Litton. I'm no quitter. And neither are you. I'll be beside you every step of the way."

His answering smile helped to soothe the ache in her heart.

"No, Clemmie, that's one good thing that can be said about us. For all our stubborn natures, neither of us is willing to give in and concede defeat."

In the days that followed, she reminded herself of his words often.

Now understanding the severity of his condition, she didn't urge him to take part in social activities as before, but she wouldn't allow him to stay confined in his box, either. In between tests and more tests she found a peaceful spot near the lake and encouraged Joel to go there with her. Soon it became a ritual. There, they picnicked and relaxed and laughed and talked about the old days and the present ones. At the lake, they never discussed the upcoming surgery or anything related to his condition, neither of them wanting to create a damper on the peace they'd both found and shared.

Over the next two weeks Joel suffered two of his bad headaches when Clemmie came to do her usual cleaning. Her heart clenched with fear at the terrible pain he suffered. She did her best to help, putting cold compresses on his forehead, massaging his temples, and making him hot, soothing beverages that helped when her own head ached. To her chagrin, very little she did took any pain away, but he thanked her and held on to her hand like a lifeline. Often she stayed until he managed to sleep and even past then, sitting beside his bed or quietly straightening his home.

In her heart, she felt like his wife, and all she did was with the great love she felt for Joel, which only deepened as time passed. She hoped one day he might feel the same strong affection for her, though she doubted it. He hadn't kissed her once since he discovered her identity, though he did accept her hugs and often held her hand. But she resigned herself to the idea that he'd gone back to thinking of her as a kid sister. . . .

And Sheridan Wallace clearly wanted him back.

The woman had visited Joel four times since the picnic—that Clemmie knew of, because she'd been there when it happened. She wished she could loathe the elegant blond. But irony of ironies, she found herself liking Sheridan, even coming to regard her as a friend. That Sheridan and Joel got along well didn't escape Clemmie's notice, and she resolved to bury her dream once more, if she must, in order to help Joel realize his. And if that meant having Sheridan by his side, Clemmie would learn to accept his choice and only be to him what she'd always been—a friend.

No matter her firm resolution, the idea of Joel belonging to any other woman made her heart feel as if it were breaking. Somehow, she would get through the long weeks.

Somehow, she must.

Chapter 17

Hey, ole pal. What are you doing all alone? I would have thought Clemmie would be here the day before you go under the knife." Herbert greeted Joel as he approached his porch. "As a matter of fact, with the way you two have been, I'm surprised not to find her glued to your side."

Joel took Herbert's ribbing in stride. He didn't want anyone to know he was worried he wouldn't survive. That fear was uppermost in his mind.

"She went with Hannah to the train station."

"Oh, right! Her parents are coming in today, and Darcy, too, from what I hear. It'll be swell to see them again."

"Yeah. Swell."

"I see Clemmie made one of your favorite desserts again. What's eating you? No appetite?"

Joel recalled the barely touched peach pie he'd set on the porch. "Not much. Want the rest?"

"Don't mind if I do."

Joel handed Herbert the plate, and Herbert chuckled.

"Remember the days when we would fight over who would get one of Darcy's pies for her contests? Mmm. Clemmie makes them just as good. You'd be a fool to let a doll like that go," Herbert observed with his mouth full. "And you can't tell me you just care about her like a little sister either. I've seen the way you are with her."

"I'm hardly in any shape to consider a relationship right now. Thea sent you over here to keep me company so I wouldn't brood, didn't she?"

"And then there's Sheridan. What a knockout—and sweet as Christmas candy, to boot. She's made it as obvious as the nose on your face that she's stuck on you, coming here like she does to visit and flagging you down at church every week."

"I can't see my nose, and I told you I'm not interested."

"To pass up either one of them, you must be bloodless or dead."

"No, but come tomorrow, check again."

"Hey now, don't go talking like that." Herbert's effusiveness dissolved into gruff sincerity. "You have a team of people praying—us, Clemmie and her family, Darcy, Brent, all those at the refuge, Sheridan, Paisley, their mom,

Hannah, her mom and dad. . ."

"Okay, okay. I get the picture. Still, you never know what could happen."

"Then it's a good thing you've made things right with your Maker, wouldn't you say?"

Joel couldn't agree more. He couldn't say what led him to reach out to God again—maybe a conglomeration of all that had happened in the past two months. One morning as he sat alone before Clemmie arrived, he felt so empty, so bleak, and he recalled much of the encouragement she'd given and what he had recently heard the pastor say. God's love was eternal. Nothing Joel could do would prevent God from loving him, and he'd seen a shadow of such love in the way Clemmie's father had treated him, had always treated him, no matter how badly Joel had behaved. Perhaps that had been the last blow needed to break the stony barrier that had encased his heart.

"Yes," he told Herbert, "I know the Lord will be with me. And if I wake up and see your ugly mug, then I'll know it wasn't my time to go yet. And if I wake up and see the angels and the face of God. . . Well, either way I can't lose, can I?"

Herbert clapped him on the shoulder. "That's the spirit! Just don't let Clemmie hear you talk of dying."

"No, I'd never hear the end of it. This has really hit her hard."

"She cares a lot about you."

"I know." Joel grew somber.

"Sheridan, too, for that matter. You were so afraid of stepping foot off the property, afraid to be seen and of what people would think. Now you have two sweet gals eager to wear your ring on their finger. A fella should be so lucky."

"You have no reason to complain. Thea is one great lady to put up with the likes of you. And me."

"Don't I know it? I suppose I should share the news, since it'll be obvious to everyone soon, but we're getting another little Miller this winter."

Joel's smile was genuine. "Well, what do you know? Congratulations, buddy."

"And you need to stick around longer so *all* our children can get to know their uncle Joel. The girls think the world of you, though I can't say why. You really can be incorrigible at times—my word, now I sound like our old schoolmaster!"

Joel snorted a laugh at his friend's nutty impersonation of Brent. Over the past few weeks he'd spent time with Herbert's daughters, telling them stories of his and Herbert's childhood at the refuge. He'd even learned to tolerate their wretched cat, which had developed a habit of making its home on his lap. Absentmindedly, his hand went to the silky soft fur and stroked it, a rumbling purr soon following.

"You know, old buddy, you're really not half bad with children. Maybe you should consider settling down and raising your own family."

Herbert clearly wasn't going to quit. Rather than go into both reasons again: that he couldn't ask a woman to share his life when he was out of work and that he didn't know from day to day if he'd be around long enough to put that ring on her finger, Joel settled for reason A.

"If the operation's a success, I'll need to find a job and a decent place to live. No offense, old pal, but no way am I going to continue living out my days in this shed."

"Good. And you're right. Women like windows. This place hasn't a one. They want plenty of space to decorate for all the knickknacks they bring home, too."

"Will you just get out of here?"

Herbert chuckled. "Seriously, I'll talk to my boss. I'm sure he'll take you back. He likes you. Said it was a shame to lose such a good worker. Said you might even have the makings of becoming a journalist one day."

"Mr. Thomas would disagree. I was one of his worst pupils when it came to writing reports and those awful poems." This wasn't the first time Herbert had told Joel their boss's opinion of his potential, but before, Joel hadn't cared. Now he felt that soft emotion clutch his insides again, making him tear up—something that had been happening a lot of late.

"Herbert!" Thea called from the back porch. "I need you a minute, honey."

Herbert groaned. "Duty calls. I just hope it's not about that silly painting she got at the bazaar. That woman must have made me move it fifty times already, to find the 'perfect spot.' I'm beginning to think one doesn't exist."

Joel smiled. "Thank you again, my friend. For everything. I know we rib each other a lot and don't always get along, but you've been a pal, helping me out like you have. I don't know how I would have made it without you."

"You're not going to start waxing poetic and get all sappy on me?" Herbert's mocking horror teased, but Joel heard the softness clutch his voice, proof he was also getting emotional.

"Aw, go on and get out of here before I take it all back."

"Yup, there's the Joel I know so well. But this isn't good-bye, so don't treat it like one. That said, now I'm going to get sappy—you've always been like a big brother to me. Even if you were a worm at times."

Joel laughed. "Would you just go? And Herbert," he added once he heard his friend's steps move off the porch and to the grass. "Feeling's mutual. On both counts."

Herbert's laughter as he departed made Joel smile again.

No matter what happened on the operating table, God had blessed him with a caring family at the refuge, parents who were his not by blood but by heart, and good friends. Not everyone could claim so much to be thankful for.

At least he'd had that.

❧

"Clemmie, luv, stop yer pacing before you wear a trail in the floor."

She turned toward Darcy who sat on one of several benches against the wall in the stark, white hospital corridor where relatives waited while loved ones were in the operating room. "It's been hours. Why haven't we heard anything by now?"

Her mother came up behind and hugged her. "The doctor said surgery such as his could last quite a long time, dear. There's nothing unusual about that." Clemmie felt grateful for her family's support, sure she would have fallen apart if they weren't there. She settled her head back against her mother's shoulder, holding on to the arms she'd looped around her waist. "You need to curb that impatient streak of yours and settle down, sweetheart."

"I know I should, but I just can't, Mama. This is Joel we're talking about."

"I know. And you love him, don't you? Not like a brother but as something much more."

"I've always loved him," Clemmie admitted. "But it's different from when I was a child. It's grown deeper now that I'm a woman. Matured and changed. And no, not like a brother at all." She flushed, remembering his passionate kisses.

"And how does he feel about you?"

"That's the question of the century," she replied dismally. "I wish I knew. At times I think he still regards me like a little sis and good friend. At other times I think he wishes we had more—or maybe that's my own wishful thinking?" She sighed. "I should just be grateful he didn't boot me out the door when I let him believe I was someone else and he found out I wasn't." Her words, upon hearing them, made little sense, but she felt emotionally drained and didn't bother to clarify. Nor had she slept much the night before, anxious for Joel.

"That. . .was a mistake," her mother gently admonished. "But I understand you didn't mean harm. I've done a good many things I wish I hadn't. A good many. But God always intervened when I asked Him to mend things, just like He did for you. I still wish to this day I'd never met Eric. . .yet if I never had, he might not be where he is, with his own loving family, of all things, and working in his soup kitchen mission. God certainly has a peculiar way of working things out."

Clemmie turned to look at her mother and noticed new lines of strain etched around her mouth and between her brows. Yet with her glowing skin, dark auburn hair, and pale green eyes, she had an unearthly beauty not many women did. "Have you talked to him recently?" She still found it odd that her mother and the villain who'd made her life a living purgatory, even trying to kill her more than once, had actually made amends.

"Just the yearly Christmas cards, as you know, compliments of his wife, I would imagine. Nothing more. I understand he and Bill Thomas still correspond by letter and the telephone. They were gangsters together in the old life, working for that awful Piccoli man. Oh, it just seems so strange talking about those horrid days in such a calm fashion. Time truly heals all wounds, and God does work miracles. He can for Joel, too."

"I know, Mama. Still, it's so hard."

"What you need is an amusing tale to take your mind off things." Darcy patted the empty chair next to her. "Come sit beside me, luv, and let me tell you what mischief that new boy Quentin has been up to now."

"Darcy," her mother warned with a slight laugh mixed with a groan. "It's not nice to tell tales."

"And you don't think she'll be gettin' an earful on her return? He didn't exactly do his misdeeds in private, Charleigh. Maybe she can give us an idea of how to get through to him." Darcy smiled at Clemmie while continuing to talk to her mother. "She always did have such a good head on her shoulders."

Except when it came to her own choices. Still, it did help hearing about the wild antics of the new young reformer, what the refuge's problem children called themselves. In between spurts of quiet laughter over the food fight he'd caused and shocked horror that he'd almost burned down the woodshed after experimenting with a cigar he'd snatched from Grandfather's box, with his own gang of boys who looked up to him, Clemmie realized how much like Joel the new boy was.

Soon her father, Hannah, and Hannah's parents returned with sandwiches; and Clemmie felt relieved and surprised that the nurses didn't throw them out, their number had become so large. They kept their voices to a dull murmur, respecting where they were. Clemmie's heart clenched in gratitude when her father gathered them all around to pray for Joel. She knew her father could see past her false smiles and wavering courage. He had always been able to read her well.

Hannah sat close and held her hand, offering reassurances while the hands of the clock slowly made their revolutions.

Once.

Twice.

Again.

At last a nurse came forward, and Clemmie jumped to her feet. "Joel Litton—how. . .how is he?"

"Your friend made it through surgery."

Clemmie felt as if she might fall and held strongly to Hannah's arm. "Can I see him?"

"Not until tomorrow. He's under anesthesia and will be for some time."

She didn't add what Clemmie feared most—*if he wakes up.*

"Please. I just want a peek. I won't go inside."

"He won't know you're there."

"I don't care. Please. . ."

"It's against hospital policy. . . ." The nurse's eyes gentled as if she could sense Clemmie's urgency to see for herself. "All right. Just a quick peek through the door."

"Thank you."

She followed the nurse down a series of corridors before they stopped at a room. The nurse smiled and inclined her head, opening the door.

The area was dark, but Clemmie could see his form on the bed. The top of his head and his eyes were swathed in white bandages. From the steady rise and fall of his chest, she knew what the nurse told her must be true.

Joel was alive; he had survived the dangerous operation.

"Thank You, God," she whispered and, not caring what the nurse might think, blew Joel a soft, trembling kiss before turning to rejoin her family.

Chapter 18

J oel awoke to familiar dark. And pain. Excruciating pain, more severe than
any headache; he groaned in agony. It took awhile to remember where he
was and why. The voices of those in his room—nurses? doctors?—soon
became blurred, and he began to feel woozy.

He woke off and on, with no idea how much time passed—minutes?
Hours? Days? It was too much trouble to figure out. In his more lucid moments, he listened to the murmuring voices, his sole connection to reality,
and tried to figure out their identity. Soon a soft, husky one grew familiar to
him, and he reached out.

"Clemmie?" he rasped.

Instantly, her soft, warm hand wrapped around his, and he relaxed.

"I'm here, Joel. Is the pain very bad?"

"Awful."

"Perhaps you need more morphine. Nurse?"

"Wait, no. . .before they dope me up again. . .and I forget everything. . .
thank you."

"You don't have to keep thanking me. I want to be here."

"How long. . ."

"Five days since the surgery. They. . .they weren't sure you'd wake up."

He heard the tightness of tears clutch her voice as she fought them back.

"I'm here."

"Thank God."

He heard the nurse approach and felt Clemmie begin to move away. He
tightened his hold on her hand. "Don't go."

Her other hand covered his. "I won't."

His lucidity gave way to the drug pulling him back into the dark of oblivion.

So his life progressed. He awoke at times more aware, at other times feeling as if he were in a strange dream that made no sense. Sometimes the pain
was unbearable. Others, it was more manageable, and on those days, Clemmie read to him from her book, a little at a time. He couldn't always follow
the story, but just the sound of her low, gentle voice soothed him. By the time
she reached the end of the novel, he was able to understand and felt satisfied
that Christian had met his goal and found God.

Sheridan also came to visit, as kind and concerned as Clemmie, and she often kissed his cheek in parting, telling him he must rest and get better. She would make some man a fine wife one day, he thought after one of her visits.

At times the drug tricked his mind and he felt confused. He was sure he'd called Sheridan Clemmie more than once and had done the same to Clemmie. He just hoped both women understood if he did and weren't hurt by his lack of clear thinking.

✍

Clemmie felt breathless after her run up the stairs. How, oh how could she have overslept? It was past noon!

She hurried along the corridor to Joel's room, stopping short at the sight of Sheridan sitting close to him, on the edge of his bed.

"You know I'm always here for you, Joel," Clemmie heard her say.

"Don't leave. . .I was a fool, not to know. . .not to admit how I feel. . . ."

"Shhh. It's all right. You rest now. I'm not going anywhere."

"I want you with me. . .always. . .a lifetime."

Clemmie watched in stricken horror as Sheridan took his hand in hers and bent to touch her lips to his, keeping them fixed there.

Standing in utter shock, Clemmie felt as if she'd been socked in the gut, worse than any injury from the fights she'd been in as a little tomboy. Quickly, lest Sheridan notice her, she backed away from the door and retraced her way to the entrance, her steps growing faster until she was almost at a run. Tears blinded her as she rushed from the building and hurried to cross the street. A piercing squeal of brakes made her stop in horror when she realized an oncoming car came only a few feet from hitting her.

Shakily, she stepped back to the curb. Once the glowering driver passed, she made her way across, careful this time, her heart so heavy she wasn't sure how she could walk with the weight of her understanding. Joel had clearly made his choice. She had known this could happen the moment she laid eyes on Sheridan and realized they'd once been more than friends, and she must come to terms with his decision.

But the sight of their kiss brought such fiery pain to her chest she didn't see how she'd be able to visit again, not with Sheridan there. And from the loving and personal revelations she'd heard, Joel's choice of a girlfriend never planned on leaving his side.

Clemmie had promised him she would be with him through the entire ordeal, and she had. But clearly he didn't need her anymore.

✍

"I can't believe you're going home in less than a week!" Hannah complained. "It seems like yesterday when you got here."

Clemmie finished looking through the box of movie star photos that were Hannah's treasure. Their perfect faces and slim bodies made her feel inferior, but she was what she was. It cheered her only a little to learn that Myrna, Claudette, and Greer were all redheads, too. She visited the movie theater only on rare occasions and had never seen their movies, though she'd heard about them, of course.

"Have you talked to Joel since he was discharged from the hospital?"

Clemmie gave her friend a sharp look. Hannah knew she hadn't.

"I hear they took the bandages off. Sheridan told me when I ran into her the other day. I figured you must know and just forgot to mention it?"

The query sounded strange, even to Clemmie's ears, since most of her days had been filled with Joel and keeping Hannah informed of almost every detail. Forgetting to mention such a huge milestone would be absurd.

"Yes, I know. I rang the hospital and learned the news from that nice nurse who let me see him after his surgery." She tried to look busy as she gathered the glossies and tapped them on her lap to straighten them. "He can see again. Isn't it wonderful?"

Hannah's hand rested over hers, stopping her agitated movements. Carefully she slipped the pictures from Clemmie's hands. "And you didn't think to tell me this amazing news?"

"I've had a lot on my mind, what with packing and such. I assumed you would hear from your mother. She mentioned she's gone to visit him. Your father, too."

Hannah shook her head at Clemmie's weak answer. "But you haven't gone to see him again, have you? Not since that day you came home from the hospital looking for all the world as if your best friend had just died."

"No. I haven't."

"Why?" Hannah insisted. "Did you two have a quarrel?"

"Nothing like that. Life doesn't always make sense, Hannah. That's something you'll learn one day." Seeing that her friend wouldn't give up, Clemmie sought a more complete explanation. "I just felt it was time he took charge of his life without my help, now that he's past the surgery."

"So you've said before—and it still doesn't make one bit of sense! He was everything to you, and now you're pushing him aside?"

Clemmie shrugged.

Hannah exhaled loudly. "I'm not a child, Clemmie. I know life doesn't always play fair, though I haven't had much to complain about. But, well, you are going to tell him good-bye before you go home, aren't you?"

"I don't know. Maybe."

"Maybe?" Hannah threw the pictures back into the box, a sign of just how frustrated she was. "If it weren't for you, he would never have had that surgery in the first place. He'd still be living alone in his box."

"He still is. Though he's been trying to find a place." She clamped her lips shut, realizing her slip.

"So you *have* been keeping tabs on him!"

"Of course. I can't just forget him. I still talk to Thea on occasion."

"Then why. . . ?"

Clemmie rose from Hannah's bed, where they'd been poring over photos for the umpteenth time since her arrival in Connecticut. "I don't want to talk about this right now—please. I think I'll take a walk by the pond. I need some fresh air."

"I'll come with you." Hannah was already putting the lid on her box and sliding off the bed.

"No, please. I—I just need time alone to think." She smiled. "Don't worry. I'll be back in time for supper."

Hannah nodded, clearly concerned, but Clemmie couldn't talk about Joel. She knew her friend was right: She couldn't leave without telling him good-bye. But she dreaded finding Sheridan there and didn't think she could handle seeing them together. No, she had to do it. She simply must stop behaving like a wounded pup licking her wounds and face him again. She wasn't a child; it was time to stop behaving like one. Yes, she hurt. But she had to learn to face her pain head-on and not hide from it. Isn't that what she'd told Joel for weeks?

The air was brisk, invigorating from the coming autumn. She took deep breaths as she strolled along the beautiful grounds to the gardens and beyond, to the tranquil pond sheltered among towering trees whose foliage had begun to blaze with color. Strangely, though the area didn't look the same, it reminded her of her spot at the lake with Joel and the ease they'd shared with one another there.

She felt grateful God had used her, even her mistake, to help Joel, and that their friendship had strengthened beyond what it ever was. But she couldn't help the tears that trickled past her lashes as she wished for something that would never be.

How long she stood there, she didn't know, but she had the oddest sensation of being watched. A prickle danced along her neck down to her spine. She wiped her eyes with her sleeve then looked over her shoulder.

And froze.

Joel stood not ten feet away.

⚘

Weeks after his surgery Joel wondered and worried when Clemmie never showed up to visit again. He asked Herbert and Thea, but they had no idea why she stayed away. He had phoned Hannah's, but the butler always stated that Miss Lyons wasn't home. It wasn't like Clemmie to disappear from his life when she had forced her way into it more than three months before. He was sure she would be there when the doctor removed the bandages and share with him either the pain of failure or the triumph of sight. The doctor had waited as long as he could until he told Joel he had other patients and could wait no longer. Joel reluctantly agreed. Sheridan had come, and he'd been grateful for her company, but he'd wanted Clemmie there since she'd been a huge support to him and the reason he'd made the leap to pursue the operation.

Upon opening his eyes once the doctor removed the final bandage, Joel had at first been blinded by the doctor's flashlight, though the room had been darkened. After more than a year of empty black and dark gray, colors had come back to his world—colors and shapes—a world he remembered and now appreciated all the more for having lost it.

But nothing prepared him for his first sight of Clemmie as a woman.

The sun's rays slanted through the trees and reflected off her hair—a lively mix of light reds and golds that almost touched her shoulders in a wavy fashion of the day. Her eyes were the most fascinating shade of dusky green with the sun bringing out yellow flecks, obvious even at this distance, her brows gently sloping in light brown arcs. Her face appeared as smooth and fair as porcelain. Her lips were wide, full, perfect, and her cheeks rosy— whether natural or from her walk or embarrassment at finding him there, he couldn't guess. Full-figured like her mother—not slender, not plump— she wore a simple brown skirt and creamy white blouse that outlined every curve of her, and she used none of the cosmetics that so many women seemed to feel necessary.

Joel stood thunderstruck. She wasn't plain, as she'd led him to believe. Nor did she have Sheridan's fair, classic beauty. Clemmie was so much more than common or a carbon copy of others who tried to emulate the movie starlets of the day. In her simplicity and with her unique coloring, she was magnificent!

As long as he lived, he knew he would never forget this moment. . . .

"Joel?" She licked her lower lip nervously. "I—I didn't expect you. Is something the matter?"

His eyes on her mouth, he answered her. "I could ask you the same thing." He lifted his gaze to hers. "Why did you stop visiting me?"

She pressed a pale hand to her heart. "I–I'm sorry. And I'm so glad you got your sight back."

"Are you?"

"Of course! You really need to ask such a silly question?"

He moved closer and noticed a light sprinkling of adorable freckles dotting her nose and cheeks. "Why weren't you there?"

"What?"

He noticed how her chest rose and fell sharply, could see the pulse that beat in the hollow of her creamy throat and the manner in which her natural, pale rose–colored lips parted in uncertainty. He could feast his eyes upon the vision of her all day.

"You heard me. Why weren't you there when the bandages came off?"

"Oh." She lifted her chin a little as if bolstering herself. "I knew Sheridan would be there for you."

He closed the remaining distance between them. "I wanted you."

She inhaled a shaky breath, her incredible eyes flickering wider. "I–I'm sorry." She took a sudden step back, clearly flustered. "How's your girlfriend these days?"

He drew his brows together at her odd choice of words. "My girlfriend?"

"Sheridan," she clarified as if he should know it.

"Sheridan's not my girlfriend."

"Of course she is! I saw her kiss you—"

He watched as the flush on her face spread, extending down the slim column of her neck, and her green-gold eyes flared wider. This close, he could see the curly spikes of each fringe of her soft brown lashes. Wet lashes. She'd been crying.

"Sheridan's not my girlfriend," he repeated. "And I don't want her to be."

"But I heard you!"

"Heard me?"

Her skin took on a deeper shade of rose, and she bit the lip she had moistened again. "At the hospital. Y–you asked her never to leave you. Told her that you'd been wrong about not admitting something and. . .and that you wanted her with you forever. I heard you. . . ." Her voice trailed off weakly as he opened his eyes wider in understanding.

"Clemmie, I thought Sheridan was you."

"What? That's impossible. We sound nothing alike."

"The drugs they gave me confused me, making voices hard to understand. Remember how sometimes I called you Sheridan? I did the same with her and called her Clemmie."

"I. . ."

She stood, her mouth open wide, her eyes dazed.

He moved forward, closing the distance between them, and took her hands in his. "I wasn't going to speak up, not until I had a chance to talk with your father, not until you turned eighteen, not until I understood the distance you'd put between us. Now that I know, I can't wait any longer. There's no girlfriend, Clemmie. Do you understand?"

Dully, she nodded.

"But there is this girl who nagged me and tormented me and wouldn't let me concede to failure. Who helped me face my fears and put my past behind me so I could dream again. And it's this girl, this amazing woman, I want to call my wife. I held back saying anything because my life was so uncertain, especially with the prospect of death hanging over my head. But now there's no reason to hold back."

Motionless, she stared as if turned to a porcelain doll. She didn't even blink.

"Clemmie. . .do you understand what I'm saying?" He dropped to one knee and felt her hands tremble in his. "I love you. Only you. I have for some time, but I was too stubborn to admit it. Now I do." His eyes searched her face for some sign, some encouragement, and he blindly struck forward. "Clementine Lyons, will you do me the honor of becoming my wife? I don't want to live another day in this world without you."

She blinked, hard and repeatedly, her breaths coming fast. All the rose color that had suffused her face drained away, leaving it almost stark white. Worried about her reaction and thinking he would need to catch her if she should suddenly collapse, he jumped to his feet. "Is this too soon—"

"You want to marry me? *Me*? . . .You love me?" she whispered in disbelief, such a look of utter astonishment crossing her features that Joel couldn't help himself. He cradled her face in his hands and kissed her, taking pleasure in tasting her lips after so long denying himself the satisfaction and learning their soft, warm texture again. When he pulled away, they were both breathless.

"Are you convinced yet?"

She gave a sobbing little laugh. He felt entranced by her smile, which lit up her face. Her eyes, already beautiful, shone with happiness, like jewels. "I'm not sure." Her voice came a little stronger, an intriguing mix of teasing and shyness. "It takes awhile to get facts straight in my head sometimes. I might need more convincing?"

With a low chuckle at her hopeful suggestion, Joel gladly accepted the challenge.

Chapter 19

Pinch me."

With a mischievous grin, Hannah obeyed.

"Ow." Clemmie laughed. "Not so hard. You don't want to bruise me, do you?"

"You wanted to make certain you're awake, right?"

Clemmie smiled. She hadn't been able to stop smiling all morning. "Oh, Hannah, is it true? Am I getting the dream I always wished for?"

"To have me for your maid of honor?" Hannah teased. "Or to wear such a pretty dress and have so many people fawning over you?"

Darcy, who'd just finished pinning up Clemmie's hair, snorted out a laugh.

"To marry Joel, silly," Clemmie replied, rolling her eyes heavenward.

"Oh, then yes, I'd have to say you're getting your dream. And you do look gorgeous in that dress."

"Don't I look go-geous in my dress?" Clemmie's eight-year-old sister, Belle, demanded, twirling so the satin folds billowed out.

"You'd look a mite prettier if you didn't still have traces of that black eye," her mother reproved.

"Can't help it, Mama. Quentin started it. He's so dumb."

"Reminds you of Clint and Miranda, doesn't it?" Clemmie's mother asked Darcy. "Those two were at each other's throats night and day as children. Now they're married with two children of their own!"

"Eww!" Belle wrinkled her nose. "I'm never gonna marry, not in a million jillion years. And I'd never marry him!"

"Oh dear. That sounds like what Miranda used to say about Clint when she was your age."

"Better take good care of that wedding dress of your mother's, Clemmie," Darcy teased. "Your sister might be needing it soon."

"Perish the thought," Clemmie's mother said with a laugh. "I'm losing one daughter today. Don't go and marry off my baby years before her time."

"You're not losing me, Mama. We'll visit every holiday. More, if Joel's job at the paper allows it."

"Or you could both move back to the refuge," her mother said hopefully. "Plenty of room there. And I'm sure we can find something for Joel to do."

Across the room, Angel laughed, and Clemmie turned her attention to another of her dearest friends.

"Better elope with Joel while you can," Angel teased. "Before your mother takes it into her head to pack you both up in her trunk and take you back home to live."

"Now there's an idea," Darcy teased as if she were serious.

Clemmie smiled at their banter, thankful for her family and friends, even if they were a bit absurd at times. In her pale lilac bridesmaid's dress, Angel looked splendid. They all did. Thea, advanced with child, hadn't been able to be a bridesmaid, but Angel, who was only four months into her second pregnancy and bloomed like a flower, had yet to show. Clemmie had defied convention to have her married friend in her wedding party, thrilled to be with her again. Roland and Angel had come from their home, thirty minutes away by train, while Angel's mother, Lila, never fond of crowds after the horrors of living in a circus freak show, stayed home with little Everett.

Many from the refuge had arrived at the home of Hannah's uncle. Although he hadn't expected them, old boyhood chums of Joel's, now married and moved on, made an appearance: Tommy, Lance, and the childhood rivals Clint and Miranda. Not only were Clint and Miranda parents, but Miranda had also achieved her dream of becoming a teacher.

Clemmie's heart felt near to bursting with joy. She'd heard other women sometimes suffered from pre-wedding jitters. But Clemmie had known what she wanted since she was a young girl: Joel. The only emotion she felt besides delirium was eagerness to begin the ceremony that would transform her dream into reality.

"You look lovely." Her mother moved forward, attaching her filmy veil and adjusting it. With teary eyes, she examined every inch of Clemmie's appearance, smiling with approval. "I'm so happy for you, dear. Joel may have been a rapscallion as a lad, but he's turned into a fine man."

"The best, Mama."

"Are you ready? We should be leaving for the church."

"I think I've been ready for Joel all my life."

Her mother laughed. "Well then, let's go and make you his bride."

⁂

"Nervous, old man?" Herbert stood beside Joel, checking his image in the mirror.

Joel wrenched the confounded drooping tie from his neck. Normal ties were bad enough. With a bow tie he might as well be all thumbs. "I'm managing."

"I can tell. You're shaking so bad it's a wonder I don't hear your knees knocking together."

"You're supposed to be my best man," Joel groused. "Not my worst."

"Mind if I barge in?"

"Mr. Lyons." Joel's nervousness peaked. "Sir. . ."

"Now, Joel, none of that. I told you, you're to call me Dad." Stewart Lyons walked into the room, as impressive as ever, his height and build rivaling any young man's. His hair had turned almost all silver, and Joel reckoned he was responsible for a number of them. "Having trouble, I see. I always did hate those things. Mind if I take a go at it?"

Joel shook his head. "No, sir. Dad." He swallowed hard.

"Sir Dad—now that would make for an interesting byline," Herbert observed in amusement. "Picture it: Sir Dad gives Fair Daughter away to Black Knight."

"One more crack and I'm booting you out the door," Joel darkly replied.

Mr. Lyons chuckled as he took the ends of the offending tie and expertly twisted and turned the material until he'd achieved a perfect bow. "You boys still have trouble getting along?"

"Not all the time, sir—Dad."

Herbert snorted.

Joel didn't mind Herbert's ribbing as much as he pretended. It took his mind off the upcoming minutes, which were advancing like a herd of wild cattle. He loved Clemmie, didn't doubt that. And he wanted her as his wife. It was this ceremony, which had grown from the intended private nuptials to a gigantic circus, courtesy of Clemmie's wealthy grandfather and Hannah's just as wealthy uncle, who'd offered his full staff and banquet hall for the reception. Clemmie had been in her element during the past two months of planning, thrilled with the prospect of the whole elaborate shindig, so for his bride, Joel would bear it. Strange that he used to always enjoy being the center of attention and now wanted to run from it. He assumed more than a year of being a hermit had caused the change.

"Herbert," Clemmie's father said, "can you give us a moment?"

"Sure." Herbert looked back and forth between them before leaving the small room where the pastor's aide had led them to wait.

Joel swallowed nervously, the awkward bow tie pushing against his Adam's apple.

"I know we talked last night in depth, but there are a few things I want to say before you go out there."

Uh-oh. Here it comes. The warning never to treat Clemmie badly, not that he would, but the threat of what might happen if he should.

Joel gave a tense nod, preparing himself.

"I'm proud of you, son. Proud of who you are today. Your life has been riddled with bad choices and mistakes, and it takes a real man of strong character to learn from those bad decisions and strive to better himself. Sometimes adversity brings great strength—and you've shown that. Even your boss at the paper raves about what a remarkable employee you are. I only wish Brent could hear for himself what an upstanding man his wayward pupil became, but of course someone had to stay behind with the children."

Joel blinked furiously, fighting back the tears that stung his eyes. "Sir. . . Dad. If it weren't for your patience and generosity and this past summer with your daughter, I would have never tried."

"My daughter, soon to be your wife, eh?" He smiled. "I never would have believed this day would come all those years ago, but having seen you together, you two do make a fine couple. I can see how much you love my baby girl, and I know you'll treat her well."

"Yes. . .Dad. Clemmie means everything to me. I only want to make her happy."

Her father clapped a hand to Joel's back. "Well then, what do you say we go and take the first step in making that possible?"

With Herbert behind him, Joel followed Mr. Lyons to the front of the church, his eyes widening at the number of people who filled the pews. *Good gravy!* He didn't remember them inviting this many—but word must have spread. Spotting old faces from his past with a shock, he had a feeling he knew who'd been the culprit. He glanced his best man's way with narrowed eyes.

"You told everyone who knows me, didn't you?" Joel whispered to Herbert as Clemmie's father took a side aisle to the back of the church.

"So, what's the problem? Now that you can see and are about to marry the gal who probably loves you most in this world, there's no longer any reason for the big secret. It's about time people knew you're back among the living, and today is a major cause for celebration. Wouldn't you say?"

"Hmm. Maybe I chose my best man right after all."

"Who else were you going to ask, the cat?"

Joel softly chuckled. "No. The job would only do for my best brother."

The organ music started, and they turned to face the back. Joel watched the short procession of bridesmaids accompanied by Clemmie's brother and two friends at the paper who Joel had asked to be his groomsmen. Then Clemmie appeared in a satin ivory gown, and Joel forgot all else.

She looked stunning. Amazing.

And she was his. Minutes away from becoming his wife.

Why had God blessed him so profoundly?

Because He loves you, Joel.

Clemmie's answer to him during his weeks of soul-searching rose in his mind at the moment her gaze found and held his.

To deserve such love, as God's, as Clemmie's. . .he couldn't begin to understand it, but he would do all he could to honor them both the rest of his life.

As the pastor asked who gave this woman to be his wife, and her father answered "I do," taking her hand and putting it in Joel's, he wondered if there was such a thing as heaven on earth because he felt he must be living in it.

⚘

Clemmie floated on clouds. Throughout the ceremony, she never took her gaze from Joel's, and he only glanced away when accepting the ring from Herbert.

"I take you, Clementine Marielle Lyons, as my lawfully wedded wife. . . ." The vows he quietly spoke were sweet music to her ears.

"I take you, Joel Timothy Litton, as my lawfully wedded husband. . . ." She made her promise to him softly, the expression of all that was in her heart, and saw the shine of tears in his eyes that must reflect her own.

"I now pronounce you man and wife," the pastor said moments later. Joel drew Clemmie close and kissed her before the pastor could finish saying, "You may now kiss your bride," earning low chuckles from some guests and making Clemmie and Joel smile.

Caught up in the resulting flurry, the ceremony complete, they were whisked away to the estate of Hannah's uncle, where an elaborate feast awaited on covered tables.

The affair was extravagant, with friends, family, and neighbors from present and past converging to wish the happy couple well. Clemmie found herself in constant demand, and to her frustration, she barely saw her new husband, who'd been detained by others eager to see him, glad to know he was alive. Suddenly Clemmie came face-to-face with Sheridan. They had sent her an invitation, but Clemmie hadn't believed the woman would attend.

"I wish you all the best." Sheridan's eyes were sincere. "You and Joel both."

Clemmie didn't know what to say and felt bad that if the situation were reversed, she probably wouldn't have shown such graciousness. "I'm glad you came, Sheridan. Really."

"Thank you. I hope we can be friends."

"Of course." Clemmie still felt at a loss.

"Clemmie, it's okay." Sheridan patted her arm. "Everything happened the way it was meant to. Joel loves you very much. He told me so, and I'm just happy to see you both happy."

In that moment, Clemmie became Sheridan's fan, too. "Thank you." She hugged her. "And you're always welcome at our home."

"Clemmie, sweetheart. . ." Joel came up behind her and slipped his arm around her waist. "Everything okay here?"

"Wonderful." She turned a beaming smile on him. "I was just telling Sheridan she must come and pay us a visit—when we find a home, of course."

Joel raised his brow as if surprised, and then he smiled at Sheridan. "I second that invitation."

Sheridan laughed. "Then I accept you both. But right now I think you're being paged."

Clemmie and Joel turned to look behind them. Clint, Miranda, Tommy, and Lance eagerly waved to them.

"Uh-oh," Joel said. "I don't like the looks of this."

The fellows moved into a straight line in the middle of the ballroom floor, facing them, linking arm in arm. Joel's face turned red. "Now I know I don't like it."

Clemmie knew what was coming and bit her lip in an effort not to laugh. After all the mischievous serenading Joel had led his gang in when they were boys, it seemed proper that he should get a taste of his own.

Tommy pulled his harmonica from his pocket and blew a few notes, gaining everyone's attention. Joel groaned and closed his eyes.

The men all hummed off-key notes, getting in tune, then belted out their tribute to the happy couple: "Oh my darlin', oh my darlin', Oh, my daaarlin' Clementine..."

The red flush in Joel's face rushed to his ears. Clemmie giggled.

"You were lost and gone forever, oh my daaarlin' Clementine...."

"Kill me now," he joked under his breath. "Did we really sound that bad?"

"They're just hamming it up. You should be used to it."

"Hmm."

Somehow he lived through the rest of the song, the words changed to reflect what an idiot Joel had been to almost lose her and what a saint she was to take him back.

"Nice to know how they really feel," he said, but she could tell he was amused.

Afterward, amid a lot of backslapping and jibes, Tommy made a toast to the happy couple and expressed his delight that the original "Gang of Reformers" was reunited. "May it be the first of many occasions!" he added. His new wife, Angel's cousin Faye, smiled and winked at him, earning her a huge smile; it was good to see Tommy so happy.

Joel clapped his hands to Tommy's and Lance's shoulders. "Okay, I gotta admit—it's great to see all you lugheads again."

Amid much laughing and jesting, the old gang hugged as a group then split up to gather around one of the tables and talk of old days and new. Clemmie, who'd seen some of their antics and heard about the rest, greatly enjoyed all of it. Miranda excused herself to take care of her and Clint's youngest boy, and the men were in heated discussion over who was the culprit behind an old prank on the schoolmaster. Everyone had a theory. Joel turned to whisper in Clemmie's ear.

"Let's get out of here."

"You mean just leave?"

"I've had enough commotion for one day. But if you want to stay for them showering us in rice and all that..."

"Lead the way, husband. I'm with you."

Her words earned her a quick kiss. He took her hand, both of them furtively sneaking to get their coats, the guests too absorbed in their own good time to notice.

"Henley," Joel said to the driver who stood in the entryway. "Would you drive us home?"

"Very good, sir. And may I offer my congratulations."

"Thank you."

"Home?" Clemmie looked at him strangely as they hurried into the brisk air. Henley opened the door to the Rolls, and Joel helped her inside. "I thought you rented a room at the hotel."

"Hush." He winked and hurried around to the other side of the car.

During the drive, he held her hand, at times bringing it to his mouth to kiss it, but he wouldn't answer her questions as to their destination. When the car reached Herbert's street, she groaned.

"Oh, Joel. Not the shed."

He laughed outright. "What kind of husband would I be to take my new wife to spend our first night together in a box?"

She flushed with warmth at his words and smiled. "Actually, I'd stay anywhere with you. Be it your box of a shed or a fancy hotel."

"Oh good. Well, in that case. . ."

"Joel." She laughed. "Don't you dare!"

The chauffeur drove past Herbert's home and stopped two houses down the street.

"What?" Clemmie pulled her brows together. "Why are we stopping here?"

Joel didn't wait for Henley, hurrying out of the car to come around and help her to the sidewalk. She raised the hem of her long gown, taking his hand as he helped her over an icy puddle.

"Thank you, Henley. We can take it from here."

"Very good, sir."

Clemmie watched in confusion as the chauffeur drove away then turned to her new husband.

"Explain yourself, Joel Litton."

"Open your eyes and look," he said while taking hold of her shoulders and turning her to see the SOLD sign in the front yard.

Clemmie blinked as realization dawned. "Joel, you didn't. . ." He barely made enough at the paper. She turned to him. "I meant what I said. I'd live with you anywhere. Even your shed."

"Shhh." He placed his finger against her lips, sending a tingle down her spine. "I didn't. This is a wedding gift from your grandfather. I didn't want to accept, but he seemed hurt when I wouldn't, and I wasn't about to make you live in that shed."

"So you buried your pride to make an old man happy and ensure that we have a good place to live at a time when such things like homes are hard to come by," she said in wonder, realizing just how far Joel had come for a man who refused handouts.

"It was a gift. And he's family."

Clemmie's smile grew wide. "Joel Litton, have I told you how much I love you?"

He swept her off her feet, making her squeal, and held her close.

"Mrs. Litton, let me show you just how much I love you. I've been waiting for this day a long time."

His words partly took away her breath.

"Joel, you have no idea how long I've waited for you. Is this truly real?"

"Let's find out." His kiss finished the job his words had started. "Yeah," he whispered. "It's real."

Breathless with the emotions he'd sparked inside her—from ecstasy at becoming his wife to eagerness at fully belonging to him—she clung to her first and only love as he carried her over the threshold of their new home and into the start of their life together.

Epilogue

Six months later

O h, aren't you the fussy one?"
Thea tended to her baby, putting him over her shoulder to burp him, while Clemmie made sandwiches for the girls. Loretta and Bethany sat at the table, drinking their milk and giggling over their pretend game of being mamas, one of their dolls in a chair between them.

"There you two go." Clemmie set their lunches in front of them. "And if you eat every bit, we have cookies for dessert."

"Yay!" Loretta squealed. "Chocowit chip?"

"Of course."

Clemmie's answer produced another squeal.

"You're good with the girls," Thea said. "With little Rupert, too. You'll make a fine mother one day."

Clemmie flushed with warmth. "I had plenty of experience at the refuge, taking care of my brothers and sisters and even some of the reformers."

"Strange name, that."

Clemmie shrugged. "It's what they chose to be called. Once-upon-a-time hooligans learning to better themselves so they can reform the world."

"Well, when you put it that way, I like it! It's catchy."

"I can't take the credit. That's Hannah's line. She's started writing plays for amusement and comes up with witty little slogans all the time."

Thea patted Rupert's back, smoothing circles over it. "I can't tell you how thrilled I am that we're neighbors. It's swell to be able to chat anytime with you, living only two houses away."

"I agree. That house can feel empty while Joel's at work. I'm used to a big family." The winter had been lonesome in the hours without him, and with the arrival of spring and warmer weather, Clemmie visited Thea's when her own housework was done.

The cat suddenly made a beeline for the door. Loretta jumped from her chair to let her outside and squealed. "Daddy and Uncle Joel are home!"

Clemmie quickly untied her apron and hurried outdoors to greet her husband.

"Hello, Herbert." She nodded then turned her full attention to the man of her dreams. "Joel."

She smiled, moving into his arms to give him a welcoming hug and kiss.

"Where's my wife?" Herbert complained. "I want some of that, too."

"Rupert's being fussy." At that moment, Thea appeared at the door, the baby in her arms. With a smile, Herbert went to his wife and embraced her.

"Let's go home," Clemmie suggested.

"All right."

They waved to their friends and walked to their house, whose front Clemmie planned to soon brighten with lilac bushes. Inside, Joel took her in his arms for a real kiss, scrambling her thoughts and her breath.

"How is my darling Clementine today?"

"Swell. Are you hungry?"

"Only for you."

His words and the light in his eyes left no doubt what he meant, making her go warm inside. Before he so delightfully diverted her from her mission, she wanted to say what she'd waited to say for hours.

"There's something I need to tell you."

"Mmm?" He touched his lips to hers again, trailing little kisses from her mouth to her jaw and her ear. "Did you know your hair shines like fire in the sun?" he whispered. His fingers wove into the strands as she struggled to think clearly.

"I had an appointment today."

"With the hairdresser? Don't change the color, Clemmie." Another kiss to her neck. "I know you've never been happy with it and talked of going platinum, but I love my feisty carrottop."

"It's not orange, it's almost auburn, and I didn't see a beautician. I went to a doctor."

He froze and moved to look at her. "Are you sick?"

"I'll be much better this coming winter. But before that, we need to decorate the spare room. Perhaps with a theme of fluffy little bunnies?"

He shook his head in confusion.

"Honestly, Joel." She smiled, wrapping her arms around his neck. "Your senses may have sharpened when you were blind, but sometimes you can be so dull. You might have two carrot-tops come December, could even be on my birthday—so, what do you think of that?"

His eyes widened in sudden comprehension. "You mean. . ."

"Yes." She giggled at his dazed reaction. She'd never known him to be at such a loss for words. "We're going to have a little carrottop. And I'm so glad you accepted Grandfather's gift, because with three of us, it might have gotten crowded in that box of a shed."

At that, Joel laughed and scooped her up, holding her tightly against him, his arms around her waist. She looked down at him, clutching his strong shoulders.

"You *are* happy then?" she asked softly.

"I can't think of news that would make me happier. Hot dog! I'm gonna be a father." He said the words as if he could scarcely believe them.

"Yes. The start of the big family I've always dreamed of. I want as many children—more—than my parents had. A dozen at least."

"A dozen? Hmm." Joel's eyes twinkled. "Well, sweetheart, you might be getting that wish sooner than you think."

"What do you mean?"

"Did I ever mention twins run in my family?"

Clemmie's eyes widened with shock. "You're teasing me again, right?"

His eyebrows lifted high, his blue eyes dancing, his smile wide.

"You *are* teasing."

Joel laughed and kissed her soundly, soon scattering all her thoughts and making her forget all else but this man she loved. . .

Her dream come true.

IN SEARCH OF SERENITY

Dedication

Thank you to my wonderful and faithful critique partners—
my mother and my good friend Theo, both of whom are always
there for me in a pinch. You are a blessing beyond compare.
Dedicated to my Lord and Savior, the God of second chances,
of lasting redemption, of impossible reunions. And to all the
families out there in need of these, this book is for you.

Chapter 1

*B*efore she could scream, a red-skinned man wearing hides and feathers
clapped a hand over her mouth. With her back against the wall, she stared
in horror. A sudden pounding shook the door of the cabin as whoever stood
on the other side demanded entrance.

*Would it be another wild man, such as the Sequoia who had come to raid her
father's cabin, or one of the settlers, come to rescue her? Attempting to wrest free,
she bit the hand of her captor and cried out at the top of her lungs for hel—*

"Hannah!"

Hannah Thomas slashed a long *scrrritch* through the rest of the word, ripping through the paper with the nib of her pen. She compressed her lips in
irritation.

"Hannah!"

"What *is* it, Abbie?" Hannah woefully eyed the ruined notepaper bearing
the past hour of her hard labor.

"Mama wants you."

"And you had to tell me that, caterwauling my name at the top of your
lungs as you raced into the parlor like a feline in a catfight?" Hannah eyed
her little sister sternly.

"What's a feline?"

"A cat."

"I wanna be a bird instead."

"You're neither a bird nor a cat, but sometimes you act like a little wild
Indian."

"Can I be the little Indian girl in your play? The one who makes friends
with the collynith?"

"The colonist, and never mind. You're too young to remember all the lines."

"Am not!" Abbie crossed her arms over her chest with another pout that
some thought cute but only irritated Hannah. A curious sparkle came into
Abbie's eyes. "Whatcha writing?"

"Nothing." Hannah folded her hands over the ruined words as Abbie moved closer.

"Ooo—you're writing them shameful stories of intreak again! Mama said stories like that are sensatial claptrap. You shouldn't write them, Hannah."

"There's nothing shameful about my stories of *intrigue*, and they're far from being sensational claptrap. Anyhow, it's none of your business."

"I'm telling Mama you're being mean."

"I'm not being mean. I'm being truthful. And how do you know that I might not be working on the Founder's Day play?"

"If you were, you wouldn't have hid it from me."

Hannah blew out an exasperated breath. "Don't you have something to do? Dolls to play with or imaginary tea parties to hold?"

Abbie frowned. "They're not 'maginary. They're real."

"Fine. Go have one then."

"Can't. Mama said I have to go to bed."

"Good idea. Go back to bed."

"There's toys all over the top. And my bedsheet's all mussed up."

"Then pick them up. And straighten your sheets."

Abbie pouted. "I wish *we* had servants like Uncle Bernard does. How come we had to move to this dumb ole house, anyway?"

Hannah sympathized with her sister. She also had grown accustomed to being waited on during the five years they'd lived in her wealthy great-uncle's manor and didn't relish this new turn of events. Why her mother insisted that life at their great-uncle's wasn't beneficial for the children, Hannah couldn't understand. But Daddy had succumbed to Mother's wishes and bought the old Fairaday house for a song. Little wonder he'd acquired it so cheap. With the way it creaked and groaned, Hannah wondered if the place might be haunted by old Fairaday's ghost—perhaps his entire lineage.

And now her father was paying the price for his foolish mistake. What if it had been a ghost that caused him to fall from the roof, and not the sudden shock of hearing some wild animal chatter in a tree branch near his head? She wondered what kind of tale her pen could craft from that.

"Hannah!"

Her little sister's demand broke Hannah's imagination from spiraling down the latest path.

"How come we had to move?"

"I don't know, Abbie. But what's done is done."

"I don't like it here." Abbie stomped her bare foot. "I wanna go back to Uncle's. I want Mary to pick up my clothes and toys so I don't have to."

You and me both, kiddo. I don't like it here, either. She didn't air her futile thoughts, not wanting to set Abbie off on another tangent. "You just have to learn to make the best of things."

"I don't want to make the best of things. I *hate* this place!"

The doorbell rang, to Hannah's relief. She waited for the newcomer to be escorted into the parlor, thus putting an end to Abbie's complaints—then remembered they had no maid and she must answer the door herself. Mother was tending to Daddy, and Hannah's younger brothers and sisters were at school, where Abbie should be, if she hadn't come down with the sniffles and Mama hadn't sent her to bed. She certainly appeared recovered.

Hannah moved to receive their guest, then thought twice and grabbed up her notebook of loose-leaf papers. No sense putting temptation in Abbie's way, though she couldn't read well, not enough to understand the novel Hannah toiled over at every opportunity. But she didn't want to return to find her pages colored on, either.

Holding her story close to her heart, snippets of what she wrote revolved in her mind. Theatrically she wondered if the person on the opposite side of the door was indeed her rescuer. . .or a wild man come to wreak havoc.

The thumping of her heart increased as she opened the door. A stranger stood waiting. Taller than herself by at least half a foot, with wheat-colored hair and riveting blue eyes that reminded her of the bottom of a slow flame, the man took her breath away. His fair, patrician features could be described as romantic, even angelic, but the firm set of his jaw and intensity of his gaze beneath thick sable brows gave him the air of a rogue.

Wild man or rescuer?

It was difficult to tell from appearance alone.

She blinked, and he raised his brows. At that, she realized she'd been staring while holding her story clutched to her breast. "Can I help you?" she uttered breathlessly and pulled the notebook away. Unfortunately, she didn't have a good hold on the edges, and a shower of papers rushed to the ground between them. Still in a daze, she could only stare at the top of his hat and the broad girth of his shoulders outlined by the gray suit jacket he wore as he bent to retrieve the escaped pages of her story.

Surely, a rescuer. . .

Her face warmed as his gaze dropped to and remained on one of the papers in his hand—long enough to take a look at the first sentences, surely—but he didn't comment. She hoped he hadn't read any of it. He handed over the last sheaf of papers as he rose to stand. Again, she felt emotionally wrung by his intense blue gaze.

Perhaps a wild man. . .

Maybe both.

"Are you all right, mademoiselle?"

His voice, rich and warm, had the opposite effect and made her shiver.

"Yes, of course." Recalling that she still didn't know why he'd come to their ramshackle house, and figuring that in his herringbone suit with empty hands he didn't look like a salesman or a workman—not that her father would agree to hire one of those—she rephrased her question. "How may I help you?"

"Actually"—he gave her a smile that threatened to make her knees melt into goo—"I came here for your family."

"Pardon?"

"This is the Thomas residence?"

"Yes?" Her reply came wary.

"Then this is where I was told to come." He slipped his hand inside his coat. Alarmed, Hannah backed up a step, opening her eyes as wide as they would go. Surely, he wasn't going for his gun?

He drew his brows together in clear confusion, and she wondered if she'd gone white as a sheet. Clutching her notebook to her chest as if it were a shield of armor, she watched as he withdrew an envelope, her relief that it wasn't a weapon helping her marginally relax. She stared at the paper he handed her.

"It won't bite."

At his amused tone, she snapped out of her foolish trance. "What is it exactly?"

"I'm Eric Fontaine. . .and you weren't expecting me." The introduction he offered in calm confidence; the rest he added with uneasy knowledge.

"No, we weren't." His obvious embarrassment made her feel bad for him, also easing her anxiety. "The name is familiar though. Are you a friend of my father's?"

"My father and your father are old associates. My father sent me to help out. He heard about your father's accident. It's all in the letter."

His explanation erased any lingering doubt about his character, and she took the envelope, offering him a smile and stepping aside to let him enter. "Please, come in. Father's upstairs. He's unable to leave his bed because he broke his leg, but then, I imagine you already know that if your father sent you." She closed the door behind him and led him to the parlor.

"I thought he would have phoned by now. I apologize for coming unannounced."

"Oh dear. There's one mystery solved. Our phone line isn't working. This place. . ." She gave a little shake of her head, spreading her hands in apology. "It's not in the best of shape on a good day, and—"

"Han-nah!"

She winced at Abbie's banshee yell and tried to cover her embarrassment with a short laugh. "My little sister. She stayed home from school because she had a smidgeon of a temperature. She's been restless all day."

"Han-nah!" Abbie shot around the corner and stopped in surprise to see their guest. "Who are you?"

Hannah sighed. "What do you want, Abbie?"

"Mama said you're to go up there right away."

"Oh right. I forgot." She turned to the man she wasn't yet sure how to classify, as friend or foe. Surely, if he came to help, he was their rescuer and not a rogue. "The parlor's through there. Make yourself comfortable—well, as comfortable as you can. The room's rather cold. It's certainly not the Ritz, not that I've been there. But, well, it's a wonder this place doesn't fall down around our heads. I'll just go give Father your letter. I'll be back shortly."

She bounced from one topic to another, as she often did when nervous or excited, then bit her tongue to prevent further rambling. With a parting nod, she exited the room. The moment she left his line of vision, she raced upstairs, too excited to share with her parents the news of their unexpected caller to walk at a more sedate pace.

Eric took a seat on the edge of a lumpy sofa, curbing the strong impulse to walk out the front door. The drafty house and uncomfortable surroundings didn't bother him; he was accustomed to sparser conditions. What made him ill at ease was the intent inspection he now received from the child who sat in a nightdress on a chair across from him, her legs too short for her bare feet to reach the ground as she swung them like small pendulums back and forth, back and forth. . . .

And stared.

He glanced away several times. He should be accustomed to children, but the unusual circumstances of his arrival put him on edge. He threaded the brim of his hat through his fingers.

"So," he said in an attempt to fill the uneasy silence, "your name is Abbie?"

A narrow-eyed nod was his reply.

"How old are you, Abbie?"

"Almost six."

"Really? I have a sister your age. Her name is Marguerite. We call her Merry, because she laughs a lot and likes to play games. Do you like to play games?"

This time her nod didn't seem as if it veiled a spitting kitten.

"Merry likes to hold tea parties. We run a mission, and sometimes she holds them with a few of our guests who've become like family."

A spark of reluctant curiosity lit her dark eyes. "What's a mission?"

"A place where people go to get help."

"Papa doesn't want no man's help. He said so."

Eric wondered just how welcome he would be at the Thomas residence. His father had led him to believe a pair of willing hands would be appreciated.

"Has your family lived here long?"

She shrugged. "I don't like this place. It smells funny. And nothing works right."

Eric withheld a smile, her little miseries reminding him of something his youngest brother might say. "Old houses do tend to have a musty odor. But what would you say if, assuming your daddy gives permission, I make things work right again?"

Curiosity warred with suspicion in her eyes. "How?"

"I have some experience fixing up old places."

"This place is really, really old."

He grinned. "I have experience with those places, too. The mission my family owns is really, really old."

For the first time, the girl smiled. "Are Merry's tea parties 'maginary?"

"Imaginary?"

"Like people in the stories Hannah writes."

"Ah." His smile grew. "No, I would have to say they're very real."

Chapter 2

Hannah stood at the foot of her father's bed, curiously watching his face lose color, then flush darker as he read the letter. She wondered what Eric's father had written and almost wished she had slipped the contents from the envelope earlier, to see for herself.

Her father's lips thinned as he lowered the paper, his eyes lifting to Hannah. "He's downstairs?"

"Yes. I left him in the parlor."

"Tell him thanks, but we don't need his help."

"Bill, you must not speak so."

Her mother stood by his bedside, her bearing as regal as ever, her fluid voice soothing to hear after his terse words. Hannah often wished she could emulate her mother who behaved like the princess her name, Sarah, meant. But Hannah didn't come close, her behavior too strong-willed and animated to be compared to quiet aristocracy. Her great-grandfather may have been chieftain of his tribe on the island where her mother was born and lived the greater part of her life, as the only child of an island princess and an American missionary. Yet though such royalty existed in Hannah's bloodline, regrettably any outward manner of the nobles would never reign in Hannah.

"With winter soon here and your need of recuperation, any help this young man could give would be welcome," her mother continued quietly.

Her father glanced from her mother to Hannah, his manner furtive. Her mother followed suit and addressed her. "Hannah, please go downstairs and tell Mr. Fontaine that I'll be down shortly to receive him."

Disappointed to be dismissed yet again, she stubbornly hesitated. Why were so many secrets kept from her? What about the intriguing man downstairs did Hannah's father not want her to hear? At her mother's raised eyebrows, she whirled on her heel and left the room.

Seventeen years old and they still treated her as a child!

She brought the door to a close, losing her grip on the notebook. Her precious story fluttered to the floor. Aggravated, she bent to retrieve it, the door barely ajar. Her parents must not have heard the rustle of pages, for they resumed their conversation, unaware Hannah knelt close by.

"I won't have any son of *his* under my roof!" Her father used a harsh tone she'd rarely heard, except when events went beyond his control. Like when the doctor told him he must remain in bed several weeks to allow the break in his leg to heal.

"He told you he has changed when you last saw him," her mother replied in her quiet, logical way.

"That was over ten years ago! How do I know it's true? That he hasn't reverted to his old schemes and taught his offspring the same? What if this is all some huge con of Eric's for power or revenge? He was a master at manipulation. He knew tricks I'd never dreamed of."

"*You* have changed." The reminder was delivered gently. "Besides, what would he have to be vengeful of? You saved his life. He saved yours."

Stunned, Hannah stopped gathering papers. Eric Fontaine Sr. had saved her father's life? From whom? The Piccoli gang?

She knew little of her father's past—only that he'd been the target of a mobster long ago when he washed up on her mother's island. There, he found the Lord through Hannah's grandfather. But the mobster who had been pursuing him, Vittorio Piccoli, struck out in revenge against Hannah's father once he returned to America with his new wife, and as a result, her mother had almost died, like their child she'd been carrying. Those facts Hannah overheard one night, many years before, when all the children were thought to be in bed asleep and her parents were visiting with Uncle Brent and Aunt Darcy, Aunt Charleigh and Uncle Stewart. The adults had quietly been reliving the past after a few of them had gone to see Eric Sr. that day, having received the startling news of his proximity through a guest visiting the Refuge. Any other details regarding her father's life before Christ had been omitted from Hannah's curious knowledge.

Though she knew she shouldn't, she gathered the papers more slowly while craning her ear to the door, eager to hear more of the past she'd never known.

"Sarah, there's one thing I learned when it came to dealing with a man like Eric Fontaine, and that is the moment you begin to trust him is the moment you've put your life in jeopardy."

"Surely things are different now. He and his wife run a mission at the wharf for the destitute."

"I know. I remember what he told us: how he found God in prison and forgave Charleigh and Darcy for putting him there and is no longer out to seek vengeance." Her father's voice held an impatient edge. "But now I have to ask myself, was it all a cover? He was a master at getting anyone to believe anything. It was all part of his twisted genius."

"But again, Bill, what would he hold against you?"

"Maybe nothing. Doesn't matter. I don't want any son of Eric's near my girls." All was quiet a moment.

"Could a man who delivered such a testimony as you have told me, years ago, when you and the others returned from visiting him, have a soul so black?"

"I don't know, Sarah. But I won't risk my family's lives by taking chances. Never again."

"Bill..." Hannah heard the mattress springs creak and assumed her mother took a seat beside her father. "You're not to blame for what happened to me and our baby."

"If I had never gotten involved with the Piccolis—with men like Eric—that thug would have never shot you."

"Still you hold such guilt in your heart, my love?" The soft sound of a kiss came to Hannah. "You must release this torment. I want you to at last know peace."

"Pretty Sarah, you are everything to me. You, the children. . .I couldn't risk losing you again."

"Hannah?"

At the sound of her sister's voice, Hannah jumped so sharply she almost fell through the door. She just stopped herself, slapping her palm to the wall. Certain now her parents must know she'd been eavesdropping, she scampered up off her knees, papers retrieved, and hurried down the hall to where Esther stood.

"What are you doing here? Were you spying on me?"

"Me, spying?" Esther scowled in disbelief. "I wasn't the one on my hands and knees crawling around in front of Mama and Daddy's door. Who's the suave fellah in the parlor?"

"No one that need concern you. Are you skipping classes?"

"It's past three, birdbrain."

Hannah sighed. "I had no idea it was so late. Come downstairs. Where's David?"

"Probably in the kitchen, stuffing his face with milk and cookies."

Her thirteen-year-old sister seemed to be in as disagreeable a mood as Abbie.

"Bad day at school?" she sympathized.

Esther shrugged. "The same. . ."

"But?" Hannah took her sister's arm, turning her around to walk with her as she began to descend the stairs. She expected her parents' door to open any moment and her mother to catch her lurking there.

Esther let out a frustrated sigh. "Betty and Claudia wanted to come over and work on a report the teacher gave. I told them no, of course. I wouldn't *dream* of letting them see this hovel. Not after them seeing the grandeur of Great-Uncle's manor!"

Hannah understood implicitly. Betty and Claudia were the young sisters of two of her own friends, Julia and Muffy. The mayor's daughter and a judge's daughter. She had yet to surrender to their persistent requests for Hannah's new address and feared she would soon run out of excuses.

"Never mind that now," Hannah instructed. "Be on your best behavior."

Esther nodded at the familiar rule enforced at her great-uncle's mansion and which her family had carried on. When guests were present in the home, frowns altered into smiles, however false, and current troubles were conveniently swept under the carpet until they had the house to themselves again.

In short, they put on a grand act. Hannah only hoped her baby sister had finally learned that rule and wondered about her choice to leave Abbie alone with their guest.

Had Abbie aired all the family secrets by now?

What rare secrets the children knew.

Hannah moved with Esther into the parlor, relieved to hear Abbie tell Eric of her intricate doll collection. Their childless great-uncle had brought her a doll from every country he'd visited while on business, and they'd become Abbie's frequent tea party guests.

At Hannah's approach, Eric turned her way. Her heart gave that unexpected lurch again.

"Mother will be down presently." She felt surprised her voice came out naturally when he looked at her with those blue, blue eyes. "May I bring you something to drink?" She winced, realizing she should have asked before she'd gone upstairs. Her great-uncle's maid usually took care of such trivialities. "We have coffee that Mother put on earlier."

"We have lemonade, too!" Abbie put in enthusiastically.

"I'll have some of that. *Merci*."

Eric smiled, and Hannah felt the now familiar *thump-thump* hammering in her chest before she whirled on her heel and hurried for the kitchen. *Oh my, he speaks French, too?* Once she retrieved his lemonade and returned to the parlor, she noticed her mother had joined him.

"My husband and I wish to extend our thanks for your offer of help."

Hannah's stomach dipped as she handed Eric the glass. Her mother's tone didn't bode well.

"As you know, he's incapacitated at the moment and unable to come downstairs to speak with you. He's expressed a desire for you to come upstairs and meet with him, instead."

Hannah blinked. From what she'd heard of her parents' conversation, she had expected Eric would be given the bum's rush. Not an invitation for a meeting.

"Of course." He took a sip of lemonade and set it down on the end table.

"Hannah, dear, will you start dinner?"

Disappointed that she couldn't tag along, she gave a short nod. If she hurried, she might be able to catch the tail end of their conversation.

❧

Eric followed the stately woman up the split staircase. Pictures of flower arrangements had been used to cover the worst water stains on the faded wallpaper, and when Mrs. Thomas switched it on, the electrical light flickered on the landing.

"The wiring up here is an abysmal mess. Please, watch your step."

As he walked, Eric's calculating mind took note of repairs needed, along with an educated guess of how long it would take to accomplish each task. She led him through a door at the east end of the house with a huge window that would let in the morning sun. This room, at a glance, appeared in better condition than what he'd seen of the rest of the place.

"*Good. . .night!*"

At the slow exclamation of profound shock, Eric looked toward the large bed and its occupant, who'd spoken. Mr. Thomas lay with his leg in a cast, his shoulders powerful and body lean—clearly an outdoorsman. His manner was reminiscent of a lion that had been caged for an eternity. He had hair a shade darker than Eric's with graying sideburns, a smattering of whiskers, and intense, light blue eyes that burned a hole through Eric.

"If I didn't know better, I could swear time rolled back twenty years." Mr. Thomas pushed himself up on his palms so he sat upright against the mountain of pillows at his back. "You're the spitting image of your father."

"So I've been told, sir." The manner in which the man offered the remark didn't resemble a compliment, and Eric refrained from saying more.

"So he sent you all the way to Connecticut to help us."

"Yes, sir."

The man took him in from head to toe. "What experience have you had with home renovations?"

"My family runs a soup kitchen, as you know. All of us have learned to be industrious in repairs. One of my uncles is a building contractor, and I also have some experience with electrical wiring."

At this revelation, Mrs. Thomas smiled hopefully.

"Why should Eric send you? How'd he learn about my accident? I haven't spoken with him in years."

"My father mentioned he owed you a great debt and asked if I'd be willing to help. As for how he found out, I don't know." His father had contacts everywhere. Through the years, his knowledge of others and of their business had been commonly acknowledged fact—and its sources had remained secret. As a result, Eric and his siblings were never able to get away with anything as children. Their shrewd father had always been one step ahead of any mischief.

"Humph. Shouldn't be surprised. Eric always did have a knack for figuring things out." Mr. Thomas's words reflected Eric's thoughts. "You sound well educated." His tone matched the skepticism in his eyes.

"Yes, sir. I took a year's schooling at our local university."

"Really? A college education yet? Makes one wonder why you do your own home repairs," he scoffed.

"Bill," his wife gently reproved.

"You haven't got a job elsewhere?"

"*Non.* I've spent most of my time helping out at the mission."

"To run a place like that seems as if it would incur a great deal of expense. Your father must have a lot of money."

"Bill, please." His wife again spoke softly, putting her hand to his shoulder as if to restrain him, and Mr. Thomas briefly shut his eyes.

"We get by." Outwardly, Eric remained unflappable. The man's thinly veiled accusations brought to mind just how his father had gained some of the money, stolen in his youth, but all of it now put to a worthy cause. His maternal grandfather had also left a sizable sum to Eric's mother before he passed away, and they received donations for the mission. The majority of financial help had dwindled with the crash of the stock market and the ensuing Great Depression.

Mr. Thomas continued to eye Eric as though he might suddenly abscond with the family silver and make a mad dash for the door. Eric tried not to feel offended. His father had warned him that being his son and a replica of his appearance, those from Eric Sr.'s past might be suspicious of his character, though Eric Jr. hadn't guessed they would be outright rude. He had offered to help them without compensation, for pity's sake!

No one from his father's past lived near the mission, or if any did, no one visited, save for that one time over a decade ago. Eric had been a small boy then, barely able to recall this man and others coming to see his father about former days, involving a stolen diamond necklace that passed through many hands. Affable by nature, never having had difficulty making friends, Eric now found himself for the first time regarded with great suspicion.

"Where are you staying?"

Even that question was delivered with wariness.

"I haven't found a place. I was hoping you might recommend somewhere I can board, as I'm not familiar with your town."

"Humph." His interrogator snorted a disgruntled reply. "Good luck finding a room."

"My husband's correct," Mrs. Thomas said pensively. "What is made available is ridiculously steep in price. But if you should come work for us, I wouldn't feel comfortable with you giving of your time and receiving nothing in return. We will give you room and board."

"Sarah?" Mr. Thomas gave her a bug-eyed look, his mouth agape.

She offered him an apologetic glance then again looked at Eric. "Would you excuse us for a moment?"

"Of course. I'll just step outside."

Once in the corridor, even after shutting the door, he could hear their faint words.

"It is only right, Bill. And we need the help. With Josiah away at school and David too young to mastermind any project, we need someone capable to take on such a load. The roof leaks, the walls need to be patched, and soon the snows will come. If we cannot get the house ready by winter, I fear we will need to move back to the mansion. And that can be detrimental, especially for the children. You've seen how they've become. Self-centered. Snobbish. With no concept of what is of true value. I was wrong to beg you to let us stay with Uncle Bernard all those years ago. I better understand now the rift between Uncle and Father. Uncle's ideals are shallow, and his concept of Christianity so ungodly. . . . I only pray it's not to late to save our children."

"Sarah, it's not your fault. I understood your desire to want to get to know your only other living relative, and I wanted to make you happy by staying there. As the children's father, I should have realized what that lifestyle was doing to them. I should have made the decision to move us out earlier. Maybe I should have quit working for him, but with the way the economy is and so many mouths to feed, it wouldn't be wise—though after so much time away, I wonder if I'll still have a job there."

"My uncle would be a fool to let you go, as much help as you've been to him. The situation's not your fault, either. You've always done what is best for the children and me. But Bill, what does it say for us if we shun this young man and judge him for what he cannot help being—Eric's son? We taught the children not to judge rashly and never on outward appearances alone."

Mr. Thomas grumbled something Eric couldn't make out.

"Yes, he *is* Eric's son, but he's also honorable. I sense this about him."

"On one meeting alone?" Her husband's tone soared in disbelief.

"I think we should give him a chance."

"You're far too trusting, Sarah."

"And you're filled with too much mistrust. I know this is because of your former life as a criminal. But darling, he isn't going to murder us in our beds."

"How can you be so sure?"

"Any man who forfeits his college education to help his parents run a soup kitchen for the needy doesn't strike me as someone so selfish that he would seek to harm others."

It was a moment before he replied.

"I still don't like the idea of him in our home, but I can't fight such logic, and you're right about one thing: We need the help since I'm laid up and no good to anyone right now."

"That's not true. Without you, I would fall apart."

"Truth be told, pretty Sarah, you're the glue that holds this family together. But just so you know, I'll be keeping an eye on him. First sign of trouble, he's out the door. I want a record of what he does every minute of the day. And warn the girls to stay away from him."

"Yes, my love. I will do all you ask."

All went quiet, leaving Eric to his thoughts.

If he was smart, he'd just walk out that door Mr. Thomas had threatened to throw him out of. But he couldn't. He'd made a promise to his father.

A rapid tread on the stairwell brought his attention to the landing. The lovely brunette he'd met earlier raced up them. Her short hair bounced with her steps. Upon reaching the landing, she caught sight of Eric and abruptly came to a stop, her cheeks flushing a pretty rose.

"Oh! Hello. . ." She glanced at her parents' closed door then back at him.

"The jury's still out," he explained.

"I see." Her face cleared, and she smiled. "Did Daddy seem. . .agreeable?"

"Let's just say he wasn't happy with the prospect of having me for a house-guest."

Her big, almond-shaped eyes opened wider. "Houseguest?"

"Your mother extended an invitation for me to room here while I fix up the place."

The door suddenly opened, and Mrs. Thomas appeared. She looked from Eric to her daughter, her eyes filled with clear question to see her there. "Hannah?"

"I went to light the range, but we're out of matches."

"Oh dear. I don't think there are any more in the house."

Eric pulled a matchbook from his pocket. "Here. Use this."

The older woman's eyebrows went up in surprise then sailed even higher when she saw the name of a nightclub inscribed on the paper flap.

"You don't smoke or drink?" she asked worriedly.

"No. Before I left, Father wanted to give me the number to your home in case I couldn't find it. We didn't have paper handy, and one of the visitors at the mission had this on him. Father wrote it down. There." He felt ill at ease as he pointed out the numbers penned inside. Of all the idiotic things to do. He already wavered at the edge of their decency list. Producing a matchbook that advertised a New York nightclub wasn't going to win him approval.

"Yes, well, all right." Mrs. Thomas smiled faintly and handed the matches over to her daughter. "Start a pot of water to boil for noodles. I'll be down shortly."

"Yes, Mama." Hannah offered Eric another shy, friendly smile and moved back downstairs.

"My husband and I have agreed you should stay. We are both grateful for whatever help you can offer."

Eric thanked her, tending to believe Hannah's mother was the only one with any true gratitude.

"You may have the room we plan for Josiah to use when he comes home on Christmas break." She walked with him past several closed doors he assumed opened into other bedrooms and turned the glass doorknob of a room at the end of the corridor, where a window stood. Before following her inside, he glanced out the spotted pane, noticing that here, too, a rich panorama of maples, firs, elms, and oaks grew in abundance. A vivid array of brightly hued leaves covered the grounds.

Two windows brought light into a musty room with a stately, four-poster bed and dark furnishings. A bureau held more drawers than he would need.

"The dust has collected," she apologized. "I'll tidy and make up your bed with fresh linens."

"You don't have to do that—"

"Nonsense. If you would like, you may relax here before dinner. The lavatory is across the hall."

He smiled, warming to the woman. "I came here to help *you*."

She chuckled in disbelief. "Surely you don't plan to start work now?"

"Whenever you need me."

"Rest tonight. I imagine it was a long trip from New York. I remember how tedious train travel can be."

He nodded. "All right. I'll just go collect my things. I left them outside." He had set his duffel bag at the end of the stoop, out of sight and hidden by shrubbery, having felt odd to appear at their door with luggage in hand.

She smiled kindly. "Dinner is at seven. And please, Mr. Fontaine, during your stay with us, consider our home yours."

What benevolence her husband lacked, Sarah Thomas made up for in spades.

He thanked her and went downstairs to collect his bag. Outside, he bent down to grab it.

"My, my, my," a feminine purr came from behind. "What have we here?"

Chapter 3

With the stove lit and noodles simmering, Hannah smoothed her skirts and left the kitchen.

She glanced into the parlor.

Empty.

Where was Eric? Still upstairs?

She cast a curious glance up the staircase just as the front door opened.

Her heart jumped at the sight of him then fell when she noticed her two visitors.

"Julia! Muffy!" She hoped they couldn't see her dismay. "What are you doing here?"

"You were so secretive about your new home, we just couldn't help ourselves." The look in Julia's eyes as she studied the foyer made her disapproval clear. Hannah was surprised she didn't swipe her manicured finger along the entry table to check for dust.

"No wonder you didn't invite us over, you naughty girl." Muffy glanced at Eric, squeezing his arm. "Clearly you've been keeping secrets!"

Eric smiled at Hannah's friend. "If you ladies will excuse me, I'll be going to my room." He took the stairs.

"His *room*?" Muffy's eyes grew round. "So what is he, Hannah? A distant cousin? A friend of your brother's?"

"Actually, he's here to help out."

"Help out?"

She watched Eric reach the top landing, feeling a sting of rejection that he'd ignored her when earlier he'd been most attentive. "He's working for my father."

"Do tell!" Muffy grabbed Hannah's arm eagerly.

"Your father certainly picked a. . .distinctive house to purchase." The condescension fairly dripped off Julia's words. "So much different from your great-uncle's beautiful manor."

Embarrassment brought a surge of heat to Hannah's face.

"Yes, it certainly is different." With Eric gone, Muffy took notice of her surroundings for the first time.

Hannah's mother descended the stairs. She nodded in distant greeting. "Girls."

"Mrs. Thomas." Julia's attitude underwent a dramatic change. "What a lovely home you have."

Her mother's smile seemed frosty. "I hadn't realized you were having guests for dinner, Hannah."

"They just popped in for a minute."

"Oh yes," Julia agreed with a syrupy smile. "We were on our way to that divine new little boutique and dropped by to invite Hannah. My sister mentioned where you now live, and Muffy and I were eager to see your charming home for ourselves."

"Really." Her mother's aloofly polite manner didn't alter. "It's rather late for a trip into town. You wouldn't be back before nightfall, surely, and we've not yet had dinner."

"Yes, well. . ." Julia seemed a bit taken aback and grabbed Muffy's arm. "We'll just be going then. We should hurry before the boutique closes. We'll call you, Hannah."

Hannah refrained from mentioning that they didn't yet have a working phone, still mortified that her elite friends had seen her deprived set of circumstances. And, oh dear! She stood there wearing an *apron* of all things! Like a servant! Hurriedly, she whipped it off—though they might not have noticed her poor state of dress at all, after spending all their time gawking at Eric and the sad condition of the foyer.

Both girls had already turned for the door.

Her mother, however, noticed her flustered action and regarded her with a raised brow once they were alone. "You know how I feel about your spending time with those girls, Hannah. It was bad enough when you attended the ladies' academy with them."

"I didn't ask them to come, Mother."

She nodded with a slight smile, her tension easing. "Come, help me and Esther with dinner, dear. Together we will master this art of cooking, no?" Hannah followed her to the kitchen, and her mother continued, "Cooking with a stove is much different from cooking over an open flame as I did on the island."

"Perhaps we should hire a chef," Hannah suggested hopefully. "Especially since we have a guest staying with us."

Her mother turned from collecting eggs from the icebox and gave her a level look. "Money isn't the answer to all problems in life."

"But it helps—"

"We will get by without servants. It will be a challenge, but a good one. You'll see."

"Yes, Mama," Hannah replied with scant enthusiasm.

Together, they prepared eggs and noodles, and Hannah sliced bread. Esther remained quiet but sullen as she set plates and silverware on the table. Abbie wandered in, still in her nightgown. "I wanna help."

Their mother shook her head. "You should be in bed."

"I feel fine, Mama. I'll pour the tea."

"No, Abbie—"

But Abbie had already lifted the full pitcher over a glass. The lip of it fell onto the edge, knocking the glass over. Tea rushed in a torrent over the table and nearest plate, also soaking Abbie's gown and splashing Esther.

"Abbie!" Esther wailed, grabbing a napkin. "Now see what you've done!"

"I'm sorry." Tears glazed Abbie's eyes as she set the pitcher down. "I didn' mean to."

"You can't do anything right! You're such a big baby!"

"Esther, that's enough," their mother scolded. "Abbie, you must learn to mind. Now go change into another nightgown and get back into bed."

Hannah glanced at Abbie's crestfallen expression, feeling a twinge of sympathy. "I'll take her, Mother."

"Yes, do. And please tell Mr. Fontaine that dinner is ready."

Hannah took her little sister's hand and went with her upstairs. In Abbie's room, she helped her change into dry clothing, tucked the child into bed, and pulled the sheets beneath her chin. Feeling remorseful for having lashed out at Abbie before Eric's arrival, she brushed the girl's curls from her forehead. "Don't feel bad, sweetheart. Accidents happen."

"I can't do anything right," Abbie moaned. "And nobody ever lets me try."

Hannah smiled. "Oh, that won't last forever. You're only five."

"Almost six!"

"Yes, all right, never mind. Get some sleep. Things will look brighter in the morning."

"I'm hungry."

"I'll bring you a plate."

Abbie crossed her arms over her chest and pouted, clearly not happy to be stuck in her room. Hannah departed, leaving the small lamp by the bedside lit.

She spotted their guest standing with his arms crossed and looking out the window that stood at the corridor's end.

With her heart fluttering, Hannah approached, noticing how the waning daylight boldly framed his lean physique and brought it into clear view. His coat now absent, Eric wearing only a white shirt and dark trousers, she took in the broad length of his shoulders and back that tapered to a narrow waist, slim hips, and long legs. Clearly whatever work he did at their family's mission kept him in fine form.

Feeling a sudden rush of weakness, she swallowed hard.

Perhaps, a wild man after all. . .

"Mr. Fontaine?"

He turned and looked at her. Since he wasn't wearing his hat, she more easily noticed the slight curl to his thick hair.

"Um, Mother asked me to tell you that dinner is ready."

"Merci. I'll be down shortly." He turned back to the window.

"All right. . ." Confused, she hesitated then walked away.

Why did it seem that he wished to avoid her?

Dinner with the Thomases was nothing like the circus at home, with Eric's nine siblings often all talking at once to be heard. The youngest girl, Abbie, was absent; Hannah's sister Esther acted sullen; and their little brother, David, stared at Eric across the table with blatant curiosity. But for all that, they executed proper table etiquette he'd never seen in children so young. He sensed Hannah's frequent glances but didn't look at her. In the conversation he'd overheard, Hannah's father had made it clear Eric was to have no association with his daughters. He had no wish to cause problems, and he wasn't here to make friends. He would do the job he came to do then return home to New York.

"Tell us what life is like where you come from, Mr. Fontaine," Hannah spoke suddenly.

He glanced at her then away. "We live near the wharf. Our home is split in half: the back part housing our family and the front part the soup kitchen. Basically, it's a huge room with nothing but tables and chairs and a few cots by the wall for those in need of a place to sleep for the night—though Mother has taken a few into our home on occasion."

"Really?" Esther's eyes bulged. "You take bums off the street into your *house*?"

"Esther," her mother said in low reprimand.

The girl's eyes lowered to her plate.

"Mother has a very generous heart," Eric explained. "There have been times when she's given one of my sister's beds to a destitute woman in need—often a runaway or a child thrown out of her parents' home."

Hannah gasped. "People do that? Throw their children out on the streets? I thought that was just in fiction, like in the movies."

Eric regarded her in disbelief. Where had she been the last several years? Didn't she see the effects that the depressed economy had wrought on so many lives?

"Your mother sounds like a wonderful woman," Mrs. Thomas said with a smile. "And your father—he also helps with the mission?"

He recognized her careful question to gain more information. Under the circumstances, he didn't blame her. "Mother is the heart of the mission, but Father is the soul. He runs the place practically single-handedly. He makes a real difference. The difference of hundreds of people not starving. Of making sure that each night everyone who needs it has a hot meal. He treats every man, woman, and child as if they're a guest, not a liability, and cares about each one of them."

He realized he was getting a little too aggressive in pointing out his father's finer qualities and calmed, taking a sip of tea.

"He sounds like a wonderful man." Mrs. Thomas's voice became soothing. "I admire those who sacrifice their needs to put others first, just as our Lord did when He walked the earth."

He smiled at the genteel lady, whose bearing reminded him of benign royalty.

271

During the remainder of the meal, he fielded more questions about his family from the children, especially regarding his siblings. When Mrs. Thomas brought out a pie for dessert, less tension prickled in the atmosphere than when he'd first sat down.

"I bought this at the bakery." Her words sounded like an apology. "I still haven't learned how to master the oven."

Eric regarded her with a curious smile. "We don't have pies, except at Christmas, so it will be a treat."

David looked at him as if he'd come from a foreign country. "Golly, that's awful. We had dessert every night when we lived at Uncle's. Wish we could go back. This place is dumb."

"David." His mother eyed him sternly. "Language. And we must be thankful for what the Lord has provided. I have long prayed that we could live together under one roof as a family."

"I think maybe you should've prayed harder, Mama. 'Cause this roof leaks."

"Weren't we a family at Uncle's?" Esther insisted.

Mrs. Thomas glanced Eric's way, as if in apology, then at her daughter. "We will discuss this another time."

Eric pondered the children's words. Clearly they lived an affluent life before moving. But this huge house with its many rooms could hardly be called one of poverty. What must it be like to have servants take over the most basic of tasks? And what had caused them to leave such a pampered existence? It seemed a useless sort of life, and he felt sorry they'd missed out on the experience of real living up until now.

He found his gaze wandering to Hannah. She used her fork to flake away her piecrust, showing little interest in eating it. She frowned suddenly, then lifted her gaze to his. He inhaled a swift breath, as he looked into her eyes, huge, like those of a doe, but blue-gray in color.

Looking away, he thanked Mrs. Thomas for the meal and excused himself from the table.

Upstairs in his room, he prepared for bed. He had just tied a robe around his pajamas when a light knock sounded on the door. He opened it, surprised to see Hannah. She blinked, taking him in from head to foot.

"You're not going to retire?" she asked in shock.

"It's going on eight thirty."

"Exactly. I thought perhaps you might like to play a game of cards or listen to the radio."

"Thanks, no. If I want to rise before dawn, I should go to bed."

"Before *dawn*?"

At her stunned response, he felt it necessary to ask, "What time do you and your family usually get up?" He didn't want his hammering to wake anyone.

"Mama is up before any of us. I often sleep 'til noon, and so do the others on weekends."

"Noon?" He shook his head in disbelief. He would obviously have to wait on roof repairs and would inspect the lower floor until then. "I appreciate your letting me know. I'll be as quiet as I can."

She appeared at a loss for words. "Well, I suppose there's nothing else. . . . Do you have everything you need?"

"Your mother took care of that earlier."

"Oh. Well, then. Good night."

"Good night."

Eric closed the door, wondering if he'd misread her quiet disappointment.

Minutes later, he found it difficult to concentrate on the scripture passage he'd chosen before retiring, his thoughts centered on this odd family and one member in particular. Recalling a pair of large doe eyes shining up at him with expectation, he closed the book and crawled into bed, dousing the light. He wished he could douse the image of her in his mind as easily. He got the distinct impression that his need to create distance would soon be challenged.

Chapter 4

Hannah awoke and blinked at her clock. Ten o'clock? Thoughts of their houseguest had made it difficult to sleep; she'd been unable to think of little else but Eric and felt surprised at the earliness of the hour.

She dressed and hurried downstairs. There was no sign of their guest, and she stifled a rush of disappointment. She poured herself a cup of coffee from the pot on the stove and took a bagel from the bakery box. Had they been at her great-uncle's, she would have indulged in a four-course breakfast the servants prepared. But stuck with the task of making her own, she decided to dispense with it altogether.

She found Eric in the parlor, pulling back frayed paper to inspect the walls. He turned at her step. "Good. You're up. I need to work on the roof."

"So soon?" she blurted, not wanting him to leave the moment she walked inside.

"I've lost a good four hours of daylight. If you could tell me where your father's tools are? I didn't bring my own."

"I imagine he put them in the shed out back."

He nodded and began to walk away.

"Will you—will you be wanting lunch?"

He looked at her strangely. "You eat lunch this early?"

"No, of course not." Flustered, she tried to think. "I just wanted to know if you would be wanting any." Her words sounded inane, and she wished she could erase the last few minutes and start over again.

He stared as if not sure what to make of her. "Just call me when it's ready."

He disappeared out the door, and she released an aggravated breath. "Fine." Clearly he wanted little to do with her. What had she done to make him lose interest so quickly? He had been so charming when he first arrived, quickly swooping to her rescue when she dropped her story.

Thinking of her manuscript, she sighed and went to the library. Standing on a chair, she pulled her notebook from its hiding place on a top shelf. Abbie would never think to look there, and Hannah's room contained no true area of concealment.

She was well into the third chapter when the doorbell rang.

Reluctant to quit, she set down her pen and answered the door. Her stomach dropped when she saw her guests.

"Bet you didn't think you'd see us again so soon," Muffy gushed as both she and Julia practically shouldered their way past Hannah into the shabby foyer. "We have so much to discuss, but first, where is your simply divine house-guest?" Muffy eagerly looked around the area. "He is such a sheik!"

Hannah's face flamed with embarrassment at Muffy's effusive words and the disparaging glance that Julia offered the stained, papered walls.

"This is quite a...fascinating little place your father found." The adjective came across as *condemned* and *horrid*, befitting a poorhouse.

The two girls moved farther inside without invitation. "Does this...place... have a parlor?" Julia asked in polite disdain.

Hannah felt surprised the mayor's daughter would condescend to remain. "Of course. But Mother might not wish me to entertain company today." She never understood her mother's antipathy toward her socialite friends, whose esteem she'd worked so hard to win, but at this moment, she shared her mother's desire to have them gone.

"Silly Billy." Muffy grabbed her arm. "Did you forget we're part of the theatrical committee for the presentation?"

"But that's a few months away."

"My mother wants to ensure that all goes smoothly." Julia took the lead as if she knew every room in the old house.

Hannah hurried ahead, thankful that the library, at least, wasn't in as ter-rible a condition as the other rooms. "I have the information in here."

Julia's assessing glance of the library could hardly be called accommodat-ing, but Hannah had new problems when she caught sight of Eric walking past.

"There you are!" Muffy practically squealed and rushed into the corridor to snag his arm and pull him inside. "You naughty boy, you're not avoiding us, are you? Where are you off to in such a hurry? The gymnasium? I've never seen such muscles. Tell me, do you lift barbells, too?"

Eric glanced at Hannah, and she winced with embarrassment at Muffy's behavior. He wore no suit coat or tie; his shirtsleeves rolled past his elbows exposed skin baked golden by the sun. His exertions had caused his shirt to cling to his strong physique, and the ends of his hair curled from dampness. Hannah swallowed and put her hand to the desk to support her suddenly weak limbs. Deciding it would be wiser to take a chair, she sat down. Eric looked away from her and smiled at Muffy.

"No, mademoiselle. Just hard, honest labor."

"*Mademoiselle?*" Muffy glanced at Hannah, never letting go of Eric. "He's French? Oh, tell me where you found him. He's just too scrumptious for words!"

"Are you from this area?" Julia's words were almost a purr as she moved with feline grace toward him. "I don't recall seeing you at any society functions."

"I'm from New York."

"New York!" Muffy responded as if the state were on the other side of the world instead of a few hours away by train. "Not that I'm complaining, but whatever are you doing in our small community?" She sidled closer to him.

With a frown, Hannah noticed Eric didn't pull away, didn't even try.

"Eric Fontaine is the son of an old associate of my father's," Hannah explained. "Eric, these are my friends, Muffy and Julia."

"Oh, this is intriguing," Muffy gushed again, smiling up at him. "And Eric is so powerful a name."

Hannah wanted to groan at Muffy's display, wanted to push her out the door and tell both girls to leave her father's pathetic old house.

"So have you come for a visit?" Julia's eyes also shone with interest, looking him up and down as a possible new conquest. She had a habit of acquiring and disposing of beaus whenever she suffered a case of ennui.

"Actually, I've come to help the Thomases."

"Help them?" Muffy looked back and forth from Hannah to Eric in curiosity, as if she'd forgotten Hannah had stated the same thing the previous day.

"I've come to help with repairs on the house."

"You're a handyman?" Julia's eyes widened.

"In this case, yes. If you'll excuse me, ladies. . ."

"I'll call you when lunch is ready," Hannah said before he could leave, perturbed that except for one initial glance in her direction, he had ignored her since entering the room.

"Lunch?" Muffy huffed a little laugh in disbelief. "It's gone past three, dear."

"Past three?" Hannah had been so involved in writing she hadn't realized how much time had elapsed. Her mother must have left the house, not to call them to the meal. "I'm so sorry. . ."

He shrugged. "I found an apple. Ladies, if you'll excuse me." He smiled at her friends, again ignoring Hannah.

"Must you go?" Muffy asked.

"*Oui*, I have a lot of work to finish before sundown."

"My, my. . .a real man. . .off to toil in the great outdoors."

Hannah couldn't be sure if Julia's reply sounded intrigued or insulting.

"I'll call you when dinner's ready then," Hannah called out after him.

He directed the barest of glances her way, without the smile he'd given the others. "Merci. I would appreciate it."

Once he left, the girls turned on her. "What did you do to get on his bad side?" Muffy asked. "Was that just about skipping his lunch?"

"Really, Hannah, the handyman?"

Hannah ignored Julia's evident amused disdain and addressed Muffy. "I'm not on his bad side." She moved away from the desk. "He's just. . .exhausted." And probably hungry. She should have offered to fix him a plate.

"Of course he is." Julia's tone was condescending.

"No wonder you didn't want us to visit your home, you naughty girl." With a mocking smile, Muffy shook her finger at her. "You wanted to keep the goods all to yourself."

"Not that she could." Julia laughed. "The 'goods' are obviously not interested in what Hannah has to offer."

"You're both so wrong." Annoyed with their taunts, Hannah spoke before she thought. "I could get him interested if I wanted to."

"Sure you could." Muffy giggled.

"Yes, I could." Hannah straightened her shoulders. "Actually, he and I got along quite splendidly when he first arrived. If I wanted to, I could interest him like that." She snapped her fingers.

"Care to make a wager?"

"A wager?" Uneasy, she glanced at the door, hoping her mother or another family member wouldn't appear. Or, heaven help her, if Eric should walk by. . .

"Chickening out?" Julia's smile came catty.

"No. I just. . .I don't gamble."

Julia's thin brows shot high. "Oh, we don't have to bet money." She walked a short distance, holding her arm up and slowly shaking her finger, as if contemplating an idea. She turned to face Hannah. "That new boutique on the avenue has the most divine hats. If you can make the handyman fall for you in. . .one month's time, I'll buy you the hat of your choice. But if you can't make him love you, then you owe me a hat of my choice. Deal?"

Hannah winced. Julia's choices were crème de la crème, the most expensive the boutiques had to offer.

"What about me?" Muffy complained. "I want in on this, too."

"Fine." Julia smiled as if she had the upper hand. "You win, you get two hats. You lose, you owe us both one."

Hannah stared at the floor, brooding over her predicament. If she still lived with her great-uncle, such a wager wouldn't have presented a problem. Uncle Bernard always gave her whatever she asked. And Julia knew right where to strike, knowing Hannah's weakness for pretty hats.

"I don't know." She hedged.

"Well, if you don't believe you can hook him, that's understandable." Julia gave a superior little shake of her head. "You're still, shall we say, inexperienced when it comes to matters of how to win a man's interest. I understand your fear of failure, dear."

Hannah set her jaw like flint. "I'm not afraid to fail."

"Then we have a bet?" Julia asked silkily.

"Yes!" Her determination to protect her pride wavered when she realized what she'd done. "Only, maybe we shouldn't—"

"Hannah?"

Before she could attempt to extricate herself from this mess, she heard the taps of her mother's pumps in the corridor. Mother appeared at the door, her expression cooling when she saw Hannah's guests. "I didn't realize you had company."

"They came to discuss plans for the Founder's Day celebration."

Her mother's features calmed. "Oh. Very well, then. I'll leave you to your discussion."

"No need, Mrs. Thomas," Julia said quickly. "We were just leaving."

"We were?" Muffy stared, at a loss.

"Yes." Julia grabbed Muffy's arm, drawing her to the door. She glanced back at Hannah. "Remember—one month. We'll be in touch." Julia left. Muffy gave a little wave and followed.

"One month?"

"Oh, it's nothing. Just a silly idea of Julia's." Hannah's face burned. Relieved her mother hadn't entered earlier and heard the challenge, she gathered the loose pages of her play and tapped them on one end, more to look busy than for any real need to have them straightened.

Her mother looked as if she might speak but instead gave a tight little nod and smile, then left the room. Hannah let the papers drop back to the desk, her eyes falling closed as her shoulders slumped in dismay.

What had she done?

If she lost, she could never afford the hats and Julia would spread her failure far and wide. She had *no choice* but to win. Somehow, before the month was out, she had to make Eric Fontaine Jr. fall madly in love with her.

❧

Rather than retire to his room after dinner, Eric decided to check out the library. Relaxing with a good book would be a pleasurable end to an exhausting day.

He stood before five shelves spread across one entire wall, surprised to see such a vast array of reading material. Tolstoy, Keats, Alcott—the list went on.

Curious to see a novel he'd heard about, he pulled a thick volume from the shelf. The subject dealt with the Civil War; the characters of the book, plantation owners of the Deep South.

A light step at the door announced he had company. He looked up as Hannah breezed in. His heart gave a funny little jolt as it did every time he came across the spoiled young beauty. She had an appealing, unique quality about her—inherited from her exotic mother, no doubt—that blended with a classic refinement suggesting years of privileged breeding.

"Hello." She smiled in approach. Clearly she was happy to see him.

He gave a stiff, unwelcoming nod, looking back at the book in his hands. As he had done so often when she came near, he recalled her father's warning that Eric was to have nothing to do with his daughters. Eric's father had cautioned him not to do anything that would stir the pot of Eric Sr.'s past crimes, since Eric's presence there would serve as a continual reminder. "Be on your best behavior," he had told Eric. "Do nothing that would cause them a moment's grief to have you in their home."

Eric had solemnly agreed, not realizing the true extent of Father's words until he'd arrived at the Thomas residence. To ignore Hannah seemed the wisest course. Unfortunately, she was having none of it.

"What's that you have?" An intoxicating aroma of sweet flowers rushed toward him as she came close and looked over his shoulder. "Ooo—

Margaret Mitchell's classic. How I would've loved to have been in that audience in California earlier this month when David O. Selznick released his preview at that charming little theater! I heard they locked the doors and told the patrons only that another movie would air in place of the one they'd come to see. Once her name rolled across the screen, the people yelled and stood up on their seats, and when the title came on, the crowd was thunderous."

He lifted his brows at her eager recounting of the story.

"I hope it comes to our theater. To have a novel made into a screenplay and received in such a delightful manner is a dream of mine, now that I've contented myself to write the stories I'll never act in. Papa wouldn't let Uncle send me to Hollywood, though I begged him to change his mind. He said I was too young, but really, it's best to start young, don't you agree?"

"I wouldn't know." Eric moved to replace the book on the shelf, and she put her hand to his sleeve. At the unexpected contact, he froze then looked at her.

"Please feel free to read it. I don't mind. If the film is released here soon, we could then compare notes on the novel versus the movie. Who's your favorite motion picture star?" She moved into her question without taking a breath, her manner making him feel a little breathless himself. "Mine is Bette Davis, though I also like Myrna Loy and Claudette Colbert. I find their acting extraordinary, don't you?"

"I've never seen them."

"Never seen them?" Her hand fell from his sleeve, and she blinked her doelike eyes, her painted mouth agape as if he'd committed a cardinal sin. "They are only the crème de la crème of the motion picture industry!"

"I've been to one movie in my life, when I was a boy, before the talkies became popular."

Her mouth dropped a little wider before she closed it and smiled. "You almost had me convinced. You naughty boy for teasing me."

That was twice in one day he'd been addressed by the title, and he didn't like it.

"If you'll excuse me, I'm heading up to my room."

Before he could leave, she grabbed his sleeve again. "Oh, please don't go! I'll simply *expire* from boredom if you don't stay and talk. Or perhaps we might listen to the radio?" The last she offered hopefully, again dropping her hand from his sleeve, slowly this time as if embarrassed.

He looked at her shining face and glowing eyes. She looked far from expiring.

"I have another long day ahead. I should get some sleep."

"But—it's hardly gone past nine o' clock!"

"Exactly. I prefer getting to bed by ten so I can rise before dawn."

She blinked at him as if he spoke an unfamiliar language.

He managed a polite smile. "Good night, mademoiselle. Pleasant dreams."

Eric barely heard her soft good night in return.

Once he closed himself off in his room, he realized he still held her book.

He didn't dare return to the library with her there and decided he may as well give it a shot and read a chapter or two before retiring.

✍

Distressed with her failed attempt at what she had hoped would be a splendid evening with Eric at her beck and call, Hannah paced the library. She could scarcely believe he'd been to only one motion picture in his entire life—surely he had been joking. She stared at the ceiling and wondered if his explanation for an early night had also been delivered in jest. He lived in New York, for pity's sake! The home of Broadway and Times Square. She had never been there, but she'd heard all about the city's glamour from Julia and Muffy, both of them frequent visitors to the Big Apple and its plethora of nightclubs.

She thought about the matchbook Eric had pulled from his pocket. Surely he had visited one or two of those places. Hannah doubted his excuse for ownership of the matches had been valid. And yet. . .he was rather an odd duck in his way of thinking.

In bed before ten?

She decided to ask him about the nightlife at her next opportunity and wondered when that might be. Certainly not tomorrow, since she'd promised to help her mother catalog items for the Ladies' Bazaar. She smiled fondly when she recalled the first of her mother's charities for which she'd volunteered. At the time, her best friend, Clemmie, had been reunited with the love of her life, a man she'd adored since childhood, the dashing Joel. Now they were happily married and living a few miles away, with a little girl on whom they both doted.

Hannah crossed her arms over her chest, hugging herself. Once she had written and sold her best-selling novel and was rolling in the dough from the profits, with her perfect house and devoted servants, she wished for what her dear friend had found. She would be eighteen soon and anticipated finding her own Romeo to her Juliet in the future. No, wait. . .that story ended in tragedy. . .a Rhett to her Scarlett, then.

She frowned, thinking of her book that their guest had taken with him to his room.

That novel also ended without Scarlett gaining her man, not even desiring his love until it was too late. Hannah enjoyed fictional drama but didn't wish to live out their tragic stories—though not all were so heartrending, only the more memorable ones.

With her head drifting in the clouds of imaginary lore, she took the staircase to her room. Once she reached the top landing, her father called out, "Who's there?"

Breaking from her trance, Hannah moved to his doorway. "It's me, Daddy." She whisked a tear from her eye before he could see.

"Kitten. . ." He called her by the pet name he used, then frowned. "Are you crying?"

"It's nothing." He would never understand her sorrow over a tale of fiction.

"Did that Fontaine character have anything to do with your tears?"

At her father's low, stern words, she blinked in confusion. "Eric?" At her familiar use of his name, her father's brows drew farther downward. "No, of course not. I was only thinking of a movie I'd seen."

He sighed and settled back, calm again. "You need to pull your head out of those dream clouds you walk in and learn to live in the real world, Hannah."

"Yes, Daddy." She'd heard his speech a hundred times, if not more. "But if I want to be a novel writer, since I can't be an actress, I have to delve in a bit of fantasy, don't I?"

"Still nursing foolish dreams?"

She frowned. "They're not foolish. Once upon a time, women had to use a man's pseudonym for their books to be published and well received, but those days are long past. Margaret Mitchell proved that with her best seller! And others besides her."

"All right, all right. . ." He lifted his hands in a placating manner. "I know when I'm sunk. But books and movies aren't what I wanted to talk to you about."

While he spoke, her defensiveness gave way to relief, then nervousness. "Oh?"

"While our. . .houseguest is staying here, I want you to keep out of his way. He's not the kind of man I want my daughters consorting with."

That puzzled her. Of all the young men she'd known, Eric seemed the least dangerous. One certainly couldn't accuse him of a life spent in dissipation— he'd probably only had acquaintance with the word when browsing through a dictionary. And she knew his economic status didn't matter—her parents had conceived this plan of moving into the rickety old farmhouse to take their children *away* from associating with the privileged class.

"I don't understand, Daddy." She voiced her confusion. "He seems like a nice man."

"Don't let appearances deceive you, Hannah. I don't trust him, and you'd be wise to follow my lead."

Hannah could barely believe what she was hearing. Eric had done nothing to merit disfavor. He'd done his utmost to seclude himself in his room, away from the family, at every opportunity. Hadn't her parents endlessly told her not to judge people for others' mistakes and to give second chances? Her father hadn't known she'd eavesdropped on his conversation with her mother, but Hannah realized that's exactly what he was doing—judging Eric Jr. for Eric Sr.'s crimes.

The thought made her feel defensive for Eric and upset with her father. "It hardly seems fair to judge him so harshly since he's done nothing wrong."

"Han–*nah*," he stressed, "I don't want you getting involved with the man."

Involved? No, not that. The challenge to hook Eric's interest was just a challenge. If she surrendered now, the girls would spread it all over town that poor little Hannah couldn't gain the interest of the handyman. She would be whispered about and laughed at wherever she went. Once she won the bet, she would come up with a plausible excuse of why it would be best not to spend time with Eric any longer, perhaps using her father's own rule that she avoid him.

But she had no interest in getting involved with the man. He must be dull as dishwater, to retire so early and rise at dawn and have no knowledge of the entertainment industry.

She sighed. "All right, I'll be careful, Daddy. If there's nothing else, I'm going to bed."

"Good night then. I love you, Hannah. That's why I care."

Her heart warmed at his tender words, and she moved forward to kiss his cheek before retiring. She couldn't help glancing toward the opposite end of the corridor, where Eric's door stood closed.

As she prepared for bed, Hannah considered her plan. She wasn't really going against her father's wishes since she wasn't truly getting involved. Yet she didn't understand why her parents were so strict; after all, she was no longer a child.

Mother was barely seventeen when she'd married Daddy, and Clemmie a couple of weeks shy of eighteen when she married Joel. Hannah had no desire to marry anyone anytime soon, but why couldn't her parents trust her to make her own choices as they had? Besides, her little plan wouldn't hurt anyone; she would make sure of that.

Her father was so wrong about Eric. He just couldn't see it right now. But all would work out well in the end. Daddy would laugh away his groundless fears, Eric would profess his undying love, after which she would let him down easy so that perhaps they might remain friends, and she would become the proud owner of two adorable new hats from the snazziest boutique the town had to offer.

Long into the night, she mulled over Operation Hook Eric. He had barely shown her any attention the few times she had tried. Grimly, she realized if she were to succeed, she would have to resort to the most desperate of measures.

Chapter 5

His third day at the Thomas residence, Eric rose before dawn, read his morning devotions, groomed, dressed, and went downstairs. A light rain tapped against the kitchen window when he greeted Mrs. Thomas as he did every morning. She always gave him breakfast, after which they drank a cup of coffee and engaged in pleasant conversation.

"I obviously won't be working on the roof today." He took a seat at the table. "I had hoped to have it finished by the end of this week. I was able to make some patches, so the leaks should be fixed over the bedrooms."

She turned from buttering toast. "Thank you! It will be so nice not to worry about these rains that come and the leaks with them." She set a plate of eggs, bacon, and toast before him.

"Merci."

"My pleasure." She retrieved their cups of coffee and took the chair across from him. "What do you feel should be the next order of business?"

"Working on the parlor walls. It gets so cold in there. My expertise extends only to patching up cracks, like with the roof. You'll want to hire professionals to replace both in the spring."

"At present, patching up is all we can manage, and we're very grateful for whatever help you can give. . . ." Her words trailed off as she looked beyond him, her expression surprised. "Hannah? Are you feeling all right, dear?"

"Of course, Mother."

At the hoarse words, Eric cast a glance over his shoulder. Hannah stood in the doorway, *stood* being a relative term since she leaned against the lintel as if it were the sole thing supporting her from sinking to the tiles. Her hair didn't look as well combed as usual, and the skin beneath her eyes appeared slightly puffy. Yet such minor flaws did nothing to detract from her rare beauty, and Eric turned back to his meal, ill at ease.

Esther scampered into the kitchen, holding a strap that buckled her schoolbooks together. She stared at Hannah. "Hello. You're up early. Are you going into New York with Muffy and Julia?"

"What's this?" Mrs. Thomas retorted sharply. "Hannah, I'll not have you go to such a city, and certainly not with those girls!"

"I'm not, Mother, I'm—"

David clomped into the kitchen, casting a curious glance at his oldest sister. "Great balls of fire! What are you doing up so early?"

"Can't a girl rise with the sun without getting the third degree?" Hannah snapped miserably.

"It's just that you've never done so before, dear." A hint of amusement touched her mother's voice.

"Why bother?" David complained. "If I didn't have to get up so darn early to walk to school, I'd sure be sleeping now."

"David, watch your language," their mother reproved.

The boy grumbled something that resembled an apology. "Wish we still lived at Uncle's and had his chauffeur to drive us."

"Eat your eggs, and be thankful for what you do have." His mother set a plate in front of him. "Many children don't have breakfast. Or nice clothes. Or a roof over their heads."

"A leaky roof," the boy complained.

"Not anymore, thanks to Mr. Fontaine." She directed a grateful smile his way.

"Humph." The boy grouched. "I'd trade it all in for a few more hours of sleep."

Mrs. Thomas sighed. Hannah moved toward the stove, poured herself a cup of coffee, and selected a piece of toast. She brought her items to the table, taking the empty chair beside Eric. He looked back to his food before she could notice him staring.

The meal passed in relative silence.

"I need a pencil for school, Mama," Esther suddenly announced.

"What happened to the one I gave you?"

"I must have lost it on the walk home yesterday."

Her mother sighed. "You need to be more careful with your things, Esther. Very well, come with me, and I'll see if I can locate another one in the library."

"And I need more paper." David jumped up from his chair to follow.

"You wouldn't if you didn't use what I gave you on spit wads. Don't think I don't know what you've been doing, young man. . . ."

"Hard to believe they were once model children, isn't it?"

Hannah's question to Eric broke the silence that settled around them once the others left.

"They're not that much different from my brothers and sisters." Eric glanced her way—into huge, light-colored eyes, noting how soft the thick fringes of her long black lashes were—which suddenly made him realize how close she'd scooted to him.

He stood and grabbed his plate, taking it to the sink.

"You're not leaving?" she asked, clearly unhappy with the idea.

"I have work to do."

"But you haven't finished your coffee."

Eric glanced at his half-filled cup, wanting both the warmth and the boost before entering the cold parlor. "I'll take it with me." He picked it up by its saucer and left.

Inside the parlor, he took sips of the hot brew as he walked around the room, studying its walls and figuring out his next course of action. He'd told Mrs. Thomas he would need to rip away the paper to make repairs, which meant the walls would be an eyesore, but she'd assured him that the room's temperature was more important than dingy displays of cabbage roses and that she hoped to repaper the walls in any case.

He had pulled the furniture away from the baseboards when a footfall from behind captured his attention. He looked over his shoulder.

Hannah entered the room.

≈❧

"Please, don't let me disturb you." Hannah smiled and moved toward the desk he'd pulled away from the wall. She laid down her notebook and sat down, noting he still stared as if uncertain why she'd come.

Simpering in the same way Muffy did hadn't gained her an ounce of coveted attention or the kind smile he'd given her friend. She wasn't so bold as to come on to him like gangbusters as Julia had done, either, so she needed to devise her own schemes.

"I work best in this room because it has the most windows for light," she explained, opening the notebook she'd unearthed from its hiding place in the library. "The ladies' committee has commissioned me to write a play for the Founder's Day picnic." Though she received no pay for her volunteer work, she hoped her words sounded important enough to impress him.

He gave a little grunt and turned back to study the wall. "I can start in another room so I won't bother you."

"No! I mean, you won't bother me." She could also move to another room, but that would defeat her purpose in being here—to put herself wherever he was so he couldn't help but notice her.

Of course, that proved difficult when his back was constantly turned her way.

Lightly tapping pen on paper, she, on the other hand, had a clear and constant view of his fine physique as he cut sections of the old, brittle wallpaper with a knife and peeled it from the wall. She wondered if he engaged in sports to be so toned, trim, and agile, or if his work at the mission had honed him to perfection.

He turned suddenly and caught her staring.

Her face flushed hot, and she dropped her gaze to the paper where she'd written three whole words: *We will prevail.*

He moved toward the door, arresting her attention.

"Where are you going?"

At her breathless rush of words, he looked at her a little strangely. "To the shed. I'm hoping your father has a bag of plaster to caulk up the cracks and provide temporary insulation."

She shrugged, relieved that he was coming back. "I'm not sure what's out there, but he purchased a number of items he would need before he had his accident."

Eric nodded and left the parlor.

Hannah sighed, dropped her pen, and gracefully slumped back in the chair. Perhaps the colonists in her play had prevailed, but she wasn't doing so well.

This would take more thought. If she were bold like Julia, she would un-button the top two buttons of her blouse and sit so as to bring attention to her shapely legs. If she were gregarious like Muffy, she might continuously clear her throat or make little humming noises now and then to remind Eric of her presence. But she was no seductress, and she certainly didn't want to come across as annoying. Since planting herself against the wall in his line of vision was clearly out of the question, she would have to resort to a different method.

A possibility came to mind that held no appeal. However, she didn't see how it could fail and dourly resigned herself to initiate a new phase to her plan.

With the items he needed located and prepared, Eric drew out his time in the shed until he felt sure Hannah would have given up and left the parlor. Upon his return, he realized his mistake.

"I was beginning to think we might need to send a search party after you." Hard at work with whatever she wrote, Hannah looked over her shoulder and greeted him with a bright smile, dimples flashing in her cheeks. "Oh my. How'd you get so wet?"

"It is raining." Struck anew by her beauty, he attempted a return smile and moved back to the wall. He used a piece of sheeting to rub most of the dampness from his clothes, keeping his back to her. At least that way he could almost forget her existence in the room; whatever perfume she wore filled the air with the scent of flowers. He tossed down his makeshift towel and set to work.

When he heard the chair skid back and her footfall, followed by a stronger wash of those flowers, his hand tightened on the mixing stick.

She dropped to her knees close beside him. He turned a startled glance her way.

"Hannah?" Her mother's voice preceded her as she approached the door.

Eric jumped up so fast he almost knocked over the pail of plaster paste.

Dressed in a slicker, Mrs. Thomas lifted her brow but thankfully didn't ad-dress the issue of why they'd been kneeling so close to one another. He didn't want her mother getting the wrong idea.

"The rain is coming down harder. I'll need to run the children to school. I don't want them coming down with what Abbie has."

"Mother, are you sure?"

Eric detected worry in Hannah's voice and glanced at her as she slowly rose to her feet.

"You know Daddy won't like it."

Mrs. Thomas smiled. "I'll be fine as long as there are no sudden stops. It's only a couple of miles."

She disappeared, and Hannah grabbed Eric's sleeve. He had the impression she didn't even realize she'd done so. "Daddy doesn't like her driving in bad weather; she's not good at the wheel. She gets very nervous in thunderstorms."

He nodded and hurried after her mother. "Mrs. Thomas!" He caught her just walking out the door. "Why not let me drive them? I need to drop by the drugstore and pick up a few things I forgot. This would give me the opportunity."

"But you don't know your way around town."

"I'll go along too," Hannah offered quickly.

"Well, I don't know. . . ."

"I'm a good driver," Eric assured. "I often use the family car to run errands for the mission."

"And if you're gone when Daddy wakes up," Hannah added, "he won't like it."

"You're right about that. Very well. Thank you." Mrs. Thomas handed Eric the keys. "Children, hurry. You don't want to be late."

David and Esther appeared in yellow slickers and matching bonnets. "Do we have to go? Can't we stay home since it's raining?" David groused.

"Of course not."

Hannah rummaged through the coats in the front closet and retrieved a black slicker.

"Have you no raincoat?" she asked Eric.

"I'll be fine."

"You'll be soaked in this deluge, and we wouldn't want you to catch a cold, either. Here. It's Josiah's. He left it behind."

He nodded his thanks and shrugged into the borrowed raincoat while she did the same with a smaller version in a navy color. He grabbed his hat, and she pulled a rain bonnet over her disheveled hair, then led him to a Packard beside the house. Eric pulled up the collar of the slicker, hunching his shoulders against the rain. The children ran behind and jumped in the car. Eric opened Hannah's door, waiting for her to get inside and shutting it before hurrying to duck in behind the wheel.

Visibility was poor, the flashes of lightning in the distance filling the skies and causing Esther to squeal each time. Eric drove carefully along the country road and across a covered bridge, the stream below frothing in its mad rush along the rocks.

Soon Hannah told him to make a right turn, which took them into the business district of the small community. At the schoolhouse, they dropped off the children, and Hannah instructed him how to find the drugstore. Once there, he ran inside, ducking the storm as best he could, and bought a box of baking soda to brush his teeth and extra shaving supplies. He had no idea how long he would be staying at the Thomas residence, but with the miserable shape of the house and the uncooperative weather, it could be awhile.

On the drive back, the storm began to diminish, enough to be heard without practically shouting over the rain, and Hannah took the opportunity. "Does New York get much bad weather?"

"We live beside the Atlantic Ocean." He grinned, casting her a sidelong glance. "What do you think?"

"I've never been to the ocean, never been much of anywhere, though we did live upstate when I was a child—in a children's reformatory on a farm. My father worked there, helping to keep things in repair, and my uncle was—still is—the schoolmaster."

"At the Lyons farm?" he asked in surprise.

"You know them?"

"My father didn't name names in public, of course, but he told my family. The Lyonses came to see him years ago."

"Yes, I remember that day; I was six." Her voice sounded tight. "My father went to see him with Uncle Stewart and Aunt Charleigh—they're not really my aunt and uncle by blood, but I call them that because our families are close. Lady Annabelle's son and his fiancé were staying at the farm. They were running from a gangster and seeking refuge. That's how they found out about your father living close by."

"Really?" His brows went up.

"Yes, I overheard them talking one night. So tell me, what's it like in New York City? It must be wonderful on Broadway, with the glamour and lights. Both Julia and Muffy have said it's spectacular. Of course, I know that live entertainment is different from motion pictures, but it's still entertainment, isn't it? I once aspired to be an actress, but Mama wouldn't allow the lessons." She scarcely took a breath. "Oh dear. I'm doing it again, aren't I? I have a tendency to ramble in conversation."

"No, it's fine." Her mix of breathless sentences hadn't annoyed him. At least now she acted more like herself and less like her friends: gushing in the library the previous evening and being so bold that morning.

"But you still haven't told me. What's Broadway like?" She twisted to sit sideways for a better look at him. "I'd like to hear a man's perspective."

"I've never been."

"What?"

He didn't miss the profound shock in her voice. "I thought you lived close to the city."

"We do."

"But. . ." She shook her head as if unable to fathom the idea. "How can you live there all your life and never visit Broadway? I know you've been to the nightclubs. I saw your matchbook."

"Like I told your mother, it wasn't mine."

She gaped at him. "You're serious."

"Not everyone who lives in New York takes part in the nightlife."

"But you live so close! It just seems odd that you would never have visited."

"Mother warned all of us, as far back as I can remember, never to go there. Father agreed."

"But I thought he—" She ended her words abruptly, but he understood what she didn't say.

"Prowled the city, engaging in all the depravity it had to offer? He did at one point. Before he met Mother. The gangsters he'd been involved with who live there still pose a threat, another reason my parents warned us not to go there. My father really has changed."

"I believe you." Her tone came soft, barely heard above the patter of rain.

He glanced her way, for the first time relaxing. "Thank you for that. Still, I'm certain your parents—your father especially—will be relieved once I'm gone. My father and your father had quite an illustrious association with those gangsters."

"My father? Oh, you mean how he got involved with those men. Owing them money for a loan, I imagine."

"I don't know about that." He shook his head. "I meant when they worked together for Vittorio Piccoli."

"My father worked for the Piccoli mob?"

"You didn't know?"

"I—I knew some—"

At her stunned behavior, he winced, realizing too late he shouldn't have spoken. His father had never withheld one sordid act he'd done, sharing his testimony with the suffering as a means of offering hope that God could forgive them, too. It hadn't crossed Eric's mind that Hannah wouldn't know about her father's past.

With relief, he noticed the farmhouse come into view and pulled into the drive. He walked around and opened the door for Hannah. She didn't move, staring straight ahead.

"Are you all right?"

His quiet words snapped her out of whatever trance held her spellbound, and she accepted his help from the car. "Thank you."

He nodded and walked with her into the house. Once he put away his borrowed rain gear, he returned to the parlor and resumed his task. Not to his surprise, Hannah came in behind him.

He heard the chair slide away as she took a seat behind the desk. After a short time, the chair again skidded on the floor, and he heard her approach. He didn't look her way until she sank to her knees beside him, as she'd done before. This time, she didn't do it boldly, as if she might pounce, but seemed insecure, her palms touching each other, clasped between her legs in the folds of her skirt.

"Can I help?"

His mouth parted in shock. "You want to help me?"

"I find it difficult to concentrate on my play."

"I'm sorry." He felt bad. "I shouldn't have told you like that."

"It's all right." She smiled faintly. "I'm glad at least someone in this house is honest with me."

He winced, hearing a hint of underlying anger in her tone. "Don't be upset with your father. He must have had good reason for not telling you."

"Hmm." She averted her attention to the pail. "Show me how it's done?"

"No, really, I can handle it. You don't have to—"

"I want to. I'm bored, and it might be fun."

Fun? "I only have one stick."

"I can remedy that." Before he could stop her, she broke it in half. "Now we have two."

At the bright smile she gave, her bleak mood lifting, he managed to curb a groan.

"Oui, it seems we do." The shorter stick would make it harder to dip into the paste without submerging his fingers, but he didn't really want to wade back through the storm to the shed to find another.

He made one, last-ditch effort. "You might end up ruining that pretty dress."

His warning had the opposite effect as her expression softened. "You think my dress is pretty?"

He did, but not half as pretty as the girl wearing it. At the sudden thought, he looked away from her shimmering eyes and focused on his task, dipping the decapitated stick into the goo and smearing it over a crack. "It's all right, as ladies' dresses go. Point is, you'll get it dirty, and it looks as if it cost a small fortune."

"Yes, that's true." She looked uncertain; then her face brightened again. "I'll be right back. Don't go anywhere!"

Before he could respond, she jumped up and dashed out of the parlor.

Chapter 6

Hannah sorted through the box of charity items her mother had collected for the next bazaar, recalling she'd thrown in some of Josiah's ill-fitting clothes. Finding a pair of denim jeans and a flannel shirt, she held them up to her. Baggy, but a sash belt would hold them up, and she could roll up the sleeves.

Excited that the first step of her plan was working, she ducked into her room to change.

Rising at dawn had been a challenge; every muscle in her young body had complained at leaving her soft warm bed. A dusting of powder had done little to eliminate signs of weariness beneath her eyes, and her hair had frizzed due to the humidity. The pretty blue dress and coat of lipstick had helped, but she'd been tempted to crawl back into bed and forget the whole thing. A glance at one of her hats had brutally reminded her of the challenge and acted as the push to send her out the door.

Now, she tied her thick hair back with a ribbon, the thought of combing out plaster bits not appealing. She glanced in the mirror, wincing at the thought of Julia and Muffy dropping by unannounced and catching her in such drab clothes, and men's clothes at that! But sometimes sacrifice was imperative to achieve success.

Her door opened as she knotted the silk sash around her waist. She watched in the mirror as her mother entered, her arms full of folded linens. Her eyes widened in surprise to see Hannah's attire. She turned to face her mother, bolstering her courage.

"I've decided to help Eric—that is, Mr. Fontaine—with the repairs."

"Really?" Her mother drew out the word softly. She looked at Hannah a moment before moving to the bureau and opening the top drawer, tucking several items inside. "May I ask what brought about this sudden decision?"

In the face of her mother's seeming calm, Hannah floundered for an answer. "If he has help, it will mean we'll have a warm house much sooner, if not a better one. Though I still don't see why we had to leave Uncle's in the first place."

"Your father and I have our reasons."

A twinge of resentment made her blurt, "Just like you had your reasons for keeping it secret about Daddy being a gangster?" Her mother swung around, her lips parting in dread surprise and confirming Eric's words. "Yes, Mother, I know. Why did you never tell me?"

"Did Mr. Fontaine tell you this?"

"It slipped out in conversation. He had the mistaken impression that our family is truthful with one another."

Her mother sighed. "We thought it best to leave such details in the past, where they belong. They no longer concern our family."

"Don't they?" Hannah spread her hands in confusion. "How can Daddy hate Eric's father so much, if he was also a criminal?"

"It's complicated, Hannah. And he doesn't hate him, not really."

She shook her head. "I just don't understand how he can be so, so hypocritical."

"Hannah! Do not say such things about your father."

"You both taught me never to play judge and jury. What happened to giving second chances, Mother? To honesty?"

She closed her eyes on another sigh. "We felt it best to shield our children from the crimes your father once committed. We wanted. . .a fresh start."

"So why won't Daddy give Mr. Fontaine a chance for a fresh start?"

"I cannot speak for your father. But in all he does, in every decision he makes, he does so for the protection of our family."

Hannah knew that to be true, knew that he loved them, but still couldn't help feeling betrayed as well as upset over the critical words he'd spoken about Eric.

"I've had several occasions to speak with our guest," her mother continued, "and I find him to be a pleasant young man raised on good, solid principles. It may take longer for your father to see, but a person's true character always does come out."

"I hope so." A smattering of guilt made Hannah fidget and study the cracks in the floor. "Daddy warned me from spending time alone with him. But I don't understand why. He's very nice."

Regardless of her plan to hook him, Hannah had seen his kindness and felt another rush of remorse for having agreed to Julia's challenge. If her mother learned of Hannah's true reason for wanting to spend time in Eric's company, she would be ashamed of her daughter.

"I will speak with your father."

Hannah looked up sharply. "Then you don't mind if I help Eric?"

Her mother regarded her in surprise. "My feelings would matter to you?"

"Of course." Hannah felt bad for the words she'd earlier spouted. "I care about your opinion."

Her mother's rigid expression eased into relief. "Then I will tell you, my dear. You may think you're a woman, and in many ways you are, but all too often you think as a child. So I give you this advice, Hannah: Be as wise as a serpent and as harmless as a dove. Do nothing that one day you may have cause to regret."

Those words haunted Hannah as she returned downstairs. Could Mother somehow know of the challenge? No, it wasn't possible. If her mother had guessed, her words to Hannah wouldn't have been so civil.

She stepped into the parlor, and Eric looked over his shoulder. His eyes widened in clear shock at her appearance, but she trusted that with the pretty sash and hair ribbon and the dab of fresh lipstick she didn't look too bad.

"Here I am," she said needlessly.

"I've been thinking. Maybe you shouldn't help with this. I don't think your father would approve of your being in my company more than necessity allows."

She bristled at that. Did everyone think her such a child? "I've just spoken with Mother, and she approved, so there's no longer a problem." She approached and knelt back down, picking up the stick. "Just show me what to do."

Eric's attitude grudging, he did as she asked. As the morning passed into afternoon, she tried to initiate conversation, but he'd gone into a brooding silence, and she realized that whatever the reason, *he* had a problem with her being there.

She withheld a sigh. It would take patience and time, but eventually she would win him over.

☙

Eric couldn't figure Hannah out. When they met, she had seemed reserved and anxious, which made sense, given the circumstances. After the last visit from her socialite friends, for some curious reason she'd tried to imitate their annoying traits. But when she appeared in unfashionable men's work clothes, which made her look home-girl cute and not at all boyish, ready to help, as she'd done every day this week, he'd been entirely flummoxed.

Just what was her game?

He had relented, hoping the two of them working together could speed the process up and he'd be out of everyone's way that much faster. Though "help" could hardly describe her actions, and instead of speeding things up, she'd slowed them down.

He wondered why he even put up with her shoddy attempts, her ignorance in the most basic of tasks not coming as a surprise due to her former privileged life. He felt sorry for the spoiled little princess, even befriended her, though he hoped he hadn't made a mistake in doing that.

Today they'd spackled the last wall in the parlor. Already he could tell a difference in the room's temperature and no longer felt as if he walked inside a refrigerated box. Splotches of hardened gray plaster covered damaged spots where paper had been torn away. He wondered if he would be asked to help with the wallpapering, then decided he should offer since his repairs had been responsible for making the walls a monstrosity.

The family hardly seemed impoverished, at least in matters of money; they certainly didn't suffer like those who visited the mission. But Eric reasoned that Mr. Thomas had little to no money left, after buying the property, to hire professional help. The house was huge, with six bedrooms and three baths, and who knew how many more rooms? He hadn't counted and had no idea how long it would take to go through each and accomplish any necessary repairs. With Hannah's sloppy work and his need to redo her mistakes, additional cleanup amounted to hours. He wondered if he would be out of here by Christmas.

Still, as he told himself numerous times a day, it was for a good cause. This family needed his help, though he sensed the eldest daughter needed a far different kind of help, help he wasn't sure he knew how to give.

What made him think of her?

And where could she be?

She had told him she would return soon. That had been at least a quarter of an hour ago. Likely she was again working on her little play or fantasizing over some movie, playing it out in her mind, her head, as usual, in the clouds. How many times had he repeated her name when she was immersed in some movie fantasy, as she'd then explained to him and in great detail?

Shaking his head to scatter thoughts of Hannah, whom he certainly did not need to think about, Eric saw he needed more plaster. He picked up the bucket and left the room to make another trip to the shed. He stopped in his tracks, across from the stairwell, stunned at the sight that met his eyes.

Hannah lay draped over the top of the newly waxed split-level banister, stomach down. As he gaped, he watched her push at the bevel post to catapult her descent. Like butter over a griddle, she flew down the narrow rail. Anxious when he saw her teeter to one side, Eric dropped the pail and rushed forward, lifting his arms to catch her.

His hands made contact with her hips, sliding to a stop at her waist before her bottom could hit the large beveled post at the main landing. She let out a startled gasp and tried to look over her shoulder, almost losing her grip on the banister and toppling to the stairs.

"Steady," Eric warned, keeping his hands fixed on her as she pulled one denim-clad leg up over the rail to meet with the other on the bottom stair.

"What were you doing?" He addressed her in stupefied disbelief the moment she faced him. Her fair skin flushed the color of a pink rose, her gaze skittering from her feet to the front door.

A burst of clapping came from above, drawing Eric's attention to the top landing, where Abbie leaned over the rail in excitement. "You did it, Hannah! You did it!" She ran to the railing. "Watch me! Catch me, too!"

Before Eric could bat an eyelid, Abbie came hurtling toward him. He raised his hands to catch her before she could make painful contact with the post. "I did it, I did it!" she squealed as he peeled her off the railing and set her on her feet.

He looked back and forth between sisters. Hannah now looked at him, embarrassment in her eyes.

"Hannah used to slide down the banister at Uncle's house," Abbie explained, "but I was too scared. Mama just polished them, and Hannah said that's when they're best for sliding. I said it was too scary, and she said it wasn't so bad as it was at Uncle's 'cause they're split-level here and not so high—"

"Abbie, that's enough," Hannah reproved quietly. "I'm sure Mr. Thomas doesn't care to hear of our silly doings."

"Wait'll Esther hears. She always calls me a baby. Just wait'll she hears." With that, Abbie ran from the foyer, leaving the two of them alone.

"Um, thanks for catching me. I'd forgotten how slick those rails could be." Eric nodded and retraced his steps to pick up the pail.

"You must think me rather foolish." She followed him. "The children miss the other place, and I had hoped to cheer Abbie."

"You don't owe me any explanations." Eric studied her. "Though it does seem that you take having fun a little too seriously."

Her eyes were curious. "I'm not sure I understand."

"I've been here over a week and have noticed, if you're not lost in some fantasy, all you can think about is the next good time to be had. You take the idea to a new extreme. I'm not sure why you offered to help me, because you even try making a game out of that."

She frowned. "And what's so wrong with operating on the bright side of things? As long as the job gets done."

"Do you ever notice a darker side exists?"

She shook her head in confusion. "Why should I try?"

"Because there's more to life than silly parties and fantasy stories."

She gaped at him in clear shock. "I'm not sure why you would say that to me. When have I talked about parties? Okay, yes, I did ask about the nightlife in New York City—is that what you mean? But writing the play is my life right now. Is that so wrong? Besides, I do other things. I've helped Mother with cataloging her bazaars. And that can be awfully tedious work. And I've helped you this past week, haven't I? I'm not entirely helpless, as you seem to think."

He refrained from telling her he could have finished three rooms alone in the time it took to do one with her help, keeping in mind her inexperience and not wanting to hurt her feelings after hearing her impassioned speech.

"I never said you're helpless. It's not that I'm ungrateful. I realize you're trying to help." He shook his head as he struggled with what should be said and what should remain silent. "Let's just drop it, all right?" He moved to the door and opened it, walking across the grounds to the shed. He heard her footsteps rustle in the leaves behind him.

"No, let's not drop it. I want to know what you meant."

He turned, and she backed up a quick step. He hadn't realized how close to his heels she'd been. "You really want to know?"

"I said so, didn't I?"

"You have no concept of the real world."

She laughed. "That's absurd. Of course I do."

"Do you?" He waved a hand toward the house in back of her. "You turn your cute little nose up at the house your father bought your family"—he realized the terminology he'd used to describe her nose and hurried ahead, hoping she didn't catch his slip—"and I couldn't begin to count how many families would consider this place a godsend and be grateful for such a roof over their heads, even with all its flaws."

She blinked and he wondered what she was thinking. "It's just beneath what we're used to."

"Yes, I know. Your great-uncle's vast mansion. Tell me, do you even know that this country has been suffering a major depression for the past ten years?"

"Of course. I haven't been living in a cave."

"Haven't you? You concentrate on such foolish nonsense when there are more worthwhile endeavors to pursue."

"Tell me that you are not calling my play foolish nonsense! One day my works will achieve nationwide acclaim—you'll see. Then you'll have to eat those words, Eric Fontaine!"

He snorted. "Who cares about a silly play when a person's belly is cramping from starvation? When they don't have a dime to buy a meal and use boxes in the alley for a bed?"

She winced. "Not everyone can run a mission."

"Maybe not, but you don't have to turn a blind eye to the suffering of a nation."

She threw her hands up to shoulder level. "What do you want me to do about it? I'm just one person."

"If everyone had that attitude, our country would have gone to the dogs a long time ago. It takes only one person to make a difference, Hannah. Instead of focusing on all the recent motion picture releases and the stars who make them, try looking at the actual world around you for a change. Life isn't composed of a celluloid movie. Those stories and characters aren't even real!"

She tilted her chin up defensively. "My Aunt Darcy taught me there should be a balance in life. That a person shouldn't spend all their time working but should have fun, too. 'All work and no play makes Jack a dull boy'—isn't that how the saying goes? She made even work fun—holding fence-painting contests with her pies as a prize, and the like. Your problem is the same as my uncle's was: You think everything has to be work, work, work."

"It seems to me, since he owns a mansion and spends most of his time globetrotting, he's an A-1 candidate for a good time."

"Wrong uncle. I'm talking about Uncle Brent and Aunt Darcy, who live at Lyons Refuge—the children's reformatory farm I told you about. Uncle Brent didn't know how to have fun, either, until Aunt Darcy came along." A smug expression tilted her mouth. "Besides, I heard that since Europe made requests for weaponry due to the war with Hitler raging over there, Connecticut has opened jobs at the munitions factories to many people in our state who were out of work."

His surprise at her knowledge of the affairs of her state, much less that there was a war going on, must have shown, because she scowled at him and lifted her chin higher. "I'm not a dunce. I do hear about current affairs."

"Hearing about them isn't the same as experiencing them firsthand."

"So, let me get this straight: You think I should sleep in a box or go without a meal to experience what the unfortunate in our country are suffering."

"I think you should open your eyes to the real world and stop living with your head in the clouds."

"And I think you should learn that a little fun won't kill you and can make the drudgery of a task disappear."

"I know how to have fun."

"Do you?"

Eric shook his head in exasperation, suddenly realizing they stood toe-to-toe in the middle of the yard, arguing at a level to be heard from inside the house. She smiled sweetly, alerting him to possible trouble.

"I have a proposition for you."

He narrowed his eyes. "What sort of proposition?"

"You seem to think I have no concept of the real world. I question if you know what it's like to have fun. You choose something for me to experience that will satisfy your idea of what's 'real.' But you have to agree to spend an afternoon doing something I think is fun. Agreed?" She stuck out her hand.

He glanced down at it then back into her eyes. "Your parents might not go along with that."

She frowned. "I can make my own decisions. But if it'll make you feel better, I'll clear it with Mother first."

He put out his hand, but before she could grasp it, he pulled away. "If both your parents agree, then we have a deal."

"Of course."

He brought his hand forward and clasped hers, noticing how his large hand engulfed her small one. A rush of warmth made him swiftly pull his hand away.

"I need to get back to work on the roof."

"I thought we were finishing the wall."

He felt the need to distance himself from Hannah. "While we finally have a sunny day, I should be up on that roof, finishing repairs. I should have resumed this morning."

"All right. Let me throw a coat on. It's a bit nippy."

"What—why?" He stopped her with a hand to her sleeve then instantly dropped it away.

"To help you, of course."

"*You* are not going up on that roof."

She cast a doubtful glance upward then at the ladder he'd left leaning on the side of the house. "I could bring you what you need—"

"Non. Your parents would never forgive me if you fell."

She sighed. "All right then. I suppose I should spend time working on the play. Clear your calendar for Saturday, though, and I'll plan our outing then."

"After you talk to your mother."

"I told you I would." She pouted, and he nodded, the deal made.

She turned to go then pivoted on her heel. "Remember, this Saturday. . ."

"I won't forget."

He wished he could.

Chapter 7

Once Saturday arrived, Hannah sat in a muddle of confusion, unable to concentrate on her story. At least she'd finished the first act of the play, but she was having kittens trying to finish the next chapter of her novel. Worse, the hero rescuer had begun to develop the physical traits of a certain houseguest.

She threw down her pen. This was getting her nowhere. Maybe if she had Great-Uncle Bernard's typewriter. . . . Who was she trying to fool? The writing implement wasn't the problem. The real problem hammered up on the roof. She turned her eyes up to the ceiling and wished. . .what?

Nothing about getting involved, surely. Among other good reasons for why it would be a very bad idea: If she allowed her feelings to get in the way, they might prevent her from following through with her plan.

She didn't need two new hats but certainly couldn't afford to buy them. Where would she get the money? She supposed she could somehow find a ride to the mansion, but if her mother ever got wind that she'd asked Great-Uncle Bernard for money, Hannah would be in bigger trouble than if her mother learned she had agreed to the challenge. For some reason, lately her mother wanted nothing to do with her uncle, and that forced distance included the rest of the family, as well.

Hannah had no choice but to win.

Looking at the clock, she shrieked. Only an hour left before her outing with Eric. Pushing away from the desk, she hurried to her room. Her plan was ingenious really, similar to the agreement Aunt Darcy once made with Uncle Brent. Deciding against wearing boys' jeans, she chose a skirt that would give ample leg room but was fitted enough not to risk getting tangled in the bike gears or chain. If anyone outside her home spotted her in drab men's attire, she would be humiliated. Besides, she had to look her best if she was going to interest Eric, who still seemed to prefer being anywhere else than with her.

Tying a paisley silk scarf at her neck to match her pale yellow sweater, she nodded in approval, then pulled on her hat and coat.

After collecting a wicker basket from the kitchen, she met Eric downstairs. He appeared ill at ease, his eyes taking in certain areas of the room, as if they refused to settle on her for long.

"You still haven't told me where we're going," he greeted.

She smiled. "I thought it high time you saw more of Cedarbrook."

"We're going for a drive?"

"Even better." She crooked her finger playfully. "Come along. You won't be disappointed."

He held back, as if he might refuse, then gave a short nod and followed her outside to the shed.

"We're going to work on more home improvements?" he asked, puzzled.

"No, silly. This." She moved to the side of the shed where she'd pulled out the bike earlier, when a sudden worrisome thought struck. "You do know how to ride one of these?"

He eyed the long bicycle. "I've never ridden a two-seater."

"Oh, it's a breeze. You'll get the hang of it in no time. I'll sit here." She patted the front seat. "And you take the back." She congratulated herself on her idea. This way she would be in his line of vision the entire time, since she would need to steer, due to his inexperience.

"I'm not sure. . . ." He glanced up at the overcast skies. "It might rain."

"The sky has looked like that for days, and no rain yet. Chicken?" she inquired sweetly. "I assumed you were the type to boldly take on new challenges, unafraid. Was I wrong?" With innocent playfulness, she batted her eyelashes.

"Lead the way," he growled with a narrow-eyed smile.

She laughed and, with some instruction to him, put her basket in the wire container at the front. They mounted their separate seats, Hannah tucking her skirt up as best she could so it wouldn't get in the way. After a wobbly start, they headed down the drive and to the empty country road.

Here the ground lay flat, though inclines and descents loomed in the distance, but she felt that together they could manage without a problem. On both sides, trees of all types loomed overhead, their branches forming a shadowed canopy. Many still bloomed in chaotic hues encompassing a bold spectrum of reds, oranges, and yellows. Some had lost their leaves, while the evergreens remained refreshing pillars of green scattered among the deciduous trees.

Despite the brisk air that blew into her face, Hannah glowed with warmth. She had finally achieved her purpose—to pull Eric away from work and spend quality time with him, ending any likelihood of one of her sisters or her mother entering the room, which had happened with annoying frequency.

They came to another road that branched off to a secluded spot she enjoyed. "We're turning here," she called over her shoulder.

Soon they pulled alongside a pond, sparkling with the noonday sun that streamed through the top boughs of the dense thicket surrounding it. Once they dismounted, she grabbed the wicker basket and pulled out a cloth, spreading it on the ground.

He observed her with an expression of utter disbelief. "Isn't it a little cold for a picnic?"

"It's not so bad." She knelt on the cloth, the chill of the ground seeping through to her knees, and rethought her position and her words. She sat down, her coat blocking the chill. "Just long enough to eat a sandwich?"

He continued staring at her.

"What?"

"I just never figured you for the outdoor type. I thought you preferred functions that the socialites take part in."

"I enjoy dances and parties, certainly, but my father taught us an appreciation for the outdoors. This pond"—she waved a hand toward the water— "will soon be frozen. Daddy usually takes us here for ice skating. He's very much the American outdoorsman, and Mother is an island princess. Some might call their union strange, but they're perfect for one another."

"Your mother is a princess?" He lowered himself beside her, taking a seat. "You mean in the literary sense? Saying she's a wonderful lady?"

"Well, she's that, too, though I get frustrated with her views sometimes. But no, I mean royalty in the literal sense. Her father, my grandfather, is a missionary on a South Pacific island. The chief gave his daughter, my grandmother, to him as a gift, so to speak, though my grandfather didn't take advantage of that, of course. She served him, though he made her sleep in a separate hut, and they fell in love over the course of time and married. Mother was their only child who lived. My grandmother died in childbirth with their second child."

"I had no idea." Eric looked dazed. "That explains a lot."

Curious, she tilted her head while handing him a sandwich. "What?"

"Your life," he said distantly, as though his thoughts lay elsewhere. "Your ideas about it. Your mother's bearing. So your grandfather, where is he?"

"He's still on the island. I've never met him."

"And your Great-Uncle Bernard is your grandfather's brother?"

She nodded. "From what I understand, they didn't get along. My great-uncle never supported my grandfather's missionary work—or rather, him leaving the family tuna business to become one. He has nothing against giving to charities and has been known to support them."

They ate their sandwiches while looking out over the pond.

"What did you mean when you said Mother being a princess explains how I think about life?" she asked, his words niggling at her.

"I didn't mean that to sound like a bad thing. . . ."

She nodded for him to continue.

"It's just that you seem to live your life in fantasy after fantasy. Knowing your roots now and that your mother is a—" He stopped speaking and looked at her. "Wait. If she's a princess, that makes you one, too, doesn't it?"

"Yes. All of my sisters, actually."

"So it's no wonder you've lived such a pampered life."

She frowned. Did he think she was spoiled? At least she volunteered at her mother's charity functions. "Wrong side of the family. My mother's mother and my great-uncle aren't related."

"Oh right." He crumpled up the wax paper and tossed it into the basket. "It's so cold, I guess my brain froze there for a minute."

"Are you really that cold?" She wore layers, but the cold from the ground had started to seep through her coat to her backside. "We have chocolate cream pie from the bakery for dessert—"

He looked up at the sky. "Did you feel that?"

"Feel what?" She followed his glance upward. "I don't feel anything."

"Something wet just hit me. There it is again." He jumped to his feet. "It's going to rain."

"Are you sure?" She looked at the overcast sky that seemed rather bright for rain. "Maybe it's from the pond."

"There's no wind to carry water this way. It's going to rain, and we need to get back before the sky unleashes on our heads."

"All right, if you insist." She gave in with a little pout.

He helped her up, and she regretted when he pulled his hands away, even if they were as cold as hers. He grabbed the hamper and stuffed the blanket inside and then set the hamper in the wire basket.

Halfway home, the sky let loose with icy droplets. She squealed as they hit her face, and Eric called out to her, "How good are you on one of these things?"

"I have years of experience," she called back over her shoulder. "Why?"

"If we're going to make it to the house before we're drenched, we need to pedal faster. Can you do it?"

"Yes." She hadn't ridden the bicycle in months, but her legs felt almost numb, and her hands didn't feel like a part of her, either.

They increased pace. Regardless, the droplets fell faster. Seeing white, she opened her eyes wide in shock. "That's snow!"

Hoping they would make it back before the road grew slick, she hunched her shoulders and kept her head low, pedaling fast and wincing at the burn in her legs. To her relief, the old farmhouse soon loomed into view, and she steered them into the drive, her heart thumping against her ribs when she almost overshot her mark and sent them skidding into the leaves.

"We made it!" She braked at the shed. He got off quickly, but she had difficulty dismounting, her legs wobbly and barely feeling connected to her body.

"Are you all right?" He caught her in his arms as she brought her other leg over the bicycle. She fell into him, and he tightened his hold, both of them helplessly laughing. The bike fell against her. She groaned, and he moved them away from it.

"Better?" he asked.

"I don't think I'll walk ever again," she moaned. Being held against him, even as wet as they'd gotten, felt nice, and she didn't want it to end, though she didn't exaggerate. Her thighs and calves burned like fire, and the rest of her legs felt as if they didn't belong to her.

His hand slipped around her waist as he tried to help her walk. She stumbled, and he brought his other arm up fast around her midriff as her knees buckled. He'd barely brought them both aright, when she felt him wrenched away from her.

Frantic at the sudden loss of support, she reached for a nearby tree, her eyes widening.

"Josiah?" she whispered.

"Keep your hands off my sister!" Her older brother growled the warning from between clenched teeth as he shoved Eric back against the shed and held him there by his coat lapels. "What did you do to her?"

"Josiah—stop it!" She raised her voice to be heard. "Eric didn't do anything. We were cycling hard to get out of the bad weather, and it's taking me awhile to get my balance."

"He shouldn't have taken you anywhere." Her brother's eyes remained fixed on Eric. "Do you have any idea who his father is, Hannah? He's scum, that's what. And I'm sure his spawn is no better."

Upset that her brother judged Eric on the basis of his father's reputation alone, Hannah approached and grabbed Josiah's sleeve, trying to pull his arm away from Eric. "You have no idea what you're talking about. What are you doing home anyhow? It's not Christmas break."

"I quit school."

"Quit?"

"I suggest we all go inside before the weather gets worse. Your sister needs to get dry, and I could do with a toweling off, too."

Josiah turned a fierce glare on Eric. "This isn't over."

"Yes," Hannah said just as adamantly. "It is."

Josiah glanced at Hannah then back to Eric before he released him with a little shove. "Fine. Go inside. But we *will* talk later."

Hannah grabbed Eric's arm and pulled him to walk back with her to the house. She didn't wait to see what Josiah would do. She loved her brother, older by almost a year, but he could take the big-brother protectiveness a bit far.

"Don't mind him," she reassured Eric when they were in the mudroom. She peeled off her wet coat and scarf, as he did the same and tossed them over a chair. "He's got bigger problems when Daddy finds out he left school."

"I'm not worried. You should get into dry clothes. I'll do the same."

"Eric!" she called out before he could leave. He looked over his shoulder at her.

"I hope this doesn't mean...that is, I hope we're still on for your part of the deal, though mine was a complete washout."

At her little pun, he gave a full-blown smile that threatened to make her unsteady again. "Are you kidding? Be prepared to leave at six thirty Monday night so we can be on time for the town meeting at seven."

"Town meeting?" She barely curbed a groan. "I hear they're quite...long." And tedious. And monotonous. And every other boring word she could think of.

"You've never been. Why does that not surprise me? It's time you opened your eyes to what's going on in your community, Hannah."

"I can't wait," she replied with a forced smile.

"Cheer up." He gave her another irrepressible grin. "It might not turn out as badly as you think."

✒

Eric shed his damp clothes and toweled off, dressing in a pair of warm, dry trousers and a wool sweater. A loud knock threatened to take the door off its hinges.

Heaving a sigh, he opened it, not surprised to see Hannah's older brother glaring at him. He realized then that this was the young man's room, another reason for him to despise Eric.

"If you want me out, I can be gone in ten minutes."

Josiah narrowed his eyes. "I thought you promised my parents your *help*."

"I meant out of your room."

He scowled. "Like Mama would agree. You may have fooled her, but I know your kind. I have you figured out by a mile. And I know what your father is. A murderer, a con man, a rapist—"

"Past tense."

"Doesn't matter." Josiah punched his index finger in Eric's chest. "You've heard the old saying 'The apple doesn't fall far from the tree'? I'm wise to you. And now that I'm home, we don't need you around here anymore."

"Yet you just reminded me of the promise I made to your parents." Eric remained calm, though the man stepped on his every nerve and he felt like giving as good as he got. "If they want me out, I'll go. But with the damage to this house and winter waiting at the front door, I can't see that happening anytime soon. Can you?"

Josiah narrowed his eyes in clear hatred. "Just watch your back, Fontaine. And stay away from my sister! I'll be watching every move you make." He grimaced, turning away from the door.

Catching sight of David coming into the corridor from the stairwell, Eric gave the boy a friendly smile. David didn't smile back, his look suspicious as he moved toward Josiah, who clapped an arm around the boy's shoulders. Clearly Josiah had poisoned his little brother's mind against Eric.

Shaking his head, Eric closed the door and went to the bureau to pull out a pair of socks. Why did he stay where he wasn't wanted? He had nothing tying him to this place. Josiah seemed to think he could take over repairs, so why not let him? Why did the idea of leaving not appeal as it had a week before?

He had just tied his shoes when another knock, this one lighter, tapped at his door.

"Seems you're a popular man today," he muttered to himself as he rose from the bed and moved to admit his guest. Mrs. Thomas stood on the other side.

"I'm sorry to bother you. I would like a few moments to speak with you, if I may."

He smiled politely. "It's no bother." He waved an arm to the side. "Please, come in."

She did, and he remained standing at the open door.

"Hannah mentioned you've met my eldest son."

"Oui," Eric answered wryly. *If one could call it that.*

She sighed. "It is a sad situation, and I know it must be difficult for you that some people cannot look beyond past mistakes, choosing to judge a family for one man's sins. When loyalty comes into the balance, protecting loved ones can take on new meaning." She laid a hand on his shoulder, her eyes shining in sincerity. "I've had the advantage of spending my mornings getting to know you in our breakfast conversations. I see you are a good man. Your mother raised you with Christian ideals. I only wish my own children would learn them as well as you have."

Her praise eased the sting of Josiah's behavior. "Thanks for the vote of confidence. Besides Hannah, you're the only one who doesn't mind my presence here."

"Ah yes. My daughter." She grew pensive. "She's made many mistakes since living at my uncle's; and at the elite school she attended, she found the wrong friends. She was very young when we left the Refuge, once I learned my uncle was alive and had returned to Connecticut. But my uncle. . .he challenged my husband's and my ideas on raising our children, making us question our decisions and often going behind our backs to do the opposite of what we approved. Hannah has lived a very. . .privileged life these past five years. At the Refuge, all her needs were also met. She knows nothing of hardship. But she is smart." A reflective expression came into her eyes. "It often takes her time to come to a knowledge of the truth; she is young. But she does. And I sense you are a good influence for her."

He squinted in curiosity. "Exactly what are you saying, Mrs. Thomas?"

"I heard my son's parting words. I do not agree with Josiah. You have my blessing to befriend my daughter."

He regarded her skeptically. "And your husband supports the idea?" During one of their breakfast conversations, Eric had admitted to her that he'd overheard her conversation with Mr. Thomas.

"I will speak with my husband. Please understand, he acts out of fear from all that has happened to us connected with the Piccoli mob. Your father was part of that ring of terror and created his own as well. Also, being bedridden has not helped my husband's attitude. But if Bill knew you as I have come to know you, I do not feel he would be so. . .hesitant."

Eric could think of a better word for her husband's treatment of him but respectfully nodded. "I plan on taking Hannah to the town meeting next week."

"The town meeting?" Her surprise was evident.

"I thought seeing the day-to-day issues of what's happening in the world, in this case her own little community, might be an eye-opening experience. She mentioned she hopes to be a writer. Attending a meeting like that could be helpful."

Mrs. Thomas smiled. "Oh, no doubt. Your plan sounds like a worthy one."

Eric thought so, too, but couldn't help grin at thinking what Hannah's reaction might be.

Chapter 8

Mere boredom couldn't begin to describe Hannah's feelings as she listened to the secretary read the minutes from the last meeting. For the time period of the novel Hannah was writing, she might use *tedium, dreariness, insipidness*—the French would describe it as *ennui*. A much more sophisticated sound.

Eric leaned to whisper near her ear, "So what do you think?"

"It's lovely." She smiled and noticed a faint grin edge his mouth.

"Well, I don't know if I would call a draft lovely."

"Draft?"

He lifted an eyebrow at her puzzlement. "I asked if you were cold, with the way you keep rubbing your arms, and asked if you want to move closer."

"Oh, that." She felt a flush of warmth now. "Closer—no! I mean, I'm fine, just. . .lovely," she finished off her excuse in a weak manner. The time spent sitting beside Eric and making easy conversation before the meeting itself had been quite lovely. She wondered if she could interest him in a stroll in the park on their way home then felt amazed at the idea. She, who never liked to walk anywhere, was considering one? But to extend their night, alone, and have more time to talk, she would reconsider her former views of the activity.

"These public meetings can be a little dull at first, when they go over items already mentioned, but give them time to get to the grittier issues. You might learn something."

Learn something? Learn what? How to paralyze a person with ennui in under ten minutes? She stifled a giggle at the thought. When the chairperson went into discussion for the funds to fix one of the covered bridges and all the *yea*-ing and *nay*-ing the vote entailed from those gathered, she felt hard-pressed not to yawn. Suddenly she heard her name mentioned. Shocked, she sat up rigid, as if a teacher had caught her nodding off in class.

"Our own Miss Thomas is with us tonight, a rising young talent who will both write and direct the play being presented for our Founder's Day extravaganza."

Hannah realized then that the subject had moved from reparation of the bridge to the upcoming community celebration. She smiled, giving a nervous nod to the speaker, who stared directly at her, and hoped the man had no idea she felt adrift in the conversation.

"Miss Thomas, would you care to share a few words about your project?"

No, she wouldn't. She really wouldn't. . . .

She gave a stiff nod and clutched the empty chair in front of her as a sea of faces turned her way to look at her on the second-to-last row. She felt them blur, then chided herself. She had once wanted to be an actress. Certainly she could address these people on a matter dear to her heart.

She filled them in on the foundation of her idea, noting a few nods of approval, which gave her the boost of courage needed. She fielded questions, delighted at the interest shown and at the offer of a few volunteers to help with the set.

When the meeting drew to a close, she was fairly glowing with their praise, but Eric seemed strangely distant, as if not happy with the outcome of the meeting.

"Shall we take a walk in the park?" she asked hopefully, after the last of the attendees had come up to offer words of encouragement or introductions. "It's close."

"I don't think so. It's nearing ten now, and tomorrow is Sunday."

"Sunday?"

"Church."

"Oh right."

He glanced her way, but she averted her eyes. She went to church every week, listened to the preacher, did everything that was required of a Christian. Feeling ill at ease, she looked his way. "What?"

He shook his head. "I'm only trying to figure you out."

"Meaning?"

"When there's talk of movies and your play, you light up like a firefly. But when the subject turns to God, you tend to clam up. I've seen you do it with your mother and once when I brought up my family's mission and the testimonies given there."

She shrugged a little self-consciously and looked around the area. "Can we go? We're almost the last ones to leave."

They left the building, but in the car, she brought up the subject again, unnerved by the unnatural silence that had descended since he last spoke.

"It's not that I don't believe in God." She pulled at the tips of her gloves. "I've been raised on the teachings of Christ. But, well, Julia and Muffy tend to think that the Bible is more of a history book of. . .stories. None of it really. . .life-pressing."

"That's a strange way to put it, since scripture deals with each solitary life and what will become of it based on the decisions we make."

"Oh, I know my friends don't have all the answers, but. . . I don't know." She shrugged, unable to express her thoughts clearly.

"I think I do." His voice came solemn, and he glanced her way, his eyes a little sad, before he looked back at the road. "You've never really suffered. You don't know what it's like to reach rock bottom and need God as desperately as you need air and water, because you've had everything handed to you since you were old enough to understand the world. And the world you understand is a place of privilege and wealth."

His words hit too close to home for comfort. She couldn't remember ever being denied anything, except, of course, to go back to her great-uncle's to live. "You're pitying me?" she asked in shock. After all, his family seemed to be the ones struggling to make ends meet. If her father ever needed money, all he had to do was ask her great-uncle.

"In a way, maybe I am."

"Well don't!"

"Sorry, can't help myself. In this past week I've come to care about your welfare, *mon amie*, and by that I mean your ultimate welfare. Of your soul."

His words disconcerted her, though she clung to his first ones. And delivered in the language of love, no less. He cared about her!

"You know a lot of French, don't you?"

He looked at her strangely. "My father is from France. It is my second language."

"Right." She knew that. Why had she asked something so obvious?

"In our household both languages are spoken; my mother is also fluent in it. And I find myself sometimes fluctuating between the two when I speak."

"Oh, don't misunderstand me. I like it." She smiled, adopting a sweeter attitude to carry through with her plan. She turned a little on the seat to look at him, batting her lashes as she'd seen Muffy do. "You really are such a gentleman, Eric. I'm sorry I got upset. I don't know what got into me."

"Is something in your eye?"

"My eye? No, it's fine." She stopped her rapid blinking, now embarrassed, and cleared her throat. "I was wondering, though."

"Yes?"

"Since my plan for a good time was a complete failure, I would like a second shot."

"What do you have in mind?"

He seemed leery, which made her wonder what she had said to cause his abrupt distance this time. "How about a movie? At least if it rains, it won't be a loss since we'll have the theater roof over our heads. A favorite of mine is still playing at the movie house, though I imagine they'll take it down soon."

He hesitated so long that she feared he might decline her invitation. "All right," he said at last. "Next weekend then?"

"Can't it be sooner?"

He gave her another swift glance. "I do have your house to work on, remember."

"Right. Of course. Next Saturday then." She forced a smile, hoping for the days to fly. . .well, at least six of them.

✦

All through the following week, Eric tried to keep his mind on his work and less on the feisty brunette who seemed determined to help him. Their conversation on the way home from the meeting had sparked warnings in his mind. He found himself not only hoping she would see the danger in her cavalier attitude toward God and the Christian faith, but desperately wanting her to understand. Yet she wasn't the only one acting carelessly.

While her mother might approve if he were to take an interest in Hannah, her father and brother still considered him an irredeemable danger to the family. But the almost palpable tension in the house was now targeted toward Josiah and his decision to quit school. From Eric's room, it had been impossible to ignore Mr. Thomas's voice raised from the adjacent bedroom as he confronted his son with his "foolish choice." Josiah had countered, just as loudly, that he planned to earn a living with his roommate friend from college, working on his father's boat as a fisherman, an admission Josiah's father hadn't taken well. Hannah had been quiet ever since, clearly affected by the family tension—another reason Eric felt sorry for her and didn't refuse her laughable excuse for help. As far as any true interest went, he had no intention of taking their relationship any further than friendship.

Hannah intrigued and baffled him. Certainly that must be the reason he couldn't stop thinking of her. She was like a paper chain of people his little sisters were fond of making—entertaining but flimsy, a long line of cutout fictional characters that didn't depict her true nature—the cutouts the only parts of her persona Hannah seemed willing to display to the world, as if it were her audience. But at times, in the unexpected warmth of her smile or the sincerity of her illuminating words, he'd detected more. Hidden deep within, he sensed the original cowered, a woman of gentle sensitivity shielding an insecure little girl. Hurting. Restless. Perhaps she'd buried her real feelings so deep she didn't realize they existed. On the other hand, his emotions always seemed to surface. He'd witnessed more than his share of suffering and hopelessness growing up in the mission, and the Depression only made matters worse.

In one matter they shared a common bond. He sensed Hannah sought the same peace he did—a need for serenity. That link made him want to help her, even befriend her. He missed the times of togetherness with his huge family and assumed that's why he'd agreed to Hannah's outings for "fun."

When Saturday again rolled around, he waited in the parlor for her to join him for the matinee. He wondered, though, since she'd already seen the movie, why she would want to see it again.

Her footsteps on the top landing had him look up, just as the doorbell rang. He looked in surprise at the door a few feet from him.

"Would you mind getting that, Eric?" Hannah sounded out of breath. "I forgot my scarf. I won't be but a moment."

Eric felt odd greeting whoever stood on the other side, since it wasn't his home, but he put on a charming smile and swung open the door.

"*Bonjour*," he said to a handsome-looking woman who appeared to be the same age as Hannah's mother. Next to her stood a younger woman, both of them with blazing red hair. "I'm Eric Fontaine, a guest of the Thomases.

How can I be of service to you ladies?"

The older woman turned a pasty gray, her mouth dropping open in horrified shock. "No!" she rasped out in a whisper. Her green eyes grew huge in terror before her lids suddenly fluttered and closed. Eric barely caught her before she could sink all the way to the ground in a dead faint or hit the baby carriage the young woman rolled.

"Mama!" the girl cried, grabbing her arm. "Mama, what's wrong?"

"We need to get her inside, out of this cold wind." Eric had no idea who the woman was, but he couldn't leave her inert on the doorstep. He managed to shift her into his arms, glad he'd kept in shape, the strain on his muscles taxing as he lifted and carried her into the house. The other woman followed. In the parlor, he laid the older woman on the couch and knelt beside her, putting his fingers to her neck to check her pulse.

"What are you doing?" a man's deep voice suddenly boomed. "Get your hands off my wife!" Eric turned to see a tall and husky, silver-haired gentleman hurry into the parlor. The man stopped suddenly at the sight of his face. "No. It can't be—it's impossible."

"What's impossible, Papa?" The young woman moved to her father, grabbing his arm as if she might try to stop him from throwing a punch at Eric, though the man appeared paralyzed in his tracks as if he'd forgotten his earlier angst. She looked back and forth between them. "Do you know this man?" she whispered. "He said his name is Eric Fontaine."

Her father's eyes widened farther as if he'd seen a ghost. "Impossible. . .you, you haven't aged in all this time?"

Eric instantly understood. "My father is Eric Fontaine Sr. I'm his son." And he understood in an instant the identity of the unconscious woman, recalling the redhead his father told them he had wronged.

Hannah came into the parlor, her expression puzzled. "Clemmie?" Her welcoming smile faltered when she noticed the woman on the sofa. "What happened to your mother?" She looked up. "Eric?"

"A case of mistaken identity."

"Is it?" Josiah suddenly appeared through the door. "Or maybe she sensed the evil of your father in you."

Mrs. Thomas hurried past her son, as if she'd been privy to the whole incident, a small jar in her hand. "Stand aside, please."

Eric stood up from kneeling beside the sofa and watched her lift the woman's head, bringing the jar under her nose. The woman recoiled as she got a whiff of the smelling salts, and her eyes fluttered open. They latched onto Eric. "You. . . how?" she said hoarsely as her husband came to her side and she leaned against him in support.

"Non, madame," he said quickly. "I'm not who you think."

"You. . .you said you're Eric F–Fontaine."

"Oui. Named for my father. I'm his son."

"But. . ." She pulled her brows together in confusion. "You look so much like. . .like he did. On the *Titanic*. You could be him. Looking at you, it's as if. . ." Her breath came tense. "As if you never aged. As if you've. . .come back. . . ."

"Charleigh, sweetheart." Her husband took her hand in his and patted it. "It's not Eric." He directed an uncertain glance his way. "At least not the Eric we knew."

"I think we should go." Hannah came to stand beside Eric.

"Yes, I think that would be wise."

Charleigh cast a rapid glance back and forth between daughter and mother. "You don't mean. . .Sarah, tell me you're not actually letting him take Hannah out?"

"Mother." Josiah took Charleigh's side. "Are you crazy? You can't let Hannah go with him!"

Eric felt weary of the entire situation, tired of being judged for his father's past sins, especially by veritable strangers. "Despite what you remember about my father, he is a changed man. The man I've heard about since I've come to your town is a stranger to me. He's nothing like the person who raised me, I assure you, and I'm nothing like the person he was."

"We really should go or we'll be late." Hannah looked from Eric to the young woman. "We'll talk later."

Taking hold of Eric's arm, she walked with him out of the parlor, ignoring Josiah, who scowled at them both.

Chapter 9

Outside, Hannah vented her anger.

"They have no right to judge you!"

Taken aback by the vehemence of her low words and how her eyes flashed like hard steel, he shook his head, still stunned. "That's the woman my father abused on the *Titanic*, isn't it? The one he wronged in so many ways."

Hannah winced. "Yes. I heard about the awful things he did to Aunt Charleigh, and I'm not excusing any of it. But I happen to know that every one of those people inside have done terrible things for which they have good reason to be ashamed."

"My father warned me this might happen. That though your father and the others had visited the mission that day, over a decade ago, and made an uneasy sort of peace, they'd been wary of him. He thought they might later have questioned if his conversion were only a trick, another con, since he'd been a master of deception. Of course he had no idea when he asked me to come to Connecticut that I would run into your aunt and uncle here." He sighed. "And I'm sure they never thought they would see a Fontaine again. Especially outside of New York."

"I don't care. It's still not right. They expect mercy, but they won't give your father the same benefit, believing he can change, too? That's just. . .wrong! And why in the world should they take all this out on you? You weren't even *alive* when any of it happened. Just because you look like your father? That's a pathetic excuse. You've never done anything to warrant such treatment. Aunt Charleigh—okay, yes, I can understand her shocked reaction, but Josiah's hostility, I can't. He barely knows you and hasn't even met your father—"

"Hannah." Eric grasped her shoulders to get her to look at him and try to calm her. "It's all right." He smiled. "You're a sweet young woman to care, but don't get yourself so upset over this. I don't want to be the cause of anything that would alienate you from your family."

The fire left her eyes, her expression almost sad, making him curious, but she nodded.

On the drive to town, she didn't say much, and he found himself frequently glancing her way to make sure she was okay. What had caused such a change?

The movie house was in need of repairs like so many places, but tickets weren't expensive, the seats were comfortable, and he wore a coat so he didn't feel the chill inside the massive theater. Once the curtain opened, a short newsreel played onscreen, optimistic human-interest stories set amid the nation's suffering along with a short reel of President Roosevelt waving to a crowd while the voice-over mentioned the war in Europe and the munitions being made in Connecticut to aid the Allies. At this, a few young men in the audience gave a loud hurrah, instantly hushed by the people with them. Eric smiled at their enthusiasm, now understanding how Hannah had come by the information. He wasn't sure how he felt about the war in general, though what the power-hungry Hitler did was clearly wrong. But Eric was amazed that such an informative reel, however short, would be shown in a theater.

Another short, this time a slapstick reel, had many men gasping in laughter, followed by the main feature that brought the women to tears. Toward the end, Hannah sniffled with regularity, and Eric offered her his handkerchief, though his vision had become a bit blurred, too.

"Thank you," she whispered, taking it and dabbing at her eyes.

The picture, about a spoiled, wealthy socialite with an incurable brain disease, who sacrificed her last living minutes with her husband to send him off on his preplanned trip that would boost his career as a doctor, her first truly selfless act and her last, surprised Eric. For one, the content matter didn't seem like something Hannah might choose. He had thought she would prefer something silly or flighty, though from what he'd read of it, *Gone with the Wind* couldn't be classified as either, and he remembered her mentioning that being her favorite novel. The subject matter of the current movie drama could even be considered moralistic, the woman changing for the better due to the love of one good man who had faith in her and saw something in her others didn't. The "victory" perhaps wasn't so "dark" as the title suggested.

"Bette Davis is just so amazing," Hannah gushed once they left the theater. "I could feel her sorrow and angst at the end, couldn't you? Though she covered up her feelings with a smile so her husband wouldn't suspect she'd gone blind and the end was near. Oh, I hope I can write a novel like that. It's my fondest dream, though of course first I had hoped to go to Hollywood and be an actress—or even Broadway—but Mother and Daddy didn't approve and have never let me even visit New York."

She stopped for a breath, and he used the opportunity to speak. "It's a nice afternoon. Would you like to take a walk?" He hoped to avoid the Lyons company and felt if he drew out his and Hannah's time together, chances were strong the family wouldn't be present upon their return.

Her eyes twinkled. "I'd love to walk with you."

The town green was only a few blocks' distant, and they reached the area in less than five minutes. Towering cedars and maples provided some shade, though soon the leaves of the maples would fall to the ground in a shower of color.

"See that old building?" She pointed to a colonial house in the distance.

"That's where we'll be holding the play. Oh, I hope you'll still be here. And there's our church."

He followed her gaze toward the familiar white steeple on the far side of the green, nestled amid clusters of trees.

"My best friend, Clemmie, married there. One day I hope to have my wedding there, too."

At the wistful quality of her voice, Eric felt a little awkward.

"Clemmie. . .the woman who came to visit?"

"Yes."

"Maybe I shouldn't have taken you away. We could have done this another time."

"Are you serious?" She laughed wryly. "I wanted out of there as much as you did. Though Clemmie didn't say anything, she might have, and I didn't want to hear it. Her mother wasn't the only victim of. . ." She hesitated.

"My father," Eric put in steadily.

"Yes, well. . .Joel, Clemmie's husband, he was a victim, too."

Eric pondered her words. "I don't remember Father talking about a Joel. Charleigh and Stewart and a woman named Darcy are the ones I heard the most about."

She brightened. "Oh, you would love Aunt Darcy. Everyone does. Now there's a woman who's not afraid to speak her mind, regardless of what people think." Eric wondered if she wished she could classify herself in the same mold. "Joel was a boy when he ran across your father at a carnival. Your father wanted to make him an accomplice, since Joel was very good at cons and worked for his father, who died in prison—but I'm rambling again. Sorry." She offered a penitent smile. "Joel was, I think, twelve when your father used him to gain admittance to Lyons Refuge. His plan was to gain revenge on everyone there, and he held a gun on Aunt Charleigh and Aunt Darcy, threatening Joel if he wouldn't help."

"He wanted the diamonds, too," Eric put in, having heard the story many times.

"Yes." Hannah looked at him in surprise, as if amazed he would know that. "I didn't learn everything until Clemmie told me years ago, but he and Aunt Charleigh worked together to steal an heirloom diamond necklace from Lady Annabelle when they sailed the *Titanic*."

"And your aunt Charleigh, then known as Charlotte, changed her name to Myra, hoping to evade my father," Eric continued solemnly. "He found her and demanded she give him the necklace and come back to him, but your uncle Stewart saved her. So he bided his time and returned to the Refuge when the opportunity arose and your uncle was out of town. But Darcy's husband surprised him, and it ended with my father getting shot and later going to prison."

She stopped walking and looked at him. "You know the story well."

"I spent my lifetime being raised on it. Father spoke of the boy, but I didn't know his name was Joel. I also didn't know who the Lyonses actually were until they and their friends came to the mission that day and I overheard them talking. I was eight at the time."

Hannah hesitated, as if unsure she should speak. "How do you feel about all of it? About him?"

Eric thought about how to answer. "When I grew old enough to realize the enormity of my father's crimes and that he'd lied to Charleigh about them being married for three years—arranging a fake ceremony—then on that last night, hours before the *Titanic* sank, abusing her in his jealousy and leaving her to die. . .when I understood all that, I hated him." He shook his head in remembered confusion. "But I loved him, too. I loved the man I *knew*, not the monster he described. It was difficult to equate the two conflicting parts of one man, and I couldn't understand how he could love my mother so deeply yet hurt a woman so horribly as he had Charleigh. It's no wonder she fainted upon seeing me. People often tell me I look just like my father when he was younger."

"I never saw him, but I still say they shouldn't take his past out on you."

"It's been difficult, I won't lie to you. But I better understand their hesitance to trust me when it seems to them that my father has come to life before their eyes, the way he used to look at the time of his cons."

She considered that. "I see your point. At least your parents share the truth with you and don't hide things you ought to know."

At her bitter words, he regarded her somberly. "Sometimes it's better not knowing the past, mon amie. It took me a long time to be able to look at my father without loathing him once I fully began to understand all he'd done. I marveled that they let him out of prison at all! They couldn't prove many of his early crimes, so he didn't receive the long sentence he deserved. Perhaps also that his father was a *comte* had some bearing on the matter. Now he has the title."

She blinked in clear shock. "Your father is a French count? I had no idea. So that makes you a *vicomte*?"

He chuckled. "It's not such a big thing as it was in the nineteenth century, but oui. Before my father changed his name, it was Fontaneau."

It was a moment before she spoke again. "So what changed your mind about him?"

"My mother." He smiled sadly.

"You miss them."

"At times, yes. I would look at my mother, who seemed the closest thing to a saint I'd known, and wonder how she could love such a man. But she does. It's in every word she says to him, every look she gives, every time she touches him. She saw the worth no one else tried to, with the exception of her family, and he became a better man because of their faith in him."

"Something like Judith in *Dark Victory*."

He grinned in resignation. "*Something* like that. Mother pulled me aside one day, questioning why I would no longer speak to my father. Once I told her, she looked at me sternly and asked, 'Eric Joseph, do you consider yourself better than God?' I was thirteen and had just read about Lucifer, who thought himself better than God and waged a war against Him. So I was naturally appalled, thinking my dear sainted mother must think I was as bad as the devil." He chuckled wryly. "She said something that stuck with me through the years and helped me learn to judge no man as a lost cause, which can be very helpful when your family runs a mission. She said, 'Paul was a murderer, David an adulterer, Jacob a thief, and Peter a liar. If God could forgive every one of those men their sins and raise them to be mighty men of God, who are you to say He shouldn't or couldn't? He's a God of lost causes and is glorified when people watch the impossible accomplished right before their eyes.'"

Hannah smiled. "Your mother sounds a lot like mine." She tilted her head in curiosity. "How did your parents meet, anyhow?"

"The guard who kept watch over the cell block at the prison where my father stayed quoted scripture to him, even read from it. My father never forgot how Charleigh came to him before the police arrived and forgave him and how Darcy gave him money to buy a coat. No one had ever done anything nice for him, and their actions helped to soften his heart, so that he was open to hear the message of the gospel. His enemies repaid him with kindness, and he couldn't fathom it. Eventually, the guard led my father to Christ, and the two became friends. That guard was my uncle Joseph. After my father was released, my uncle invited him to a family dinner, and my mother was there."

"Weren't her parents upset or worried when your father took an interest in her?"

"Oh yes. Father had to prove himself before they would let him be alone in the same room with her, but they gave him that chance. They didn't just assume he could never change and treat him badly, as many had done, no matter how he tried to make amends. He came to work for my grandfather when the mission was hardly as big or as productive as it is now. My father had ideas that made it that way. Soon my grandfather saw he wasn't only brilliant, but also trustworthy. He gave the management of the mission over to my father a year after meeting him. Shortly after that, he gave his blessing for him and Mother to marry."

"That's just so. . .romantic."

At her dreamy sigh, he lifted his brows. "Romantic?"

"Oh yes. How she stuck by his side, how she had faith in him despite the odds and the mind-sets of those around them. . ."

Before she could go off into one of her dream-world soliloquies, he felt a sharp tug at the back of his coat. He turned, Hannah also stopping to look, and noticed a little girl in a drab blue dress and shabby coat, both which looked as if they could do with a washing. Her brown hair appeared clean though straggled, her face heartbreakingly thin.

"Please, mister, can you spare a dime?"

He took into account how snugly her dress fit, her ribs poking through the folds.

"When have you eaten last?"

She looked startled by his gentle question and wrinkled her brow. "We found some food in the bin behind the coffee shop yesterday."

"We?"

"My little brother and me." She looked at the shrubbery and waved in signal for someone to join her. The bushes rustled, and a small boy, possibly five, came out. His eyes, the same shade of brown as the girl's, seemed to take up most of his freckled face. "My mama got real bad sick," the girl went on to explain. "She lost her job at the mercantile. She's sick now."

"And your father?"

"He left when things got bad."

A strong twinge of sympathy made Eric hunch down and put his hands to her shoulders. "How would you like a hot meal from that coffee shop over there?" He pointed down the street.

Her eyes shone as if he'd promised her the moon and stars. "Really?" She glanced at the boy, a head shorter than herself, and took his hand. "Jimmy, too?"

Eric smiled at the boy. "Jimmy, too."

"Golly, mister, that'd be swell!"

Eric glanced at Hannah, whose expression looked a little odd, but she didn't disagree. During the entire walk to the shop, with the children following as quiet as church mice behind, Hannah didn't say a word, and to his surprise, Eric really wished to know what she was thinking.

Chapter 10

Hannah sat next to Eric, across from the children, who ate their hot soup as enthusiastically as if it were ice cream. She thought of her little brother, who turned up his nose at any form of liquid nourishment, and his informative boast to Eric of their daily intake of desserts at her great-uncle's. She wondered what Eric must think of her family. It was bad enough he'd called her a "sweet young woman." Reminded of her foolish bet with Julia and Muffy to win him over, she could hardly be considered sweet.

But more than her twinge of conscience for her lack of ethics, seeing evidence of the starvation that had plagued her town affected her strongly. To see children as young as Abbie forced to beg in the park for a meal had horrified her and pulled at her heartstrings. She knew that many in her state now had work, but apparently the suffering still existed. How had she not known or seen it? True, they now lived in a rural area and her great-uncle's mansion had been situated in the more affluent district, but not to realize the situation baffled Hannah. Were there more out there like Shirley and Jimmy? There must be, since Eric had mentioned children who'd been thrown onto the streets, children his family's mission had helped.

She sipped her coffee, having declined Eric's offer of a meal, and watched the brother and sister wolf down their roast beef sandwiches. Oddly, she felt more satisfied watching them eat than partaking of food herself. When they dug into their slabs of apple pie with equal gusto, she worried they might get tummy aches from so much good food all at once.

Once the children were satisfied, Eric ordered more sandwiches and asked the waitress to wrap them, telling her he'd pay for everything. Hannah found herself wondering where Eric had obtained so much money and asked him about it once he handed Shirley the sandwiches, with the promise from the child to take them home to their mother, the box containing enough for all three to share in two meals.

"Father didn't want me to. . .tarnish my welcome. He also didn't anticipate your mother's invitation to me as a guest in your home."

"Then your parents are wealthy?"

"Let's just say we're not poor and leave it at that."

Clearly, he didn't wish to speak of it, and Hannah wondered if their money was part of what Eric's father had received during his life of crime or in his inheritance as a count. She found it baffling that Eric's roots also stemmed from nobility. And after coming to America, Eric Sr. had also worked for a gangster. *Like Daddy did. . .*

Hannah still hadn't approached her father with what she knew. She realized she should reconcile her feelings toward him, now knowing of his criminal history, as Eric had done with his father. Yet everything she had learned since she first opened the door to Eric Jr. and he had walked across their threshold still was too much to process, and she remained silent on their return home.

Rescuer—yes. Rogue? At times. . .handyman, vicomte. . .

And what else?

Once they stepped inside the house, she almost groaned when she heard Aunt Charleigh's precise British accent drift from the parlor. She had hoped their visitors would be gone, not wishing Eric to perhaps suffer through further mistreatment.

They approached the parlor, and she sensed his tension.

Aunt Charleigh rose from the sofa when she noticed him. Instead of excusing herself and leaving, she surprised Hannah by moving their way and stopping in front of Eric. Again her eyes made a sweeping perusal, the intense shock on her face to look at his evident.

"I owe you an apology for my behavior." Her smile came polite, if shaky. "I skipped breakfast this morning in my eagerness to arrive in Connecticut and visit my daughter and her family, which in all likelihood aided my swoon."

"Under the circumstances, you owe me no apologies, Mrs. Lyons." He hesitated, as if he had more to say but wasn't sure if he should. "My father told me he'd never been taught to love because he'd never known it. His mother ran away with another man when he was very small, and his father took his anger out on him, also condemning his mother and the institute of marriage—why my father never went through with an actual marriage to you. His father led him not to believe in it. Despite his status as a comte's son, he had little, and he learned to think that to love something meant to possess it. In that sense, he came to care for you and told me that's why he always found it so difficult to let you go and searched for you to get you back. It wasn't just about the cons. But he was a mass of contradictions and ended up giving in to his rages and jealousy, treating you horribly, just as his father had done to him. He didn't know how to stop."

"Oh my. . ." Her face lost a little color, and tears glossed her eyes.

Uncle Stewart protectively moved to her side. "Why are you telling us this?"

"I think it's time Mrs. Lyons knew everything my father never could say and wished to, and then after he found Christ and love with my mother, never had an opportunity to tell her. Forgive me if I spoke out of turn, but since I've taken the brunt of his mistakes since I got here, I felt like the perfect liaison to speak. Now if you'll excuse me, I'll bid you *bon nuit.*"

Everyone gaped as he left the room.

"Hannah?" At her mother's voice, she blinked, looking away from the now empty doorway. "Will you please get more tea, dear? I think everyone could use a cup."

Hannah vaguely nodded, glancing at her aunt, whose shocked dismay was still apparent. In the kitchen, she poured herself a cup first, feeling in limbo. At a step behind her, she glanced over her shoulder to see her redheaded friend.

"If you've come to criticize Eric, save your breath, Clemmie. Maybe he shouldn't have said all that, but I'm glad he did."

"I'm the last person to offer any kind of speech. Joel was once the bad boy of the bunch, remember."

Hannah swung around to face her. "But Eric's not. That's the point. He's done nothing to warrant anyone's bad treatment. *Nothing.*"

Clemmie's green eyes narrowed in enlightenment, and self-consciously Hannah looked away. "Those are rather strong words in defense of someone who's only a visiting guest. . .or is he more than that, Hannah?"

"I don't know what you mean."

"I think you do." Clemmie approached, putting her arm around Hannah's shoulders. "Just be careful. I'd hate to see you get hurt."

Hannah winced, sure if Clemmie knew the particulars and the foolish little challenge to win Eric's favor, she would be hearing a different sort of speech.

"I'll admit, knowing that the son of the man who abused my mother is in your house—staying here—well, yes, I'm still a bit shocked and anxious. But if anyone knows how God can change hearts, I do. I'm sure Eric's father is nothing like the man Mama knew. Just from hearing Eric's admirable defense of him, I can tell that."

"Then why tell me to be careful?"

"Because you seem to be moving too fast. The way you behave, you sound like a woman in love, fighting for her man, and you've scarcely known him, what, two weeks?"

"In love?" Hannah stared at her friend in utter disbelief. "That's preposterous. I don't love Eric." She gave an incredulous huff of laughter. "But he has become a friend, and I don't like to see my friends mistreated."

Which is why you're engaging in such a demeaning bet, her conscience maliciously whispered.

"I don't want to talk about this anymore." Hannah set the teapot on the tray. "Were you able to locate anyone to make costumes for the play? I admit I've had nightmares of the little colonists and Indians running around naked in pilgrim hats and feather headdresses."

Clemmie laughed. "I assure you, we'll have something for the children to wear even if I have to try my own hand at sewing. I don't think Thea would approve of her two little girls running around in their underthings. How's the play coming along?"

"Oh, all right." She didn't admit that, since Eric's stay, she hadn't managed to concentrate long enough to add the second act.

"Maybe we can help. Joel has an old typewriter he said he was willing to give you. He was given a nicer one for his job at the newspaper office, so he has a spare."

"Oh, that would be splendid." And surely all her stories would progress much faster!

"I'll bring it Wednesday."

"Then we're still on?"

"Of course we're still on," Clemmie said with a reassuring laugh. "I would never break the tradition of our monthly standing lunch dates."

"Good. But no more warnings about Eric, all right?"

"Honey, I'm just concerned. Much like you were with me when Joel was blind and I pretended to be a stranger, to help him, so he wouldn't kick me to the curb."

"That was entirely different. You've always loved Joel, ever since we were children."

"True. But I can't help think there's more beneath the surface with you and Eric."

"And I've told you there's not, so there's no reason for concern." She managed a smile, her face warming, and quickly averted her attention to the task of gathering teacups.

*

Eric spent the next two days working on the loose wiring in the upstairs corridor. Hannah kept herself strangely absent, which surprised and oddly disappointed him. He knew she'd gone to lunch with Clemmie yesterday, after explaining to him they always met on the fifteenth of each month to catch up on their lives. Today she was home. He just wasn't sure where.

Had he really begun to rely on her companionship so much that he missed her absence? He supposed that shouldn't come as a surprise. Eric had never been a loner, always surrounded by family and those at the mission. These past weeks at the Thomas residence had been a lesson in tolerance, in being treated as an outcast.

"Whatcha doin'?"

Abbie came up behind him. He looked over his shoulder at her shadowed form before turning back to his work, almost happy to see the precocious child, even if she did tend to addle his nerves with her personal questions.

"Fixing wires."

"Can I help?"

"Non. It's too dangerous for a little thing like you."

"I'm not so little." A pout angered her voice. "I go to school now like everyone else."

"But school doesn't teach you these kinds of things, and I don't want to see you get electrocuted."

"Aw, I never get to do anything fun around here."

Eric shook his head in amusement at her idea of fun.

"You and Hannah won't let me patch up walls, either."

"Your mother doesn't think the powder used for the paste would be good for your lungs since you've been sick. Besides, a lot of it is too high for you to reach."

"I can climb a ladder, too!"

Eric decided to let the matter drop, realizing Abbie wouldn't be satisfied. The silence lasted no more than several seconds.

"You like my sister, don't you? I mean *really* like her?"

He jerked in shock at the blunt question and pulled the pliers away, deciding if he didn't want to slip and electrocute himself or pull the wrong wire, he should quit until Abbie left. He'd cut the power supply to the upstairs but didn't trust the old wiring. "Your sister is a nice girl." He purposely was evasive. Moving to his feet, he clicked off the flashlight in his other hand. The window at the end of the corridor provided enough muted lighting to be able to see.

"Hey—where are you going?" Abbie complained as she followed him to the head of the stairs.

"Time for a coffee break." He took the steps, hearing her lighter tread behind him.

"There isn't any coffee left. Hannah's friends drank it all."

So Hannah's friends were here. That explained her distance.

"I heard them talking. About you. They don't think you like Hannah much."

Abbie's matter-of-fact statement made Eric pause on the stairwell near the banister Hannah had come flying down when he'd caught her.

"She told them you do."

"Did she?" Eric narrowed his eyes in curious thought and resumed walking to the landing.

"I think you like her, too."

He turned to face her. "Don't you have homework?"

"Why is everyone always asking me that?"

He hid a smile. "Guess they don't want you to fail."

She sighed. "Oh, all right. . ." Mumbling, she took the stairs back up to her room.

With coffee no longer an option, he decided to make a second visit to the library shelves. He'd left Hannah's Civil War novel upstairs but didn't really want to return to his room to get it. He was halfway finished with the story, which hadn't turned out so bad, after all.

He'd no more than turned the handle and pushed the door aside when he realized his mistake.

Julia and Muffy turned, looks of pleased surprise spreading over their features. Hannah sat behind a typewriter on the desk, bright spots of color blooming in her cheeks. The three looked as if they'd been immersed in an intense confrontation. Hannah's lashes swept downward in apparent nervousness, and Eric wondered if he'd been the topic.

"Sorry to interrupt. I'll just go—"

"Don't be silly." Julia approached before he could make his escape, a not so subtle sway to her hips. All that was missing was a long cigarette holder dangling from her fingers along with the vamp look. "We were wondering what had become of you."

Muffy trapped him from the other side, batting her lashes and smiling. "You really shouldn't work *all* the time. Come talk with us awhile. We were just finishing up."

Eric politely smiled at them, not wanting to offend Hannah's friends. He glanced her way, catching her fixed gaze on him. Her cheeks blossomed a deeper shade of rose.

"I really don't have the time." But neither girl would relent. Each of them took one of his arms, drawing him into the room.

"You're coming to the presentation next week, aren't you?" Muffy asked.

"Presentation?" He shook his head in confusion.

"The play, of course!" The short brunette gave an exuberant giggle. "After all the time we've spent working on this, you simply must come."

"It *is* for a worthy cause," Julia added. "The Founder's Day celebration will have a drive to help aid the destitute, and Hannah did mention your family supports that kind of thing."

He wondered just what Hannah had told them, his eyes again going to hers. Again she quickly averted her gaze.

"Hannah did mention her project. I haven't decided if I'll attend or not."

He didn't miss the quick lift of Hannah's head or the injured look in her eyes.

"But you simply *must* come," Muffy urged, pulling on his arm, which she had yet to release. "There will be other things there to do, and food besides. It will be a lovely way for you to meet everyone, since most of the town will turn out for the event, I daresay."

"Yes," Julia agreed with an amused drawl. "Muffy's mother is in charge of food preparation. Their entire family has an overzealous fondness for indulging, so I'm certain there will be quite an enormous spread."

Muffy pulled her brows together in hurt at Julia's catty remark.

Eric had had enough.

"If you ladies will excuse me, I really need to get back to work."

"Surely it can wait a little longer?" Julia asked, affronted, as if she held some power over him.

"Actually, it can't." With one last glance at Hannah, who earnestly studied the paper in the typewriter, he left and returned upstairs.

No more than ten minutes passed before he heard her light tread on the stairwell. He didn't turn around to see. He didn't need to. She moved to his side and knelt down beside him.

"What are you doing?" she asked.

He glanced at her then focused back on his work. "Trying to fix this wiring, but your father should hire an electrician. My uncle taught me what he knew, but I'm no expert."

"Oh, but I most certainly disagree." Her words ended on what could be construed as fawning, and she put a hand to his shoulder. "You're so intelligent when it comes to all these confusing repairs, Eric."

The words, of themselves, seemed sincere. But the lilting note that sugared her voice and her attempt at vamping him, as she'd done his first evening there, only made him frown.

"The day you arrived on our doorstep was surely the most providential day of our lives. I simply don't know what we would have done if—"

He turned to look at her. "Stop."

Instantly, she quit batting her lashes. "Wh–what do you mean?"

He noted the confusion on her face. "Stop trying to be something you're not."

Her eyes widened a little. "I still don't know—"

"You're not Scarlett O'Hara, and you're not your friends. Don't act like those girls, Hannah. You're better than that."

She slowly dropped her hand from his shoulder. "I thought you liked that kind of attention," she all but whispered.

Liked it? He'd only been trying to be polite.

Accustomed to being straightforward, he looked at her intently. "I like you better. The real you. Not these fake interpretations you keep coming up with." He watched her head lower in clear distress. "Why do you keep company with such people, anyway?" he asked more gently. "You're not like them."

Her gaze snapped up. Though the lighting was dim, he sensed a trace of guilt beneath the anger brimming in her eyes. "You have no idea what it's like, having a mother who's half Polynesian, being whispered about and criticized all through childhood, even if she is a chieftain's granddaughter. It didn't matter to them. It made matters worse. The fact that my grandfather is a missionary didn't gain me any favor with my peers, either."

He narrowed his eyes, trying to understand. "You're ashamed of them?"

"No, of course not. I love my mother, and I respect my grandfather for his ideals, though we've never met. But try living among people who judge others for where they come from—and try to fit in despite all that. The boarding school my great-uncle sent me to was full of those kinds of girls. Girls like Muffy and Julia. I was lonely. I wanted friends, just like everybody else had. I soon found I had a gift for literary drama and helped put on school plays. A few of those classmates who would never have anything to do with me before started being kind to me. When the chance came and several of the most popular girls in my class opened their circle to accept me into their fold—two of them from my own hometown—I was determined to do whatever I could to keep their favor."

"Even if that means sacrificing what you believe in?"

She gasped. "What are you talking about?"

"It seems you would have to live a life of pretense in order to keep such friends. Pretending to go along with what they believe while burying your own values, just to be accepted. Life isn't one big stage play, Hannah—it's real, and it hurts, and it can hurt you. You can't go on assuming fantasy roles as an escape just because you're afraid to face who you are."

Flustered, she shook her head. "I'm not afraid—what makes you think I am? Just because I like having a good time and enjoy the motion pictures? Just because I don't look at life as one big depressing newsreel?" She glared at him. "You don't know anything about me."

"I've seen enough."

"All right. Maybe Julia and Muffy can be. . .overbearing. I'll give you that. But at least they offered friendship when others wouldn't give me the time of day!"

"And what kind of friends are they if their primary goal in life is to find new ways to hurt others? I've seen their type, I know what they're like. What makes you think they won't turn on you one day and pull the rug out from under *you*?"

Her mouth parted in shock, but he continued. "You told me you want my friendship. That's all I'm trying to offer. I don't want to see you hurt by those girls. Maybe I have no place to talk to you like this. But if you continue hanging around them, I'm afraid you could be hurt very badly. Your schooldays are over, mon amie. It's time you moved on. Are Julia and Muffy really the type of people you want to be with the rest of your life?"

She stood up so suddenly, he felt the rush of air. He looked up at her.

"You're right, Eric. You don't have any place to talk. Especially since you have no idea what you're talking about."

She opened her mouth to say more but instead turned on her heel and marched to her room. The slam of her door told Eric he'd overstepped the line, but he didn't feel sorry about it. He only hoped his well-meaning words had found their mark.

ℒ♥

Definitely a rogue!

Hannah felt like throwing something.

With her back pressed to her bedroom door, she swung her gaze around the room, looking for a worthy target. Her hand closed around a novel. She hesitated, looking down at the illustrated cover. The memory of his emphatic words twisted in a relentless circle in her mind.

Infuriation, rage, disbelief, mortification, guilt—all fought for pre-dominance. Guilt won.

Tears misted her eyes, and she hung her head.

Earlier, Julia and Muffy had baited Hannah about her pathetic attempts to snag Eric, before he came into the library and put a blissful end to their torment. She had watched his interaction with Muffy and Julia, had mistaken his kind smiles for delight in their interest, and had tried to attract him by emulating her friends. But she'd been wrong. . .so wrong.

He had seen right through her. . .shocked her with his knowing words, angered her with his presumptions of her character, embarrassed her with his blunt disapproval. But more than that, when he looked at her with such concern, admitting his fears to see her hurt, a blade of shame had twisted deep inside her excuse for a heart. The irony didn't escape her, since she was engaging in a plan that could wind up hurting him. Oh, she had hoped in the end it wouldn't, of course, hoped he would laugh it off and chalk it up as a good joke. Or if not that, hoped at least that he might not fall hard for her. But she'd soon discovered Eric wasn't like the boys she'd known. "Boys" in the true sense of the word, immature and insensitive. Silly rich boys who flirted with girls and fell all over themselves to gain their attention. Eric wasn't like that. . .

Eric was a man.

The boys in her social circle cared more about status, wealth, and ego, and less about other people's feelings. Perhaps they deserved to be the target of such a foolish challenge, but Eric did not. Eric put others first and volunteered his help when needed, even when he wasn't shown the appreciation he deserved. He acted more mature than all those boys put together.

"God, what have I done?" Hannah uttered the short plea and set the book down, shaking her head in distress as she moved to her bed. Her novel lay concealed for the moment in her box of photographs of her favorite motion picture stars, but she felt no desire to jump into it and lose herself in the fictional world she'd created.

The world she had control over when nothing went right in her own life.

She stared in dawning shock.

Eric had accused her of crawling within the pages of fantasy to escape life and in the process, lose who she was. Was he right?

She did love to pen her stories but now realized that desire only intensified once she'd gained recognition and acceptance because of her skill, from those who'd shunned her before. She did have talent, or they wouldn't have been impressed. But maybe she should consider a better way to use her craft, something worthier. She didn't have to give up her stories completely.

An idea teased her mind. Unable to resist the lure, she grabbed pen and paper and jotted everything down, hoping Clemmie would approve. More importantly, hoping Joel would agree. She read through what she'd written, experiencing a sense of satisfaction that had been missing with her unfinished novel. She didn't speculate about the reason too closely, her thoughts finding their way back to Eric.

With grim resolve, she knew what she must do.

And the biggest irony above all ironies. . .

She realized she was falling fast and hard for him.

Chapter 11

The air held a brisk chill, hinting of the weather to come. Eric stood on the green with the rest of the town who'd turned out for the Founder's Day celebration and watched the play unfold. The original plan had been to hold the production inside the colonial-style building, but a broken pipe had made it impossible, flooding the floors of the renovated structure. So the entire affair was being held in front of the building, outdoors.

He stood a short distance from Hannah's family and friends, her brothers giving him hostile glances on occasion. Clemmie had attended with her friend, Thea, their husbands covering the event for the newspaper. Clemmie nodded toward Eric with an uncertain smile, and he sensed her nervousness to have him there.

He hadn't planned to attend but realized how important it was to Hannah that he do so. In the end, he'd agreed, not wanting to injure her feelings. Over the past several weeks, when she wasn't swamped by work on the play or they weren't exchanging clipped words about the value or triviality of their daily lives, he saw a quality in Hannah that intrigued him. Despite everything, she had a sweet naïveté about her, so much different from her haughty friends, and he hoped that gentle part of Hannah would never change.

The play continued, the little colonists and Indians acting out one scene of many in the fictional story Hannah had composed using their town history as a guide. A boy dressed in the clothes of a former century delivered a soliloquy about the founding fathers and their first difficult year, speaking as if he'd also experienced the events by his use of the word *we*, while behind him, other children silently and dramatically acted out the roles of epidemics, crop failures, and more. At times, the boy narrator turned to the side, as if to become part of the audience, and also watched what took place. When that happened, the play became more lifelike as the characters interacted with dialogue, the overall idea unique and interesting. This went on back and forth as the narrator took them through the first hundred years, then solemnly bowed his head. Another narrator, a girl dressed in clothes of their time period, took the opposite side of the stage and continued with the last hundred years of the town's history, also using first person to portray events.

Eric watched, impressed with Hannah's talent to write and organize such a play. He had thought her desire to become a novel writer foolish, in light of all their country suffered, but maybe he'd been too quick to form an opinion. She obviously had creative skills; the play was informative without coming across as heavy or dull.

The only problem that arose she handled smoothly: One of the littlest Indian's feathers came loose from his headband, and he started chasing it over the grounds. The crowd chuckled, as did Eric, and the narrator became flustered, stumbling in his speech. Eric watched Hannah, who stood on the sidelines, quietly say something to the older boy with an encouraging smile, and the narrator resumed while the little Indian chased his feather.

Within minutes of the play's conclusion, Hannah sought Eric out.

"It was awful, wasn't it?"

Her question surprised him, as did her evident insecurity.

"I thought it was good."

"Really?" Surprise lit up her eyes. "You actually liked it?"

He couldn't blame her for her skepticism; he hadn't given her an easy time about how she chose to use her hours each day. "It was very well written."

She smiled then looked uncertain again. "It would have been better with the proper lighting. The spotlights were supposed to be on the narrators at certain moments, for effect, but who could foresee a water pipe bursting?"

"You did the best with what you had and made quick decisions when things went wrong. It was splendid. In fact"—he grinned in sheepish surrender—"maybe such entertainment is good for the soul." Everyone appeared in high spirits, even those in the community he'd rarely seen smile.

She laughed, her features relaxing. "That's high praise, coming from you."

The day continued in a whirlwind of fun, feasting, and laughter. The food was simple fare, but there was so much it practically ran off the tables. Hannah's play and the sight of the provisions made him think of the first Thanksgiving and the nation's celebration of the event, which the president had designated to happen five days from now. Eric noticed Hannah's fixed attention on the food table, her eyes distant.

"Are you hungry?" He captured her attention. "Would you like a sandwich?"

She shook her head. "I was thinking about Shirley and Jimmy."

Her admission astonished him, and he regarded her in tender approval. "Would you like to walk to the park and see if they are there?"

"Oh, could we?" Her eyes sparkled with hope. "I also thought. . .I could locate a box. Maybe we could fill it with food and take it with us?" She sounded hesitant, as if seeking his approval.

He nodded. "I like that idea, *mon amie*. Let's do that."

Once she found a container a little bigger than a shoebox, together they filled it with delicious food until it would contain no more. The hostess behind the table asked their reason for collecting so many sandwiches. When they explained, she told them to wait a moment and disappeared. She returned with a pie and set it on top of the box Eric held.

"For the children." A twinkle lit her eye. "With so much food, it won't be missed."

They thanked her and began their walk to the park. He spotted Julia and

Muffy looking at them from across the green, and Eric sensed Hannah go rigid. She grabbed his arm. "Let's go this way. I know a shortcut."

He didn't ask why she wanted to avoid her friends, curious but relieved he wouldn't have to be the victim of the fawning Muffy and the vamping Julia once again.

They strolled through a patch of rough grass, the shrubbery growing closer, clearly not the best of paths to take if it was a path at all. But Hannah's tension soon eased. Her lips turned up at the corners, her eyes bright in her excitement. He had never seen her more beautiful.

Once they reached the area where they'd first met the children, he and Hannah searched but found the park empty. No one was in sight, and he assumed it had to do with the celebration they'd left. He noticed the disappointment cloud her eyes and wanted to make it disappear.

"They said something about an alley behind the coffee shop."

Her eyes brightened again then looked troubled. "Yes, let's try there."

The walk took a short time. The streets were practically empty of traffic. Entering the alley behind the shop, Eric felt Hannah clutch his arm suddenly. "Oh Eric. . ."

Dismay trembled in her voice, and he also felt a wave of horrified sympathy.

Shirley and Jimmy scrounged through a trash bin of rotting garbage like two scrawny alley cats. Another smaller child nibbled from the well-eaten core of an apple turned brown.

"Don't eat that!" Hannah rushed forward.

The curly-haired tot lifted huge dark eyes to them, flashing with fear. The girl dropped the core, whirled away, and ran as if fearful Hannah might lash out and hurt her.

"No—don't go," Hannah called after her. "We brought better food!"

Eric was certain nothing else Hannah could have said would have stopped the panic-stricken child. But at the promise of good food, she cut short her mad retreat and warily turned.

"It's okay," Shirley said. "I know these people, Lily. They won't hurt you."

The girl peered at them distrustfully through her tousled brown curls. Her woolen dress was as dirty as the rest of her, and she wore no coat. Her face was gaunt, her eyes haunted. Eric had become accustomed to seeing such horrible poverty and misery at the mission, especially during the past years of great depression, but he saw Hannah's profound shock at this new slap of reality.

"Why don't you give them the sandwiches?" His voice came as a gentle nudge. He knew from experience that being the one to administer aid would help lift her spirits.

She glanced his way, her eyes glazed with stunned sorrow for the little ones' plight. Gingerly, she took a sandwich in each hand and approached, offering the sandwiches to Shirley and Jimmy. They grabbed the food, bringing it to their mouths in the same motion. The other child, seeing her friends' enthusiastic response, edged closer.

Hannah took another sandwich from the box and, with the same caution the littlest girl displayed, moved forward a few steps then hunched down at a level with the child, smiling and reaching across the small chasm toward her.

"It's really very good," Hannah whispered. "They're from the celebration the town is holding on the green. Did you children not know about that?"

Shirley nodded. "We thought they might throw us out or chase us down if we tried to get some food there."

"Non, it's free to everyone," Eric said when Hannah looked stricken and unable to speak.

The little girl slowly came forward, her acceptance of the sandwich just as gradual, before taking several quick steps back. Like Shirley and Jimmy, she crammed the bread in her mouth.

"Lily's scared 'cause some people yelled at her and threatened to call the cops last night," Shirley explained. "We sneaked into a snazzy food joint on the other side of town and tried to take food when no one was looking after some people got up to dance. The waiter caught Lily. Me and Jimmy got away. The woman called her filthy and told the waiter to throw her in jail, that the streets weren't safe with vermin like her. She was wearing a sweater like yours."

Eric noticed how the color seemed to rush out of Hannah's face, leaving it white and nowhere near the rose color of her sweater.

"What happened then?" he quietly prodded.

"Me and Jimmy was hiding behind some plants. Jimmy ran and kicked the waiter in the shin so he'd let go of Lily, and I dumped a plate of spaghetti in the woman's lap then grabbed Lily's hand, and we scrammed out of there fast."

"Did your mother know where you were?" Hannah's voice came as a mere wisp, and Eric shot her a concerned glance.

"No, ma'am. She was out looking for work."

"At night?" Hannah's shock didn't escape him.

"Yes, ma'am. She wouldn't have cared." Shirley shrugged. "She don't mind when we find our own meals. Says it's less of a burden on her."

"Is that pie?" Jimmy spoke for the first time, hungrily eyeing the dessert and licking his lips.

"Sure is, son." Eric handed over the box. "Take this home and share it with your little friend. But I want you to make me a promise. No more digging through garbage cans for any of you. Do we have a deal?"

Jimmy shrugged. "I s'ppose."

"You ain't gonna tell on us?" Shirley seemed surprised but relieved.

He wished he had a car to take them home, wished also that his family mission was just down the street. "Who would I tell? Now you three skedaddle before it gets dark. You shouldn't be out on the streets at night."

"Okay—thanks, mister!

"Thanks!" Jimmy echoed his sister as the two took off running. Lily gave them a shy smile before she followed.

Concerned for Hannah, Eric looked at her. "Are you all right?"

"They're so little." Her voice cracked as if it might break. "Too little for this. . ."

Understanding what she didn't say, he put his arm around her shoulders, drawing her to him. Her tight fists lay pressed against his chest. From the manner in which her body trembled, he realized she was trying hard not to cry. It seemed the most natural thing in the world to stroke her hair and bring his other arm around her waist, holding her closer.

After a moment, she lifted eyes shining with unshed tears up to him. The light from the back window of the café made them luminescent. Her lips trembled, and warmth surged through his veins.

He wanted to kiss her.

He might have done just that and had begun lowering his head toward hers, vaguely noting how Hannah's eyes fluttered closed and her chin lifted a little higher, when the back door suddenly swung open, startling them both. Hannah jumped a little in his arms.

At the sight of the cook who scowled at them, she didn't break their embrace but instead nestled against Eric, as if seeking refuge.

"You seen two brats loiterin' around here?" the man demanded.

Eric could feel Hannah bristle with indignation. "It's just us," he said before she could speak and give the children away. The cook had the stub of a cigarette dangling from his mouth, and a dirty apron covered his stout belly. His large, hairy forearms were well muscled, and Eric had a sneaking suspicion that he wouldn't hesitate to strike a child.

The cook gave them a suspicious look, clearly wondering what they were doing in an alley at twilight. Eric stared back gravely, refusing to give an inch.

"Well, then. . ." The man went back through the door. "Guess if them brats are finally gone, it's safe to leave the door open for air so my pies can cool."

Eric felt Hannah tense. "You would let little children starve?"

Eric squeezed her waist in warning. "Don't bother, Hannah." He glared at the man. "Some people you just can't get through to."

"Can't feed the whole world, now can I?" the cook defended, slamming the door—rather than keeping it open as he'd said. Eric wondered if the man thought his pies weren't safe from them.

"It's just so awful." Anger lent a sharp edge to her voice.

"It is," Eric agreed. "But this sort of thing has been going on since the beginning of time. There are always the poor, always the needy, and always those who just don't care." He didn't want to release her but couldn't hold her in the alley all night. "We've done what we could, and three small tummies are going to be satisfied tonight, thanks to you."

His reassurance earned him a grateful smile. Rather than let her go completely, he took hold of her elbow, turning her toward the street.

"Eric?"

"Yes, mon amie?"

"Tell me about your family's mission. I want to know everything."

⁊❧

Hannah stood at her bedroom window, looking out at the fresh layer of snow coating the ground. She pulled her sweater closer around her body, then glanced down at its frilled edges. . .a rose sweater of the softest merino wool with pearl buttons. . .a sweater like Julia and Muffy had, when the three bought the same style at a boutique, like sorority sisters. . .a boutique near the boarding school they'd all attended.

The woman called her filthy and told the waiter to throw her in jail, that the streets weren't safe with vermin like her. She was wearing a sweater like yours.

Hannah felt ill. Surely Muffy or Julia wouldn't be so cruel to a starving child? Both her friends had helped with the play and other charity work. . .though both their mothers were on the ladies' committee and perhaps had pressured their daughters into volunteering.

Hannah shook her head to clear it, not wanting to think such ill thoughts. She forced her mind to return to the past week. Giving to those children had brought more pleasure and satisfaction than buying a coveted hat. It had felt more like Thanksgiving to her, sharing Eric's company in an alleyway and bringing smiles to three needy children, than their own small celebration held in the kitchen, since the dining room had been under repairs. Her mother had shared a meal with her father, still bedridden, and Hannah, Eric, and her siblings had eaten their ham around the small table.

It had been pleasant enough—at least Josiah didn't start a fight with Eric, though he barely talked to him. At her mother's insistence, Eric had used their now-working phone to call his family for a distant reunion with his loved ones. But that day couldn't compare to the memory of those moments in the alley. There, for the first time in her young life, she had experienced deep sorrow based in sympathy amid moments that were pure golden.

Golden—in seeing the children's eager response to the offering of food. Golden—in that Eric had held her and almost kissed her.

She should confess the foolish challenge and beg his forgiveness—had considered it that day—but the opportunity fled forever the moment he took her in his arms.

"I can't tell him now," she whispered miserably. "God, help me. I just can't."

"Yipppeee! Hot dog!"

At the sudden booming hurrah outside her closed door, Hannah nearly jumped out of her skin. She rushed into the corridor, catching David before he could disappear into his room.

"Why did you yell like that?"

"The pond's frozen over! I just heard the news."

All Hannah's worries evaporated with the meaning of his words. She grinned at him before darting downstairs and rushing into the library.

Eric turned suddenly at her abrupt entrance, almost painting a white line across the bottom of the low windowsill. He stared at her in surprise.

"Put your paintbrush down and your tools away. You're coming with me!"

"I need to get this trim finished."

"You don't need to do any such thing, not today. Today is for fun."

He gave her a tolerant smile. "Fun again. I've been having entirely too much of that and not getting enough work done. If I want to make it home before Christmas, I need to concentrate on renovations more and recreation less."

The reminder of his upcoming departure made Hannah falter, but only for a moment. She didn't want to think about that depressing day.

"One more afternoon won't hurt. The pond is frozen over!" She expected some positive response, but he shrugged quizzically. "Ice skating," she clarified.

"I don't know how."

She gaped at him then closed her mouth and shook her head. Why should she be surprised?

"Well, now's the time to learn." She moved his way, grabbing his arm, and did her best to pull him up.

He laughed and allowed her to get him to his feet but shook his head. "I really can't, Hannah—"

"My daughter's right." Her mother walked into the room, smiling and wiping her hands with a dish towel. "I insist that you take some time off, Eric. You've been working too hard, and I'm certain with the little that you told me remains left to do you'll be finished long before Christmas." She smiled. "I even promise I'll not ask you to run more errands or take the children anywhere in the car."

Hannah smiled at her mother, grateful she took her side. He looked from one to the other, his gaze at last settling on Hannah.

"Oh, all right. The painting can wait. But I don't have any skates."

"You can use my husband's. You look to be the same size, and he'll have no need of them this winter."

"Sure he won't mind?" Eric's question came uneasily.

"I've spoken with him in great depth about you. I think he would approve."

Hannah drew a stunned breath, hoping her mother's words went deeper than a pair of ice skates.

Within the next half hour, she and Eric, with David tagging behind, took the car to the pond. David kept quiet, looking at Eric indecisively from time to time, and Hannah hoped he was questioning Josiah's lousy opinion of him.

Soon they pulled into a clearing near the snow-laden trees. Seeing a familiar car, Hannah couldn't help the little squeal that escaped and eagerly looked toward the pond.

ℒ♥

"There's Clemmie and Joel!" She waved to a couple across the pond.

Hannah grabbed Eric's hand and pulled him along. He felt amused by her enthusiasm and tense by the cold eyes of the fair-headed young man in whose direction Hannah pulled him. He and Eric were similar in coloring, Eric's hair and eyes a shade darker. When Hannah spoke of her friends, she had joked that Clemmie's husband had been a little imp in behavior, though in looks everyone compared him to an angel when he was a boy; as he grew into a man, the term evolved into warrior angel. The burning look the man gave Eric did remind him of a celestial being who would wield a fiery sword.

"I'm Eric Fontaine." He put out his hand.

The man looked down at it but didn't respond to the gesture. He lifted steady eyes. "I know who you are. I know who your father is, too."

"Joel. . ." His wife slipped her hand around his arm as though trying to restrain him.

"I heard about what he did to you." An icy calm filled Eric. "I'm sorry."

"Sorry?" The man didn't smile. "Your father almost *killed* my wife's mother and on more than one occasion."

"Oh no, not this again! Can we please not talk about this?" Hannah barely suppressed her angry disgust. "I came to enjoy the day, not fight over the past. Anyway, I'm surprised at you, Joel Litton. You weren't exactly guiltless of any of your crimes, yet you found forgiveness. Can't you offer it? Especially—and I don't know how many times I've had to say this—since Eric isn't his father and hasn't done anything wrong! Why must everyone behave so beastly toward him?"

"Hannah, it's all right." Eric squeezed her gloved hand where her fingers still clutched his, her pressure tightening with her words.

"No, it's not. And if this is how it's going to be, then we might as well go find another patch of ice to skate."

She whirled away, but Clemmie hurried forward. "Hannah, wait." She glanced at her husband. A silent message seemed to pass between them before she turned back to Hannah. "You're right. Let's enjoy the day. We rarely have time to spend together anymore. I've been so busy with Rebecca. Mother's watching her this afternoon. Did I tell you she cut another tooth?" She pulled Hannah away as the mood shifted, and arm in arm, both girls began to chatter.

The two men sized each other up.

"The girls are right," Joel said at last. "I shouldn't judge you for your father's sins."

"Since I've come to Cedarbrook, I've learned to get used to it."

"You don't have that problem where you come from?" Joel seemed surprised.

"My father is a changed man. Nothing like the cad of his youth, and I'm sincerely sorry that he endangered you when you were a boy. He told me about those days and meeting you at the carnival."

Joel's eyes narrowed. "Did he? Makes me wonder why."

"He doesn't hide his mistakes or minimize his crimes. In trying to help others find a solution to their problems, he spares himself nothing."

Joel snorted. "How noble."

Eric didn't respond. This man's opinion of his father, the man Joel remembered, was harsh, with good reason.

"I don't want to see Hannah get hurt. She grew up at the Refuge. As well as being my wife's closest and dearest friend, Hannah's like family."

"I would never hurt Hannah. You have my word on that, whatever it's worth to you."

Joel nodded. "Glad we understand each other."

A settlement reached, however shaky, the tension ebbed a few slight degrees.

"Uncle Joel!" a little girl in a bright red coat screeched as she came into view, gliding on her ice skates. "Look at me! Look at me!"

"That's really good, Bethany. You'll be a world champ in no time. Where's your sister?"

The child pointed to the flocked trees behind her, where a little girl glumly sat on the snow.

"She doesn't want to skate. She's a scaredy-cat."

Joel lifted his brows. "Well then, what do you say we go and help her?"

The girl nodded.

"Your niece?" Eric asked, and Joel looked at him.

"A good friend's daughter. At the Refuge, some developed the habit of calling the adults close to us Aunt or Uncle. Herbert's children do the same with me. He's sick in bed, his wife's busy with their baby, and Clemmie and I offered to take their girls for the day."

Eric nodded, recalling Hannah express that she used the same sort of title for her "Aunt Charleigh" and others there and realized just how close any of them who once lived at Lyons Refuge really were. Like one big family, and clearly protective of each another.

The three moved toward the small, redheaded girl, Eric following only because he spotted Hannah. Both she and Clemmie spoke to the child, who furiously shook her head.

"Don' wanna skate!" she insisted.

Eric quickly took in the situation. Being the eldest of a string of children, his youngest brother four years old, he decided to try and help. "Hi there," he said brightly to the child who sat holding her knees beneath her coat. Tears glistened in her eyes, her expression stubborn.

"I'm a friend of Hannah's. Did you know where I live we don't have a pond like this?"

She didn't respond.

"We have a really wide ocean though. But the water doesn't freeze over like it does here."

She tilted her head to one side, exhibiting a shred of interest.

He looked at the others as though nervous, then hunched down beside her. "Can I tell you a secret? I've never skated before."

Her big hazel eyes regarded him in wonder as if the idea of an adult not being able to partake in the sport was an anomaly. "Are you afraid you might fall down?"

He grinned at her faint words. "Non. Falling down doesn't hurt so much since I've got all this padding." He pulled at the thick sleeve of his coat, noting how well she was bundled up. "I'm afraid I won't be able to get up, and I'll look silly if I try."

She giggled. "Daddy looks like a fish bouncing when he tries."

Eric assumed she meant a fish out of water. "I really would like it if someone would come with me, someone else who doesn't know how, so I won't feel so alone. Would you do that for me?" A return glint of terror in her eyes had him quickly say, "Maybe if your uncle helps you and my friend helps me, we can help one another get up if we fall down. What's your name?"

"Loretta."

"That's a pretty name. So what do you say, Loretta, will you help me not be such a 'fraidy cat?"

A moment's indecision made her scrunch her brow. "Okay."

"Swell." He smiled, sitting down on the snow beside her with the foreign skates. "I'm afraid I don't know how to put these on, either." He pretended to try to pull it over his shoe, and she giggled.

"You're s'pposed to take your shoes off, silly."

"Oh." He gave her a sheepish grin. "Thanks. . .silly." He tweaked her nose, earning him a bigger giggle.

Hannah knelt in the snow to help him while Clemmie helped Loretta rise to her feet. Joel took a few steps his way. "Okay, I'm impressed." His tone came grudging, his smile faint.

"What?" Eric looked up, his expression deadpan. "I meant every word I said."

At that, Joel laughed outright.

Once the strange-feeling shoes with blades for bottoms were tied successfully to his feet, both Hannah and Joel took his hands and helped him up. Instantly his ankles buckled. "How does one walk in these things?" He stood on snow and was struggling. They expected him to go out on ice?

Amid gales of her laughter, Hannah offered tips as both she and Joel helped Eric.

"Having fun?" he asked dryly when she burst into another fit of giggles while Eric tried to keep his balance on the blades and not walk like a drunkard.

"Okay, I think you're sufficiently practiced," Hannah announced. "Time to get your feet wet on the ice."

Eric grabbed a close, low-lying branch to prevent his fall, showering a mound of snow on his shoes. He gaped at her. "You're joking, *oui*?"

"Non." She grinned. "You've got to get out there some time, *mon ami*. Remember, you have to be an example." Her eyes twinkled too merrily, and he growled in good-natured fun.

"What was I thinking? Maybe that little girl had the right idea all along. . . ."

"Come on, ole sport." Joel clapped him heavily on the back. Had Eric not been holding on to a branch, the action would have brought him to his knees. While relieved that the man had begun to warm to him, Eric questioned Joel's eagerness to get him on the ice. Maybe any friendliness was a sham and Joel looked forward to seeing Eric slam into the freezing hard surface.

Grumbling, he let go of the tree. He held fast to Hannah's hand until he was sure he'd cut off all circulation but somehow managed to plow his way through the snow. He watched as Hannah and Joel glided onto the ice. Joel did a figure eight, and Hannah twirled in a continuous circle.

He stared in disbelief. "They have got to be kidding."

"Just testing it." Hannah smiled at him. "Come on!"

While Joel took Loretta's mittened hand and cautiously helped the child along the ice, a little at a time, with Clemmie holding her other hand, Hannah did her best to support Eric with both arms wrapped around his waist. But her figure was slight compared to his heavier build, and he spent most of his time falling, occasionally bringing her down with him when she couldn't break away fast enough or keep her balance.

As he improved, very slightly, she let him go. But after countless tender landings on his backside, Eric felt thankful they now skated at the edge of the pond, where the blessed bench they'd used stood close in sight.

"Maybe that's enough for one—*agh!*"

His foot slipped out from under him, and he fell backward onto the snow. Hannah reached for him, losing her own balance, and fell frontward—right on top of Eric.

Sprawled atop the length of his body, her laughter quickly ebbed. Their faces close, Eric forgot all about the pain.

They stared into one another's eyes a long moment, their frosty breaths mingling; then his gloved hand went to the back of her head, and he slowly drew her closer.

Chapter 12

Hannah felt his breath, warm against her cool lips, and she clutched his shoulders, her eyes fluttering closed in anticipation of his kiss.

"Smoochin' in the snow! Smoochin' in the snow!"

The teasing shout came from some young boys who ran past, and Hannah's eyes flew open. Eric's hand dropped from the back of her head, but he wasn't looking toward their hecklers. Hannah followed his solemn gaze to the ice, where her brother David had stopped skating and stood, not ten feet away, glaring at them.

Hannah managed to scramble up off Eric, awkwardly but as quickly as she could. She offered her hand to help him up, but he ignored it, somehow managing to get to his feet without falling. "I think I've taken enough bruises and bumps for one lesson." His voice came calm, giving nothing of his feelings away. "How about we take a walk instead?"

Still flustered from being caught by her brother, Hannah nodded at the opportunity to find temporary sanctuary from the others. They stripped off their skates and tugged on their shoes, which Clemmie had stowed in a bag beneath the bench.

"Ahhh. . ." Eric sighed in contentment. "Flat-soled shoes are best."

Hannah giggled, relieved the mood had lightened again. They moved through the woods and along the path near the first few layers of trees that formed a ring, hiding them from the skaters on the pond.

"About what happened. . ."

"That's okay. Forget it. I didn't mind." She felt flustered, certain his quiet words related to their almost-kiss.

"You didn't mind David being angry about seeing us together?"

"Oh, that." Heat rushed to her face at her blunder. "He's barely fourteen. He needs to learn, as does Josiah, who has no good excuse." She barely knew what she was saying. "At least you and Joel seem to have reached an agreement."

"He decided to give me the benefit of the doubt."

"Good." She felt relieved she'd steered him away from her gaffe. "He's really a nice fellow, though you wouldn't believe it to have known him back in the days at the Refuge. And later, when he went blind, he—"

"Joel went blind?" Eric stopped walking. "Not because of anything my father did, I hope?"

"Oh no! It was an automobile accident. Clemmie came to Connecticut and nursed him back to health. Well, emotional health, that is. Joel was an awful curmudgeon then, but Clemmie wouldn't give up on him. Of course, she didn't tell him who she was at first. . ."

She filled him in on what she knew of their story and how Joel realized it was Clemmie he'd loved all along. She gave a wistful little sigh. "It's so romantic."

"It sounds like a novel."

"Or like that movie we saw weeks ago!" Hannah nodded. "Only it wasn't. It all happened. It was very. . .intense."

"Reality is more intense and satisfying than any movie, Hannah."

Something lingered beneath his words, but she was afraid to dig too deeply and find she'd been mistaken. "For someone who doesn't have a lot of experience visiting the motion pictures, you seem rather sure of that."

He chuckled. "It only stands to reason. The motion pictures are just copies of real life."

"But they can be satisfying. That movie we saw inspired me with how she changed toward the end, how she wanted to change. . ."

"I've noticed you've been doing a lot of that lately."

She fairly glowed with his praise. "I do feel different about some issues than before."

A few moments of easy silence passed between them as they walked through the fairy-tale land covered from topmost branch to sloping ground in a thick, fluffy coating of sparkling snow. Beyond the trees, she heard laughter and the happy shouts of skaters.

"Are you still writing your novel?" he asked.

She turned her head to look at him. "You know about that?"

"Abbie might have mentioned it."

She felt herself blushing again, which might have something to do with her hero, who'd taken on the characteristics of the man beside her.

"I dabble now and then. Actually, I've been working on another idea."

"Oh?"

At his clear interest, she wavered. She had hoped to show, not tell him, but then Joel's boss might not agree. "I wrote a piece about Shirley and Jimmy, without mentioning names, of course. A human-interest story, you could call it. But hopefully a method to help—"

He stopped and swung around to face her. "You wrote a piece about those kids?"

She nodded, unable to tell by the sudden softness of his tone matched with the intent look in his eyes if he approved or not. "Joel said he would show it to his boss. I don't know if he'll print it or not. But I tried."

"You're a special lady, mon amie. I think it's a great idea."

"Not so special." Shame made her lower her eyes to his chest when she recalled the silly challenge. She considered telling him and begging him to go along with it, only so that she wouldn't need to purchase two hats with money she didn't have. For her part, when she won, if he agreed to help her, she would tell her friends that they didn't need to pay up. She could never like any hat gained through such a deal. This moment seemed perfect to tell him. But. . .she just couldn't spoil their beautiful outing.

Nor could she bear the look of admiration in his eyes.

"I do a lot of things wrong, Eric. I constantly make mistakes and foolish choices."

"That's all part of being human."

"I'll bet you don't make half as many as I do. You seem so. . .perfect." She spoke the words sincerely, not trying to imitate anyone but herself.

"If you knew what was going through my head right now, you wouldn't say that." His glove lifted to push away her hair that had been blowing in her eyes, and Hannah felt a little thrill go through her.

"What could be so bad to make me change my opinion of you?"

"Not bad. . .just shocking."

"I think I'm intrigued." The words came in a whisper as his eyes lowered to her mouth.

"And I think I would like to kiss you."

Her breath caught on an inaudible gasp, her gaze going to his parted lips. "So, what's stopping you this time?"

At her shy invitation, he cradled her cheek against his hand. His head lowered to hers too slowly, as if he might change his mind, and Hannah did something. . .shocking. At the incredible longing that had been building for days to experience his kiss, she surged up the scant distance left, her mouth firmly meeting his. He let out a gasp of surprise at her eagerness, his warm breath against her lips making her heart pound. She felt her head swim and her hands moved to grab his lapels.

Thankfully, he didn't retreat as she feared he might after her bold gesture. Instead, he brought his free hand to cradle her other cheek while learning her lips with a gentle precision that made her go weak in the knees.

When he did pull away, she opened her eyes and stared at him in bashful wonder. She had written of kisses between the couple in her novel, in complete ignorance. Having experienced her first real one, she realized now she had no idea what she'd been writing about.

His eyes regarded her with tenderness as his thumbs gently stroked her jaw. "It's a good thing we weren't wearing skates."

His light remark alleviated the intense mood, and Hannah giggled. No doubt if they had been in skates, with the way her knees had practically buckled, she and Eric would both be lying in a snowdrift right now.

He looked at her mouth as if he would like to kiss her again, but only dropped his hands from her face. "I think it's time we return to the house. It's getting dark."

Hannah sighed. "I suppose you're right."

They turned to go, and she felt another thrill when Eric slipped his gloved hand inside hers.

The drive to the house was slow due to icy roads, with heavier snow falling. Eric sensed something wrong the moment he opened the door.

The house was too. . .still, but more than that, a strange heaviness weighted the atmosphere. He looked over at Hannah as they removed their coats and scarves. She scanned the room with a frown, and he realized she must sense it, too. David came in behind them and stomped up the stairs without a word. Eric followed Hannah to the entrance of the parlor, where she hesitated, then looked down the corridor. Light flooded the area from the open library door, and she anxiously grabbed his hand and moved that way.

Inside the room, a ladder lay on its side. The floor was covered with loose papers.

"My story!" Hannah rushed forward, dropping to her knees to scoop it up. Eric moved to help.

"No!" Her face flushed with color. "I—I can do it. Thanks."

From an earlier reaction, he had a sneaking suspicion that she didn't want him to see what she'd written.

"But how did the notebook fall all the way from up there. . . ?" Her puzzled gaze went to the highest shelf. A wave of dread washed through Eric.

"Hannah, the ladder."

"What?" She blinked his way.

"Why is the ladder lying on the floor?"

The realization hit them at the same time.

"Abbie!"

"Oh, you don't think. . .surely not. . ." Hannah paled. "She must have climbed it to get my story." With Eric's help, she scrambled to her feet. "She was so angry with me earlier. . ."

Eric groaned. "Me, too. She asked to help, and I told her no. I said she was too little to climb a ladder."

Before they could discover if their fears were true, Esther met them at the door. One look into her frightened eyes made Eric wince.

"Abbie fell off the ladder," Esther confirmed. "Mama caught her trying to get something from the shelf, and she got surprised and fell. Then the ladder fell on her. Hannah, she won't wake up. Her face is so. . .white." The girl's voice trembled.

"Where is she?" Hannah asked fearfully.

"In her room. I have to get more water. Mama's trying to rouse her with cold washcloths."

Her sister ran off. Trembling, Hannah turned into Eric's arms. He held her close.

"If only I hadn't written the stupid thing, if only I didn't always snap at her to leave it alone, to leave me alone. . ." Hannah's tears wet his shirt, and he stroked her hair and back in a gentle effort to soothe. He murmured little meaningless words of consolation, when no words would really ever do. She melted against him, sliding her arms around his waist.

They remained like that for some time, Eric calming her until her body ceased quivering, when suddenly his sleeve snagged at the back of her sweater.

He frowned. "Uh, Hannah. . .we have a small problem."

She moved her head to look at him, an awkward feat when he couldn't move his arm back to let her. "I think my button is caught on your sweater." He could tell the mohair was expensive and didn't wish to wrench his arm away and ruin it. He craned his head to try and evaluate the difficulty. Just as he'd thought, his button seemed to be snagged in the loop of one of the incredibly tiny buttons at the nape of her sweater. Or perhaps in its thread. He couldn't tell—all of it was bright white—and he couldn't tell which button snagged him, either.

"I'm, um"—a rush of heat warmed his face—"going to unbutton the top of your sweater to try to free my wrist." He only wished he could see what he was doing.

She had lowered her head at his first words, and he felt her nod, her face against his chest.

With his free hand, he felt for the top button, managing to slip it from the ridiculously tight elastic loop. His wrist remained caught. He went for the second. Again, nothing. He gave a short nervous cough, wondering how many tiny buttons covered such a small space! Why would any clothing manufacturer put them there? What if it wasn't caught in buttons at all? What if it was caught somehow in the mohair itself? He certainly couldn't undress her!

On the fourth button, he developed a cold sweat.

On the fifth, he was about ready to take off his own shirt and let her remove herself to another room to slip out of the sweater and free his sleeve.

On the sixth, he had a horrible sinking suspicion it wasn't a button his sleeve was caught in.

Just as he was about to suggest another desperate approach, like finding someone who had a clear view and could fix the problem, he heard someone in the corridor.

"What the. . ." Heavy footsteps followed the angry exclamation. Suddenly a hand grabbed the errant sleeve, wrenching it from Hannah's sweater. A button went flying to the floor, but Eric barely saw it before he felt himself swung around and a fist shot toward his mouth. Hannah let out a horrified cry as Eric fell a few steps back with the impact, just managing to stay on his feet. Tasting blood, he wiped it from his mouth.

"Stay away from my sister!" Hannah's older brother glared at Eric and came at him a second time. Eric blocked Josiah's fist before it could slam into his eye.

Hannah sandwiched herself between them. "Josiah—stop! Have you gone crazy?"

"I saw what he was doing, Hannah!" Josiah glared at Eric over her head.

"He's a filthy snake, just like his father."

Hannah's entire body shook as she planted her palms on her brother's chest and using all her strength pushed him away from Eric. "He's not! What you saw isn't what you think! His button was caught on my sweater. He was trying to get it free without ripping it—which thanks to you is no longer a possibility."

"He was undressing you, Hannah—I saw!"

"Hardly! The buttons don't go all the way down, and even if they did, Eric is too much of a gentleman to have done that!"

"At the lake, she was lying on top of him." David had appeared at the door, his expression grim. "And he left the ladder in here when he should have taken it back to the shed."

"What?" Josiah's eyes flashed with another burst of rage. Hannah did her best to keep him away from Eric.

"He fell on the ice—I fell on top of him. There's no crime in that! As for Abbie, she shouldn't have been sneaking around in my things. She knows better. I'm the one who pulled Eric away from his work, dragging him from the room, so if anyone's to blame for Abbie being hurt it's me." She glared at her brothers while keeping her restraining palms flat against Josiah's chest. "I am sick to death of the way you both treat Eric. He's not responsible for every evil under the sun as you seem to think! You've both been acting like pigheaded fools, and you should be ashamed."

Eric watched in amazement as she defended him like a growling lioness.

"Your lousy treatment has gone on long enough," she announced. "Our baby sister is upstairs, maybe fighting for her life, and all you two can think about is beating up on Eric and throwing accusations at him? Did you hear me cry for help? Did you see me try and push him away? No. You didn't even ask—you just assumed, again judging him without reason. He's done nothing wrong! And if you can't handle him being in our home, that's just too bad. Because I happen to care about him a great deal, and I want him here, and if you don't like it, well you'll just have to learn to live with it!"

A wave of color washed her cheeks once she blurted the last words. Eric felt shocked by her admission and touched that she'd defended him to her family.

Suddenly, her mother swept into the room. Lines of concern altered her usually placid expression. Her eyes were dark with worry. "What's going on here?"

Hannah told her in a few sentences what had happened.

Her mother looked back and forth between her sons. "I'm ashamed of you. Have I not taught you to keep from jumping to conclusions when you have little of the facts? Your sister is right; your behavior toward Eric has been abominable, and I certainly wouldn't blame him if he left us tomorrow. He's been a godsend to us. You've misjudged him, and it will stop now. There are more urgent matters that need to be addressed. I cannot reach the doctor."

Eric remembered meeting the man at the Founder's Day celebration and also recalled where he'd last seen him. "He's at the pond. I can take the car and tell him."

She shook her head. "No, the roads are too icy. Our neighbor has a sleigh. I will call to ask. A sleigh will be faster."

"I'll go with you." Hannah moved with Eric into the foyer, and they grabbed their coats.

Josiah suddenly appeared, tense but not looking ready to throw another punch. He addressed Eric. "You know how to rig a sleigh?"

"With Hannah's help, I can manage."

"She doesn't know how, either. I'll do it. We had one at my great-uncle's."

With that, the young man left, again surprising Eric, who'd been sure he would demand his sister stay behind. He shrugged into his coat, still cold from their earlier outing.

"They'll come around," Hannah reassured, grabbing her outerwear, "especially with Mother on your side."

"Don't worry about me," he soothed, helping her into her coat. "I'm a big boy. I can handle it."

She faced him suddenly, her fingers lifting to the corner of his mouth and taking him by surprise. "Does it hurt?"

"I have brothers, too, and we didn't always get along. A punch in the mouth is nothing." He smiled to reassure her. "Let's go find help for your little sister."

The concern deepened in her eyes, and he slipped his hand around her sleeve in consolation as they hurried to the neighbor's.

Chapter 13

On any other occasion, Hannah would have been thrilled with such an outing. The sleigh rides to the pond and back on a clear, moonlit night, while sitting nestled up against Eric, composed the essence of romance. The neighbor's two grays dashed over the ground, pulling the sleigh in a swift, crisp slice through the drifts of snow. Yet Hannah could think only of her baby sister, and she clutched Eric's hand under the blanket, grateful for his strength.

"When I said you should face reality, I never wanted you to suffer anything like this." His voice came quiet, and she squeezed his glove.

"I know. And don't apologize. You were only trying to shake me out of my dreams to see the real world."

He frowned as if unhappy with her reply. "There's nothing wrong with dreams, Hannah. Keep them. A little entertainment is good for the soul, too."

At his admission, she laid her head against his shoulder, not daring to tell him that he was good for her soul. Since he'd arrived in Cedarbrook, she'd been intrigued by him, drawn to him, enamored of him. . .and now, she knew without a doubt, in love with him. She loved Eric, and despite the current tragedy, she felt a new peace with him she'd never experienced. A sweet. . .serenity. Something she'd never known she was missing until she found it with him. He accepted her, faults and all, and didn't wish her to be anyone else.

But he doesn't know about the challenge yet, Hannah.

Her conscience nagged at her, but she closed her eyes to the thought. Now was not the time. Later. . .

Much later, after they'd arrived home and the doctor had departed once he'd seen Abbie, the family gathered in the parlor.

"Besides a broken arm, which the doctor has set," Hannah's mother informed her worried children, "Abbie took a nasty bump to the head. The doctor said if she doesn't awaken by morning, it could be bad. She mustn't be moved. Now, I must see to your father."

Hannah moved forward. "Is there anything I can do to help, Mama?"

Her mother's harried expression gentled. "Pray, my daughter. All of you children, pray." She swept out of the room.

"Yes, we all will. Won't we?" Hannah looked at her brothers. They drew closer. Hannah slipped her hand into Eric's and felt relieved when Esther took his other one. At least she'd never shown him animosity. David took Hannah's other hand, Josiah took Esther and David's, all of them forming a circle.

"Eric, you're probably better at this than we are." Hannah felt ashamed to admit that, remorseful of just how far she had slipped in her faith since living at her great-uncle's. "If you wouldn't mind?"

He dipped his head in a nod, bowed it, then offered up the most touching and heartfelt prayer for Abbie's full recovery, the doctor's wisdom, and her family's peace. Hannah stared at him in wonder. Afterward her brothers exchanged glances; then Josiah looked at Eric.

"Listen, maybe I had you figured all wrong. When I heard about the reign of terror your father caused, then seeing you with my sister and knowing you were living here, well, maybe I jumped the gun like Mother said."

"Yeah, me, too," David admitted, his grin sheepish.

"That's all right." Eric smiled and stuck out his hand in a peace offering. "I have sisters, too, and if I ever thought any man might hurt one of them. . .well, I probably would have done the same thing." Both boys took turns shaking his hand.

Josiah grinned. "How's the jaw?"

Eric rubbed his hand along the offended part of his face. "You throw a mean punch."

"I boxed one year in high school."

"It shows."

Hannah knew that was the closest her brothers would probably ever come to an apology. But Eric's response astounded her, and she felt he was being too kind. She shook her head in amazement as she watched the fellows exchange pleasantries and thanked God for small miracles.

The doorbell rang.

"I'll get that," Hannah said, but they were too deep in discussion on the subject of the economy to hear her. She glanced at her sister who'd started to pick up the papers Hannah had abandoned, looking at each. "Esther! You get the door—I'll pick those up."

She snatched the papers from her sister's hand, and Esther took off running as Hannah scooped up as much of her manuscript as she could and shoved it in the notebook. The story wasn't sinful, but it didn't make her proud, and she almost wished she'd never started it. Maybe if she hadn't been so secretive about the whole thing, Abbie wouldn't have fallen.

"Hannah?"

An uncertain yet awed element in Esther's voice brought instant alarm. Hannah noticed the fellows had stopped talking, too. They all turned toward the entrance.

An older gentleman with a solid, wiry build, his face bronzed and weathered by years as if he spent a great deal of time outdoors, came in behind a wide-eyed Esther. His hair shone gray, his eyes shimmered bright green, and Hannah realized with a curious start they were full of tears.

"Hello," she said uneasily. "May we help you?"

He smiled, and she sucked in a breath, knowing she'd seen that smile before.

"Papa!" Hannah heard the shriek and watched in wonder as her usually sedate mother ran down the stairs and toward the man. She vaulted into his arms, throwing hers around his neck. He returned her embrace with just as much gusto as tears streamed down both their faces.

"Oh Papa—you didn't say you were coming! Oh Papa, you came at just the right time. I don't know what to do."

"There, there, my little Sarah. Papa's here. It's all right. . .there, there. . ."

Hannah blinked in shock as she watched her mother fall apart in the arms of her father, whom her mother hadn't seen since she left the island when she'd gotten married.

Eric came up beside her and offered her his handkerchief. It was then Hannah realized she was also crying. She noticed her siblings gape at the emotional display. Sensing the newly reunited father and daughter needed time alone, Hannah motioned that they should all leave.

They walked past her grandfather, still holding and comforting her mother, and Hannah pulled Eric with her into the kitchen. "I never even considered all she must be going through. First Daddy, now Abbie. And I certainly never gave her an easy time of things. I just never thought. . . she's always been so strong, the rock in our family."

Seeing her mother in such a distressed state shocked Hannah more than she let on, and she couldn't stop trembling.

"Even the strongest rocks chip from time to time," Eric soothed, rubbing his hands up and down her arms as if to warm her. "Your mother will be all right. Especially now."

"I just never realized how hard it's been for her. I've had my eyes closed to a lot of things, too involved in my own little world. Well, they're open now." Her eyes widened, as if in emphasis to her words. "And my *grandfather* has come. I never thought I'd get to meet him. Now if only Abbie would recover."

"I think it's a good sign that your grandfather arrived when he did. Maybe it's God's way of offering hope."

Hannah nodded, moving into Eric's arms and resting her head against the sure, steady beating of his heart. Oh, how she loved this man! And how she had wronged him. He had easily forgiven her brothers. Could he forgive her if she told him what she'd done?

She lifted her head to look into his eyes, but again all thoughts of confessions scattered—this time when he tilted her chin farther upward and delivered the softest of kisses to her lips. Sweet warmth melted through her, and the gentlest of sighs winged through her heart as she returned his tender affection.

The door suddenly slammed open. They jumped apart in shock, looking toward the entrance.

Esther stood there, her face beaming. "Abbie's awake! And the first thing she asked was if she could now be waited on like Daddy!" She giggled. "Daddy even used a cane to go into her room, and Mama's there, too. And our grandfather!" Her eyes grew brighter. "Abbie's okay, and our grandfather's come to meet us! Oh Hannah. Isn't life grand?"

"Yes, it is, Esther. Absolutely splendid." Hannah laughed in tearful relief and smiled at Eric. "It feels as if Christmas has visited us early this year."

⚘

"My daughter tells me your family runs a mission. I'd like to hear more."

Eric looked up at Mrs. Thomas's father from across the table where the two men enjoyed sandwiches and coffee. Ever since Josiah LaRue arrived three days ago, he and Eric had bonded, spending hours in discussion. The former missionary had been the anchor his family needed, and Eric admired the man for the lifetime he'd devoted to his calling.

Eric filled him in on all his family had done to help their community, even broaching his own fledgling idea.

Mr. LaRue's eyes widened in appreciation. "That sounds like a worthy cause. I'd like to be part of it if you decide to do it. Mission work runs in my blood. Even though I retired and left the island to be with my family again, I don't want to quit the field completely."

Eric smiled. "I'd be honored for you to help us, sir."

Mr. LaRue looked at the clock and stood from the table. "My brother should be home from his trip, and I think it's time we made amends. He never did like that I chose missionary work. But he did for Sarah and her family what he could, and I must thank him for that, among other things." The older man chuckled, shaking his head in amused wonder. "You can imagine my surprise when I found out by a fluke that my brother was the anonymous donor who'd been supporting my work for years by paying for all necessary supplies to be shipped to the island. Somewhere in that stony heart of his, I believe there might be some good soil and a sprout in need of watering."

He chuckled, and Eric grinned as he walked with the man to the foyer. He turned as he opened the door. "We'll talk more about your idea later."

"I'd like that—" Eric abruptly ended his sentence when he noticed Hannah's newly arrived visitor.

"Hello, Julia." The informal greeting seemed wrong, somehow, too personal when he didn't want that at all. But he didn't know her last name.

"Hello, Eric." Her smile seemed seducing.

Hannah's grandfather, whom she completely ignored, looked from the woman to Eric, his eyes issuing a warning. *Watch out, son, this one's trouble.*

Eric nodded. He didn't need to be told twice.

Once Hannah's grandfather left, Eric tried to play the polite host and opened the door for her to enter. "Hannah's upstairs with her sister. I'll tell her you're here."

"Oh, that's not necessary." She grabbed his sleeve before he could leave. "I came to inquire about Abbie." Her features softened in concern, and Eric wondered if he'd misread her. She seemed to care about the little tyke. And he knew the pain of being judged for a crime not committed.

"Abbie's improving every day. She's demanding and fussy, and I understand those are her usual traits, so I'm sure she'll be fine."

Julia laughed. For a moment the mask seemed to break as her coolly collected features showed a flash of warmth. "That's wonderful." She seemed suddenly uncertain. "Might we talk? Somewhere more private?"

Eric narrowed his eyes in suspicion, wondering what she was up to.

"Please. I need to talk to someone, and you seem so nice. Like the type who really cares about people."

He didn't bother asking why she didn't confide in her own friends; her last comment explained that. Still uneasy, he motioned to the parlor door. "We can talk in there."

"Yes, please. Thank you."

Her sudden switch to meek behavior took him aback. He allowed her to precede him into the finished room, now warmer and brighter with new flowered paper covering the walls.

"I have a confession to make," she began softly.

He nodded for her to go on, wondering what she'd done to cause him harm.

"I didn't want to do it, but Hannah insisted."

Chapter 14

Against the pillows that supported her, Abbie bowed her bandaged head in shame. "I'm really sorry I tried to take your story, Hannah. I won't do it again."

Hannah, grateful her sister was alive and well, felt she could forgive anything. "And I'm sorry I treated you badly when we first moved here and at Uncle's, too. You're so important to me, Abbie." Carefully, she leaned forward and embraced her baby sister, who wrapped her one good arm around Hannah's back. Abbie's other arm hung encased in plaster in a sling about her neck. The poor girl looked like a war orphan, and Hannah kissed her forehead beneath the white bandage, then the tip of her nose, cradling her small chin with her fingers to look her in the eye.

"No more climbing ladders, though."

Abbie sighed. "Yes, I know. But no one ever lets me do *anything*. You say I'm just a baby, but I'm not."

"Hmm. I see now how that's upset you. And it takes a really big girl not to cry when I know how it must hurt. So, you get better, and we'll see about changing that old rule. Deal?"

Abbie grinned. "Deal!"

"Good. Get some rest now." Hannah moved away. She never made it out the door.

"Can you bring more hot cocoa? And cookies?"

Hannah affected a stern countenance. "Any more sweets, and you'll be dealing with a tummy ache, too."

"Please, Hannah," her sister cajoled. "I'm still hungry."

"Well. . ." She smiled, knowing she would surrender in the end. These past three days, Abbie had reigned supreme as a little princess in the Thomas home, no one able to refuse her anything. "All right, but don't say I didn't warn you."

At the bottom of the staircase, Hannah heard voices in the parlor. Curious, she moved to the open doorway, shocked when she saw Eric offer Julia his handkerchief, and she dabbed at her eyes with it.

"Thank you, Eric. You don't know what a relief it is to get that burden off my chest. Hannah should never have done such a horrid thing. I thought you should be warned, since I don't want to see you hurt. You're so sweet, any girl would be lucky to have you, and Hannah was wrong to treat you so callously."

In gaping shock, Hannah watched Julia slip her hand behind Eric's neck and move up to kiss him. He averted his face at the last moment and stepped back, causing her lips to brush his jawline instead.

Hannah moved forward, hurt and angry, the truth a harsh slap in the face. They turned at her entrance. Julia's face paled, but her eyes sparked in triumph. "It's over, Hannah. I told him. I just could no longer take part in your cruel little scheme."

"Is it true?"

Eric's low, quiet voice broke through Hannah's rage. She swung her gaze to his, her anger fading as she looked at him, her eyes going wide and anxious.

He knows. . . . Dear God, help me. He knows.

"Yes," she said simply, weary of the deception and realizing she deserved every bit of his censure.

"You wanted to make me fall madly in love with you?" His brows drew together in curiosity as he moved toward her. "Why?"

She swallowed hard, nervous by his slow advance, unable to admit her reprehensible part in the foolish challenge and her desire to prevent any wounded pride. She realized she'd been as shallow and selfish as Julia and dropped her eyes in shame.

He stopped before her while she waited for the hammer to drop. Gently he tilted her chin up to force her wary eyes to meet his serious blue ones.

"When falling in love with you was the easiest thing to do, *ma chère*," he continued, then dropped a kiss to Hannah's parted lips that left no doubt he meant what he said.

Stunned by the turn of events, she felt her knees buckle and clasped his arms tightly, barely hearing Julia's huff of disgust as her former friend whisked from the room. The slam of the front door hardly registered, as incredible warmth rushed through Hannah. Eric deepened the kiss with a small groan, as though he couldn't help himself, and cradled her head in his hands. Her heart pounded harder. For the first time, she wished for the old chill of the parlor in the now uncomfortably hot room.

He abruptly pulled away, his breathing as uneven as hers, and looked into her eyes as if to gauge her thoughts. She saw the hurt there and sensed his mood change.

"Did you mean it?" she whispered.

"Did you?"

She knew what he referred to and that no way existed to make it sound less awful than it was. She lowered her hands from his shoulders where they had slid. "I felt cornered into Julia's challenge. She instigated it, not me. I didn't want to be thought of as juvenile. I really did like you from the start, and I hoped you would see it as a harmless prank." She swallowed, nervous. "Then I began to care about you more, about hurting you, and I realized how juvenile I'd really been. But I didn't see a way out of it. The more time we spent together, the worse I felt. I never meant to hurt you, Eric, and I never should have agreed to that silly challenge."

"No, you shouldn't have." She lowered her chin in distress, and again he lifted it, his eyes gentle. "But I forgive you."

She blinked. "How? I mean. . ." She struggled for words. "I hoped you would—I'd planned to tell you sooner. And I'm relieved, you have no idea how much! But how can you always so quickly forgive, no matter how badly you've been hurt?"

He smiled wryly. "I've had a lifetime of lessons. After hearing my father's testimony on a continual basis and understanding the terror he inflicted on so many—especially your own family—I can hardly hold grudges, Hannah. Your aunts, despite any lingering fear they might still possess, *did* forgive my father, and he never forgot that. It's what helped lead him on the road to salvation, and he instilled that lesson of forgiveness into all his children. Life is too short to hold animosity against anyone. We all make mistakes, ma chère. I've made them, too."

Her heart full by his quiet admission and her newest feelings for him, she whispered, "I truly do love you, Eric." Her eyes widened when she realized she'd spoken her thoughts, but he only smiled.

"Enough to marry me, *mon amour?*"

"Wha—" Sure she'd heard wrong, her legs grew unstable again, and she grabbed his arms a second time.

"Maybe we should sit down."

She nodded, and he helped her to the sofa, taking a seat beside her.

"I've spoken with your grandfather and still need to discuss it with my parents. But I have an idea and want you to be part of it. Actually, you gave me the idea when you mentioned you wished your town had a mission. I want to start one here for people like Shirley and Jimmy and Lily to come and get at least one hot meal a day. A place where they can hear about Jesus' love, a place that can offer help to families and perhaps even find them work."

She tried to follow his eager news, her brain still whirling with his former question. "That sounds wonderful—but. . .did you just ask me to marry you?"

He grinned. "Oui. I've been wanting to for a while. Maybe I should have waited until your father was at least tolerant of the idea of me for a son-in-law, but I couldn't hold back any longer. I'm sorry if it wasn't very romantic."

Not romantic? Any more romance, and he would have had to fetch the smelling salts. She shook her head in wonder. "Despite all I've done, how selfish I've been, you want me for your wife?" The words seemed incredible; she could scarcely believe them.

"Like I said, everyone makes mistakes. That's not who you are. I've watched you since I've been here. You've changed, mon amour. I've watched you evolve, like a butterfly breaking out of a cocoon. I said so earlier, and I'll say it again—loving you was the easiest thing to do."

His poetic words and French endearments warmed her heart; she could listen to them forever. "Yes, I'll marry you, Eric." After another breathless kiss that made her grateful for the sofa now supporting her legs, she softly breathed, "When?"

"Whenever you'd like."

"I've always wanted a Christmas wedding."

His eyes flared a bit in surprise. "That's only a few weeks away. Don't you have to prepare and get things ready and do whatever it is you women do?"

She laughed. "Right now I don't care if we get married by a justice of the peace. I just want to be your wife as soon as I can and live out our dream together!"

Elated, she kissed him again. Certain nothing could burst her bubble of joy, she then grabbed his hand and pulled him with her out of the parlor. "Let's tell Mother and Daddy now. I can't wait another second!"

❧

"No—absolutely not!"

"Bill. . ." Mrs. Thomas put a hand to her husband's shoulder as he bolted upright in bed.

Eric remained somber, not surprised. He felt Hannah's hand tighten around his.

"Daddy!" she insisted, "You're not being fair. Mama's told you what a wonderful man Eric is, and so has Grandfather. Can't you take their word for it if you can't take mine?"

The expression in his eyes softened as he turned toward his daughter. "This has nothing to do with Eric's character. I'll admit, I was wrong about him. After these last months of having him in our home and hearing your mother's praises of him every single day, I realized there must be some good there for my Sarah to think so highly of him."

Hannah shook her head in confusion. "Then what. . . ?"

"You're too young. You're seventeen, and you're what?" He looked at Eric. "Eighteen?"

Eric gave a swift nod. "Nineteen in January, sir."

"That's just too young."

"Mama was barely seventeen when she married you," Hannah argued, a hurt tone to her voice, "and Clemmie was only a little over my age when she married Joel."

"They were more mature. They both faced struggles in their young lives, which made them mature far past their years. You've had life handed to you on a silver platter for so long and are just learning how to deal with adult issues."

"I may be young, but at least I never judged Eric falsely like so many in this household did. At least I gave him the benefit of the doubt and trusted him. Something you never did."

Eric squeezed her hand in both comfort and warning. But the angry tears in her eyes showed she wouldn't be stopped.

"You lied to me, Daddy. Why? You never said you were a gangster and that was why you were the target of that awful man who shot Mama and killed my unborn sister or brother. You've taught us to be honest. But the truth is you really don't like Eric any more than before, isn't that right?"

"Hannah!" her mother reprimanded sharply, and Hannah lowered her eyes.

"Did you tell her?" Her father's eyes snapped to Eric's.

"He assumed I knew already. It wasn't his fault. You shouldn't have hidden the truth from me, Daddy."

"Perhaps we should wait to speak of this when we've all calmed down," her mother suggested quietly.

Hannah's father patted her mother's hand resting on his shoulder. Looking to Eric, then Hannah again, he spoke. "No. Now that she knows that much, she should know the rest."

They shared a grave look, and her mother nodded.

"I didn't tell you about my time as a gangster for two reasons, Hannah. I kept it hidden, not wanting it to affect your life—not wanting your friends to somehow learn and give you grief, making you an outcast among them. We had decided to leave New York and the Refuge after Eric's father sent us a message, warning us of danger. The Piccoli bunch found us before we could, and well, you know what happened after that." He closed his eyes a moment in remembered pain. "When you were little, we learned your mother's uncle was alive and living in Connecticut, and we took the opportunity to put New York behind us for good. Those men I worked for are ruthless, honey. Every day, I regret joining up with their organization. But that doesn't change the fact that I did."

Hannah gasped. "That's why you never allowed me to go to New York City, isn't it?"

"That's part of it. Years have passed with no sign of trouble, but you can never be too careful. When Eric arrived, it felt like the old dangers had resurfaced, since his father was my associate. That's one reason I treated you so badly." He met Eric's eyes. "I'm sorry, son."

Eric nodded, too stunned by the man's confession to respond. Hannah released his hand and hurried to embrace her father. "I'm sorry, too, Daddy. I've been so angry with you ever since I found out. I should have just come straight out and told you that I knew. I understand now."

Her father smoothed her hair. "Unless you've lived through such an ordeal, you can't begin to know the fear, Hannah. I almost lost your mother. I did lose our child. God forgave me, but it took a long time before I could forgive myself. And I couldn't bear for you to look at me with hatred, knowing all I'd done."

"Oh Daddy, I could never hate you."

They embraced again, and Eric felt he also understood much more than before. That her father would speak so freely in front of him showed Eric something else: He had won his trust.

"I never said you two couldn't get married." Her father brought the subject back around to them. "Just that you wait. One year. You two have known each other such a short time. It's too soon to talk of marriage. If the love is there, if this is what God wants for you, then nothing will prevent it from happening." He reached for his wife's hand, and she shared a tender look with him, forged through long years of shared devotion, tragedy, and trust. One day Eric hoped to share such a look with Hannah.

"Your father's right," Eric spoke, earning him a grateful look from her parents. "I know my feelings for you are true, Hannah, but it's best to wait. There's much I need to accomplish, and this way you'll get your dream wedding." He smiled. "You can't tell me you don't still wish for one, knowing you as I do."

Her face aglow, she rose from her father's side and approached Eric. "I promise you this, Eric Fontaine Jr. In one year's time, I'll be walking toward you in our church on the green to become your bride."

"I love you, Hannah. That won't change. I'll wait for you forever if I have to."

She slipped her arms around his waist, tilting her head back, her smile warming him. He glanced toward her parents, grateful to note they didn't seem displeased by their daughter's public affection. Likewise, he slipped his arm around her back.

"I've already told Hannah. I want to make Cedarbrook my home, to start a mission here. I like the peacefulness of your small town, and I like what it has to offer." At this, he again looked at Hannah and smiled. "The best in all of Connecticut."

Chapter 15

A little over one year to the day, Hannah stood in the back of the church, ready to take her first steps down the aisle and become Eric's wife.

She smiled at her sisters, who carefully smoothed the satin folds of her gown, and also at Muffy, her bridesmaid, who straightened the veil Hannah's mother had attached to her upswept hair. Muffy had grown weary of Julia's cattiness and cruel games and appeared one day to volunteer at the new mission Eric and Hannah's grandfather ran. At first Hannah had been wary, remembering her friend's designs on Eric, which Muffy later apologized for. It also came as a relief to learn Muffy hadn't been the woman diner in the rose sweater to hurt Lily—evident when the child shyly offered her hand and smiled upon meeting Muffy. Clearly it had been Julia, which came as no shock. Like Hannah, Muffy had been raised in wealth, but insecure in her own skin, she fed off people like Julia for reassurance. Muffy and her family had become one of the mission's strongest supporters, and Clemmie, Hannah, and Muffy had become fast friends.

Throughout the past year, Hannah and Eric wrote to one another constantly, and he visited often to oversee the building of the mission and to see Hannah. She'd been shocked to learn that Eric came from old money on his mother's side. His father was also wealthy, though their family lived modestly. Eric Sr. used his ill-gotten gains long-ago stolen from his nameless victims to help the needy, and a good chunk of his inheritance as comte he'd put aside for his grandchildren. Eric Jr. had been supportive of Hannah's journalistic efforts, which Joel also encouraged, the human-interest stories she wrote gaining recognition for the mission. She'd never abandoned her novel entirely, even adding to it to make it more inspiring, but it was no longer her focus. Fame wasn't her goal.

Her goal waited at the end of the aisle.

Their love had grown, ever changing, into something rich and indefinable. In the past year, Hannah had matured in her quest to help the needy, now grateful her father had made them wait to marry. She'd been such a child, too foolish and silly to take on the role of Eric's wife. But now. . .now she was ready to take on all of what that entailed.

Hannah felt a momentary unease at the thought of how her entire family would react to having Eric's father in their presence once again. Her brothers and friends had at last accepted her fiancé, and now Eric and Joel were good pals. She'd even heard her brothers ask Eric for advice, and Hannah's heart warmed every time she heard her father call him *son*.

But she knew old grievances, especially those Eric Sr. had caused, could bring lasting bitterness. Everyone had struggled to accept Eric Jr., who'd done nothing wrong, judging him by his father's many sins.

And now his father was present among them.

Long ago, Aunt Charleigh and Aunt Darcy had forgiven him, then walked away, never expecting to see him again. Could they—her entire family—accept Eric's father as part of their family?

She'd met him the previous evening at their hotel room, a little awed, nervous, and fearful to approach despite knowing that he'd changed. Nevertheless, the old horror stories of all he'd done whirled within her mind as the tall and slender, leonine man—her soon to be father-in-law—stood to greet her. He bowed over her hand with a charm that must have won many in his cons. She gasped a faint greeting, vaguely noting where her fiancé had received his heart-stopping, attractive looks, indeed his whole manner.

Eric Sr.'s dark blue eyes twinkled with reassurance and kindness, nothing dangerous or frightening in their depths. "Don't worry. I don't bite," he greeted her lightly with the faint lilt of a French accent, instantly setting her at ease. "Ma chère, it is a pleasure to welcome you into my family. To finally meet the woman whom my son speaks of day and night—"

"Father. . ." Eric Jr. fidgeted in embarrassment but grinned at Hannah.

She had smiled as Eric's father kissed her hand. She then surprised them all by moving forward to kiss his cheeks, as she knew the French did from the movies she'd seen. "Merci, I'm happy to meet you at last. Your son speaks highly of you and your work at the mission."

"Then I think I enjoyed the better of the conversations," his father said with a wink.

Eric's mother, Janine, a lovely brunette, was sweet and gentle, greeting Hannah with a warm hug. It was clear she doted on her husband, often touching his arm or hand, and Eric's nine siblings clearly loved their father.

"It's time. Are you ready?" Clemmie squeezed Hannah's arm, bringing her to the present. Hannah had insisted that Clemmie be her matron of honor, dispensing with the idea of a maid of honor.

"Oh yes. As you once said on your wedding day—I think I've been ready forever."

The girls softly chuckled, and Clemmie left to join the bridesmaids at the front of the sanctuary. Smiling, Hannah took her father's arm, prepared to take the first step into her new future.

The church, decorated with white satin ribbons and matching roses, was indeed lovely, but Hannah only had eyes for Eric. He looked handsome in his tuxedo, and she inhaled a swift breath to realize that their day had really arrived.

"I love you, kitten," her father whispered before they began the march down the aisle as the music played. "I hope you'll be very happy together."

"I love you, too, Daddy. And I know we will be, just like you and Mama."

Within minutes, she exchanged vows with Eric, reverently, the moments passing as if in a dream, a fantasy.

But this was better than any novel or motion picture ever made.

A reformed princess and a missionary vicomte. . .

A benevolent handyman and an amateur writer. . .

Soon to embark on their own life story.

Once the final blessing was given, Eric's lips touched hers, and Hannah laid her hand against his cheek, leaning into the warmth of his kiss.

Oh yes, much better. . .

The best reality had to give.

✑❤

The sweet feel of Hannah's lips against his made every long, excruciating day Eric had spent without her this past year dissolve. He almost forgot where they were, but at Joel's amused clearing of his throat, Eric remembered and managed to let her go. For now.

"Plenty of time for that later," his best man said low enough that only Eric could hear. He had learned of his friend's partiality for mischief and ignored him, taking Hannah's arm.

"Shall we, Mrs. Fontaine?"

Her eyes sparkled in delighted wonder. "Gladly, my husband."

They smiled at each other, then hurried to exit the church, many of the guests already waiting to shower them with rice. Squealing, Hannah grabbed his arm as they tried to duck the showers of grain thrown their way.

A short time later, Eric and Hannah arrived at Great-Uncle Bernard's manor for the reception, both of them anxious about how Eric's father would be received.

Hannah's great-uncle had mellowed, according to Hannah. Similar in looks to her grandfather, his skin sallow instead of bronzed and weathered, her great-uncle was a congenial host and offered them his best wishes, happily receiving Hannah's fervent hug. Ever since the two brothers had reunited, they'd been close. Her parents and great-uncle had also mended their differences, and shortly afterward Hannah's grandfather had brought his older brother to Christ. Hannah's great-uncle had become a staunch supporter of the mission, and with so much capital, Eric now hoped to build a bigger shelter where the homeless could not only enjoy a hot meal and hear of God's love, but also have a bed and find rooms devoted to entire families. It was a dream for the future, but he'd learned that God did make dreams come true.

The reception was held in the grand hall, the curtains of the wide window drawn for a breathtaking view of the softly falling snow and the white-coated wood beyond. White roses garnished with satin ribbons decorated the area, and friends and family filled the room.

Shirley and Jimmy giggled nearby, sneaking swipes of frosting from the bottom of a seven-tiered cake. Their mother, working as a maid for Hannah's great-uncle, lightly slapped their wandering hands and told them to behave.

Catching sight of Hannah and Eric, the children immediately ran to them as they always did at the mission. Hannah didn't seem to mind that Jimmy crumpled the satin bows on her gown, laughing in delight as she reached down and returned his exuberant hug.

"You're pretty," Jimmy said with awe, staring at Hannah.

Eric pushed a lock of tousled hair from the boy's eyes. "Hands off, son. She's mine," he teasingly warned, earning him a big smile from the little boy. Both children glowed with vitality and health.

"Where's Lily?"

Their small friend never tagged far behind. Shirley pointed, and Eric was amazed to see Lily half sitting and half standing on his father's lap, excitedly chattering to him. The five-year-old had come a long way from the frightened little scarecrow he'd once met scrounging for food in an alley. Hannah's great-uncle had also hired Lily's mother, in fact, giving jobs whether in his home or his offices to whomever Hannah and Eric presented to him.

But while Lily had clearly accepted his father as her friend, Eric noticed Hannah's family and friends had not. They remained on the opposite side of the room, casting his father wary glances at best, hostile ones at worst. At least the children from both families seemed to play well together. Eric hoped that as the evening progressed and the gaiety multiplied, their parents' hesitation would decrease.

He hoped in vain.

"Is everything all right, darling?"

Hannah came up beside him, slipping her hand into his, her endearment touching his heart. He lifted her hand to his lips for a brief kiss. "Our plan to bring the families together is at a standstill, mon amour."

Hannah's brow creased with concern. "Should I talk to them?"

Mr. LaRue approached, fiercely hugging his granddaughter and offering Eric the heartiest of congratulations. "What's this?" Hannah's grandfather held her by the shoulders, peering closely at her. "Is that sadness I see in those beautiful eyes? What's wrong, my girl?"

Hannah grimly told him the situation.

"Is that so?" He looked her family's way, then smiled thinly in determination. "This is your wedding day, and I know how long you've both waited for it. You should be enjoying it, not worrying about other people's foolishness. Let's see what your old grandfather can do to help."

Eric had never admired the man more than when he watched him walk across the floor to Eric's father and heartily greet him, shaking his hand. Abbie and Eric's littlest sister, Merry, shyly approached Lily, likely asking her to play tea party. Lily's bright curls bobbed up and down as the three walked off holding hands, while Hannah's grandfather took a seat across from her father and engaged him in lively conversation.

Occasionally, both men let out bursts of laughter, bringing attention their way. Soon Hannah's parents joined them, and Eric felt his bride slip her hand against the back of his shoulder in relief at their public show of acceptance. As the evening elapsed, the circle increased, others slowly drifting over to meet the father of the groom and his wife, who now sat beside him.

Hannah gripped Eric's arm suddenly. "Look."

He turned. Clemmie's parents moved across the floor, somewhat stiffly, Charleigh clutching her husband's arm. He stood a little taller than Eric's father and had a stronger build; Eric knew Stewart had always been Charleigh's protector. The man looked the part. Brent and Darcy, who were both amazing and never showed any hesitance in accepting Hannah's choice for a husband, also walked with them. It still stunned Eric how much Brent and his father-in-law looked alike, almost twins, and Darcy's brash ways often made him smile.

Both couples now approached Eric Sr., and Hannah tugged on Eric's arm. "I've got to hear this."

So did Eric.

They moved to the outside of the growing circle, unobserved, an amazing feat since they'd been constantly greeted and pulled every which way since their arrival.

Eric's father, upon seeing the approaching four guests, slowly stood to his feet.

"Charleigh." His voice seemed a little hoarse as he nodded to her. "You look lovely, as always. . .Stewart." The two men shared an unfathomable look before Eric's father turned his gaze to the other couple. "Darcy. Brent. I'm glad you came."

Eric knew his father's words involved more than the wedding.

"You look like the years have been good to you."

Eric wondered if he was the only one who noticed Stewart's dry tone.

"I've been richly blessed." Eric's father reached for his mother's hand and helped her up to stand beside him. His father was a strong man, but Eric sensed his need for her support as he watched him slip an arm around her waist. "It's God who's been good to me. Not the years."

His quiet statement seemed to ease the tension, and Stewart nodded as if he understood what his old nemesis didn't say.

The ice melted, if not broken, Eric's father invited them to join their circle, explaining that they talked of mission days. Eric Jr. knew the subject was sure to interest Hannah's aunts and uncles since they ran a children's reformatory that Hannah said was more of a home for troubled orphans with a need to be loved. After hesitating slightly, both couples sat down.

"Thank God." Eric breathed the prayer in relief, sensing the hardest summit had at last been breached.

"Uh-oh." The sudden nervousness in Hannah's voice caught his attention. She looked across the room. "Um," she giggled. "There's something I forgot to tell you about Joel."

"Oh?"

"He developed a sort of. . .tradition with some of the boys at the Refuge, his gang. He was their leader, and well, I think we're about to become their next victims."

"What?"

At his confusion, she turned him around by the arms to look.

Joel and his buddy Herbert, who'd also become a good friend of Eric's, stood in a line with three other men, their arms linked around each other's shoulders.

"That's Clint with the brown hair, Tommy in the middle, and Lance at the end," Hannah informed him with a resigned grin. "They were childhood buddies at the Refuge, who later called themselves 'The Reformers.' We're about to be serenaded."

"Serenaded?"

The most horrendous screech came from a harmonica Tommy put to his lips to gain the attention of those not already looking their way. Eric winced, and Hannah giggled. "They really do sound better than that."

Eric felt red wash his face as the five friends let loose with a corny ballad of love and longing intended to embarrass the happy couple and wish them well. The crowning moment was when Joel dropped to one knee, holding his hands over his heart, then spreading them wide, as one by one the others followed suit.

"You've just been officially accepted into the fold," Hannah said after the last dying note, a pleased grin on her face. "They only do that for those they consider family."

"Then I guess I should feel flattered." Right now all he felt was embarrassed.

She let out a soft gasp. "Oh Eric, look."

His gaze went back to the circle, which to his surprise had grown larger. Two of his younger siblings sat near his parents' feet, and his father held Eric's youngest brother, Gerard, in his lap. Everyone listened as Eric Sr. related a humorous story, receiving smiles and chuckles all around.

Hannah grasped his arm with both hands, nestling her head against his shoulder. "I think we're going to be all right."

"Non, mon amour, we're going to be better than all right." He looked down into her eyes, and she reached up to give him a kiss, the absolute joy glowing from her face a sight to behold.

After almost three decades involving peril, fear, pain, and regret— redemption and forgiveness had finally, completely visited their households, as Hannah's family opened their circle to the Fontaines. . .and God proved once again that nothing was impossible for Him.

Epilogue

C ome in, come in!" Hannah eagerly herded the newest arrivals into her home. "Brrr. It's freezing out there! Let me take your coats."

Her father-in-law kissed her cheeks then shook the snow off his coat before handing it to Hannah. Her mother-in-law moved forward, embracing her. "Hello, dear, you look lovely as always."

Hannah thanked her, taking her coat as well. "The others are in front of the fire in the parlor getting warm."

"Where do I put these?"

Eric's sixteen-year-old brother, Stefan, held what looked like a mountain of presents. He was followed by his seventeen-year-old sister, Lynnette, holding little Gerard's hand, then a giggling Merry, and the rest until all nine children stood inside, and Hannah gratefully closed the door.

"Oh my! It looks like Christmas here already. What did you do?" she laughingly accused her in-laws. "On the coffee table is fine," she told Stefan, who struggled to hold the stack.

Excited to hold her first family gathering, the first time she'd felt well enough for any sort of party, Hannah smiled. Usually they met for cozy gatherings at her parents', at her great-uncle's, at the mission, or at the Refuge.

She addressed the Fontaine children. "Why don't you join the others in the kitchen? Abbie made hot cocoa and cookies for everyone."

Eagerly they nodded and hurried away. She grinned, wondering if her cozy little kitchen would hold them all.

"Eric, good to see you." Uncle Stewart moved across the room to shake his hand. "This weather is for the Eskimos."

"It is, but I couldn't miss my granddaughter's coming out—so, where is she?"

Aunt Charleigh laughed and moved forward to hug him. "Patience never was your strong suit."

"Non," Eric Sr. admitted sheepishly. "You know me too well, ma chère."

In past months after such a personal remark involving the old life, delivered in haste and without thought, an awkward silence followed. Her father-in-law had once conned Aunt Charleigh into believing they were married, so the two had been close at one point in their lives.

Hannah felt relieved to hear her aunt's teasing answer of, "We *all* know you better than you think, Eric Fontaine!"

He stared in mock concern. "Does that mean I'm in trouble?"

"Only if you don't turn around and wish me well, Guv'ner." Aunt Darcy came up behind him from the direction of the kitchen, where she'd left two of her scrumptious berry pies.

He swung around and returned her exuberant embrace. "You've gotten thinner," she chided, pulling away and looking him over with a critical eye. "Keeping too busy at the mission, I'll warrant."

"You're so right, Darcy," Hannah's mother-in-law agreed. "I constantly need to remind him to rest or eat."

"One of your famous pies should do the trick." Hannah's father-in-law gave her aunt a hopeful grin as Uncle Brent appeared from the kitchen with a slice of said pie in hand.

"I call foul," Eric Sr. complained jovially. "The celebration hasn't even started."

Aunt Darcy's eyes twinkled as she moved to Uncle Brent's side and slipped her hand through his arm. "Aye, but he's my husband. He gets special privileges."

Hannah laughed along with the others, grateful the mood hadn't faltered at her father-in-law's slip of the tongue with Charleigh. Clearly enough time had passed, with God's touch, to heal even the deep wounds of decades before.

Her parents entered from the dining room, followed by her grandfather and Great-Uncle Bernard, and greetings were once more exchanged all around. The doorbell rang again, and Hannah answered, relieved to see Clemmie and Joel at last.

"Oh, it's so good to see you." Awkwardly she hugged her dearest friend, then threw her arms around Joel's neck. "I was getting worried."

"I wasn't going to come," Clemmie admitted. "I feel as big as a house with this one." She groaned in laughter, putting a hand to her protruding stomach.

"Unh-uh." Joel's eyes twinkled as he set down their little girl with a kiss to her temple, pulling off her coat, then moving to help his wife out of hers. "Make that two."

Clemmie looked at him grimly, and Joel laughed, dropping a kiss to her nose.

"I wasn't teasing when I said twins run in my family, darling. I really think this could be it."

Hannah didn't voice her opinion, but for once, she didn't think Joel was being mischievous. Clemmie wasn't due for two months and already looked past due. "Hi, Rebecca," Hannah greeted their small, redheaded daughter, who with her fair skin and the outside cold looked as if roses bloomed in her cheeks. The child smiled shyly.

"Where's Eric?" Joel asked, handing her their coats.

"That's a good question. I'll just put these away and see what's keeping him."

Leaving the pleasant buzz of conversation and occasional hearty laughter of her guests behind, Hannah hurried to deposit all the coats on their bed, then went to the nursery, certain she knew where to find her husband.

She paused at the doorway, her heart melting with love to see Eric bent over the cradle, his finger caressing their tiny daughter's cheek.

". . .And that's my side of the family. On your mother's side, there's your Grandma Sarah, who's also a princess, and Grandpa Bill. Your Great-Grandpa Josiah and Great-Uncle Bernard. . .Esther, Abbie, David, Josiah, and Aunt Darcy and Uncle Brent, and all their children. . ."

Hannah grinned, moving forward. "As big as our family is, you'll confuse the poor child."

"Non, she's smart. Do you see how her eyes are lit up with interest?"

"And you're not the least bit biased."

"Is it my fault if we have the most beautiful and intelligent child on the planet?"

Hannah laughed and moved into her husband's arms, lifting her lips to receive his kiss. He held her close, and she sighed in satisfaction, her ear pressed against his chest and the steady beats of his heart.

"They've all arrived."

He sighed. "So I guess that means I should let you go?"

"Never."

For several precious moments, they stood lost in one another, sharing in the joy of their little girl and enclosed in their serene world, while outside the door the laughter and conversation of their loved ones rose and fell like a comforting wave surrounding them.

"They'll wonder where we are," Hannah said after a while.

"*Oui, ma belle princesse.*" With another little sigh, he released her. Carefully, he picked up their tiny daughter, who'd inherited her father's flame blue eyes and Hannah's dimpled smile. Giving their child a kiss on her rosy cheek, he handed her to Hannah.

She smiled at her husband. "Time for her big debut."

"And she'll outshine any starlet ever born."

Hannah laughed as together they moved into the parlor. At their entrance, the family quieted, many gathering around, all looking with eager expectation at the swaddled bundle in her arms. She smiled, and Eric rested his hand upon her shoulder.

"Mothers, fathers, aunts, uncles, cousins, and friends, may we introduce you to Erica Rose Fontaine. . . ."

To her husband's announcement, Hannah silently added, *The precious link that now bonds our families and has helped to make us whole.*

A Letter to Our Readers

Dear Readers:

In order that we might better contribute to your reading enjoyment, we would appreciate you taking a few minutes to respond to the following questions. When completed, please return to the following: Fiction Editor, Barbour Publishing, Inc., P.O. Box 719, Uhrichsville, OH 44683.

1. Did you enjoy reading *Connecticut Brides* by Pamela Griffin?
   ❏ Very much. I would like to see more books like this.
   ❏ Moderately—I would have enjoyed it more if _____
   _____

   _____

2. What influenced your decision to purchase this book?
   (Check those that apply.)
   ❏ Cover   ❏ Back cover copy   ❏ Title   ❏ Price
   ❏ Friends   ❏ Publicity   ❏ Other

3. Which story was your favorite?
   ❏ *In Search of a Memory*   ❏ *In Search of Serenity*
   ❏ *In Search of a Dream*

4. Please check your age range:
   ❏ Under 18   ❏ 18–24   ❏ 25–34
   ❏ 35–45   ❏ 46–55   ❏ Over 55

5. How many hours per week do you read? _____

Name _____

Occupation _____

Address _____

City_____ State _____ Zip_____

E-mail _____

HEARTSONG
PRESENTS

If you love Christian romance…